PLAYING WITH FIRE

Kerry Wilkinson is a bit less of an accidental author than he once was. His debut, *Locked In*, the first title in the detective Jessica Daniel series, was written as a challenge to himself but, after self-publishing, it became a UK Number One Kindle bestseller within three months of release. His three initial Jessica Daniel books sold over 250,000 copies in under six months, making him Amazon UK's top-selling author for the final quarter of 2011. *Think of the Children* followed, making *Playing with Fire* the fifth title in the series.

Kerry has a degree in journalism and works for a national media company. He was born in Somerset but now lives in Lancashire.

For more information about Kerry and his books visit:

Website: www.kerrywilkinson.com or
www.panmacmillan.com
Twitter: http://twitter.com/kerrywk
Facebook: http://www.facebook.com/JessicaDanielBooks

Or you can email Kerry at

kerryawilkinson@googlemail.com

By Kerry Wilkinson

LOCKED IN

VIGILANTE

THE WOMAN IN BLACK

THINK OF THE CHILDREN

PLAYING WITH FIRE

KERRY WILKINSON

PLAYING WITH FIRE

PAN BOOKS

First published 2013 by Pan Books
an imprint of Pan Macmillan, a division of Macmillan Publishers Limited
Pan Macmillan, 20 New Wharf Road, London N1 9RR
Basingstoke and Oxford
Associated companies throughout the world
www.panmacmillan.com

ISBN 978-1-4472-2341-2

1 3 5 7 9 8 6 4 2

A CIP catalogue record for this book is available from the British Library.

Typeset by Ellipsis Digital Limited, Glasgow
Printed and bound by CPI Group (UK) Ltd, Croydon, CR0 4YY

Visit **www.panmacmillan.com** to read more about all our books
and to buy them. You will also find features, author interviews and
news of any author events, and you can sign up for e-newsletters
so that you're always first to hear about our new releases.

PLAYING WITH FIRE

1

Andrew Hunter put his feet on the desk and leant back in his chair. In what was a less-than-impressive office, the chair was worth more than the rest of the furniture put together. The estate agent's advert had enthusiastically declared the place came 'fully furnished' which, Andrew had to admit, it did – up to a point. What the advert hadn't revealed was that the furnishings were apparently part of a job-lot of junk being cleared out from a school. He had already paid the deposit to secure the space when he realised the underside of the thick wooden table that served as his desk was plastered with dried chewing gum and felt-tip declarations that 'Ian iz bent'. Among other things, 'Ian' certainly seemed to have a very varied sexual appetite.

The chair he'd inherited had a dreadful blue canvas covering and the back wouldn't stay fixed in place. As part of a lavish exhibition of spending which he hoped at the time would impress prospective clients, he bought a brand-new leather-backed seat which the website dubbed 'the Big Daddy' of office chairs. It didn't mention that it came flat-packed, which somewhat took away from Andrew's enjoyment at receiving it. Two days later, he finally managed to relax in the height of luxury. Well, it would have been if he could have figured out how to make it go up and down.

Andrew pushed back into his new purchase and wondered why he once thought a chair would be enough to woo clients. Then he jumped as someone rapped hard on the frosted glass of his office. He tried to spin around but somehow mixed up his limbs, catching his knee hard on the solid wood of the desk. He shouted 'Come in', at the same time stifling a swear word and rubbing his knee.

A man in a sharp, perfectly fitting grey suit entered the office. He was somewhere in his late fifties, possibly early sixties, and had a bright pink tie with matching handkerchief sticking out from his jacket pocket. His grey hair was immaculately swept backwards, while his six-foot-plus height made Andrew, with his five-foot-eight frame, feel instantly insecure. Andrew watched his visitor peer from one side of the office to the other, taking in the white, largely empty walls and potted plant in the corner before turning to face him. It was pretty clear that he was underwhelmed.

'Is this Andrew Hunter's office?' he asked abruptly.

Andrew stood, trying not to wince from the pain in his knee. 'I'm Andrew,' he said, stretching out a hand.

The man gripped it firmly. 'You're a private investigator?'

'Er, yes,' Andrew replied, wondering if he could match the iron handshake. He couldn't and the man quickly released him.

'I'm Harley Todd,' the man said, still looking around. 'You're definitely *the* Andrew Hunter?'

Andrew wondered if his fame – or lack of – had somehow preceded him. 'I am Andrew Hunter, yes. I'm a private investigator. Can I help you . . . ?' He pointed towards the chair on the opposite side of the desk, the blue canvas one he had rejected for himself.

Harley edged around the table, as if making a special effort not to touch anything. Andrew didn't think his office was dirty but it was somewhat sparse. Aside from the two chairs, the large desk and his computer, there was an empty bookshelf, the potted plant he had inherited and kept forgetting to water, and a stack of boxes which contained junk he didn't have room for in his flat. To prospective clients, he figured the closed boxes might seem as if they contained vital paperwork. The fact they didn't was something they didn't need to know.

Light spilled through the window, partially obscured by the boxes, glinting from the man's expensive-looking cufflinks. Harley carefully sat in the chair, instantly annoyed as the backrest fell backwards.

'Sorry about that,' Andrew said. 'I'm waiting on a replacement. Delivery companies, hey?' It was a lie which Harley didn't seem convinced by. He certainly didn't respond to Andrew's lighthearted chuckle.

'I'm not sure this is what I expected,' Harley said. His voice was full of authority, the type of terrifying tone that made Andrew think of teachers and parents. Or worse, his former father-in-law.

'I can assure you, I run a very professional service,' Andrew said, only half-believing his words. He swivelled slightly in his chair, wondering if 'the Big Daddy' would impress this prospective client.

If it did, then the man hid it well. 'I've never come to a

private investigator before. I found you in the phone book. I think I was expecting some sort of ex-policeman around my age.'

Andrew had forgotten about the phone-book advert as he had been focusing mainly on Internet advertising. 'I offer the highest class of service . . .'

The investigator tried to look confident as Harley again scanned him up and down. 'How old are you?'

'Thirty-four,' Andrew replied without thinking.

'Hmmm . . .' Harley was squinting slightly, apparently wondering what to ask next. 'It might be better that you're younger . . .'

Andrew sat up straighter, thinking he might be on to something. 'How can I help you?'

The man ignored his question. 'Are you married? Kids?'

It wasn't the response Andrew expected but, given the man's resonating tone, he felt obliged to answer. 'I was married, I'm not any longer. I don't have children.'

'Hmmm . . .'

Andrew watched Harley repeat the examination. He was beginning to grow more and more uneasy under the older man's gaze. The suit he was wearing was a little tight and compared to the quality of the garment the man in front of him was wearing it felt insufficient for the air of professionalism he was trying to portray.

'Did you leave her or the other way around?' Harley's query was as direct as before.

'I'm sorry, I . . .' Andrew was stammering, uncomfortable with the question.

Harley fired straight back. 'I know it's not my business

but I like to work with certain types of people, Mr Hunter. I have a very important job and I'll pay you very well.'

Andrew paused for a moment. He dropped any pretence of being someone he wasn't and leant forward in his seat, allowing himself to slump. 'She left me.'

'Hmmm . . .'

'It wasn't as simple as that,' Andrew added, keen to justify himself. 'We were very different. She has a very rich family, while I . . . don't. Her dad never liked me. Her mum did but, well, that didn't really matter. In the end, when we were thinking about kids, it fell apart.'

'So her father didn't approve?'

Andrew thought he sensed a flicker of sympathy in the man's voice but he wasn't sure. 'No.'

Harley nodded slowly, scratching his chin. 'We're hard people to please when it comes to our little girls. You'll learn that if you have children.'

Andrew said nothing but held the man's gaze until Harley clapped his hands together loudly. For the first time, Andrew noticed how big they were. He'd felt his hand being squeezed when they shook hands but hadn't noticed how brutish they now seemed. The clap echoed around the room.

'I think you might be exactly who I'm looking for, Mr Hunter.'

Andrew nodded. 'So how can I help you?'

Harley smiled and shook his head gently. 'First tell me how you came to do this. Are you ex-police? Marines?'

Andrew snorted before he could stop himself. Just

thinking of the marines' training he had seen on television made him feel slightly sick. His idea of exercise was the walk it took to climb the stairs to his office each morning. His slightly overweight physique was certainly not the type to be accepted into the navy. He wouldn't describe himself as 'fat' but he had noticed his suit clinging to his thighs in recent weeks. The football he used to play as a teenager seemed increasingly as if it was something from another life.

Harley was sitting impatiently with his legs crossed and fingers interlocked, waiting for a reply.

'I have a degree in criminology,' Andrew said.

The older man nodded. 'But why are you doing this? Why aren't you off with the police or MI5 or something?'

Andrew didn't know why he continued to entertain Harley's questions. It wasn't because of the promise of money but perhaps it was because Harley had said he was the person he was looking for. Beyond money, Andrew was looking for something to stimulate his mind.

'Do you want me to be honest?' he said.

As if expecting something exciting, Harley leant in, licking his lips. 'Always.'

'It's a bit of a complicated story. I studied criminology at university and met a girl, Keira, while I was there.'

'The ex-wife?' Harley interrupted.

Andrew nodded. 'Her father is high up with a bank in London. They own this giant mansion in Cheshire which they use at the weekends. It's unbelievable. Keira took me there one time while we were still first years. I thought the weekend had gone well but she was really upset on the drive home. She said her mum told her that her dad hated me and insisted we break up.'

Harley said nothing but Andrew looked up to see him nodding. He didn't know if it was because the man had taken a dislike to him as well, or because he had children of a similar age of whom he was equally protective.

'We didn't break up,' Andrew went on. 'We stayed together through university and then flew to Vegas and got married the day after Keira's final exam.'

The older man coughed and unlocked his fingers. He hadn't said it explicitly but Andrew knew for sure that he had a daughter who was most likely a young adult, possibly with an equally troubling boyfriend.

'Anyway, that didn't go down too well,' Andrew continued. 'But her mum was great and her dad seemed to accept it in the end. Well, sort of. He got me a job in his bank. It wasn't what I wanted to do but I didn't have much choice.'

'So how did you end up back here?' Harley asked.

Andrew found the man hard to read. His legs were still crossed, while he was staring intently across the table, seemingly interested in Andrew's story.

'Guess.'

Andrew didn't know why he'd said it but he suspected Harley Todd shared much in common with his former father-in-law. Harley seemed to relish the challenge. His eyes narrowed and he broke into a wide smile for the first time since entering the office. 'He paid you off.'

Andrew laughed and spun his chair a quarter of the way

around, before returning to face the other man. 'How did you know?'

'It's what I would do.'

The answer was clinical and Andrew knew the person he was dealing with was uncannily like Keira's father.

Andrew nodded slowly. 'He told me he would make sure we broke up one way or another before we had children. He said that if I took the money, at least I'd have that. If I didn't then he'd make sure I ended up with nothing.'

The other man didn't speak for a few moments. 'Smart man,' he said eventually. 'So you took the money?'

Andrew shrugged. 'He didn't give me much choice.'

'How long ago?'

'Seven years.'

Harley waved his arms around to indicate the office. 'And this is what you did with the money?' His tone sounded mocking but Andrew didn't think he was trying to be cruel; it was simply the way he phrased things.

'Among other things. I only started this six months ago.'

Harley nodded with a smile on his face. 'Do you need my money?'

'No.' Andrew didn't know why he continued to answer. It was almost as if he was facing his ex-father-in-law, unable to stop revealing his inner thoughts.

'How much have you got left?'

'Lots.'

'So why do you do this?'

Andrew shrugged. 'Because I want to.'

Harley made a point of looking around the room. 'Why haven't you got a better office if you have so much money?'

'Money doesn't interest me. It's just there. I spend what I need to.'

Apart from nodding almost non-stop, Harley wasn't moving. He stared at Andrew, as if fascinated by a new creature he had never seen before.

'You're perfect,' he said, almost purring. Andrew didn't respond. He didn't know if he wanted to work for the man in any case. 'Do you want to know what the job is?' Harley asked.

Andrew sat up straighter, deciding that he would face the man, no matter if he felt intimidated. 'Whatever it is, it's going to cost you.'

'I thought you had money?'

'I do.'

Harley leant back into the broken seat, splaying his legs. He laughed loudly, the sound echoing around the room. 'I'm really going to like you,' he said.

'So, what's the problem with your daughter?' Andrew asked.

The other man stopped laughing. 'Who said I have a problem with my daughter?'

It was Andrew's turn to smile defiantly at the man, waiting for a reply. Harley stared back before turning away.

'Sienna,' he said. 'She's just turned eighteen. She goes to college in the city. I wanted to take her away from the area but she insisted. In the end we agreed that she had to go to the university of my choice if she got to go to this college place with her friends.'

'Why are you choosing where she goes?' Andrew wanted to get a rise out of the man.

Harley didn't react. '"We're hard people to please when it comes to our little girls",' he repeated.

Andrew nodded. 'What's the problem?'

'She's pregnant. Well, she was . . .'

For the first time, Andrew thought he saw a small chink in Harley's demeanour. One of his eyes twitched as if he was winking but it was clearly not deliberate.

'What happened?'

'What do you think happened?' Harley said irritably. 'I paid to make it go away.'

'You made her have an abortion?'

The two men locked eyes but Harley ignored the question. 'You're on thin ice,' he said and Andrew realised their roles had completely reversed.

'I don't mind if you walk away,' Andrew said, indicating towards the door.

Harley didn't move. 'I made it go away.'

'So what do you need from me?'

Any trace of a smile had disappeared from the man's face. His eyes were narrow, the rest of his features fixed. 'I want to know who the father was.'

2

Detective Sergeant Jessica Daniel glanced up from her plate to face the man sitting opposite. She put the metal fork on the table, loudly enough to ensure he knew she wanted his attention.

'So, Garry,' Jessica began. 'Who the hell is Sebastian Lowe?'

She watched Garry Ashford squirm. Despite the fact she had known the journalist for a few years, she knew he was still that little bit afraid of her.

Garry looked up from his breakfast, where a congealed fried egg yolk had blended into the leftover baked-bean juice. All that was left of his breakfast was a final piece of black pudding, which he was chewing on while swirling his hand in the air, as if pointing out to Jessica that he would answer when he had finished. She had purposely picked her moment to ask the question, so that he was at his most uncomfortable. Jessica fixed Garry with a steady stare, telling him with her eyes that she was waiting for the answer.

The journalist swallowed and started to speak before spluttering and gulping the final mouthful of tea from his mug.

'Sorry,' he coughed. 'I was just finishing off.' He smiled apologetically but Jessica didn't relax her glare. 'Sebastian's newish,' he went on. 'He's been working for me for around six months. I hired him but he's just been bumped up to senior news reporter.'

'When did you start hiring people?' Jessica replied, failing to hide her surprise.

'Since I was promoted to news editor.'

Jessica weighed up his response, not overly satisfied with it. 'What's he like? A bit of a troublemaker?'

Garry shook his head. 'Sebastian? No, he's a bit like I was. He gets by story to story, although he seems to come up with better stuff than I did.'

Jessica looked sideways at the man, flicking her long dark-blonde hair away from her face and wishing she had tied it back. When she had invited Garry for breakfast, she hadn't known if she wanted to play on the fact he was scared of her, or that she was pretty sure he still fancied her – despite apparently having a girlfriend. Torn between the two, she opted for a bit of both and left her hair down.

As they waited for their food to arrive in the cafe around the corner from his newspaper's office, Jessica hadn't said too much. She allowed the tension to build, watching him devour a full English and deciding she would definitely be going down the 'scare' route. She quickly finished her sausage sandwich, wondering if the large breakfast was a usual thing for him, or if he had ordered it because she was paying.

'Does he have better dress sense than you?' Jessica asked.

Garry peered down at his brown corduroy trousers, before realising what he was doing. In fairness, Jessica had to admit he was looking as smart as she had ever seen him. His previously long scruffy hair had been cut short and was tidily shaped, with the goatee on his chin looking as if it was there by design, as opposed to because he hadn't bothered to shave. His cord trousers were perhaps a little outdated but, for as long as she had known him, that seemed to be his style.

'Why do you want to know about Seb?' Garry asked, not taking the bait.

Jessica reached into the bag under her seat and scooped out a copy of the previous day's *Manchester Morning Herald*. She pushed a ketchup bottle to one side and unfolded the paper before turning it around so Garry could see the front page, pointing at Sebastian's byline on the lead story.

'Did you have anything to do with this?' she asked.

The headline read 'FLAMING HELL' with 'Killer Out This Month' underneath.

Garry must have known what was coming but he still fidgeted awkwardly. 'I didn't write the headline but I knew about Seb's story.'

Jessica pushed the paper away. 'Didn't anyone think about the implications? What if this guy gets hurt when they let him out of prison?'

The journalist sank into his seat and Jessica began to feel a little sorry for him. 'That's exactly what I said,' Garry insisted. 'I told my editor that. I told Seb that. I said we should be careful if we were going to run it.'

From her earlier dealings with Garry, Jessica knew he had a pretty good grasp of what was right and wrong. Or, more specifically, what she considered to be right or wrong. She wasn't as prejudiced against the media as some at the station but, as with all professions, she knew there were good guys and bad guys. Garry was one of the better ones. He had certainly helped her in the past, although she was loath to admit it – especially to him.

'I've been assigned to keep an eye on Martin when he comes out of prison,' Jessica said. 'It's not even our job but after this,' she pointed to the paper again, 'we don't have much choice.'

Garry looked a little apologetic, his eyes slightly wider than before. 'You have to admit it's a good story.'

Jessica knew it was and had made that exact point in the staff briefing the previous day. It was probably that which prompted Detective Chief Inspector Jack Cole to give her the job of escorting Martin Chadwick when he left prison in a few days' time. Unknown to Garry – she hoped – everything had been moved forward by a day in an attempt to avoid any further publicity.

'Where did Sebastian get the story from?' Jessica asked, fully aware Garry would never give her the answer. She was curious because the day of a prisoner's release wasn't the type of information that should have been freely available. All they had managed to come up with in the briefing was that the second subject of the article – who would have been told by the prison service that Martin was due to be released – had taken it to the media.

Garry shook his head. 'You know I won't tell you that.'

'Was it Anthony Thompson?' Jessica asked, hoping Garry's body language would give him away. As he had grown older, the man had clearly learned his lessons from dealing with her. He sat impassively, refusing to answer. 'Don't get me wrong,' Jessica added. 'I know Anthony might have every reason to want to hurt Martin – but flagging it up for the world to see isn't going to do anyone any good.'

Garry nodded slowly and Jessica could see he agreed with her, although the congealed egg yolk on his chin did detract slightly from the serious conversation she was trying to cultivate. She leant across the table and wiped the yellow liquid from Garry's face as he writhed away from her. 'You're not my mum,' he said with a smile.

Jessica grinned back, the atmosphere lost. 'Believe it or not, I didn't invite you to breakfast to simply bollock you. Whoever this Sebastian is should do his homework. There are mistakes in the piece and, although it's not my job to clean up after you, my boss and I thought it would be much better if we gave you some proper facts for next time.'

'On the record?'

Jessica shook her head. 'You give me your source and I'll give you something on the record.' Garry smiled back but didn't answer.

'Fine,' she said. 'Off the record it is. Have you got a pen?'

The journalist stacked his empty plate on top of Jessica's and moved them into the middle of the table, before fumbling in a shoulder bag hanging over the back of his chair and taking out a notepad and pen.

When it was clear he was ready, Jessica began. 'You got most of it right. Martin Chadwick is due out of prison but you know I can't confirm exactly when that's going to happen. Up until seven years ago, he was a bit of a pest with sporadic criminal offences, none of which was very serious. Then he set fire to a pub he thought was empty. Unfortunately, a twenty-one-year-old man named Alfie Thompson was sleeping inside.'

Garry was making notes, although Jessica hadn't yet told him anything he wouldn't already know. She paused to let him catch up, continuing when his pen scratched to a halt. 'Martin was so drunk, he was picked up sleeping on a bench less than a hundred yards away from the pub. The lighter and empty bottle of vodka he used to start the fire were still in his possession. He didn't exactly confess, largely because he said he couldn't remember doing it. With the CCTV footage and forensic evidence, he pleaded guilty to manslaughter and received his prison sentence.'

The journalist looked up from his pad. 'We know this . . .'

Jessica interrupted. 'What you don't know is that Martin had an eleven-year-old son who was taken into care when his father went into prison. He is now eighteen and, apparently, he's been in regular contact with his dad. I don't know much about his mother but the son is called Ryan. Although I've not met him yet, strictly unofficially we would rather you be careful of mentioning him. He doesn't have anything to do with this and I am only telling you because I know you will find it out at some point anyway.'

She let her words hang. Garry hadn't written down any of the last pieces of information. 'All I can do is ask,' he said.

Jessica nodded. 'Obviously you know about Anthony

Thompson. It was his son killed in the fire. I'm assuming he was your source about Martin's release because he was informed. We don't know that much about Anthony, except for what you printed.'

She picked the paper back up and began to read. '"There's no bringing back my Alfie but everyone has to pay for what they've done".'

She looked up to see Garry wince. 'I know it's ambiguous,' he said.

'Deliberately so?' Jessica asked. She fell silent as a waitress came close to their table and picked up the plates.

'Can I get you anything else?' she asked sweetly, although the twang of her local accent made it sound as if she was offering them a fight. The woman was somewhere in her early twenties, with bleached hair tied neatly in a bun on top of her head. Jessica watched Garry eye the waitress up and down, before stopping himself when he realised she was observing him.

Jessica giggled slightly, shaking her head. 'No thanks, just the bill.'

When the woman had moved away, she raised her eyebrows. 'Are you really a ladies' man now?'

Garry offered an apologetic 'No' but Jessica already knew he was far from the type. He might have wandering eyes, as did most men she knew, but the journalist lacked the social grace to be discreet.

Jessica lowered her voice. 'From what Anthony says, I don't know if he's referring to the jail sentence as Martin "paying" for what he's done, or if there's a veiled threat there.'

Garry spoke slowly and cautiously. 'I don't know. Sebastian did the interview. I know you can read it both ways. I said we should take it out.'

Jessica returned the paper to her bag. 'I don't think any of us want something stupid happening when Martin comes out. Whatever you think of the guy, or the punishment, he's done his time.'

Garry put down his pen and nervously wiped his chin with a napkin from the table.

'How are things anyway?' Jessica asked in a lighter tone.

He stopped dabbing his face and smiled. 'Are you actually being nice to me?'

Jessica grinned. 'Hey, I left my hair down for this impromptu bollocking. I'm not all bad.'

Garry shrugged. 'I'm doing okay. I've been promoted and I've moved in with my girlfriend.'

'Is she the blind one?'

The journalist snorted gently and shook his head. 'I thought you were being nice?'

'This is me being nice,' Jessica replied with a wink.

'What about you?' Garry asked. 'I heard you were loved-up, engaged and all that?'

Jessica tried not to fidget but couldn't stop herself. Instead of answering his question, she shunted her chair backwards and picked up her jacket, before crouching to retrieve her bag. 'I've gotta go,' she said.

Garry laughed. 'Thanks for the breakfast.'

'Judging by the amount you left on your chin and shirt, it certainly looked like you enjoyed it.' He glanced down at his clean shirt before looking back up at a smiling Jessica. 'Gotcha,' she said.

The journalist put his coat on while Jessica paid at the counter. As she turned, he looped his bag over his shoulder and stretched out his hand for her to shake. 'It was good seeing you again, Jess,' he said.

Jessica rolled her eyes but shook his hand anyway. 'Can you deliver a message for me?'

'What?'

'Tell this "Sebastian" that I will kick his arse if anything happens to Martin.'

3

'So much for bringing it forward a day so no one knew,' Jessica said agitatedly. She deliberately elbowed a reporter she didn't recognise as she fought her way through the crowd of journalists assembled outside the prison gates. She heard the man grunt but kept moving, wondering if the person she had 'accidentally' caught was Sebastian Lowe. She didn't know what he looked like but she could only hope.

Detective Inspector Jason Reynolds and Jessica stepped through the gate, where they were met by a man in a suit. Reynolds was around six feet tall but the man was taller and stooped, stretching out a hand for Jessica and then the inspector to shake. He had brown hair combed and smoothed to one side and introduced himself as the deputy governor of the prison. Jessica thought he seemed younger than other people in similar positions she had met in the past. She would have placed him somewhere in his forties, but his sharp eyes gave the impression of someone who knew what they were doing.

The man turned and started to lead them towards the main part of the prison. 'We're not used to this sort of attention out here,' he said, referring to the throng of photographers and journalists waiting outside. 'Have you ever been to Wymott before?'

Jessica exchanged a look with Reynolds but let him answer 'No'. They had spent the best part of an hour driving through the back lanes of Lancashire, with Jessica complaining at every turn how remote the institution was. Wymott was a category C prison not far from Leyland, around thirty miles north of Manchester. She had grown up in Cumbria, where the roads were even narrower and harder to negotiate. Since then, she had lived most of her adult life in Manchester, largely forgetting how fiddly country lanes could be. Judging by the way Reynolds had ignored her complaints, she guessed he didn't share her annoyance.

Martin Chadwick had been moved to the low-risk prison a few years previously when it became apparent to the authorities that he posed no particular danger to anyone.

In the days since the original story about his release, Chadwick's case had gradually received greater interest through the local media. Even a few national papers had got hold of it, all adding to a feeling at Longsight Police Station, where Jessica worked, that they would have to play things carefully.

Both Martin and Anthony Thompson lived in their district and although supervising newly freed prisoners was largely out of their remit, the police were working closely with the probation service over Martin's release in an effort to prevent any trouble.

Unfortunately, someone with a big mouth had told the media that the man's discharge had been brought forward, leading to the presence of journalists, photographers and television cameras at the front of the prison. As ever, the police, prison and probation service blamed each other.

The deputy governor held a door open for them as they entered the prison's visiting hall. Aside from the three of them, the room was empty. The man closed the door behind the two officers and followed them into the room.

Reynolds spoke. 'Do you have some sort of rear exit?' he asked, although Jessica realised his choice of words was clumsy. 'I know everything had been arranged for Martin's release but we didn't expect all of this attention.'

The deputy governor screwed up his face awkwardly. Jessica knew prisoner releases were generally straightforward things, although, depending on the people and category involved, they might need meticulous planning.

'It's a bit late to be changing things now . . .' he said.

Jessica was regretting wearing one of her better suits as she stretched out her legs in an unsuccessful effort to get comfortable in the back of the van. She didn't know how clean the floor was and it was too dimly lit to make out exactly what she was sitting on. The man across from her offered a weak smile as if sensing her discomfort. He was also wearing a suit, although it was far too big for him. As she peered through the gloom, Jessica could make out his thinning grey hair, the crinkles around his eyes making him look older than his fifty years.

'You got the short straw,' Martin Chadwick said with a small, unconvincing laugh.

Before Jessica could reply, the van bucked upwards over a hump in the road, sending her flying sideways.

After the deputy governor had told them it was unlikely

he could find a better way to get them out of the prison without going through the media crowd, Jessica had uttered the words she was now wishing she hadn't: 'Isn't there a service van or something similar we could sneak out in?'

At the time, it sounded like a good idea. With Martin's unwillingness to face the media, it became an even better one. Unfortunately, Jessica hadn't thought through the part where someone was supposed to be escorting the former prisoner off-site.

As the catering van reversed towards the prison's main building after dropping off its daily delivery, Jessica had looked at the deputy governor and then Reynolds, before it dawned on her that the inspector was going to pull rank. While he and the probation officer were to leave the prison via the gates they'd come in through – much to the confusion of the waiting media – she would be in the back of a van with Martin.

Apart from the tinted windows at the rear, the rest of the back of the vehicle was enclosed, a wooden panel separating Jessica and Martin from the driver's compartment. She tried to steady herself, thinking it was almost certainly illegal to be travelling in such a way without seatbelts. The plan was for the van to drive them to a nearby petrol station, where they would transfer back into Reynolds's car.

'Sorry about this,' Martin said, sounding genuinely apologetic.

'It's all right, it isn't your fault.'

Jessica was wary of getting into too much of a conversation with Chadwick. Although when she'd told Garry

Ashford that Martin had served his time, she meant it, that didn't mean she had to like a person who had burned someone else to death, whether it was on purpose or not.

'At least it's not raining,' Martin added, clearly trying to make conversation.

Regardless of her personal opinion, the more he spoke, the harder Jessica found it not to be charmed by him. She couldn't explain it but there was a fatherly tone to his voice. Some people came out of the prison system broken but Martin's voice had no resigned quality to it. Instead, there was hope. She wondered how he'd got to the point years earlier where he was so drunk he burned down a building.

'It's not been wet, just cold,' Jessica told him but the man didn't seem to be listening.

They went over more bumps as Martin continued. 'My son Ryan visited a few days ago. He says he's been getting the house ready for us to move back into.'

Jessica was curious. 'Is it the house you used to live in?'

Martin barely stopped for breath. 'Yes. I've lived there since I was a boy. It was passed through the family, so there was never any rent or anything. I've been . . . away but Ryan was too young to live on his own so one of my cousins stayed in it for a while. It's been empty for some time though.'

'Has Ryan been living there since he turned eighteen?'

Martin sounded pleased with Jessica's interest. 'Yes. It's in his name – it's his house now. I told him I'd sign the papers when he became an adult. It's only fair after what . . . I did to him.' The man's voice tailed off as he finished the sentence.

The van momentarily dropped into a pot hole before leaping out, sending Jessica and Martin sprawling again. Jessica was beginning to think she should find out exactly who Sebastian Lowe was, so she could blame him for her predicament, when Martin began crying.

At first, she just heard him sniffing but then it became a full-blown sob. Jessica felt a moment of panic she wasn't used to. She had seen people break down in interviews but this was an entirely new situation where she didn't feel comfortable offering any form of reassurance. She wanted to stay neutral, reminding herself that the person across from her, like it or not, was a killer.

She reached into the inside pocket of her suit. 'Tissue?' she asked, trying not to sound as feeble as she felt. Martin shuffled across the hard floor as Jessica reached forward, passing him a small packet. After various accidents with food over the years, she kept tissues on her just in case.

Chadwick pressed himself back into the side of the van and blew his nose loudly. 'I'm sorry,' he said just loudly enough for Jessica to hear over the sound of the engine.

She didn't want to get into a conversation about it but, for some reason, couldn't stop herself. 'What are you sorry for?'

Martin continued to sniff. 'This. Everything. I've made such a mess of it all.' He ran his hand through what was left of his hair. 'You know what I did, don't you?'

Jessica replied firmly. 'Yes.'

The man gulped and blew his nose a second time. 'My wife left me and I lost my job. I couldn't deal with having

Ryan on my own and I . . . got pissed all the time.' Martin paused for a moment and the quiver in his voice had gone when he spoke again. 'Looking back, it doesn't feel like me. I haven't had a drop since I was arrested. I don't know why I did it with the fire and everything. I guess it was one of those things that seem clever when you've had too much to drink.'

Martin let out another sob and tried to dry his eyes. Jessica was lost for words. It would have been unsettling in any situation but as the van they were sitting in bumped along the country lane and she shuffled to try to get comfortable, it was almost surreal. She thought about the types of people the man would have encountered over recent years. As well as fellow inmates, there would have been counsellors and chaplains who might have heard similar confessions. She wondered if Martin had spoken to any of them, or if the contrition was something that had grown inside him as his release date neared.

'I'm sorry for doing this now,' Martin added.

'You don't have to apologise.'

'I can't believe I'm out. I can't believe I'm going to live at home again. It doesn't feel fair, not after what happened to that boy.'

Jessica never knew how to take statements of remorse. When she was younger, she would take everything at face value but years of seeing people's sentences reduced because of guilty pleas and the 'remorse' they showed had left her cynical about the whole thing. Despite that, Martin did appear to be sorry for what he had done. Jessica couldn't think of a reason why he would break down in front of her. He certainly had nothing to gain by doing so because he had already served his sentence.

'It's up to you what you do with your second chance now,' she said.

Jessica was wondering whether the rapid switch in Martin's mood was something that should worry her as the revs of the engine dropped. The vehicle was slowing, presumably because they had reached the garage where they were swapping back into the car. As she watched Martin nodding gently in the dim light, she thought the media attention could be the least of her worries.

Reynolds parked the car outside Martin's house and switched off the engine. The journey from the petrol station to Manchester had been an almost silent affair although, somehow, their plan had worked and none of the assembled media had followed them. Martin and the probation officer opened the rear doors as Jessica opened the one on the passenger's side. Together with the inspector, they all walked towards Martin's house.

The man's property was on a tight maze of roads just south of Crowcroft Park, barely a mile away from Longsight Police Station. On one side of the road was a long row of dark red-brick terraced houses but the homes on the opposite side were semi-detached and had been built in a different era. An empty driveway ran along the side of Martin's house but the tarmac was beginning to crack and chunks of it had been swept to the side. As he opened a small metal gate, Jessica looked to her left where a scruffy paved area was becoming overrun with weeds growing in the gaps between the slabs.

Before Martin could knock on his own front door, someone opened it. Jessica knew Ryan Chadwick was eighteen but he looked a year or two younger. He was thin with short spiky blond hair and was wearing a pair of jeans with holes in the knees and a hooded top. Ryan reached forward and pulled his father towards him into an embrace. As they held each other, Jessica watched the younger man's eyes stare over his dad's shoulder, darting from Reynolds to the probation officer before fixing on her. They may have been blue but, in the light, looked grey and had a piercing, steely quality to them. Jessica suppressed a shiver as Ryan watched her before he eventually released his father.

'Welcome home,' Ryan said, turning to lead them into the house.

As the younger man went towards the rear of the house to make tea, Martin took them into a living room with wooden floorboards where the varnish had long since started to rub off. From the smell, it seemed as if the walls had been repainted recently but Jessica guessed the rest of the furniture was exactly as it had been seven years ago. A cream-coloured sofa with a faded pink pattern was pushed towards the wall facing them, with an armchair in a matching pattern opposite the bay window. A large mirror hung on the wall above the sofa and, aside from a low coffee table and television, the room was otherwise empty and felt cold.

The probation officer opened his briefcase and set down some papers on the table as Jessica and Reynolds sat on the sofa. The officer talked Martin through some formalities regarding when they would have to meet and handed over some contact numbers. He didn't seem too keen on hanging around and was packing up his papers when Ryan returned with five mugs of tea. Martin showed the officer out as Ryan put the cups on the table and then sat cross-legged on the floor leaning up against the wall. Jessica could feel him staring at her but refused to meet his eyes, instead reaching forward and taking one of the teas from the table, cradling it in her hand.

A few moments after the front door closed, Martin returned, picking up a mug and settling in his armchair.

'We just wanted to make sure you were happy with everything before we left,' Reynolds said. 'I know we have spoken briefly about the recent media coverage but you should know we haven't had any specific threats made towards you.'

Ryan snorted. 'Didn't you see that stuff in the paper?'

Martin shushed his son. 'I appreciate you coming around,' he said, addressing the two officers and sounding sincere.

Jessica sipped her tea before replying. 'I'll leave you my direct number but you've also got the number for the station and, of course, you should call 999 if you feel unsafe.'

Martin leant back in his chair and smiled gently. His earlier tears seemed long gone and he had reverted to the gentle fatherly type. 'You didn't have to go to all this trouble.'

Reynolds picked up one of the full mugs from the table.

'Are you likely to be alone much? Obviously that's not a problem, it would just help us to know.'

Martin scratched his head and ran his hand through his hair. It was the second time Jessica had noticed him do it and it appeared to be some sort of nervous reaction.

'I'm not sure,' he replied. 'Ryan goes to college a few times a week and works at a local garage. I'd quite like to get myself a job but I'm not really sure how things like that will work. The probation guy told me we'll talk about it at our first session. I think being out here is going to take a bit of getting used to.'

The man was interrupted by a clatter of crockery as Ryan loudly put his mug down on the floor. Jessica had been deliberately ignoring him, feeling his stare but not acknowledging it. As she turned to look at him, she could see the fire in his eyes. Their colour hadn't changed since he moved indoors – grey, focused on Jessica, and furious. 'This is utter shite,' he spat. 'You read what was in the paper. Why haven't you arrested this Thompson clown? Are you going to wait until he's actually done something?'

Martin started to intervene but Jessica spoke over him, meeting Ryan's eyes. 'We saw what was in the paper and officers have been to speak to Mr Thompson. He says he was misquoted in the article and that he didn't threaten your father.'

'And you believe him?'

Jessica could see the venom in Ryan. Whereas his father sat passively and – at least from what she'd observed – let his emotions overflow through tears and remorse, his son expressed himself through anger. She said nothing at first, watching the teenager's fists ball and arm muscles tense.

Jessica held his gaze. 'I think you should calm down.'

She knew that telling people to calm down was frequently one of the biggest causes of people actually flaring up. The policy of certain forces was to avoid using the words because of the negative effect they could have on people, especially those who were drunk. Jessica didn't for one minute think Ryan was affected by drink but she wanted to see how he would respond. She felt the inspector next to her shuffle uncomfortably and wondered if he knew why she had said what she had. On the floor, Ryan's back straightened, his eyes narrowing. His fists were still clenched tightly, his lips thin.

Just as Jessica was wondering what the teenager might say, Martin spoke. 'It's okay, Ry. They're trying their best.'

Reynolds stood quickly and awkwardly, placing his empty mug on the table. It was clearly an indication they should go. Jessica stood too, turning to face Martin.

She reached into the pocket of her jacket and handed him one of her business cards. 'Call me any time of day or night if you have a problem but always dial 999 first if it's an emergency.'

Martin took the card and stood, before ushering the two officers into the hallway. 'Thanks again for coming,' he said, closing the door that separated the living room from the rest of the house. He lowered his voice. 'Sorry about Ryan. He's really not a bad lad; he's just not had his dad around for all this time. I don't know everything but some of the things that happened to him in care . . .'

He didn't finish his sentence but didn't need to. With Ryan's aggression, it was easy to forget he hadn't had much of a life for the past few years. That didn't stop Jessica thinking she might need to keep an eye on him.

The two officers exited the house after a final 'Thank you' from Martin, Reynolds leading them back to the car. A few years before, they had shared an office when they had both been sergeants. After his promotion to inspector, very little had changed initially but recently Jessica had begun to feel less comfortable around the man. It was something that was hard to pinpoint. A few months previously, while investigating the case of a missing child, she'd had what was a minor disagreement with the chief inspector. Largely because of her stubbornness, things hadn't been addressed. Anyone who wasn't familiar with the internal dynamics between Jessica and her colleagues might not notice anything different and she sometimes thought it was all in her head. Regardless of the truth, Jessica was feeling a little ostracised by her workmates.

It didn't help that she was struggling to deal with the guilt of how she had broken the law trying to solve that case. Apart from Detective Constable David Rowlands, whom she had involved in her plan, no one knew what she had done.

Jessica slid into the passenger seat, slamming the door harder than she meant to. Reynolds sat in the driver's seat and put the keys in the ignition without starting it.

'Are you okay?' he asked.

In the same way that 'calm down' could infuriate drunk or angry people, Jessica knew that someone asking how she was feeling was her trigger. 'I'm fine,' she replied, forcing an upbeat tone.

The inspector laughed gently. 'How was the back of the van?'

'Bumpy.'

'Did Martin say much?'

'No.'

Jessica's reply was instant. She didn't know why but she wanted to keep the man's breakdown to herself – at least for now. Very little about her morning's work had turned out how she'd expected but she was feeling a sense of responsibility for Martin she wasn't sure she should have.

Jessica lay awake staring through the darkness at the ceiling. She stretched a hand across to rest on Adam's hip as he slept facing away from her. She listened to his breathing. It wasn't quite at snoring levels but he was certainly exhaling loudly through his nostrils. She wanted to blame him for waking her up but knew it was entirely down to her restlessness. She traced the outline of the man's side with her fingers. His skin was smooth and tight, his hip bone jagged.

Rolling away, Jessica squinted to look at the alarm clock on her side of the bed. The red LED letters glowed 03.33 through the gloom. It was utterly irrational but Jessica had always found something satisfying about the numbers matching on a clock. It was small comfort in a house that still felt unfamiliar, even though she had been living there for a few months.

It was the home Adam had lived in with his grandmother before her death and Jessica was still coming to terms with being somewhere that didn't feel like 'hers'.

After leaving home, she had either shared a flat with her best friend Caroline Morrison, or lived by herself. The last few months had been a learning curve as she had never lived with a man before. Despite Adam's insistence that the things in the house were 'theirs', she didn't see them like that. Everything felt like it was his and that she was somehow trespassing. She even felt guilty about eating food from the fridge if she hadn't bought it. At first she had confided in Adam about her discomfort but she wasn't sure he understood her feelings. She didn't think he was being insensitive, simply that, because the house was his, he couldn't grasp why she didn't feel it was home.

Jessica's daze was broken by a buzzing sound from the small table next to the bed. The light on her mobile phone's screen was flashing and the ringtone sounded after a second or two. She could feel Adam beginning to stir, his legs stretching as he rolled over. Jessica wondered if she was awake or asleep, blinking rapidly at the ceiling as she reached out and pulled the phone towards her. The grey haze around her vision prevented her from reading the name on the screen, so she simply stabbed the front to answer it.

'Hello,' she said groggily. Her throat felt dry and she squinted towards the table to see if the glass she left there had water in it.

'Sergeant Daniel?'

It was a man's voice. He spoke quickly and frantically.

'Yes.'

'It's Martin Chadwick. Sorry, something's happening. Please come quickly.'

4

Despite having lived at Adam's house for months, Jessica still wasn't sure of the best way to get from where they were in Salford to where she worked in Longsight. After the first night, she got lost trying to drive off the estate in the dark the following morning. She had stayed at his house before moving in but each time had left during daylight. It was only when she found herself turning back onto his road that she realised she had somehow gone the wrong way. After a few months, Jessica had a better grasp of the general area but still hadn't mastered the shortcuts that avoided the queues.

As she pressed down on the accelerator and neared the turn onto Mancunian Way, Jessica figured driving to work at four in the morning was definitely the future given the complete lack of traffic holding her up. Getting up at four in the morning was definitely not the future, however. Well, unless it was a future where people enjoyed seeing her very tired and annoyed by mid-afternoon.

Reluctantly, she had to admit it was nice to have a car that started first time on a cold dark morning. Six weeks previously, she had finally given up on her beloved Punto and gone with Adam's advice about a new vehicle. It was roughly the same size as her old car but had none of the character. Yes, it might start first time every time, yes, it might be fuel-efficient, yes, it might be quiet – but it didn't have a cigarette lighter that fell out and rolled under the pedals, making braking something of a lottery. It didn't make a growling noise of annoyance each time she hit exactly forty-two miles per hour. It didn't even have that little dent in the passenger door from when she reversed into a concrete post in a multi-storey car park.

After she had pointed that out at the showroom, Adam told her there were many more concrete posts out there just waiting for her to collide with them. Jessica smiled as she remembered his cheeky grin, then her phone rang, snapping her back to the present.

Reaching forward, Jessica pressed a button next to the dashboard. The Bluetooth answering function was another benefit of the new vehicle. 'Yep,' she said.

'Jess, it's Dave. Are you on your way to Martin Chadwick's?'

Detective Constable David Rowlands didn't sound anywhere near as tired as she might have expected him to, given the hour. He had been her first call as she headed out of the house.

'I'm ten minutes away,' Jessica replied. 'Are you there yet?'

'Yes.'

'I woke Jason up. He's on his way too.'

'What's going on?'

'It's probably best if you see for yourself.'

She drove through a red light and turned right towards Stockport Road. 'Are Martin and Ryan okay?' she asked.

'Sort of. They're not hurt.' Jessica heard a muffled noise,

as if the constable had broken away from the conversation to talk to someone. He quickly returned. 'I've got to go, sorry, Jess. I'll see you in a minute.'

Jessica focused back on the road, adding extra pressure to the accelerator as she headed past the turn for the station and kept driving, passing Crowcroft Park before turning left into the estate where Martin lived. A police van was blocking the entrance to the road, so Jessica parked on the adjacent street and walked briskly past the van. A female uniformed officer was standing next to the vehicle and nodded as she neared. 'Are you all right?' she asked.

'Four in the morning is not a time I recognise,' Jessica replied.

In the distance, she could see a small crowd gathered under a street light. When she was within a few feet, she saw Martin sipping from a mug of tea with Rowlands standing next to him.

Martin saw her before anyone else. 'Sergeant,' he said.

'Are you okay? What's happened?'

Martin pointed through the gloom towards his house where Jessica could see the front window had a hole roughly in the centre with cracks that had spread towards the corners. 'Is that why you called?' she asked.

Martin nodded. 'I'm sorry. I know I should have called 999 first. I wasn't thinking.'

Before she could reply, Jessica heard a raised voice. She turned towards the house, where Ryan was storming out of the front door, pointing towards her aggressively. 'Where the fuck were you lot?' he shouted. Jessica tried to shush him, aware it was still the early hours of the morning. 'Don't you fuckin' shush me,' the young man shouted, even louder. 'Where were you?'

He was within a few feet of her and she could see the saliva around his mouth as he spat the words, his eyes wide and the whites illuminated in the street light.

'Hey,' Martin said sharply to his son. Ryan turned to his father and screwed his lips together. 'Anything could have happened,' he said, slightly more quietly than before, this time addressing his dad.

'We'll sort out some sort of panic button,' Jessica said, trying to sound reassuring. She wasn't surprised by Ryan's aggression but wanted him to calm himself, rather than having to have an officer step in.

'It's not just the window,' Rowlands said.

His words sounded ominous. Jessica turned to face him as he gently gripped her arm and started to walk her forward. She could hear Ryan ranting to his father behind them as they opened the gate, leaving the pavement.

'He's a happy chap, isn't he?' Dave said.

'Ryan? I think he's on something,' Jessica replied. 'Did you see his eyes?'

'Shall we take him in?'

Jessica sighed. 'Not tonight. Someone's going to have to keep a close eye on him though.'

Rowlands pointed towards the side wall of the house that adjoined the property's driveway but he didn't need to say anything. The graffiti had been sprayed in bright yellow paint, the letters half a metre high. The message was easy enough to make out, even in the limited light.

'DEAD MAN'

Jessica sighed again, louder the second time. 'Oh for f—'

'I know,' Rowlands said. 'At least they can spell.'

She couldn't stop herself from laughing. 'You're such a dick sometimes.'

The constable didn't miss a beat. 'Who do you think did it? Anthony Thompson?'

Jessica puffed through her teeth. 'I bloody hope not. The last thing we need is to arrest him. The media will kick our arses.'

'Someone's going to have to visit him either way, if only to find out where he was this evening.'

'Shite.'

Jessica knew it was true – and that she would be dispatched to ask Anthony the question someone had to but nobody wanted to. If he had done it, it wouldn't be good for anyone. If he hadn't, they were harassing a man because his son had been killed seven years previously.

'It could be anyone,' Jessica added. 'Martin's release was in the papers and on the Internet. All it takes is some nutter who has read the story.'

'Are you trying to convince me or yourself?'

Rowlands leant sideways, deliberately nudging her with his shoulder. Jessica rocked to one side and then back again, hitting the constable with her own shoulder.

'How's Chloe?' she asked, referring to his live-in girl-friend.

'Pissed off at my phone going off at half-three in the morning.'

Jessica laughed but moved the constable further away from the road because she didn't want either Martin or Ryan to think she was enjoying the situation. 'I knew you only lived a few minutes away. It was quicker than phoning the station and I told Martin to call 999 anyway.'

'What about Adam?'

'He barely stirred. He just farted and rolled over.'

'Classy.'

Jessica giggled again. 'He's been saying the four of us should go out for a meal again.'

'Chloe was going on about that too. She reckons she had fun last time.'

'That's because she didn't have to stay in alone with you all night.' Jessica nudged her colleague with her shoulder again. 'What are we going to do with Ryan?' she asked.

'I thought you wanted to leave him be?'

'For now, but you didn't see him earlier. If it was Anthony who did this, Christ knows what might happen.'

Rowlands cupped his hands around his mouth, blowing into them for warmth. 'Do you think he might go looking for some sort of revenge?'

'I don't know. He seems like a very angry young man. Not that I blame him; he has grown up without any parents.'

'Where's his mum?'

Jessica shook her head, although it was gloomy enough that she realised she wouldn't be seen. 'I don't know. I think she left when he was young. It's not been mentioned but she's not in the picture.'

Rowlands blew into his hands again. 'Aren't you cold?'

Jessica pulled up the lapels on her jacket. 'I nicked a coat off uniform.'

The constable gripped Jessica's arm and nodded towards the road, where Ryan was striding towards them. At first she could make out only his silhouette against the street lamp but he kept walking until he was within a few feet of the two officers.

'I want to say sorry,' he said. 'I know it's not your fault. I'm just worried about my dad.' His voice still contained a menacing undercurrent and Jessica suspected his father had sent him across.

'We understand,' Jessica replied, although she said it with enough fire in her voice to let him know she wasn't prepared to allow him to speak to her in that way too often.

She could tell from the angle of Ryan's body that he was looking towards her but it was too dark to see his facial reactions. There was an uncomfortable pause before the teenager grunted some sort of acknowledgement, then he turned and headed back towards the road.

Jessica knocked on the door and stepped backwards, accidentally standing on Rowlands's toe. She turned to see her colleague leaping sideways with a scowl on his face.

'Will you stop being such a baby?' Jessica said with a frown of her own as she heard the door unlocking.

By the time she turned around, a small crack had appeared between the door and its frame. Jessica could see an eye peering through the gap at her. Faded red paint was flaking from the wood and the man's blotched skin was almost the same colour as the emulsion.

'Mr Thompson?' Jessica asked in the friendly tone she saved only for visits such as this. She deliberately raised the pitch of her voice, but also had a slower, more serious version for the moments when she had to break bad news to someone. Her semi-aggressive, slightly lower-pitched voice was what she most often used – although that was usually followed shortly after by a threat that someone would break the door down if whoever she was after didn't open it. Jessica could feel Rowlands eyeing the back of her head, no doubt partly amused by her method.

The eye flickered from side to side before a low gravelly voice answered. 'Who's asking?'

Jessica introduced herself and offered her identification so the man could have a better view. His eye darted around it before he added, 'So?'

'Can we come in, Mr Thompson?' Jessica asked, even more sweetly than before.

'What do you want?'

'Just a chat. We'll be quick if you're busy.'

For a fraction of a second, Jessica caught the gaze of the single eye. It widened, the white lined with deep red veins, and then blinked shut. The face disappeared from the crack and the door opened inwards slightly. Jessica took a half-step forward but, as she did, it was slammed in her face with a bang that sent a rush of air into her face. Jessica stepped backwards quickly, again standing on Rowlands's toe. He yelped and she felt his hand pressing into the small of her back through the borrowed coat.

'Can you stop doing that?' he said, his voice decidedly squeaky.

'I'm only a little girl, stop whingeing.'

'Not so "little" any more.'

Jessica didn't get a chance to reply before the door rattled in front of her. At first it stuck in its frame and then it was wrenched open.

The pictures of Anthony Thompson that had been in the newspapers looked hardly anything like the man standing in front of her. In the media, he had sensible brown hair cut almost into a basin style and had been wearing an open-necked shirt. Jessica wondered how long ago the photo had been taken because the man in front of her had straggly grey hair that hung to his shoulders, his cheeks puffy and glowing red. He was wearing a thick green jumper with a hole in one of the shoulders and Jessica could smell the alcohol without having to cross the threshold. The only thing that told her this was the man she was after was a scar that ran across his chin, finishing somewhere before it reached his neck. In the photos it had been visible, although somewhat faded. On the man in front of her, it was white against the crimson of his skin. She knew from their files he was in his early fifties but he looked much older.

Without a word, Anthony turned and walked through a doorway. Jessica glanced around at Rowlands, shrugging before stepping inside. As she wiped her feet on a thinning grey mat, she couldn't help but notice everything seemed to be as faded as the paint of the front door. It reminded her a little of Adam's house in that there wasn't necessarily anything wrong with it but its style was twenty years out of date. The crusty wallpaper had a raised oval pattern that had been painted over in white gloss that was also beginning to flake. Apart from the reek of alcohol, there was also a stale smell which Jessica associated with the boot of her old car.

Jessica headed to the doorway she had seen Anthony go through. It was no surprise as she walked into the living room to see it had the same carpet and wallpaper as the hallway. Directly across from the door was a white cabinet filled with books – except for one slot in the centre where there was a large framed photo. Without going any closer, Jessica knew it was of Alfie Thompson. She had seen similar pictures in the file they had and, given the length of time since his death, she knew the photo had to be somewhere between eight and ten years old.

Anthony was sitting in a rocking chair steadily going forwards and backwards. It was made out of dark wood and creaked noisily each time it moved. He was holding a glass filled with a dark brown liquid that Jessica assumed was whisky. She walked around the room until she was standing in front of him, Rowlands staying close to the door awkwardly leaning to one side.

'Are you okay, Mr Thompson?' Jessica asked.

Anthony sipped from his glass before answering with a croaky 'Yup'.

'Do you live alone?'

The man's rocking increased in tempo, the back of the curved wood touching the floor. 'Yup.'

With the obvious tension, Jessica didn't think it was

worth wasting any more time. 'Can you tell me where you were between three and four this morning, Mr Thompson?'

She tried to use her sweetest tone again but it seemed to agitate the man further. The speed of Anthony's rocking increased again, causing a few drops of his drink to splash over the top of his glass.

'Mr Thompson?' Jessica persisted.

Abruptly, Anthony planted his feet on the floor and stopped the chair, springing up in a way that was totally at odds with his age and appearance. With an elegance Jessica could barely believe, he switched from rocking to walking in one fluid movement, striding from one end of the room to the other. He sat in a brown armchair closest to the photograph of his son and leant back, pointing at a matching seat across from where he was sitting. The whole incident had lasted a few seconds. As she walked towards the seat he was indicating, Jessica caught Rowlands's eye but he too seemed stunned by Anthony's sprightly movement.

'I was sleeping,' Anthony said crisply, still holding the drink in his hand.

'On your own?' Jessica asked, already knowing the answer.

'Yes.'

'Did some officers visit you a couple of days ago?' Jessica again knew the answer.

'Yes.'

'And you told them you hadn't threatened Mr Chadwick?'

Anthony downed the rest of his drink in one and winced slightly. 'Yes,' he replied, his voice hoarser.

'Have you had any contact with him since then?'

The reply came instantly, although the man was staring at his empty glass, refusing to acknowledge Jessica. 'No.'

From her first impression, Jessica would have doubted Anthony being able to throw a brick but it was now clear the man was a lot more agile than he looked. They had no evidence to connect him to the scene of vandalism at Martin's house and, although the specialist team were looking for footprints or anything else of note, she didn't expect them to come up with anything. Jessica didn't want to tell Anthony what had happened; for now, she wanted to get a feel of what he was like, especially after the time she had spent with Martin and Ryan.

She'd been hoping Anthony's words had been taken out of context by the newspaper. Instead, her fears that something could happen between the two parties had only increased.

After a host of one-word replies and general lack of cooperation from Anthony, Jessica glanced sideways at Rowlands, who had a blank look on his face. It was clear they weren't going to get anything. Jessica stood and offered her hand for the man to shake. She didn't know if he would, but the man reciprocated, sending a shiver through her from the coldness of his hand. Jessica left him one of her cards and followed Rowlands out of the house. Anthony hadn't moved to show them out, so Jessica closed the door behind them.

'He's friendly,' Rowlands said once they were outside.

Jessica clicked her tongue into the top of her mouth. 'Did you see how quickly he moved?'

The constable hummed in acknowledgement. 'I thought he was going straight towards you before he went for the armchair.'

'I hope we can keep him and Ryan apart. I don't trust either of them.'

As she was talking, Jessica bumped into the back of Rowlands, failing to notice he had stopped in front of her. She peered around him and saw why: at the end of the pathway leading to Anthony's house was a woman with a camera with a telephoto lens pointing towards them. Even at this distance, Jessica could hear the click and whirr as the person took their photo.

She pushed ahead of Rowlands and strode purposefully towards the gate, opening it as the photographer stepped backwards, still taking pictures.

'Who are you?' Jessica demanded.

The photographer answered without lowering her camera. 'Press.'

'I can see that,' Jessica snapped, trying not to take the bait. 'Where are you from?'

The woman finally moved her camera down to her hip. '*Herald*.' Jessica turned and realised there were two more photographers a few metres away also taking her photo.

Before she could say anything, a male voice sounded from behind her. 'Sergeant Daniel?'

Jessica turned to see a man holding a silver metal device towards her. He was somewhere in his mid to late twenties with spiky dark hair, wearing a black pinstripe suit that looked as if it was tailored specifically for him. It fitted perfectly around his trim physique and he was also sporting a thin dark tie. His smartness coupled with the fact he was standing on a pavement uttering her name made Jessica take a step backwards in surprise.

'Who are you?' Jessica asked, noticing that the electrical object had what looked like a small microphone pointing out of it.

The man's response was as sharp as his attire. 'Sebastian Lowe, *Manchester Morning Herald*. Why are you visiting Anthony Thompson, Ms Daniel?'

Jessica winced at the use of the word 'Ms'. She hated it and had long figured you were either a 'Miss' or a 'Mrs'. Or an idiot. She wondered if he had said it to deliberately annoy her.

'It's Sergeant Daniel,' Jessica replied. She hardly ever asked anyone to use her title but the man's directness had annoyed her.

'Why are you visiting Anthony Thompson, Sergeant Daniel?' he asked.

'Detective Sergeant Daniel.'

Jessica could hear the click of one of the cameras behind her as she locked eyes with Sebastian. She was annoyed with herself for noticing how attractive he was. He had long dark eyelashes, his eyes an intoxicating mix of brown and black. His high cheekbones and blemish-free skin only added to the impression with his short dark brown hair stylishly pointed to one side. He stared back, expecting an answer. 'Detective Sergeant Daniel,' he added sarcastically.

'None of your business,' Jessica replied loud enough for the small crowd of photographers to hear. She motioned to stride past Sebastian but, before completely passing him, she stepped close enough so she could hiss in his ear. 'Stop stirring this up.'

Before he could react, Jessica strolled past him towards her car, forcing herself not to turn around to see if his suit fitted him as well at the back as it did in the front.

5

Blending in was something Andrew Hunter had always felt able to do. Some people turned heads when they walked into a room, their natural charisma drawing people towards them. Others would attract attention for negative reasons, exuding a lack of confidence as strongly as somebody else might exert natural magnetism. Andrew knew he fell almost exactly in the middle of those two extremes. He first realised it at school when he was eleven. His form tutor, who had been his teacher for eighteen months, couldn't remember his name one morning. She had asked a question and, when Andrew had raised his arm, the teacher pointed at him. She stuttered and, as her face turned to confusion, the woman reached across her desk and checked the register book. Eventually she looked up and said, 'Yes, Andrew'. Some students didn't understand what had happened but Andrew did. She had simply forgotten who he was.

Keira was the first person who saw him in a different way. For whatever reason, she saw something in him most others didn't.

Andrew was thinking of his ex-wife as he leant back into the chair and tried to avoid touching the armrest, which he had discovered rather disgustedly had a distinctly sticky coating. He glanced sideways towards where

Sienna Todd was staring at her mobile phone and chatting to her friend, seemingly oblivious to the film playing on the cinema screen in front of them.

If Andrew had any interest in the movie, he might have been annoyed by the distraction but he was more interested in keeping an eye on Sienna. He had followed her unnoticed from the college she attended to her friend's house, then to the more-or-less empty cinema for an early-evening screening. The first thing that struck him about the young woman was how striking she was – although how much of it was natural he didn't know. She had long bright blonde hair and a glow to her skin that most likely came from either a sunbed or a bottle. Despite that, she possessed that invisible attraction that didn't just come from her looks. If anything, her friend was the more physically eye-catching of the two with her tighter clothing and loosely tied black hair – but Andrew would have felt more drawn to Sienna even if he wasn't being paid to find out who the father of her aborted baby was. Despite being just eighteen, there was something about her that seemed older. He figured it could come from the growing up she had to do after discovering her pregnancy and the subsequent termination. Either way, there was something alluring about her that went far beyond her looks.

Sienna started giggling as she held the phone up for her friend to see. Even through the darkness, Andrew could tell there was something about the laugh that was forced. Someone towards the back shushed loudly but the young women didn't seem to notice as Sienna dropped it into the large bag she had been carrying all afternoon.

Andrew glanced towards the screen where something apparently funny was happening. A man towards the rear of the cinema, possibly the person who had made the shush noise, was laughing hysterically to himself as the character on screen said something that Andrew didn't think could have amused anyone.

The investigator was across the aisle, five rows behind the two women. He switched his eyeline back towards the pair, who were leaning in close whispering to each other. Because of the way the screen flickered, it was hard to tell exactly what was happening but what seemed like light-hearted chatter moments before now appeared to be becoming a little heated. Their whispers grew in volume until Sienna uttered a perfectly clear and taut, 'Right, well, fuck off then', only to be shushed by the person at the back again.

Sienna stood and, for a moment, Andrew thought she was going to storm down the aisle out of the room. That would leave him in an awkward position considering how tough it would be to follow her without being obvious. As he held his breath, Andrew watched the young woman straighten her loose-fitting tracksuit bottoms, and then sit down again. He realised that not only had she been talking into the phone rather than to her friend, but also that he had been oblivious to her taking it back out of her bag in the first place.

Focusing back on the women instead of the film, or the laughing buffoon at the back, Andrew watched them lean in and begin whispering – this time definitely to each other. The friend put an arm around Sienna's shoulders

and pulled her closer, seemingly consoling her about whatever had been said on the phone.

Apart from Andrew wondering if the man at the back
might have some sort of medical condition that made him
laugh at incredibly unfunny situations, the final hour of the
film passed without incident. As soon as the credits began
to scroll and the lights came up, Andrew heard shuffling at
the back and turned to see a massively overweight man in a
blue uniform bounding down the aisle with a dustpan and
brush. The middle-aged laughing man from the back was
brushing a mass of uneaten popcorn from his jumper and
trousers. In a snap judgement Andrew decided he probably
worked in insurance and had a wife and two kids. He didn't
know why those things seemed true – or why that might
equate to the type of enjoyment he had apparently taken
from a bad movie. Either way, Andrew followed him out
before stopping to one side and untying his laces.

As he crouched on the floor slowly retying them,
Andrew watched Sienna and her friend walk past, both
talking on their respective mobile phones. He waited until
they had reached the corner that led back to the foyer
and then stood, walking briskly in the direction they had
gone in. Sienna's powder-blue tracksuit was hard to miss
and her friend's skirt was so short, the two of them were
attracting looks from both males and females as Andrew
followed around thirty metres behind them. They walked
through the heavy front doors, before stopping to talk to
each other. Andrew had little choice than to carry on past
them but he took his phone out of his pocket and held it
to his ear, speaking to a non-existent person as he passed.

As well as his interest and degree in criminology, Andrew felt it was his ability to blend into his surroundings that made him a good private investigator when he was doing something that motivated him. He wasn't bothered who the father of Sienna's aborted child was – but he was engrossed enough in her father's story to take the man's money and trail his daughter.

A handful of people passed Andrew as he leant against a thick brick pillar. He continued to talk into his phone, half-watching the two young women chat with each other. Eventually, Sienna spun around and started walking along the pathway that ran around the giant car park. The complex comprised the cinema, a couple of restaurants, half-a-dozen large electrical outlets and a few fast-food chains. In the far corner, Andrew could see a small blue hatchback racing along before handbrake-turning to the delight of the handful of young people standing around watching. Other than that, the area was surprisingly quiet, with a smattering of vehicles manoeuvring around the car park and even fewer people meandering along the walkways.

Andrew pocketed his phone and walked towards his car, entering the driver's side without taking his eyes from the two females who were now around a hundred metres away. From the direction they were heading in, the pair seemed to be returning to the bus stop on the main road. He started the engine and began to crawl towards the exit when the women moved off the pathway and started crossing the car park towards a burger place. Andrew eased his car forward, before edging into the separate parking area that served the restaurant. He watched Sienna and her friend enter the restaurant, still chatting to each other, and then reversed his vehicle into a space that ensured he could see most of the inside of the building.

Sitting up straighter to get a better view, Andrew watched the women sit at a table without approaching the counter. The investigator was wondering what they might be up to when he heard a screeching noise. He turned to see a small blue car racing into the car park, its wheels squealing from the harshness of the turn. For a moment, Andrew didn't think it would stop before cannoning into a bollard, but the vehicle skidded to a halt mere centimetres before colliding with it. All four doors opened in unison and Andrew could hear thumping music blaring before it stopped abruptly. Three young men and a female stepped out of the car. Andrew could see they were all in their late teens or early twenties, the woman wearing a pink tracksuit very similar to Sienna's in style. One of the men pulled up his jeans so they were covering the lower third of his backside, allowing his white boxer shorts to hang over the top, as another focused on straightening a baseball cap.

It was faced with groups like this that Andrew felt his age. Being in his mid-thirties he wasn't that old but the types of young people he saw around were so alien to those of his own youth that he couldn't comprehend how much things had changed in what felt like a relatively short period of time.

The group of four slouched their way towards the restaurant, bumping through the door at the front, before Andrew watched Sienna and the other girl stand up. Sienna kissed the female on the cheek and then hugged each of the three men individually. Andrew watched the final one squeeze her bottom, for which he received a playful slap.

Sitting up further, Andrew reached into the footwell of the seat behind and picked up his camera. He had never had much of an interest in photography but it was a necessary part of his job. As such, and with money not being a big issue, he had bought the third most expensive one from the biggest camera shop in the Arndale Centre. He figured the one that cost the most was probably over-priced, with the next one down inferior to the first. He guessed the third one would probably have most of the same functions as the first but likely be better than the second, albeit with a lesser-known brand name. It wasn't the most scientific of theories but, either way, he was happy with what he ended up with.

The six young people approached the serving counter and Andrew snapped multiple photographs as they turned with their food to walk back to the table. He focused especially on the males, wondering if any of them – partic-ularly the bottom-squeezer – was the person he was being paid to find. In the fifteen minutes it took them to finish eating, the sun had dipped towards the tops of the trees on the far side of the car park.

One of the males whispered something in Sienna's ear, making her laugh, while the third fed her chips as she sucked his fingers seductively just a few moments later. Andrew took photos of it all, barely managing to capture everything before the light faded too much.

By the time he had finished, all three of the young men had enjoyed some sort of potentially erotic interaction with Sienna. Andrew wondered how Harley would take it if he could see the way his daughter acted around the young men.

It had been hard to judge in the cinema when she was with only her friend but the investigator could see she exuded sexuality, despite her age. There was an absolute confidence about the way she treated the males and, despite her unflattering attire, all three of them were clearly entranced by her at the expense of the other girls. Andrew didn't need to see her around other men to know she would have this effect on pretty much anyone, especially the young, inexperienced ones. He watched the way she smiled at them and the way she flicked her blonde hair to one side each time she was halfway through a conversation. Everything about her movement appeared so natural and yet, at the same time, there was something that didn't feel quite right.

Apart from the flirtatious hair flicks, Sienna touched her face a lot, almost as a way of self-reassurance. It was very subtle but Andrew also noticed that she barely ate anything. Aside from the chips she had been fed, most of her food was played with and then discarded back into the brown paper bag it had come from, in such a way that you wouldn't know she was doing it unless you were watching her closely.

The six young people left the fast-food restaurant together, and Andrew watched a weary-looking cleaner shake his head at the mess left on their table. At first, he thought they were heading for the car but the group continued past it, walking in the direction of the cinema. Unsure of the best way to follow them with the light fading quickly, Andrew started the ignition and drove on slowly to the main part of the car park with his headlights switched off. He weaved in and out of the parked vehicles, keeping his revs low and watching the young adults skirt around the outside of the area. Andrew pulled into a space and left the engine idling. He used the viewfinder of the camera to zoom in on the group and could see Sienna holding hands with one of the men. The light wasn't clear enough to be sure but Andrew thought it was the bottom-squeezer.

From where he was sitting, Andrew had a view of the entire complex. More people had appeared since he had left the cinema and couples were steadily streaming into nearby restaurants.

For a few moments Andrew lost sight of the six people as they disappeared behind a thick pillar that was similar to the one he had leant on outside the cinema. As two of the girls at the front emerged on the other side, the investigator felt a moment of panic as Sienna didn't appear. He shunted over to the passenger seat to see if he could get a better view but there was still no sign of her. Andrew reached across and turned off the engine, stepping out of the car and walking in an arc across the car park in an effort to see her again.

Two of the other men were following the women closely but none of them were looking backwards. As he moved quickly, Andrew heard a car's wheels squeal and then the sound of a horn. Bright lights illuminated him in the rapidly increasing darkness as he realised he had walked straight across the road in front of a car. Before drawing any more attention to himself, Andrew stepped out of the vehicle's way and slid between two parked cars. From where he was, he should have been able to see fully behind the post but it was too dark. The other four people from the group were now close to the front of the cinema, at least fifty metres away from where Sienna had dropped out of his view.

Andrew walked as quickly as he thought he could get away with without attracting further attention. He dashed between two more parked cars before reaching the walk-way and striding past Sienna's friends in the opposite direction. At first he couldn't work out where Sienna might have gone as there didn't appear to be a gap between the buildings. As he neared the corner, Andrew saw what had happened. One of the young men had Sienna pinned up against the wall. One of his hands was inside her tracksuit top and she had a hand hooked around the back of his neck pulling him into her. For a moment, Andrew thought about taking a photograph but he realised there wasn't enough light unless he used a flash. He took a few steps closer to establish the male involved was the bottom-squeezer and then turned and walked back to his car, taking extra care not to stride in front of any other vehicles.

Back in the driver's seat, Andrew picked up his camera and skimmed through the images he had taken, half-watching the pillar to make sure no one emerged from behind it. He eyed the photographs of the male, wondering if he should take them to Harley. They offered no proof of who had got his daughter pregnant – but they showed that Sienna was in a relationship of sorts with someone.

He was beginning to wonder how much longer the couple could get away with such a public display of affection when he saw Sienna emerge from one side of the post walking back towards the fast-food restaurant. She was on her own, moving quickly and smoothing her top down. The man was walking in the opposite direction, towards where their friends had headed. Andrew's fingers hovered over the key in the ignition, unsure of where Sienna was going. She strode past her friend's car in the direction of the bus stop but then cut diagonally across the car park towards a large electrical store.

He took the keys out of the ignition and stepped quickly out of the car. Because of the speed and direction in which Sienna was moving, she had moved out of his line of vision. He jogged towards where she had headed, looking from side to side to see where she could have gone. She had been out of his eyesight for less than thirty seconds and there wasn't enough of a crowd for her to have disappeared into. Andrew reached the front of the store, thinking her pale blue outfit was distinctive enough that he couldn't miss her, even with the fading light.

With no obvious idea of where she could have gone, Andrew entered the store. Three washing machines were stacked in a pyramid directly in front of him and a female shop assistant with a smile that may as well have been painted on lurched towards him asking if she could help. Andrew ignored her, striding past the tills before attempting to peer over the top of the display cases to see if Sienna was anywhere obvious. He walked as quickly as he thought he could manage without drawing unwanted attention, bounding along the width of the store, checking the aisles for any sign of the woman. After retracing his steps, it became clear she wasn't in the shop.

Andrew exited and continued walking in a straight line off the pavement onto the car park. He stopped and turned, trying to see what he had missed. If Sienna hadn't entered the store, he couldn't see where else she might have gone. Even if she had sprinted, she wouldn't have reached another shop before he saw her and there was nowhere else for her to have gone unless she had got into a car.

The area of the complex he was standing in was relatively empty, with fewer than two dozen parked cars. Andrew was confused, wondering if Sienna somehow knew he was watching her, when he noticed a narrow gap between the store he had just exited and the one adjacent to it. Because of the angle he had approached the shop from, a pillar with the same brickwork as the store had obscured his view.

Annoyed with himself for missing it, Andrew walked purposefully towards the alley, not knowing exactly what he was planning to do. He had no idea where it came out or, if Sienna had headed through the gap between the buildings, how he could explain his appearance if she was waiting at the end.

Without a plan, Andrew broke into a run. The alley was only a metre wide with gravel underfoot. He crunched his way to the end, where it opened out into a concreted yard. Ahead, Andrew could see tall metal gates where he guessed delivery lorries would enter. He squinted towards the corners of the yard, trying to look for any sign of Sienna but the light had faded to such a degree that he could barely see the shape of anything except the gates. One spotlight hooked high on the store illuminated the middle part of the area – but there was nothing there, except an upturned plastic crate.

Andrew stood still, frustrated with his own carelessness. He didn't have a brief to follow Sienna wherever she went but something about the way she had left her friends and moved away from the path didn't seem right.

He walked along the length of the gates and then followed the wall they intersected with. The corners were dark and disorientating and Andrew took out his mobile phone, using the screen as a light. He had no idea what he might be looking for but continued to trace his way around the yard.

As he neared the corner closest to the alley's entrance, Andrew could see a pile of wooden pallets. He flashed the light across them before realising they were arranged in a U-shape, meaning there would be a gap in the middle. The investigator walked steadily around the objects, being careful not to trip over any of the scattered pieces of wood.

As his foot squelched and skidded slightly, Andrew felt his heart jump. He shone the light of his phone towards his feet where deep, dark liquid was pooled around his black leather shoes. Time seemed to slow as Andrew lifted his phone upwards, following the trail of liquid to Sienna, who was sitting on the floor, bent over and slumped against one of the pallets. The hems of her tracksuit bottoms were stained with the same liquid as his shoe and, as Andrew scanned the light across her, he could see the slash marks diagonally across her wrists and a pair of scissors splayed on the floor.

6

Jessica was halfway back to Salford after finishing for the day when the call came through on her mobile to say an eighteen-year-old woman had been found with her wrists slashed. She didn't necessarily have to return to deal with things – especially after being called to Martin Chadwick's house in the early hours of the morning – but, for a reason Jessica didn't want to think too deeply about, she wasn't that desperate to get back to Adam's house.

Adam's house.

Jessica pulled her car over to the side of the road and sent a text message to tell Adam she was going to be late, and then turned the vehicle around, heading back the way she had come.

If she hadn't left work, it would have barely been a five-minute journey from Longsight Police Station to the entertainment complex on Hyde Road. Having reached the city centre before turning around, it took her closer to forty-five. By the time Jessica arrived, three police vans and two ambulances were parked in front of an electrical store. Two uniformed officers were blocking the entrance to a narrow alley which separated two shops. One of the officers recognised her, offering a 'didn't you go home for the day?' look which Jessica ignored.

'Are they out back?' Jessica asked.

The officer nodded towards the alleyway. 'There's a service yard back there and a separate road where delivery lorries come down. Scene of Crime are already here.'

'What's it like?'

The officer didn't answer but the sideways glance he gave his colleague told Jessica all she needed to know: it was messy.

Jessica edged into the alley, following it until the end where another officer was waiting. At first he stuck out an arm to block her path but then he recognised her. 'I thought you'd gone?' he said.

'Me too.'

Three pylons had been set up in a triangle, each with a bright white light on the top angled to illuminate an area surrounded by wooden pallets. A white screen had also been erected and Jessica watched a figure in a white paper suit lift a flap and enter the shielded area.

As she walked towards it, Jessica could see Cole's familiar shape speaking into his mobile phone. While he talked, he raised his free hand to acknowledge her presence and then pointed to the phone, rolling his eyes. After a few moments, he removed it from his ear, pressing a button before pocketing it. 'The wife's not happy,' he said with a weary half-smile. 'We were supposed to be going out for a meal tonight.'

'I was supposed to be sitting in with a microwave lasagne watching TV,' Jessica replied with a smile.

Although they hadn't been getting on, she couldn't stop herself from trying to get a laugh.

Cole's smile widened but he didn't crack. 'I told them

not to call you but apparently you'd left instructions that you were available all night . . .'

Jessica ignored his part-question, part-fish-for-information. 'What's going on?'

The chief inspector nodded behind her towards a man who was talking to a uniformed officer close to one of the pylons. 'He called 999, saying he'd found the body of a teenage girl. Her wrists have been slit but quite high up and it looks like an artery was hit rather than the vein. There's blood everywhere. You can go have a look if you want but there's not much to see if you're not a haemo . . . what's the name for that blood weirdo we picked up the other month?'

Jessica pulled a face to show she was happy to stay where she was. 'A haemogoblin. You shouldn't know what something like that is. Anyway, who's the girl?' She saw the DCI's face harden. 'What?' she added.

The chief inspector nodded at the man again. 'He knows her – he says her name is Sienna Todd.'

Jessica knew immediately that things weren't straight-forward. 'What am I missing? What's her body doing back here?' she asked, not knowing the best question to go for.

She saw Cole's eyes narrow slightly. 'You're better talking to him directly,' he said. 'You won't like it – I'm not sure I do.'

Confused, Jessica turned and walked towards the man. The uniformed officer was in the process of pocketing a notebook and then stepped backwards, giving her a nod of acknowledgement. Jessica turned her attention to the man. He was somewhere around her age, not a lot taller, with a slightly overweight physique. He didn't seem to have a large stomach but his white shirt was a little too small for him, giving the impression that he had breasts. Even though it wasn't a particularly warm evening, Jessica could see beads of sweat on his forehead, illuminated in the glow from the white lights.

Jessica had often thought Cole had relatively plain features but, as he aged, his looks had become more distinctive, the worry lines and crinkles around his eyes giving him more of a personality. His plainness was nothing compared to that of the man in front of her. He had a face that was instantly forgettable and, although Jessica had dealt with hundreds of situations where she had been frustrated by witnesses' lack of attention to detail, she wasn't sure she would have been able to describe his features – even while she was staring straight at him.

'I'm told you found the body?' Jessica asked tentatively, remembering Cole's suggestion that she might not like what the man would say.

'Yes, are you . . . ?' The man was staring past her towards the stack of pallets.

Jessica introduced herself and then asked for the man's name.

'I'm Andrew Hunter,' he replied. 'I'm an, er . . . private investigator.'

She knew why Cole had been hesitant and felt herself rolling her eyes without thinking.

'Is she something to do with you?' Jessica asked, knowing the man could be a suspect if there was anything suspicious about the young woman's death.

Andrew stuttered his way through a reply. 'I was following her. I lost sight for maybe five minutes – ten minutes at most – before I found her like . . . this.'

'Why were you trailing her?'

Andrew explained that Sienna's father had paid him to find out who had impregnated his daughter. Cole was exactly right in his assessment – Jessica didn't like it. She asked if Andrew had seen anyone else following the young woman but he said he hadn't.

After double-checking they had his details, Jessica told the man he could go but that she would visit him the following morning. He said he had photographs of a young man who Sienna seemed to be romantically involved with which she wanted to see.

Jessica walked across to Cole, who raised his eyebrows and smiled. His tired eyes didn't offer the same sentiment his lips did.

'Making friends?' he asked.

Jessica snorted as a response. 'At least you warned me.'

'What do you think about his story?'

Jessica stepped closer to her supervisor, partly so she wouldn't be overheard but also because her hands were beginning to feel cold. She blew onto her skin, before burying her hands deep into the pockets of the jacket she still hadn't returned. 'It sounds about right. I don't think he would have called us if something else was going on. There are cameras around so we'll get the footage. I told him I'll visit him tomorrow to pick up some of the photographs he has of Sienna.'

Cole nodded. Jessica had always been given a relatively

free rein to do what she wanted for a case. It had brought results in the past and she played on that. If the chief inspector had any objections then he didn't raise them.

'Is it definitely a suicide?' Jessica asked.

Cole tilted his head to one side and bit his lip. 'It looks like it. I only saw it briefly but one of the crime scene guys says there are cuts diagonally across her wrists, rather than up and down or side to side. He seemed to know his stuff.'

Jessica nodded. 'I had a witness a couple of years back who self-harmed. She said there are all sorts of websites out there with the information. She told me about how different blades offered varying amounts of pain and relief. She knew more about arteries, veins and blood than I ever will. Maybe it was just her – but the impression I got was that self-harmers generally know what they're doing and only go this far if they want to.'

Cole stared beyond her into the darkness. 'Why would you do it?'

Jessica didn't know if he was talking about self-harming or the apparent suicide. She knew he had younger children and wondered if he was associating them with Sienna.

She rested a hand on his shoulder, the most contact they had had in months. 'Some people cut themselves because the physical pain helps with whatever it is they're dealing with emotionally. But she would probably know the difference between veins and arteries if she was a regular self-harmer. If you cut a vein, you wouldn't bleed to death that quickly, which would make this a deliberate thing. If this was the first time she had tried something, she might have cut herself in the wrong place. The post mortem should give us a few answers.' Jessica paused for a moment. 'I take it there's a knife or something?'

'We found some small, curved nail scissors near her feet.'

A shiver went through Jessica. She knew the kind of blades he was talking about because Adam had a pair in the bathroom cabinet. For whatever reason, that made things seem more real.

'Has someone gone to tell her family?' she asked.

Cole sighed. 'That's sorted. I'm going to head home as soon as the body has been moved. You may as well head off too.' Jessica knew there wasn't much more they could do. By the morning, they would have a reasonable idea of whether it was suicide. 'What about Chadwick and Thompson?' the chief inspector added.

Jessica had briefed Reynolds about her morning's work. She wondered if Cole had read the notes and wanted clarification, or if he was trying to rebuild bridges with her after months with very little interaction. As long as she didn't have to apologise, she didn't mind either way.

'I'm hoping it will be a quiet night,' Jessica replied. 'There's tension on both sides. I don't know if it was Anthony with the brick and graffiti but he knows we're keeping an eye out now. Hopefully it will all blow over with a quiet week or two.'

Cole started laughing quietly to himself. It was not only out of character but Jessica thought it was also slightly inappropriate. 'What's up?' she asked.

'Sorry, I'm just tired,' he replied. 'It's not all of this. Sometimes I wonder what things would be like if these cases happened a few miles out of our way. How much different would our lives be? Imagine if Martin Chadwick lived in Prestwich or Stretford or something like that. We probably wouldn't even know his name.'

Jessica didn't know why he had brought it up but it was something that crept into her mind some evenings when she was struggling to sleep. With all the things she had dealt with over the past few years, she wondered how much different her life might have been if she had either worked in a district that didn't serve the centre of Manchester – or if the respective criminals had operated in the areas covered by the north, south, east or west CID divisions instead of her metropolitan one. She had never heard her supervisor bring it up and wondered why he had.

'Are you okay?' she asked.

Cole paused for a moment before replying. 'I'm just wondering how my wife's going to react when I get in. Things haven't been . . . great recently.'

Jessica didn't want to dwell too much on her own relationship. Sometimes she thought it was Manchester itself that seemed to drain everyone. The grey skies, the endless rain, the winters that went on and on. If you judged a place by its weather then this really was the end of the earth.

Not convinced by her own words, she said: 'I'm sure things will be all right.'

The chief inspector nodded, although his smile told her that he knew her words were just that. 'I'll see you tomorrow,' he said.

Jessica put a hand on his shoulder, turning and walking towards the alleyway that led back to the car park. She could see her breath in front of her and snuggled her hands deep into the jacket's pockets in an effort to keep them warm. At the far end of the cut-through was a police van. Its siren was off but the lights were spinning around, casting blue shadows that stretched the full length of the alley.

As she reached the far end, Jessica tapped one of the uniformed officers on the side and offered him a thin smile as he stepped away. He started to say something but Jessica heard another voice speaking over him before he could get the words out.

Sebastian Lowe was standing next to a pillar adjacent to the electrical store. He looked as perfectly turned-out as he had hours before and Jessica had half a mind to ask what his secret was. That was until he thrust the recording device out towards her as he strode forward. 'Detective Sergeant Daniel,' he said, trying to get her attention. She wasn't sure if the emphasis he put on her title was politeness or sarcasm because of the way she had demanded it the previous time they met.

'Go home, Sebastian,' Jessica said, walking away from him towards her car.

She could hear him jogging after her. 'Can I have a quick word?' he called.

Jessica reached her car as Sebastian caught up, turning to face him as he stopped behind her. Despite the fact he'd been running, he wasn't out of breath. She had left her car under one of the high lamps illuminating the car park.

The overhead light was a hazy yellow but, even with that, his dark eyes were as striking as they had been in the daylight. Jessica was desperate to dislike him but had to fight back a grin as his mouth cracked into a lop-sided smile.

'Thanks for stopping,' Sebastian said.

'What do you want?'

'I had a call from the office that something was happening here – something about a girl. Can you tell me anything?'

Jessica ignored his question. 'Why did you write about Martin Chadwick and Anthony Thompson?'

If her question had rattled him, Sebastian kept a straight face. 'Because it was a good story.'

'Did you contact Anthony Thompson, or did he come to you?'

Sebastian met her eyes and smiled wider. 'I don't think I should tell you.'

Jessica finally broke and was unable to stop herself grinning back. 'Honestly? You should go home. You're not going to get any information waiting here. There's a service yard at the back of that alley and everything will be removed without you even knowing it's happened. Call the press office tomorrow and they'll have something for you.'

The journalist lowered the recording device he had been holding. 'Can I call you tomorrow?'

Jessica wasn't sure but it looked as if he had winked at her as he spoke. She didn't acknowledge it, just in case it was a trick of the light. 'I don't give my number to journalists,' she said, although she hoped he didn't know that Garry had it.

Sebastian nodded without replying for a few moments. Jessica studied his face, hoping to notice a mole or unsightly hair – anything that would reduce his appeal. There was nothing she could see.

'How about giving me your number so we can go out sometime?' He stared into her face, his smile unmoving.

Jessica held up her left hand, wiggling her ring finger at him. 'I'm engaged.'

Sebastian's smile widened even further. 'Let me leave you my card,' he said, reaching into his pocket.

'I told you I'm engaged,' Jessica replied sharply.

Sebastian tilted his head to the side and laughed. 'I meant for if you want to talk to me for professional reasons.'

Jessica took the card and unlocked her car door. Sebastian made to turn around but she wasn't ready to let him have the final word. 'I meant what I told you before,' Jessica said. 'Stop stirring things up.'

She wrenched the door open, ready to duck down to climb in but Sebastian called out without turning around. 'Oooh. I love it when you talk tough.'

7

'What is wrong with this bloody chair?' Jessica said, reaching under the seat to try to adjust the controls.

The man opposite her grimaced, looking on apologetically. 'Sorry about that, I've got another one on order. It should be here any day.'

Jessica frowned across Andrew Hunter's desk at him, trying to look menacing but, as they locked eyes, she lifted what she quickly discovered was the wrong lever under the chair. The piston mechanism hissed and Jessica felt a rush of blood as the height of the seat dropped dramatically, leaving her at eye level with the desk, her knees bent uncomfortably. She stood quickly, unhappily glaring at Andrew to make sure he wasn't laughing.

'You should really fix this thing,' she said.

'Do you want to swap seats?' Andrew offered.

Jessica looked at the man's high leather-backed seat and nodded. 'Go on then.'

She moved to one side as the confused-looking man stood up. He clearly hadn't expected her to accept his offer. As they swapped positions and she moved behind his desk, Jessica struggled not to make an appreciative groan as she reclined into what was definitely the most comfortable office chair she had ever sat on. Meanwhile,

Andrew adjusted and then fidgeted uncomfortably into the broken one she had just vacated.

Jessica wheeled herself closer to the desk. 'Right, now that's sorted, we can get on with it. I read through the statement you gave last night and we have been in contact with the medical investigation team this morning. We don't have a post mortem yet but there are no concerns that Sienna Todd's death was anything other than a suicide.' She thought she was giving the man good news, considering it meant he was definitely not a suspect. The uneasy look Andrew was giving her didn't seem that relieved. 'Are you okay?' Jessica added, feeling a little embarrassed about stealing his chair.

Andrew was clearly trying to keep his face neutral as he replied but his bobbing Adam's apple gave him away. 'Yeah . . .'

A thought occurred to Jessica. 'Is that the first . . . ?'

She didn't finish the sentence as the look on Andrew's face gave her the answer that Sienna's was the first dead body he had ever seen. She had already checked out his story to see if he could be a suspect but everything he said was confirmed. His horror was so real that any suspicions there could have been around him seemed ridiculous. She had not looked behind the sheeted-off area herself – but had seen the photos that morning. Even in less than perfect light, the amount of blood was astonishing.

Andrew clearly didn't want to dwell on it, so Jessica moved on. 'Are you still working for the girl's father?'

He paused for a moment, apparently thinking his answer through before responding. 'Is that important?'

'There's a conflict of interest if you're our only witness but you're also being paid by Sienna's father. As long as you cooperate, there's not much we can do – but it would be nice to know.'

The man nodded. 'I spoke to him last night after your people had been around. He was devastated, not the man I met a few days ago. He doesn't think it was suicide.'

Jessica wondered if Andrew was offering his own opinion on the death but she didn't question it. 'Is he paying you to find out if someone killed her?'

Andrew didn't reply but nodded gently.

'Great, so we're investigating a suicide while you're blundering around getting in the way.'

The man was instantly defensive. 'It's not like that. I'll share anything I find.'

'What makes you think you'll find something I won't?' Jessica was being deliberately inflammatory.

'I don't, I . . .'

Jessica spoke over him. 'There are certain things I'm going to share with you because you're a witness and it might jog your memory about the things you saw last night. I want to be clear that I am not passing these on in any sort of professional capacity and that I'm trusting you not to hand this information over to Sienna's father. Is that understood?'

Andrew was looking flustered, nodding but confused.

'Good,' Jessica continued. 'Although we're pretty sure it was a suicide, what we don't know is if it was deliberate or accidental. We found cut marks high on Sienna's inside thigh where they wouldn't be seen unless she wanted to show someone. We're pretty sure they are self-harm cuts. Most self-harmers would do that to their arms, not their legs, but not everyone.'

Andrew was wide-eyed and Jessica thought he was likely remembering the previous night, which was what she wanted him to do. She did have a few pangs of regret given the shocked look on his face.

'Are you sure you're all right to hear this?' Jessica added.

'I just . . . I've never heard about the thigh thing before.'

Jessica didn't like to think too much about it herself. She untied her hair and then knotted it tighter into a ponytail as she replied. 'Apparently it's fairly common. What we don't know is whether she cut her wrists trying to self-harm in a similar way – but accidentally hit the artery – or if she knew what she was doing.'

She watched Andrew lean back into the chair, apparently able to ignore the collapsing backrest. 'I'm not sure I can help you. Once I saw the blood I just . . . I can't even remember it. I called you and that's about all I know.'

Jessica nodded, thinking the visit to see the private investigator hadn't been one of her best ideas. He seemed a little wet.

'We have recovered the CCTV footage of the complex,' she said. 'Although there isn't one specifically watching the area where Sienna was found, we're pretty sure no one else was present. We have also rounded up a couple of her friends who were with her earlier in the evening. We haven't managed to identify or speak to everyone she was with but the two we have statements from say they didn't know why she might have a reason to kill herself. I'm going back to see them all at some point but, for now, all we have to go on are the surveillance images you told us about.'

Andrew leant forward. 'I'm going to need my computer back if that's all right . . . ?'

Jessica stood up from the desk. 'Go on then. I guess it is your desk.'

He lifted himself up from the seat and Jessica saw him wince slightly as he reached towards his lower back. She thought it would serve him right for trying to stitch her up by making her sit in that chair but she didn't say anything.

'What time is it?' Andrew asked, looking at his watch. Jessica didn't reply as the only time-keeping device she had was her phone, which was in her jacket pocket. She wondered if he was asking as a hint because he wanted to get away. Seemingly realising what he had done, Andrew met Jessica's curious eyes. 'Sorry, I do that.'

Jessica shrugged, ready to swap seats but, instead, Andrew turned around and walked to the window where he twisted a plastic pole hanging from the top to close the blinds. It had been gradually getting darker and she realised why the man had queried the time. Jessica took her phone out of her pocket and saw that it was half past six. The day really had flown by.

'Sorry for keeping you,' Jessica said.

Andrew waved his hand in acknowledgement before sitting down. She stood behind his chair, watching as he dug into the bottom drawer to take out a camera. He placed it on the desk and then hunted through the next drawer up, pulling out a lead which he connected from the camera to the computer.

'Sorry, it's a bit slow,' he said apologetically.

Jessica wandered to the other side of the desk and started pacing the room. She was feeling restless, so started poking at the plant in the corner. It was almost as tall as she was, its green leaves waxy and bright.

'Do you know what it is?' Andrew asked. Jessica looked up to see him pointing at the foliage.

She shook her head. 'Some sort of plant, I think.'

She knew it sounded pathetic but she was unable to stop herself laughing. As Andrew joined in, Jessica began to feel a bond of sorts with him. Outwardly, he was plain but there was something about his personality that was delightfully charming. He reminded her of Adam in the way there was something incredibly likeable that was hard to specifically identify.

They were the exact opposite of Sebastian.

'What's it like being a shit version of a detective?' Jessica asked in a way that let Andrew know she was joking. Well, half-joking.

Andrew stopped laughing but he still had a smile on his face as he tapped on the computer's keyboard. 'I dunno. What's it like being a shit detective?'

'Ha!' Jessica liked the boldness of his response. 'Touché. You don't know my colleagues, do you?'

Andrew chuckled as a reply. 'It's all right. I never wanted to be a police officer or anything like that.'

'What did you want to be?'

The man continued typing on the keyboard while he spoke. 'My mum reckons I wanted to be a dustman when I was four.'

'Nice. Are you still aiming that high?'

Andrew laughed again. 'I don't know why I'm doing this. I have a degree in criminology so I know a bit about it. The truth is, I don't know what I want to be when I grow up.'

He laughed at his own joke but Jessica could see the truth in the statement. So many people fell into jobs and careers without knowing if they actually enjoyed them.

'What kind of things do you usually do?'

Jessica remembered how squeamish he seemed at the blood. She didn't blame him but figured he rarely dealt with anything that had any real intensity to it.

The man looked up from the computer. 'It's mainly affairs and stuff like that. Husbands cheating on wives, wives cheating on husbands.'

'What do you do? Follow them?' Jessica was genuinely interested, wondering if it was rewarding.

Andrew removed the wire from the camera and plugged it back in before returning to typing on the keyboard. 'Pretty much. You follow one of them, maybe take pictures depending on where you are. It's not that hard.'

'Is that mainly men?'

'Actually no. Most of the ones I end up trailing are women – but that's probably because it's the men who are willing to pay to find out what their wife is up to. I think a lot of the females checking up on their husbands go to agencies in the city where they run these honeytrap things. They have these young women who look like models on their books who go into pubs and clubs and flirt with the men to see how they respond.'

'I've heard,' Jessica replied. One of her previous cases involved a man being murdered having being caught up in a honeytrap sting. She wondered how Adam might respond if a female with model looks tried to chat him up, remembering how shy he was when they first started going out. Jessica thought of the way he would trip over words and apologise all the time and figured it would be funny to watch him in action.

Andrew looked up and shrugged. 'That's not my thing anyway. If you're hiring a girl to chat up your husband, I reckon you've got bigger problems.' Jessica wanted to ask what else he did, thinking it couldn't all be affair-related, when he added, 'This is ready, by the way.'

She stopped playing with the plant's leaves and went to stand behind Andrew. He brought up a window on the screen and started clicking through the photographs of Sienna.

'You do know that a grown man following around an eighteen-year-old and taking photos doesn't look good, don't you?' Jessica asked.

Andrew said nothing but he continued to click. There were a handful of photos of the young woman with another female friend, before a selection that showed her in a fast-food restaurant.

'Go slower,' Jessica said.

'That's the one I saw her kissing,' Andrew said as they reached a photograph of Sienna having her bottom squeezed by one of the males. Jessica nodded and said they would need a copy of it. They had already interviewed some of the friends she had been out with but, with that picture, they might have a few more direct questions to ask the male in question. 'There are two others as well,' Andrew added.

He continued to scroll through the images. Jessica noted one that showed a male appearing to whisper something and another showing a young man feeding Sienna chips while having his fingers sucked.

'She's a popular girl,' Jessica said, trying not to sound overly disapproving.

Andrew skimmed to the next photograph but Jessica was suddenly serious. 'Go back one,' she said. The man clicked forward before correcting himself and returning to the previous image. 'Can you zoom in?' Jessica asked.

'Hang on.' Andrew struggled with the controls, first zooming in on Sienna's chest, which Jessica managed to resist teasing him about and then eventually focusing on the two people's faces. Sienna was accepting a chip from one of the males with a grin on her face. 'What is it?' Andrew asked but Jessica didn't reply. He turned around to face her. 'Do you know him?'

'Can you print it off for me?' Jessica asked, ignoring his question. Andrew clicked the mouse and a printer under his desk whirred to life. He pulled out two pieces of paper, handing them to her. 'Print the other ones off too,' she added.

Of the first ones she had been handed, one had the full photograph, while the other had the two people's faces enlarged. Jessica put them down on the table, the zoomed-in picture on top.

'This is a very familiar face,' she said quietly, partly to herself but mainly to let Andrew know she was on to something, even though she had no intention of telling him what it was.

Andrew was holding onto the other printouts but, before he could say anything, Jessica felt her phone vibrating through the pocket of her jacket. A fraction of a second later the ringtone sounded. Jessica took out the device, noting the call was from the station.

As she received the news she had been dreading, Jessica tried to keep a straight face. She hung up and reached into her other pocket, fumbling for car keys, but she could tell from Andrew's expression that he knew something was wrong.

'What is it?' he asked.

Jessica had to compose herself before replying. 'There's been a fire.'

8

As Jessica drove closer to the estate where Martin Chadwick's house was situated, the air began to thicken, almost as if a cloud had dropped on top of the area. Although it was evening, it felt to Jessica like a Manchester morning, where you woke up to see heavy mist outside your window and condensation clinging to the glass.

The difference was the smell.

Even with her car vents closed, the heavy burned aroma was apparent. Jessica parked at the bottom of Martin's road. As soon as she opened the car door, the stench hit her.

She had attended her first fire scene when she was in uniform. From various television shows and training sessions, she had preconceptions of how things might unfold – but no one ever said what the smell would be like. Jessica wasn't sure she would be able to describe it fully to someone else who had not experienced it. Saying it was like burned toast but a lot worse was true in some ways but far too simplistic. The combination of charred bricks, fried electrical cables, melted plastic and the fire itself created an almost overwhelming odour that could be sensed as much through the mouth as the nose. Although it was evening, Jessica felt a strong sense of déjà vu from the previous time she had been called out to Martin's house in the dark.

As she strode along towards the flashing blue lights, Jessica struggled not to gag on the taste of the fire. She could see residents lining the road, standing outside their own houses, looking nervously in the direction of the fire engines and police cars. Some of them were holding tea towels in front of their mouths and she could see flecks of ash drifting in the haze of the street lights.

A fire officer had erected a cordon around the house as she neared. Although there was still a haze of heat, she could not see any flames. On the ground, a pair of hoses snaked limply, stretching from the pair of fire engines across the pavement towards Martin's house. Knowing fire investigators weren't always impressed with police officers trampling around their scene, Jessica made sure she asked the officer on duty where he was happy for her to stand. If the fire had still been burning, she wouldn't have been allowed anywhere near the house. She walked around the first fire engine, noticing a small group standing in between that vehicle and another similar one. Most of them were fire officers, their heavy outfits making them appear enormous in the distorted light from the street lamps.

She could see the outlines of Reynolds and Rowlands, as well as a smattering of uniformed officers and residents. An older woman exited the house opposite carrying a tray. Even from the distance she was at, Jessica could hear the rattling of the teacups as the woman approached the fire crew and started handing out drinks. Jessica was still trying to ignore the almost overpowering smell from the scene but couldn't resist smiling to herself. She dealt with many types of characters through her job and sometimes it was easy to forget the other side of things, where little old ladies with a tray of tea reminded you what most people were like.

Jessica turned to face what should have been Martin's house. It was too dark to see everything but she could tell that much of the front of the property had collapsed or burned away. The side wall where she had seen the graffiti was largely intact but she squinted to check where the top floor had collapsed onto the lower one.

'What do you reckon?'

Jessica heard Rowlands's voice from just behind her. From the hum of activity, she didn't notice him approach but he appeared next to her and together they looked at the destroyed property.

'How long have you been here?' Jessica asked, ignoring his question.

'Maybe twenty minutes? I'm not sure. They had just finished putting the fire out when I arrived.' As he finished, the constable let out a small cough. Jessica could feel something building at the top of her lungs too, almost as if there was something tickling her that was out of reach.

'Did Martin . . . ?' Jessica had been putting off approaching the other officers because she wasn't sure she wanted to know the answer.

'He's in an ambulance over there,' Rowlands said, pointing towards the other side of a fire engine. 'I think he's okay but no one has really spoken to him yet.'

'What about Ryan?'

'I don't know. I haven't seen him but I heard one of the fire guys shouting that everyone was out so he must be around somewhere. The neighbours are fine too.'

Jessica hadn't noticed the attached property, largely because it was in a spot that fell between the two closest street lamps. She stepped forward, peering through the gloom. From the outline, it looked as if the house next door was in a worse state than Martin's. While the shell of the Chadwicks' house seemed relatively intact, the neighbouring property had almost imploded upon itself, as if someone had stood inside and sucked everything inwards. Charred silhouettes of debris were scattered across the ground in front of the house.

'What on earth happened?' Jessica said to herself more than anyone. She was afraid of what the answer might be. Rowlands sensed her discomfort, taking a step closer to her but not replying. 'Do you know how Martin is?' Jessica asked.

'No idea, sorry.'

'Let's go see.' Jessica and the constable walked around the front of the fire engine towards an ambulance which was parked in such a way that the rear doors were facing the other vehicle, shielding the inside from both the rest of the street and any overlooking properties. Jessica could see a paramedic standing next to the open doors talking to someone inside. As he spotted her walking towards him, he motioned to wave her away but she could hear Martin's voice from inside the vehicle.

'Can I just . . . ?' Jessica began before the paramedic cut her off.

'He needs space, you'll have to come back.'

Reluctantly Jessica halted but Martin's voice called out. 'Sergeant Daniel?' She didn't want to defy the medical worker, who looked inside the ambulance and then back to Jessica before moving to one side.

Jessica and Rowlands approached the rear of the vehicle, where Martin was sitting on the end of a bed wrapped in a thick warm-looking blanket. On the bed next to him was an oxygen mask, which his hand was twitching towards.

'Are you okay?' Jessica asked.

Almost as if on cue, the man launched into a guttural cough before picking up the mask and taking a deep breath. 'We can leave you . . . ?' Jessica added. Martin's face had a smudge of black on one of his cheeks, as if someone had tried colouring him in with a piece of charcoal. Even from where she was standing, Jessica could see the man's eyes were painfully bloodshot.

Martin shook his head rapidly and his 'No, it's fine' came out as one hurried word.

Jessica took a few moments to understand what he had said. 'Is Ryan okay?'

The man nodded. 'He wasn't in.'

She wanted to go easy on Martin, knowing full well he would have a proper interview at some point. There was only one question that seemed to matter. 'What happened?'

Martin took another breath from the mask and, surprisingly, smiled gently. 'I was watching TV and must have fallen asleep on the sofa in the living room. All of a sudden I heard this bang from the letterbox. I was in a bit of a daze and thought it was just the postman being loud or something, so went out into the hallway. By then, the door was on fire. I'd only just woken up so I wasn't sure if I was dreaming but it was so hot and I was coughing. Then I thought that I couldn't be dreaming if I was coughing.'

The man had obviously experienced fire in the past but Jessica couldn't begin to imagine how terrifying it must be to be on the inside. Alfie Thompson popped into her mind and it was impossible not to think about how he would have gone through something similar when Martin had set fire to the building he was in.

Could it really be his father who did this as some sort of revenge?

Jessica tried to push the thoughts of Alfie out of her mind. Regardless of the rights and wrongs of what had happened in the past, she knew she had to deal with what was in front of her.

'How did you get out?' she asked.

'Out of the top window at the back. I had to jump.'

'What about the back door?' For the first time, his eyes widened in fear. 'It was blocked,' he said solemnly.

Jessica didn't mean to sound so abrupt but the word just spilled out. 'How?'

Martin spoke as quietly as before. 'I only saw when I landed. Someone tied the door handle to the window handle, meaning neither of them could be pulled down.'

Jessica felt a chill run through her that didn't relate to the temperature. Someone hadn't just set fire to the house as a scare tactic, somebody had deliberately tried to burn it down with Martin inside.

'Are you okay?' she repeated, rather feebly.

Chadwick nodded. 'I landed on my ankle and I've got a bit of a cough but . . .' Jessica didn't hear the end of the sentence because of a man's voice shouting from somewhere near the front of the ambulance. The paramedic who had been standing behind her walked around but Ryan's voice was distinctive and his anger obvious.

Jessica followed the medical worker to see Ryan stomping towards her, pointing furiously. The paramedic started to say something before Rowlands added a stern, 'Listen, mate . . .' Ryan shoved him aggressively to one side before moving to within a few inches of Jessica.

'Where's my dad?' he stormed, spit flying from his mouth and landing on Jessica's chin.

She winced in disgust but tried to stay calm. Ryan didn't seem to notice. 'He's fine, Ryan. Can you . . .' Jessica didn't get a chance to add anything else as the young man barged past her, his shoulder connecting painfully with hers as he stomped over to the rear of the ambulance.

Jessica looked up to see Rowlands staring at her, clearly stunned by what had happened.

'Are you okay?' he asked. She didn't say anything but her eyes must have given her anger away because the constable followed it with a gentle, 'Stay calm, Jess.'

If she hadn't been looking directly at him, there was every chance Jessica would have snapped but the constable's gaze was composed and she knew he was right. She spun around, returning to the rear of the ambulance where Ryan was sitting on the floor next to his father. He looked as if the fury in his dark eyes was helping to hold back tears that could begin at any moment. His fists were balled and shaking. Martin was muttering something under his breath that Jessica didn't catch but he stopped speaking as she neared.

Jessica caught Martin's eye and he stared from her to his son. 'Is everything all right?' he asked.

'A word,' Jessica replied sternly, adjusting her eye line so she was glaring at Ryan. She could feel a dull thudding pain in her shoulder but didn't want to let on.

The younger man looked up but didn't move until Martin added a curious, 'Ry?'

Clearly not wanting his father to be involved, Ryan clambered to his feet, finally unballing his fists. 'I'll be back in a minute,' he said, not looking at either Jessica or his father.

She walked backwards until she was on a clear piece of tarmac twenty metres away from the ambulance. No one could overhear them but Jessica could see that Rowlands was standing midway between them and the emergency vehicle, watching nervously.

Ryan was staring at his house which was no longer there. 'Are you okay?' Jessica asked.

'What's it to you?' he replied, not meeting her eyes.

'I know this must be quite a shock to you . . .'

'What are you going to do about it?' Ryan turned to face Jessica. His face was half in shadow but she could see him shaking.

'We'll do what we always do. We will investigate what

happened and hopefully, at the end of it, we will find out who did it and prosecute them.'

Jessica spoke as calmly as she could, deliberately slowing her words. On the previous occasion they had met she had wanted to see how Ryan might react to a gentle bit of winding up but this time she needed him to stay composed.

Ryan turned back to the house and replied, barely moving his lips with his teeth clenched tight. 'You know who did it.'

'No we don't.'

'It was in the paper. He said he was going to do this.'

Jessica stifled a sigh. 'He didn't, Ryan. I promise we will go talk to Anthony but you'll have to be patient.'

The man said nothing for a while and Jessica watched the plume of air from his nose evaporating into the cold evening air. He was still staring at the destroyed property. 'He could have killed my dad.'

'There's something else I've got to ask you about.'

'I wasn't here. I was out with friends.'

Jessica spoke firmly. 'That's not what I was going to ask. Can you come for a walk to my car?' Ryan looked over his shoulder. 'Your dad will be fine. He's being well looked after.'

He seemed reluctant but silently followed Jessica as she headed along the road towards where she had parked. Jessica heard Rowlands jogging behind them to catch them up before appearing at her side.

'Where are you going?' he muttered quietly so only Jessica could hear.

'Stay close.'

As they walked, she could see that even more people

were outside the houses than when she had first arrived. Some were taking photographs on their phones as others chattered away. She smiled as she saw a burly fireman sipping from a small teacup, thinking he could crush it with one hand if he so chose. The older lady from before was standing next to him gossiping as if it was a coffee morning at a local church, instead of a major residential fire.

Jessica unlocked her car and reached into the passenger seat, picking out a cardboard document wallet. She put it on her bonnet, separating out the contents, the overhead street lamp offering enough light for what she needed.

'What's going on here?' she asked.

Ryan picked up the piece of paper with a puzzled look on his face. 'Where did you get it?'

'I'm asking the questions, Ryan. What's going on?' Jessica kept a firm but steady tone.

He didn't answer for a moment and she wondered if he was thinking of what the best answer to give might be, rather than simply telling the truth.

'I'm feeding one of my friends a chip by the look of it,' Ryan said.

Jessica couldn't detect any emotion in his voice. 'Do you know she's dead?'

'Sienna?'

'She killed herself last night some time after this was taken.' Jessica knew this hadn't been confirmed but was watching Ryan to see if he would react. They hadn't tracked down all of Sienna's friends from the previous evening, largely because they didn't know the names. At least initially, they hadn't had Andrew's photographs to work with. Jessica wondered if Ryan knew. With mobile phones, news travelled quickly among friends.

Ryan didn't react to the news that the young woman he apparently seemed very friendly with had died, continuing to stare at the photo, apparently transfixed.

'It wasn't anything to do with me.'

'I never said it was. In fact, I said she killed herself.'

'I know what you were thinking though. Why aren't you out arresting Anthony Thompson instead of harassing me?' Ryan's tone had risen again and he thrust the picture towards Jessica.

'Were you in a relationship with Sienna Todd?'

'No.'

'Then why is she sucking your fingers?'

Ryan shrugged dismissively. 'I dunno.'

Jessica passed him the next photo, the one that had a male squeezing Sienna's backside. 'Who's this?' she asked. They already had a name because one of the witnesses they had spoken to that morning passed it on. At the time, they hadn't known he might be romantically involved with Sienna, given that Andrew had seen them kissing, but Jessica wanted to know if Ryan would tell her who it was.

He glanced at the picture, before quickly looking up. 'I can't tell from that photo.'

'Are you sure? I've been told you turned up in a car with whoever this is. You must have a pretty good idea who it is?'

'Have you got someone watching me?'

Jessica didn't want to spell out explicitly that she didn't. 'Who says they were watching you? I just happen to know a keen birdwatcher who was taking pictures of the creatures perched on the roof of the building you were in. Unfortunately their aim wasn't too good.'

'Is he in trouble?'

'I don't know. I just want to know who he is.'

Ryan bit his bottom lip before finally relenting. 'It's Finn. Finlay Pierce. We went to college together but he finished last year.'

Jessica knew that matched the name they already had. 'Was he Sienna's boyfriend?'

'Not really.'

'Were you?'

'No.' Ryan handed the photo back to Jessica. 'Can I go see my dad now?'

He went to step away but Jessica held out an arm, although she didn't touch him. Rowlands, who had been standing silently, stepped sideways to block Ryan from moving.

'Why do you think she killed herself, Ryan?'

'What?'

'Sienna. Why do you think she killed herself? You seem pretty close in these pictures.'

Ryan laughed, a snort that sounded genuinely menacing. Until that moment, Jessica had seen him as something of a troubled teenager but the way he dismissively cackled was unnerving.

'Close? Sienna was close to everyone.'

Jessica wasn't sure she wanted to hear any more but couldn't stop herself. 'How do you mean?'

The man raised his eyebrows mockingly. 'You need me

to spell it out? She fuckin' loved it. Finn might have been her boyfriend yesterday but he was one of many. She was absolutely filthy.'

Jessica didn't know if any of what Ryan had said was true but she was disgusted with the spite with which he had spoken.

The teenager seemed to sense that he had got to Jessica as he broke into a smile. 'Can I go now?'

When she didn't respond, Ryan took a step forward but Jessica acted without thinking. She grabbed his arm, yanking his thin frame around so she was forcing him up against the side of her car. She could still feel pain in her shoulder from where he had barged her but ignored it, digging her elbow into his chest. Almost involuntarily, he let out an 'ow' before correcting himself and pushing back. Jessica felt Rowlands's hand on her shoulder.

She leant in so Ryan had no choice other than to look at her and spoke firmly but ruthlessly, letting him know she was serious. 'I'll let you off the way you spoke to us the other day and I'll forget the fact that you shoved Constable Rowlands and barged me with your shoulder. But this is your final warning. If I come across you being a shit once more, there will be trouble. And not just, "We'll come knocking at your door and ask you a few questions" trouble but big, bad, "I will kick your arse in front of all your mates" trouble.'

Jessica stepped back, allowing Ryan to straighten his clothing. She kept her eyes on him. 'I've taken on much bigger, much meaner people than you in the past and I'm still here,' she added, spreading her arms as if to prove the point. 'Now go look after your dad and stop acting like a dick.'

9

Jessica changed gear and pushed down on the accelerator, missing how her old car would have made a crunching sound in protest. There had been something intensely satisfying about punishing her previous vehicle's gearbox and driving the newer one just wasn't the same.

'Why is it always you?' Rowlands asked with a gentle laugh. Jessica eased onto the brake as the set of traffic lights ahead flicked over to red. She knew that there was a lot of truth in what her colleague was saying despite his amusement. It did frequently seem to be her that brought out the aggression in people. Was it because she was a woman and some found that intimidating? Or was it something more intrinsic to her personality? Jessica didn't want to think too deeply, fearing what the truth might be.

'I didn't see you stepping in,' she replied.

'I didn't know what was going on,' the constable protested. 'I didn't know what those photos were of, or what you were asking him about.'

Jessica felt a pang of regret at the way she had spoken to Ryan. She had to keep reminding herself that he hadn't had the upbringing she had. Her parents had always been there to support her and, if anything, showed too much interest. She found herself ignoring their calls when their number appeared on her phone because she didn't want to put aside an hour of her day. Ryan had never had that and it was no surprise he was upset having just lost his house and almost his father. But there was something about the way he talked of Sienna that didn't sit right. He had a harsh, unforgiving attitude towards a young woman who had killed herself without giving any indication of why he felt like that. With that and his general attitude towards the police, something had snapped inside her.

The content of what he had said also didn't ring quite true. Sienna had cut herself high on the inside of her thighs, presumably to hide it from anyone else. If she was as 'easy' as Ryan claimed, lots of different people would have known about them.

'It's green,' Rowlands said gently. Jessica snapped back to the present, wondering if she had dozed off for a second or two. She eased the car away from the lights. 'Have you heard from Iz?'

Detective Constable Isobel Diamond was their colleague and friend who had recently gone on maternity leave. 'She texted me earlier to say that she and baby Amber are doing fine,' Jessica replied. 'Apparently her husband is waiting on her hand and foot, so there's a lesson for you.'

Dave snorted. 'If I ever have a kid, I'm going to make sure it's a boy. I read this article about how you can guarantee the sex of your child if you eat certain things.'

'What's so special about boys?'

'You can take 'em to the park and play football, things like that. They get all the cool toys.' Rowlands spoke as if his argument was the most obvious one going.

'You can do that with girls too. Or, better yet, you could

let them develop their own interests, then get involved with that,' Jessica pointed out.

'Nah.'

'You just want a mini you, don't you?'

Rowlands laughed and replied in a put-on accent that was either American or Australian. Jessica wasn't sure which. 'There's only one of me, baby.'

She couldn't stop herself from giggling, observing that she was laughing at him, not with him and adding: 'You're such an idiot.'

After a few moments, Dave spoke again, but more seriously. 'What are we going to do when we get to Anthony's? We can't keep turning up at his house.'

Jessica knew he was right. 'We can't do much else at the moment. The fire investigators say they won't have even the basics from Martin's house until tomorrow, although they are pretty sure it was arson. Regardless of what they end up with, the fact the back door and window were secured to try to keep Chadwick in shows it was a deliberate act. This was attempted murder. None of the neighbours say they saw anything – at least not yet – so he's our only lead.'

'How do you think he'll take it?'

She didn't reply, instead reaching forward to turn up the heaters. Jessica didn't know if Anthony was responsible but felt trapped in the middle of a dispute between two sides which was only going to end with one or both parties either locked up or dead. From her only encounter with him, Anthony seemed too eccentric to get through to, while Ryan was fuelled by hatred. Martin was also caught between them – although it was down to his actions.

Jessica parked a few doors away from Anthony Thompson's house and the two officers got out of the car, although not before Jessica had reached onto the back seat for the jacket she hadn't yet returned.

'Is it just us two?' Rowlands asked.

Jessica slammed her door and walked around to the pavement where he was waiting.

'For now. We still have no evidence that Anthony is involved, so we can't go stomping in. I want to make sure that everything I told him the other day has sunk in. It won't do any harm to ask where he was this evening either.'

She led the way to the house, pointing towards the front window as they walked along the short path. 'Curtains open but no lights on,' Jessica said.

She knocked as quietly as she could on the door so as not to disturb the neighbours. Given the time of the evening, she didn't want to draw attention to what they were doing. As she knocked a second time, Rowlands edged along the window frame, pushing his face up to the glass.

'See anything?' Jessica whispered loudly.

'No. Why are we whispering?'

Jessica noted that he had lowered his own voice. 'Because it's dark and we don't want to annoy the neighbours.'

The constable stepped away from the window, walking backwards across the small patch of lawn. 'I can't see anything upstairs,' he said out loud.

Jessica knocked a third time, although she knew it wouldn't be answered. Rowlands rejoined her at the door. 'It doesn't look good, does it? This guy threatens revenge and is nowhere to be found on the night the other person's house burns down.'

'Anthony didn't threaten revenge,' Jessica said. 'He said that people had to pay for what they had done.'

'What's the difference?'

Jessica sighed. 'At the moment, I don't know. He might have been referring to the price Martin had already paid by being in prison.'

She was hoping there was a simple explanation for the man not being at home. Hopefully he was somewhere public where his presence could be checked. Jessica nodded towards the path that stretched around the side of the house.

'Let's check around the back,' she said, leading the way.

A high overgrown hedge shielded their trespassing from any potential onlookers as Rowlands helped to lift Jessica over the top of a wooden gate that was taller than she was. Landing with a grunt on the other side, Jessica unbolted the lock to let the constable through.

As they walked into the back garden, the hedge height dropped, allowing a row of houses at the end of the property to be clearly visible. One of them had a light shining through a top-floor window.

'Should we go back?' Rowlands asked, nodding towards the house.

'Nah, it's too dark for anyone to see,' Jessica replied. The light of the moon, along with a faint glow from a street lamp on the other side of the hedge, gave them just enough illumination to see the area. A roll of carpet had been left directly ahead of the side entrance and Jessica stepped over it, attempting not to stand on anything that could show they had been there. She turned to check there were no lights on at the rear of the house as Rowlands again peered through the window.

'Nothing,' he said without prompting.

The garden was a mix of uneven paving slabs and overgrown, muddy grass areas with seemingly no plan of what should be where. A flower bed ran the length of the hedge near to the discarded carpet but, although it was spring, Jessica could see nothing was sprouting. Instead, it comprised piles of earth and a bush which had been hacked back in the corner.

As she traced her way along the hedge at the end of the garden, Jessica's eyes were drawn to a shed in the far corner that was largely hidden in the shadows. The only thing that gave it away was the sloping A-shaped roof, with long windowless sides almost camouflaged against the background.

Jessica was edging towards the outhouse when she felt a jolt shoot through her. At first she thought it was pain from her shoulder but then she heard her phone's ringtone start, and realised it was the vibration of the device through her jacket pocket that had made her jump. Desperate not to draw the attention of a nosy neighbour, Jessica fumbled for the phone, stabbing at the screen.

'Adam?' she whispered loudly.

'Er, yeah. Are you okay?'

For some irrational reason, Jessica felt him talking at full volume could expose where she was and shushed agitatedly into the phone.

'I'm fine,' she said, trying to keep her voice down. 'I'm sorry I'm late, I'll be home soon. Do you want me to pick up a takeaway?'

Adam had lowered his voice when he next spoke. 'I'm going to sort myself out. You're definitely going to be home soon?'

'Yes but I've got to go.' Jessica ended the call abruptly. She remembered a few weeks previously when she had been in the station's canteen and caught the tail-end of Rowlands finishing a phone conversation with Chloe as each refused to hang up on the other. He eventually relented when he noticed Jessica watching but public displays of affection were another part of being in a relationship she hadn't come to terms with.

Jessica returned the phone to her pocket and stood silently in case a neighbour had noticed. As she was about to continue towards the shed, she heard Rowlands's voice hissing from somewhere close to the house. 'Jess.'

His tone sounded urgent and she walked as quickly as she could towards him, careful not to leave footprints on the grassed areas. He was standing by one of the windows at the rear of the house looking at her.

'What?' Jessica said.

'Look.' Rowlands pointed to a small alcove underneath the bay window, where the frame curved out, leaving a gap underneath. 'I've not touched it,' he added.

Jessica took the phone out of her pocket and crouched,

turning on the screen's light. In the white glow, she could see a faded green plastic petrol can pushed towards the back, lying on its side. The lid was unscrewed, resting on the ground, attached by a thin synthetic strip. There were a few drops of liquid on the concrete next to it but it otherwise seemed empty.

Jessica stood up as the light on her phone turned itself off. 'Shit.'

'It doesn't look good, does it?' Rowlands said.

She leant against the window, facing the rest of the garden, and breathed out deeply, watching the steam drift upwards into the air and then evaporate.

'Maybe . . .' Jessica replied, pausing. 'But, if Anthony set fire to the other house, why would he come back here, leave the can and then disappear? Also, it's sort of hidden where you found it but, if he wanted to properly hide it, why wouldn't he dump it in a bin, a hedge, a field or anywhere on his way back? It's only a plastic can, so it's not as if it can have any sentimental value.'

'True but why would it be here at all? Why wouldn't it be in the back of his car where anyone else would keep it?'

Jessica pressed against the glass and stared up at the clear sky. The moon was a bright white and she could see the blinking red lights of a plane passing overhead.

'What if he was out here when we knocked?' Rowlands added. 'He might have heard us and then shoved it in there to hide it and run off.'

Jessica wasn't convinced but a thought skipped through her mind. 'There is a shed at the other end.' She pointed towards the shadowed corner. The constable stepped forward but Jessica held a hand across him. 'Be careful, we're not supposed to be here. Don't leave any footprints.'

Together they navigated their way across the uneven flags, carefully stepping on the parts of the lawn with the most grass when they had to. Jessica knew they wouldn't have a good reason for trampling on his property if Anthony was in his shed. If he wasn't, she didn't want to run the risk of having problems with evidence later.

With something like the petrol can, she couldn't simply phone into the station and say what they had picked up because they had discovered it while trespassing. If that ever found its way into a defence lawyer's argument, the evidence could be ruled as inadmissible. That didn't mean there weren't ways and means of working around the law. Jessica had already mentally rehearsed the conversation she would have with Cole later that evening. It would go along the lines of, 'Our only suspect went missing at the exact time the fire was being set, let's ask a magistrate if we can have a warrant.' It was easy to make it sound like two and two were five if really necessary. Once that warrant was granted, Jessica would either be with the team that arrived at the house, or she would have a quiet word with whoever was leading the raid, just to say that there might be something of interest under the window at the back. If they could handily forget that the side gate was unlocked, then all the better.

It was the kind of thing that happened frequently although no one ever talked about it. When they knew about a certain person who was dealing drugs, they might have no evidence but 'intelligence' would emerge of people coming and going at inopportune hours, or 'neighbours' would provide anonymous statements. By the time they'd raided the place and found the evidence as they knew they would, no one cared whether the tip was genuine.

Lost in her thoughts, Jessica almost fell into the constable as he tripped on a raised paving slab and rocked backwards to steady himself. She stumbled and stretched out as he half-turned and reached out to grab her. He caught her just in time to stop her falling but Jessica winced as he touched the shoulder Ryan had barged into.

'Are you okay?' he asked.

'Yeah, come on, let's get on with it.'

Jessica stepped past her colleague and hopped from one paved area to the next until she was in front of the shed. She hadn't been able to see it from a distance but the wood was stained a greeny-brown and large parts of it were damp and rotten, even though it hadn't rained for a few days. The door appeared as flimsy as the rest of the structure but a large metal padlock was attached. Jessica rattled the door gently but couldn't pull it forward enough to make a crack she could see through.

'Shall we go?' Rowlands whispered. 'He's obviously not here if it's padlocked from the outside.'

'Light your phone up and hold it here for me,' Jessica said, crouching next to the lock.

The constable did as he was told as Jessica reached into an inside pocket of her jacket and took out a wide hair clasp. 'What are you doing?' Rowlands asked but she ignored him.

The padlock was connected to a metal bracket and, using the clip at the back of her clasp, Jessica scraped the paint out of the grooves of a screw holding the joint in place. After clearing all three screws, she pushed the clasp into the grooves sideways then slowly began to turn it. As she twisted, Jessica thought the clasp would give way first but she gradually managed to loosen the screw before, finally, it dropped into her hand.

'That was pretty good,' Rowlands said.

'Just hold the light still,' Jessica replied grumpily as his hands shook. She started on the second screw, using both hands.

'If this was a movie, you would have just picked the lock,' the constable whispered.

'If this was a movie, I'd have a chest three times bigger than I actually do and you'd be much better looking. Now hold still.'

Steadily Jessica eased the second and third screws out from the bracket before pocketing them. Although the padlock was still connected, the door's hinge was only screwed to the frame of the shed, so Jessica could pull it open. It squeaked loudly, so she wrenched it as quickly as she could and then propped a stone in front of it.

Jessica entered the shed, holding her phone out in front of her for light. She didn't know what she expected but the interior was about as shed-like as she could have imagined. A lawnmower was in the corner although, from the state of the back garden, it didn't look as if it had been used in a while. A wooden shelf ran along the left-hand wall, stacked with jam jars, paint brushes and all kinds of tools, with potted plants lining the wall opposite.

'This is like my dad's shed,' Rowlands said unhelpfully.

'Thanks for that. I just spent five minutes tearing my fingers to pieces trying to get in here.'

'Can you see anything?'

'Junk.' Jessica turned to leave but Rowlands was blocking her way. 'Come on, move,' she said agitatedly.

Dave stepped backwards, grabbing her arm. 'Jess . . .'

Jessica turned to see where he was pointing his phone. Her eyes struggled to adjust to the light but, as she squinted, she could see an upturned bucket caked in soil. At first she didn't know what he was highlighting but then she noticed it: sitting next to the bucket was a can of spray paint with a yellow cap.

10

Jessica had reached the main road on her commute the following morning when her phone started ringing. She pressed the button on her car's dashboard to answer. Rowlands's voice sounded but he didn't even say 'hello' before getting to the point.

'Have you seen the paper?'

'Which paper?'

'The *Herald*. They've got the fire on the front page.'

'Who wrote it?'

'Some Sebastian bloke.'

Jessica edged into traffic that wasn't moving and put her handbrake on. 'What does it say about Martin and Anthony?'

Dave mumbled to himself, as if reading quickly. 'It says it happened at Martin Chadwick's house and that he was recently released from prison. It mentions the Alfie Thompson case . . . I think that's it. They've got a photo of the house so someone must have been there after we left.'

'No Anthony or Ryan?'

'I don't think so.'

'Well that's one thing.'

'There's something else.' Rowlands sounded ominous.

'What?' Jessica edged off the brake, crawling forward four car lengths before stopping again.

'It's got the girl's suicide in. The one you were asking Ryan about. It's only small but that's on the front page next to the main story.'

Because she had seen Sebastian at the scene, Jessica knew that story would be going in but was worried about the journalist finding the link she knew existed between the two cases – Ryan.

'Does it mention any names?' Jessica asked.

'No, not even the girl's.'

'Well, that's two things.' There was a pause but Jessica could sense Rowlands had more to say. 'Are you on a late today?' she asked.

'Yeah, I'm not in until this afternoon. Do you know what's going on this morning? I'd rather be with you.'

Jessica didn't want to admit it to him but she would rather Dave was with her too. With Izzy's maternity leave and the fact no one else had been hired to cover her, a detective constable was being asked to come in from a different district for a few hours at the end of the day to tidy up any of the late bits and pieces. It helped to clear the paperwork but hadn't gone down well among staff.

'I spoke to Jack last night,' Jessica said, waving a car into her lane with an exaggerated movement of her arm to let the other driver know she was doing them a massive favour. 'Someone was going to watch Anthony's house overnight while he sorted out a warrant to search the property. They might have already gone in. I told him they might want to pay attention to under the back window and in the shed.'

'What did he say?'

'He pretended he hadn't heard.'

'Ha! What about Anthony? Have we got a warrant to pick him up?'

'I don't know. Jack said they had put him on the watch lists and were going to send uniform around to knock on doors. He reckoned they'd call me overnight if he turned up but I haven't heard anything so I assume he's still missing. We still don't have anything concrete to connect him to the fire other than the fact he's not at his house. I suspect the DCI's played a bit of smoke and mirrors if he's sorted the search warrant but we probably didn't have enough for the arrest one.'

Jessica heard Rowlands yawn loudly. 'Were you up late last night?' she asked. 'What were you doing?'

Dave yawned again straight away but Jessica could hear him trying to talk through it. 'Nothing. I got in late and couldn't sleep.'

'Aye aye, so you'll have deleted the Internet history this morning before Chloe saw it?'

Rowlands's alleged web-surfing habits, which Jessica had invented to get a laugh out of Izzy a few months previously, were a frequent cause for her amusement.

Jessica laughed as the man protested. 'Hey, I was phoning you to be nice and give you a heads-up.'

'Yeah all right, your secret's safe with me. I'll see you later.'

Jessica hung up, realising she had travelled barely a quarter of a mile during the entire conversation.

*

Despite arriving late because of the traffic, Jessica reached the station in time for the morning briefing in Cole's office along with Reynolds and Detective Sergeant Louise Cornish. The DCI said the investigating fire officer had found traces of petrol or diesel which he thought had been used to start the blaze at Martin Chadwick's house. Meanwhile, they had searched Anthony Thompson's empty home earlier that morning and, as Jessica knew full well, had discovered an empty petrol can and almost-empty tin of yellow aerosol paint.

Jessica thought about the fifteen minutes it had taken her to twist the screws back into the shed the previous evening and wondered whether the tactical entry team had simply smashed the door in with a battering ram. Cole didn't mention her 'tip' to the rest of the room – but he did glance her way as he brought it up, letting her know that he knew what she had done.

As she suspected, Anthony was still missing and, with little else to go on, they were doing what they could to look for him without making it official. The items recovered from his house would be sent off for testing to see if they could be linked to the crime scene but it was unlikely. The wall where the yellow graffiti had been sprayed was badly fire-damaged, with the petrol can circumstantial at best.

As for finding Anthony, by discreetly working with the rest of Greater Manchester Police, they could coordinate things such as pulling over suspicious cars, door-to-door checks around the area he lived in, and visits to places he was known to frequent. What they didn't want to do was tip off the wider media that he could be involved with the fire. For one, they didn't know that he was but, worse than that, they didn't want to risk the negative attention it would bring to them all if there was an innocent explanation for his disappearance. Jessica thought of what Sebastian's gleeful face might look like if that happened.

The only other piece of news the DCI had was a steer from the coroner that Sienna's death would likely be ruled as suicide but that he wasn't yet discarding the chance of an inquest because there were still a few test results to come back. It was what they had suspected but Jessica still had a nagging thought in her mind about the presence of Ryan in both cases.

With the search for Anthony being kept quiet and Sienna's death not yet ruled upon, Jessica and Reynolds were assigned to visit the college that Sienna had attended. Even if the coroner did eventually decide on suicide, it would do no harm for them to find out as much background as they could to what had happened.

Jessica first called the college to check the details they would need. The Manchester College largely served sixteen-to nineteen-year-old school-leavers and they had half-a-dozen campuses dotted around the city. Sienna had been studying health and beauty at the Openshaw site which, Jessica noted from the website, was the closest to where Ryan lived. As the receptionist passed on the information, Jessica asked authoritatively which course Ryan was involved with. Although she wasn't entitled to that information, she knew that, if you used any of the words 'officer', 'detective' or 'sergeant' and asked with enough confidence, most staff would happily tell you what you wanted to know, thinking they were obliged to do so.

Ryan was studying masonry and brickwork on the same campus but the key piece of information Jessica discovered was that both he and Sienna shared the same form tutor. It had been a while since she had been in education but the receptionist told her that every student – regardless of course – was assigned to a set adult who would monitor their attendance. They were required to sign a register each day and attend bi-monthly meetings with the tutor to talk about their overall progress. Jessica noted the teacher's name – Aidan Barlow – and asked the receptionist if they could organise a time to speak to him that day. Jessica figured he would be one of the few adults to actually see Sienna and Ryan interacting.

Much of the local traffic had cleared by the time Reynolds drove them to the college but Jessica's frustration at the hours she seemed to have spent in a car that day didn't abate as they endured fifteen minutes searching for a parking spot at the campus. Her suggestion to 'just run him over' as a gormless-looking student wandered in front of them was ignored, as was her idea to 'just block him in' when they drove past the head teacher's marked space for the third time.

By the time they had reached the reception area, only to find a queue of people, Jessica was ready to snap. After another ten minutes of listening to the group of girls in front blathering on about which type of hair extensions they should get, Reynolds had resorted to resting a reassuring hand on Jessica's shoulder. The pain had largely subsided from the previous evening but she could still feel a twinge as her supervisor gave her a wide-eyed 'be calm' look.

Jessica did lots of things well. Calm was not one of them.

Despite her annoyance, she had to admit the receptionist was helpful when they reached the front. She phoned for a support staff member, who led both officers out of reception across the car park they had spent so long navigating. Although the signs proudly displayed the area as a 'campus', Jessica wasn't sure the large two-storey grey building that stretched for a hundred metres or more could really be classed as anything other than a giant warehouse with windows.

The member of staff swiped them through a set of double doors and led them up a flight of stairs that opened onto a cream-coloured corridor that looked identical to the one below it.

Eventually, they reached a door with Aidan Barlow's name printed on it and, after knocking and being called in, Jessica and Reynolds were offered seats in his office.

Aidan greeted them with a handshake and a smile, although Jessica struggled to identify his accent. At first she thought it was Irish but she also wondered if there was a hint of Scottish. The man was somewhere in his mid-thirties with a mop of straggly brown hair. He was wearing a jumper over a shirt, with thick-rimmed glasses which perfectly suited his face. In terms of looks, he wasn't as striking as Sebastian but there was definitely something about the man which Jessica felt drawn to.

She did figure that part of the appeal could be the state of his office. While his desk was placed in the centre facing the door, piles of papers and files littered the edges of the room. Some were in boxes, with others piled on top of each other. It reminded Jessica of her own 'filing system'.

'How can I help you?' Aidan asked when they were all seated and the two officers had turned down the offer of tea.

Given the way Reynolds had tried to calm her in reception, Jessica didn't know if he would want to take the lead. Usually there was something unspoken between them – between her and pretty much anyone at the station in fact – that she would ask the questions. Even Cole gave way to her, although she had never asked him why. As the inspector stayed quiet, Jessica took the cue.

'Obviously you know what occurred with Sienna Todd a few days ago,' Jessica said. 'We wanted to talk to you as her form tutor about anything that might have led up to it.'

Aidan nodded gently, ready to help. 'I heard it was suicide?'

'We're not completely sure yet.'

'Have you spoken to her friends? I'm not sure how much use I can be.'

'That's our next stop,' Jessica assured him. 'Any background you can give us would be great. Is it right Sienna had been in your form since September?'

Aidan pushed out his bottom lip, nodding. 'Yes, just this year.'

'What did you make of her?'

'Sienna? I'm not sure. She had one of those names that's a bit different, so you remember them. She seemed to be very friendly with everyone. Her course progress was good according to her marks. Generally she was here on time. She seemed very normal.'

Jessica asked for any particular friends that Aidan knew she hung around with but he didn't offer any names other than what they had from the earlier inquiries.

'What about boyfriends?' Jessica asked.

Aidan gave a knowing smile but quickly suppressed it. 'I'm not sure about a boyfriend,' he said. 'She was certainly very friendly with a few of the male students but I'm not sure I knew enough about her to answer that. You would have to speak to her friends.'

From what Andrew had told Jessica about Sienna's abortion, Ryan's claims, and now her form tutor's insinuations, a rather disturbing picture of the young woman's relationships was emerging. Jessica knew Sienna's friends might be her best bet for finding the truth although, from her own experience of adolescence, she wasn't convinced she would get the answers she needed.

'What are her friends like? Are they in your form?' she persisted.

Aidan scratched his chin and nodded. 'A couple of them. I'm not sure if it's the fairest term to use but she was in a sort of clique with four or five others. I believe they were on the same course. Every time I saw them around campus, they were together.'

The man didn't know all of the names but two of them were the girls who had already been spoken to.

'Did she ever come to you with any problems?' Reynolds asked.

The man shook his head. 'Why would she?'

'Because you're her tutor,' the inspector observed. 'Perhaps she mentioned to you problems at home, or issues with her work or something like that?'

Aidan continued to shake his head. 'We didn't have that kind of relationship, I'm afraid.'

Jessica tried to word the question in a slightly different way. 'Did you ever see her upset or depressed?'

The man continued to look blankly back at them. 'Sorry.'

Jessica could feel Reynolds trying to catch her eye, as if to say he didn't think they could get any more from the man, but she still had something else to say. Jessica asked the question already knowing the answer. 'Is Ryan Chadwick in your form?'

'Ryan? Er, yes . . .' The query had clearly taken Aidan by surprise. Jessica felt Reynolds tense slightly next to her but he didn't say anything.

'What's he like?'

'Um, I'm not sure what that has . . . ?' From sitting coolly in his seat while discussing Sienna, the man began to fidget and he looked nervously towards the wall.

'No reason,' Jessica said. 'We just know he was friends with Sienna.'

Aidan steadied himself as if his moment of nervousness had never happened. He gazed at Jessica again. 'Oh right. Um, Ryan's a . . . complicated character.'

She could not have thought of a better word herself but wanted specifics. 'How do you mean?'

'He's not the easiest person to communicate with. Sometimes he seems happy, other times not. Sometimes he'll join in with the group but then he can be a loner too. He's the type of person where you're never quite sure where you stand with him.'

Everything Aidan was saying backed up Jessica's own impressions of Ryan. 'I've heard he's perhaps a little more than just friends with Sienna,' Jessica added, trying to make it sound as if she knew more than she did and fishing for information.

Aidan seemed a little surprised at Jessica's question, his eyebrows deepening before he shrugged slightly. 'I guess. I've seen them talking in registration but I don't know much more than that. They're all at a bit of an awkward age in regards to opening up. Some of them are all right with you but others are still stuck in the moody teenager phase.'

Jessica glanced at Reynolds, letting him know she was finished. Aidan must have noticed the gesture because he continued to speak. 'I . . . um . . . it's a bit awkward . . .'

Jessica looked back to the tutor, eyebrows raised expectantly. Aidan seemed to be struggling with something. He was sucking nervously on his top lip. 'I might have something for you regarding Ryan but . . . there are confidentiality rules and I . . .' He tailed off without finishing the sentence.

Reynolds tensed further in the seat next to her. Listening to whatever Aidan might have would be a legal grey area at best, perhaps even an outright breach of various protection laws – if not on their part then certainly on his.

Jessica sensed it could be important but didn't have time to reply before the tutor spoke again. 'If you're off to talk to other people, can you give me maybe an hour? I have to check a few things out.'

Jessica didn't bother to wait for her supervisor's approval. 'We'll see you in an hour.'

11

As they exited Aidan's office, Jessica could feel Reynolds's discomfort. She waited for him to close the door and then he crossed the corridor, standing and staring at her. His dark hair was beginning to grey around his ears and at the front, the colour contrasting with the darkness of his skin.

'Well?' he said.

Jessica shrugged. 'You saw what Ryan was like when we were at the house but you didn't see the aggression after the fire or the way he talked about Sienna. It's not what he said, it's the way he said it.'

'That doesn't mean you should let his tutor break the law, let alone condone it.'

Jessica looked away, unable to meet her supervisor's eye. She wondered how he might have taken her excursion to Anthony Thompson's house. 'There's something not right,' she said.

'Like what?'

'Just . . . something.' Jessica didn't know what it was herself. 'Everything seems to be revolving around him. Did you see the way Aidan shifted around when I mentioned him? After the fire, he shoved Dave out of the way, even though he must have known he was an officer. He didn't care.'

Jessica didn't mention the way she had been barged.

'That still doesn't mean . . .'

Jessica interrupted before the inspector could finish. 'What if Aidan has something that says Ryan has done something serious?'

Reynolds looked away, staring down the deserted hallway. 'I can't be involved.'

'What if we miss something?'

The inspector turned to face Jessica, his face stern but his eyes wide. 'I can't be involved.'

His implication became clear. 'Oh,' Jessica replied. 'Right.'

As she sat listening to the endless stream of 'yeah', 'y'know' and 'y'what' responses, Jessica remembered why her friend Caroline had been the only person worth hanging around with at school. Teenage girls really were annoying. Well, maybe not all of them but certainly the four she had spoken to so far. Sienna's 'clique' as Aidan had called them didn't seem to recognise the seriousness of their so-called friend killing herself.

The first young woman Jessica spoke to looked as if she was dressed for a night out rather than a class, her nails almost long enough to be offensive weapons. Her 'Yeah, it's like really bad about Si innit, y'know?' was more or less the most literate thing she came out with.

As Jessica and Reynolds worked their way through talking to the rest of the group, the responses and concern did become a little more apparent – but Jessica had a constant nag in the back of her mind that the girls' distress seemed to be more for themselves than their dead friend. It all added to her feeling that something wasn't quite right about Sienna. None of them claimed to know she was pregnant, with all of them edgy about the nature of Sienna's relationships. They all said she had no boyfriend but admitted she was friendly with Finlay Pierce – the name Ryan had given them. Even more curious was the reaction they gave when Jessica mentioned Ryan's name. At first they all acted as if he was just a passing acquaintance, concluding that, although Sienna may have been friends with him, none of them really knew him.

Jessica knew Ryan had been in the fast-food restaurant with at least two of the girls when Andrew had taken photographs of them but she couldn't figure out why they might lie. All she was sure of was that everything seemed to be revolving around him. A thought even ran through her mind that perhaps Anthony wasn't missing through choice.

As the fourth girl left the classroom, Jessica looked at Reynolds sitting next to her. She lowered her voice as the rest of the room was empty and everything they said seemed to echo. 'They don't seem the best of friends, do they?'

The inspector shook his head and smiled wearily. 'Are all teenage girls like this?'

'I bloody wasn't. Last summer I got caught in traffic on the way home because there was some prom going on at the high school. There were limos, horse-drawn carriages, double-decker buses and all sorts trying to pull into the car park. They had these dresses like giant parasols. Do you know what I did after my final day at school?'

Reynolds rolled his eyes. 'Go on.'

'I went to the park with a few mates and a giant bottle of cheap cider and we got pissed behind the bandstand. These kids today don't know they're born.'

'Are you about to go off on one about the kids of today?' Reynolds's eyes twinkled as his smile widened.

Jessica slapped his arm. 'You're older than me.'

They were interrupted as the door opened and their final interviewee walked in. Because no one was under any suspicion and they were all eighteen, there was no need for any of the girls' parents or any legal representation to be present. Jessica had assured the head teacher they were simply looking for background on Sienna. She didn't mention that she was also trying to suss out Ryan.

The last young woman looked a little different from the four that had come before. Jessica could see it straight away from the way she walked. There was less confidence about her and she was not as dressed-up as her friends. She had short straight black hair tucked behind her ears and was wearing a pair of jeans with a checked shirt over a white vest-top. Jessica noticed a small mole in the dimple of one of the girl's cheeks and, while she could see how young males might go for the almost airbrushed looks of the other girls, there was something more naturally attractive about the woman in front of them.

'Are you Molly North?' Jessica asked, checking the note she had written.

Molly nodded nervously, shuffling from one leg to the other before Reynolds gestured towards the chair. The young woman sat but stared at the table the two officers were seated behind, rather than focusing on them.

'We wanted to talk to you about Sienna Todd, Molly. I understand you were one of her friends?' Despite her frustration with the other young women, Jessica used the same reassuring tone she had tried with them.

Molly nodded. 'Yeah.'

'How well did you know her?'

'Pretty well.'

'We have been trying to find out if there was someone Sienna might have confided in? Maybe one friend she was closer to than anyone else . . . ?' Jessica was trying to lead the girl, hoping for something other than one- or two-word responses.

Molly shrugged slightly but she appeared far more sombre than the rest of Sienna's friends. They hadn't seemed too keen to engage with the officers but the young woman in front of them was at least listening to the questions. 'We have been friends a long time,' Molly said. 'Since primary school.'

'Did Sienna ever confide in you about anything that could have led to what happened?'

Molly shook her head.

'And you weren't out with her on the night everything happened?'

Another head shake.

Jessica paused to think. 'Do you mind if I say something that might sound a little harsh?'

Molly finally looked up and met Jessica's gaze. Her eyes were wet but she wasn't crying. 'What?'

Jessica tried to sound as gentle as she could. 'You seem very different from Sienna's other friends. Perhaps Sienna herself? You dress differently, you walk differently. I don't see how you fitted into their group.'

Molly laughed with no real joy. 'You must be really good at your job to see that.'

It was a sarcastic remark but Jessica sensed no real spite to it. She tried to match the girl's half-smile. 'Tell me about Sienna.'

The young woman tucked a strand of hair behind her ear, clearly forcing herself not to cry but also suppressing a smile. 'She wasn't what you think.'

'I don't really think anything about her,' Jessica said, largely telling the truth. 'No one seems to know much other than her name and who she hung around with.'

'Those other girls aren't really her friends,' Molly said, without prompting.

'How do you mean?'

'Her dad's rich. He didn't want Si to come here because he would have rather she went to a private college. They only latched on to her because she had money and didn't mind spending it on them. That was all.'

Jessica had not met Sienna's father because a support officer had been sent to tell him about what happened to his daughter. Because there was no murder or suspicious death investigation, she'd had no need to see him since. Despite that, Andrew Hunter had told her that Sienna's father said he had allowed his daughter to go to a college he didn't approve of because of her friends.

She wondered if it was one friend in particular.

'Sienna came here to stay close to you, didn't she?' Jessica asked.

Molly smiled and nodded. 'We were at school together. Best mates and all that. Her dad wasn't rich then but he left Si's mum and moved to this house out of the city when he made his money. We were about fourteen or fifteen. Si stayed with him but refused to change schools and then she wanted to come here with me. She was on this beauty course thing, even though she's not interested in it. She was only doing it do we could carry on being friends.'

'What course do you do?' Jessica asked.

'English lit but it's on this campus.'

'Is that why Sienna chose a course to do here?' Molly shrugged but offered a half-nod at the same time. 'Why did she hang around with those other girls if they're not really her friends?' Jessica asked.

Molly scratched her forehead and wiped her eyes. 'She liked being liked.'

'What about you?'

The young woman blinked rapidly and looked towards the door. 'I liked her.' The connotations of the ways she used the word 'liked' and then emphasised 'her' on the final occasion was not lost on Jessica. She didn't know if it was fair to ask the question but Molly answered it anyway, as if sensing Jessica's dilemma. 'Si wasn't like that if you're wondering.'

'Why do you think she might have killed herself?' Jessica asked, trying not to sound overly blunt.

Molly shuffled uneasily in her chair, still looking

towards the door. 'I don't know.' Her words sounded shaky and untrue.

'Did you know Sienna had an abortion?' The young woman shook her head but Jessica could see it was a lie. The other girls had struggled to hide their surprise but Molly barely reacted. 'Do you know if Sienna was seeing anyone?'

'No.'

'You don't know or she definitely wasn't?'

'She wasn't going out with anyone.'

The fact Sienna didn't appear to have a regular boyfriend was at least something all of her friends, plus Ryan, agreed on. From the second-hand information Andrew had passed to her, it seemed that was the impression her father was under too.

'Did you know Sienna cut herself?' Jessica asked.

Molly winced slightly and tugged at the sleeve of her own shirt, pulling it down further. 'I didn't know,' she replied, although Jessica couldn't judge whether the response was genuine.

'How well do you know Ryan Chadwick?'

Jessica saw the young woman stiffen, her arms locked to her side momentarily and her expression taut. A strand of hair unhooked itself from behind Molly's ear and drifted across her face. She did nothing to move it.

'Molly?'

'He's one of the lads. Si knew him better than I did.'

'Was she ever in a relationship with him?'

Molly spoke without thinking. 'I don't know.'

'What do you think of him?'

The young woman pushed out her bottom lip and then sucked it in, chewing on it anxiously. 'I don't really know him.'

'But he hung around with the people you hung around with?' Jessica had seen similar responses from the other girls but no one seemed to want to give her any further information. She sensed that Molly was close if she could find the right way in.

The woman shrugged and stared towards the door once more. 'Can I go?'

Jessica sighed. 'Are you sure there isn't something else you might want to tell me? About your friend? Or Ryan? Something important? We're trying to help.'

Molly didn't reply but Jessica saw her gulp, her eyes blinking furiously. 'I have to go,' she eventually said.

The two women stood at the same time, Reynolds continuing to sit. Jessica could sense he felt uncomfortable and she thought how Izzy would have been a much better bet to come along if she wasn't on maternity leave.

Before Molly could reach the door, Jessica caught her. 'Hang on,' she said, taking a business card out of her jacket pocket along with a pen. The printed part included the station's phone number but Jessica turned it over and pressed against the doorframe to add her mobile number, passing it to Molly. 'Call me any time – even if it's late.'

The young woman took the card and pushed it into her jeans pocket, before opening the door and letting herself out without reply.

Jessica turned to face Reynolds, who was now standing

next to the table. 'I'm going back to the car,' he said. 'You should come too.'

'Don't you see it?' Jessica asked, stifling her frustration. 'Everyone has the same reaction when we talk to them about Ryan. There's something not right with him.'

The inspector shook his head. 'You're seeing what you want to. He was aggressive at the house because you tried to provoke him. He was always going to be upset after the fire. Then these girls, they're telling you they don't really know him but you're not listening.'

He didn't sound angry, more annoyed. If anything, that made it harder for Jessica to judge his mood. She had seen him lose his temper in the past but never with her. She didn't know if he was genuinely annoyed, or simply trying to give her advice.

'It's not just that . . .' Jessica replied.

When she failed to add anything further, Reynolds shook his head again. 'I'll see you in the car. Whatever you do, I don't want to hear about it.'

With that, he strode past Jessica out of the room.

As the door swished closed in front of her, Jessica rested her head on the doorframe. She wondered if her supervisor was right. Was she really allowing her judgement to be clouded? The truth was, she didn't know if Ryan was involved in the things that were going on. He just always seemed to be there. A few years ago she had become obsessed with her then-DCI – John Farraday. That had not ended well and, although no one except the former chief inspector knew what had happened, it was still something she thought about on nights she lay awake.

Jessica took a deep breath and then opened the class-room door. The corridor was deserted, although she could hear a low hum of voices coming from the various rooms. Jessica followed her way back through the passageways until she found Aidan's office, knocking loudly on the frame and instantly hearing a 'come in' from the inside.

Aidan was sitting in the same spot he had been in a little over an hour beforehand. On the desk in front of him was a cardboard folder. Jessica motioned to sit but the teacher simply held out the wallet for her to take.

'Can I trust you with these?' he asked before releasing his grip.

'Absolutely,' Jessica replied, taking the documents. For a moment she thought Aidan was going to add something but he stayed silent as she lifted the flap and pulled out five sheets of paper.

She skimmed through the contents, her eyes widening with each turn of the page, before Aidan cleared his throat. 'As well as being their form tutor, we run a formal social education module over the two years,' he said. 'They have to hand in three essays a year on various subjects but, for this subject only, we require them to write their work by hand as opposed to type. It's our way of ensuring they have a degree of literacy.'

'And this is Ryan's?' Jessica asked.

'Yes.'

'How long ago did he write it?'

'Maybe two months ago? Not long.'

Jessica flicked back to the first page. The sheet was covered in untidy blue ink but it wasn't the words she was interested in. Through the margins of all five sheets, Ryan had apparently been unable to stop himself doodling. Footballs and three-dimensional cubes were on the first two pages but it was the final three which concerned Jessica. Crudely drawn daggers and knives littered the third, with the fourth and fifth littered with a mass of spiky horizontal lines that was undoubtedly meant to be a wall of flames.

12

Jessica waited at the station after her shift had finished, not wanting to sit in yet more queuing traffic for her journey home. She hadn't mentioned the drawings to Reynolds but couldn't resist flicking through them as she sat in her office by herself. Jessica tried to see a way that the final sheets could be anything but flames but there was no mistaking them.

The memory of how she used to constantly draw along the bottom margins of her exercise books when she was younger was at the front of Jessica's mind. She would doodle hearts and elephants. She couldn't draw anything else with any amount of accuracy but the hearts were easy and, for whatever reason, she had a vague talent for sketching an elephant which actually looked like one.

As for Ryan's art, she might be able to accept the knives because of their simplicity in the same way that she used to draw hearts. The fire seemed too close to home considering what his father had done, not to mention his own house had burned down. The thought had crossed her mind that maybe he had set the fire, although the reasoning made little sense.

Jessica put the papers back into the cardboard folder, wedging them underneath a stack of files on the edge of her desk, not knowing what to do with them. Reynolds didn't want to know about what she had and, given where they had come from and the grey area – at best – surrounding data protection and confidentiality issues, Jessica wasn't sure she should take them to Cole, especially since he knew about her trespassing. On their own, the sketches proved very little.

After making sure the document folder wasn't exposed, Jessica made her way out to her car. From what she had been told, very little else had happened while she had been at the college. Anthony hadn't been found and initial tests on the paint tin and petrol can revealed nothing except for fingerprints they could test against Anthony's when they finally found him. Not that it would matter if they couldn't connect the objects to the scene. The team going door-to-door on the Chadwicks' street had failed to come up with any suspicious sightings or information about who could be responsible for the arson. Depending on how the Crown Prosecution Service saw things, it could even be attempted murder.

Jessica had timed her journey well and cruised home so easily that the lack of red traffic lights was almost unnerving. The stop-start nature of commuting across the city was incredibly frustrating but was always there in the same way that grey skies were.

As she walked through the front door, Jessica could smell something intoxicating drifting from the kitchen. She walked through the door ahead, where Adam was standing with his back to her facing the cooker. Even from behind, she could tell exactly which T-shirt he was wearing. It was the crimson one with an enlarged head of a comic-book character printed on the front. She'd known he was a bit of a nerd for cartoons before she moved in but only realised what she was letting herself in for when it was too late. At least a third of all his tops featured some sort of character she either didn't recognise or hadn't seen since she was a child.

'You're late,' he said, without turning around.

Jessica strolled across the kitchen and put her arms around his waist, snaking them up around his chest until she was hugging into the back of him. His straggly shoulder-length black hair tickled the side of her face as she replied playfully, 'Whatcha cooking?'

'Nothing for you.'

Jessica hugged him tighter as he stirred a pot of what looked like dark red sauce. 'That's a lot for just one person to eat.'

'It's for on-time people.'

She kissed the back of Adam's neck in the spot she knew would make him giggle. Jessica felt his body crease from his hips upwards until he turned to face her with a large smile on his face.

'That's cheating.'

Jessica grinned back. 'What can I say? I'm a cheater.' She pulled him into her and hugged him tightly. It was her way of telling him she had not been having a good day at the station. Jessica always felt cagey sharing her work thoughts with anyone and she could see Adam had learned over the short while they had been living together that she would tell him things if she wanted to. Other than that, he never asked about how everything was going.

'What's it like working a four-day week?' she asked as he released her and turned back to the stove.

'Good. What's it like working a seven-day week?'

Jessica laughed. 'I don't work seven days.'

'It seems like it.'

It didn't take any of Jessica's skills for her to know there was a lot of truth in Adam's words.

'How is the job?' she asked, trying not to dwell on what he had said.

When they had met, Adam worked in the laboratories which served the police force. Almost a year ago, when they weren't seeing each other, he had applied for a job working for the science department at Manchester Metropolitan University. After hearing nothing, he had forgotten about it until they called him unexpectedly a few months previously asking if he was still interested and, if so, whether he could start in the new year. It was a research-based job with a small amount of support teaching but Jessica was convinced he had it easy because he worked four ten-hour days and always had weekends off.

'It's hard work,' Adam replied, not turning around. 'I'm going to have to start bringing stuff home soon because we're working on a big project. It could be worth millions to the university.'

Jessica asked for more details but he replied with a string of science-sounding gobbledygook. 'You've just made those words up, haven't you?' she said.

'It's not my fault I have an education, Jess,' Adam replied with his standard argument whenever she accused him of being a 'science geek'.

The gnocchi and meatballs Adam prepared were quite a treat and Jessica even suggested sitting at the dining table in the living room, as opposed to eating from their laps, in order to do the meal justice. Adam said they could open a bottle of wine but Jessica didn't feel like having any. She wondered if he knew her well enough to realise she was refusing because she wanted to be able to drive just in case a call came through that something else had happened. If he did see through her, he didn't complain – but then he rarely did.

In some ways, that annoyed Jessica more. She wanted him to be angry with her and object to the way she left her phone on and how she stayed at work late. He would offer little digs every now and then but he was too nice to really have a go at her.

After the meal, Jessica did the dishes, which seemed only fair, before cuddling up to Adam on the sofa to watch something on television that neither of them were particularly interested in.

Jessica curled her feet underneath her, resting her head on his shoulder. 'How's Caroline?' Adam asked.

'She's all right. She sent me one of her long emails at work yesterday, saying how the divorce is all sorted but they're going to rent out the flat over on the Quays that they own. They don't want to make a loss selling. She was going out with this other lad but I don't think it's going anywhere.'

'You should invite her over.'

'I have. I think she's still a bit embarrassed about the divorce. After that, it was a bit awkward when we were living together again.'

As Jessica was talking, her phone began to ring. She unwrapped herself from Adam and reached to answer it. Mouthing a 'sorry', she pressed the button to answer Andrew Hunter's call.

'Been following any more young girls around with cameras today?' she asked jokingly, walking out of the living room.

'Good evening to you too,' he replied.

'What are you after?'

'A bit of information perhaps?'

Jessica climbed halfway up the staircase, before turning around and sitting, resting her head against the wall. 'You know there isn't much I can tell you about anything.'

'I told you everything I knew about Ryan, Sienna and Harley,' Andrew insisted.

'That's because I work for the police and you had to!'

Jessica could hear Andrew laugh at the other end of the phone. 'Yeah, I didn't think that line would work but figured it was worth a try.'

'Go on, what are you after?' Jessica put on a deliberately weary voice as if to tell the investigator she was going out of her way to even listen to him.

'I was wondering if Sienna's death had been confirmed as suicide?'

Jessica knew she shouldn't technically give any information away but Andrew had found the body and she had the feeling he was more affected by it than he was willing to let on.

'It's not a hundred per cent but it seems almost certain,' she replied.

There was a long pause at the other end of the line, except for Andrew's breathing. 'Why did she do it?' His question sounded almost desperate.

'Are you asking for personal or professional reasons?' Jessica asked. 'We haven't been able to go back to her father with anything concrete yet. He's not asking through you, is he?'

'No, sorry. I know I shouldn't be asking. Honestly it's nothing to do with Harley. I don't know why I called.'

Jessica had a feeling he was being genuine. 'We don't know why she did it. I went to talk to her school friends but none of them appeared to know very much. Her father didn't seem to know enough about her and one of the other officers questioned the boy you saw her kissing. He insists he's not her boyfriend and that he couldn't have got her pregnant because they had never slept together.'

Jessica didn't know why she had used the word 'boy' to describe Finn, who was eighteen. Despite their age, something about the behaviour of them all seemed immature. Hanging around fast-food restaurants and having a snog in a dark corner weren't the types of thing she associated with adults.

For a few seconds, she could only hear Andrew's breathing before he finally replied. 'Thank you.'

'What are you doing now?' Jessica asked.

'It's complicated. Harley is still paying me. I've told him there isn't much I can do because it's a police investigation but he says you'll never get to the bottom of it. He can't fathom why his little girl might have killed herself. He's desperate to know who got her pregnant. I guess he thinks the person could be involved with what happened.'

'If you do find out, you'd better tell me first.'

Jessica was serious. She hadn't met Harley but she didn't want to risk him getting hold of the young man before she did if he was as suspicious and angry as Andrew made him sound.

Andrew didn't reply at first and only half-answered the request when he finally did. 'I won't do anything stupid.'

'Have you got anything else?' Jessica asked.

'No, but . . . can you tell me when you get a final verdict about Sienna?'

'I'll think about it.'

'Thanks.'

Jessica ended the call and made her way down the stairs, clutching her lower back. Although the carpet was comfortable, the position she had twisted herself into ultimately was not. She had been feeling a few twinges in her back and legs in recent months and didn't want to admit to herself that it could be age-related. Adam knew better than to suggest anything along those lines.

Jessica made her way back to the sofa but Adam had changed the way he was sitting, making it uncomfortable for her to cuddle into him. She didn't know if it was deliberate.

'Everything all right?' he asked.

'Just work stuff.'

Adam didn't say anything but she knew he was annoyed, even if silently so. She thought he would sit quietly watching the television but instead he surprised her. 'Do you think it's time to set a date yet?'

It was the first time he had mentioned it in around six weeks but Jessica knew then that it would come up again. They had got engaged months previously and he bought her a ring – even though it had been her who'd popped the question. Since then, nothing had happened.

At first Adam seemed keen to look for venues and start thinking about dates but Jessica had stalled, saying she was busy at work, which was partly true. She still liked the idea of marrying him, just not everything that went with it. The dress, the cake, the tearful parents, the negotiations over guest lists and the rest of it seemed like things other people did. Things that adults did.

She also didn't know how to tell him that she wanted to live somewhere else. This house had belonged to his grandmother and he had inherited it after her death. She knew that meant he felt a connection to it and didn't want to take that away from him. As she lay awake at night, scenarios would run through her mind of the best way to bring the matter up but she had never been good at talking about serious issues or explaining her feelings to anyone. She had grown closer to Adam than anyone she had ever known, including Caroline and her parents, but, for whatever reason, she couldn't bring herself to confide her latest insecurities.

'Maybe the summer after this one,' Jessica replied, thinking it was vague enough to not commit her to anything.

Adam had also inherited some money when his grandmother died. It wasn't a huge amount but he insisted it should be used to pay for the wedding. After becoming engaged, Jessica was all for telling her parents over the phone in order to play it down as much as possible. They lived around a hundred miles north in the Lake District and Adam was adamant they should tell them in person. She agreed to do things his way and, after mockingly getting down on his knees to thank Adam for taking her off his hands, Jessica's father said he wanted to pay for the ceremony too. That all meant money wasn't a problem, leaving Jessica's own feelings the only obstacle in their way.

'Maybe we can get a few brochures?' Adam suggested. 'There are a few nice places up Lancashire way and it's around halfway towards your parents', which will help. Perhaps we can go for a drive next weekend?'

'Sounds good,' Jessica replied, thinking she would definitely be working the following Saturday and Sunday whether or not she was on the rota.

Apparently happy with her response, Adam shifted his weight, holding his arm out towards her again. Jessica obliged and rested her head on the inside of his armpit, allowing him to cuddle her. She didn't know what he was watching on the television but, whatever it was, nothing much seemed to be happening except that one woman was very angry with a man. Adam had put on a jumper over his T-shirt and the fabric was soft and inviting. Jessica felt her eyelids beginning to get heavy and she struggled to stop them closing before finally succumbing to the intoxicating lure of sleep.

*

Jessica didn't know how long she had been dozing when she felt an arm shaking her awake. 'Jess, we should go upstairs,' a man's voice said. Her mind was fuzzy and unresponsive as her eyes opened onto a room where the only light came from a muted television.

She felt someone kissing her hair as he untwined his arm from her and then the television turned off. Jessica's body flopped on the sofa before she raised herself up into a sitting position, still feeling dozy. She reached out towards the shape of the other person, who hauled her up from the sofa and put an arm around her, then leant down to kiss her. Jessica responded by chewing on his bottom lip gently and giggling before recoiling away abruptly.

'Are you okay?' he asked, clearly confused by her response.

Jessica's throat felt croaky and dry. She blinked rapidly. 'Sorry, I'm just tired.'

She gripped Adam's hand, allowing him to lead her up the stairs. Any sleepiness had drifted from her mind as he opened the bedroom door and she followed him inside. Her thoughts were a mixture of self-loathing and relief that she had stopped herself from saying something stupid for once.

Jessica started to undress, unable to face her fiancé and knowing that, if her mind had taken a second or two longer to wake up, she would have called him Sebastian.

13

Jessica was beginning to think the biggest problem with commuting wasn't the time she spent sitting in her car watching traffic lights change, cars sit still, or rain fall, it was that she felt trapped alone with her mind. Trying to think through her thought process from the previous evening wasn't something she wanted to do but she simply couldn't avoid it. Even with the radio turned on as a distraction, Jessica couldn't believe how close she had come to saying Sebastian's name. The only explanation she could come up with was that she had been dreaming about him but that didn't offer much comfort either. In many ways, the fact he had crept his way into her unconscious made it worse.

She thought of the way he had flirted with her in the car park a few nights before and the cocky charm he possessed. She wanted to dislike him but he had those delicious eyes that made it seem as if you were the only person he was focusing on.

Bastard.

Trying to forget him, Jessica turned up the radio, hoping it would take her mind away from her own guilt. The presenters wittered on inanely and took calls from members of the public who offered their opinions on everything from foreign policy to whether a female celebrity was too old to have children. It was the usual kind of nonsense which drove her crazy – and failed to take her mind away from both Adam and Sebastian. Maybe she should phone the radio station and let members of the public pass judgement on her dilemma?

Jessica arrived at Longsight just as Reynolds was walking out of the doors into the car park. 'I saw you pull in,' he said, not breaking stride. 'We have found Anthony Thompson.'

She put one hand on the still-swinging door as a gesture to show she had actually arrived at work, before turning and following the inspector towards one of the marked police cars.

On the journey he explained that Anthony had been arrested in the city centre the previous evening for being drunk and disorderly. At the time he was too drunk to give his name and had been put in a cell at the Bootle Street police station. This was located just off Deansgate and was about as central as you could get in Manchester. Jessica knew it was where a lot of the overnight drunks ended up before they were either released in the morning or, if they had been particularly abusive, cautioned or charged. The last time she had been here was when she was dealing with a series of magic-related paraphernalia that had been left around the city.

Reynolds said that Anthony had sobered up by the morning but started telling the officer who was ready to release him about how his son had been murdered and that he wanted revenge. That was when they had been called.

'Where was he picked up?' Jessica asked.

'I don't know, somewhere central. Why?'

Jessica hoped she was wrong. 'Because Martin and Ryan Chadwick have been put up in a hotel in the centre by an insurance company. What if he was found outside where they are staying?'

The staff at Bootle Street were expecting them and the first thing Jessica did was look through the paperwork. Anthony had been picked up in Piccadilly Gardens, less than a hundred metres from the hotel the Chadwicks were in. It proved nothing as there was a good chance he would have been picked up around there anyway if he had gone to the centre to get drunk. Still, along with the spray paint and petrol can, the circumstantial evidence was building.

Rather than take him across the city, Jessica and Reynolds were given an interview room in which to talk to Anthony. One of the uniformed constables told them their suspect had refused any offer of food and when told officers would be arriving to talk to him, insisted he didn't have – or want – a solicitor. As he closed the door and assured them he would return with Anthony shortly, the constable's final words of 'good luck' didn't bode too well.

A security camera hummed in a top corner. Within the last few months, every interview room in Greater Manchester had been fitted with one after complaints from a suspect that he had been assaulted in a station in the north of the city. The police officers involved denied the accusations and there was no evidence but the media outcry didn't paint them in a good light. And so, the chief constable somehow found funds in a budget that had previously had no flexibility to fit the cameras. Jessica could think of a specific incident in her past that had happened with a suspect called Wayne Lapham that she was pleased hadn't been caught on camera. It seemed strange that they were still using old-fashioned cassette tapes to record interviews considering they had the newish piece of technology as well.

After a short while, Jessica heard the clanging of doors and then theirs was opened. Anthony Thompson walked in looking slightly disorientated, as if he had just woken up. His face was as red as it had been when she had last seen him and he was wearing the same green jumper. His grey hair had begun to mat together and it hung across his face, partially obscuring his view. Anthony sat where he was told and rubbed his eyes. Jessica wondered if he recognised her. If he did, he certainly didn't acknowledge it. Reynolds asked if the man wanted a solicitor and if he was feeling okay. Jessica knew he would have been checked for drugs but there was something about the way his eyes seemed to drift in and out of focus that was disconcerting.

When the formalities were out of the way, Jessica began. 'Where have you been, Anthony?' she asked in a way that she hoped didn't sound too accusing. 'Do you know we've been looking for you?'

Anthony stared at a spot somewhere over Jessica's head and shrugged. 'Around.'

'Have you been staying with anyone in particular?'

'No.'

'We know you haven't been at home.'

'No.'

Jessica didn't know if he was saying 'no' to disagree with her, or to acknowledge that he hadn't been at his house. Either way, they'd had an officer stationed there ever since Anthony went missing, so they knew he hadn't been around. She sensed she wasn't going to get much with regard to where he had been. By the look of him, he could well have been sleeping rough. He certainly looked as if he had done plenty of drinking since going missing.

'Do you remember when I came to speak to you the first time?' Jessica asked.

Anthony didn't respond, still focusing on the spot on the wall behind her. She half-wanted to turn to see if there was anything actually there.

'It was because Martin Chadwick's house was sprayed with graffiti the night before. Did you know that?' Jessica deliberately hadn't told him at the time. A fraction of a smile appeared on Anthony's face but he didn't reply.

'We came back to your house a few days ago to look for you but you weren't there,' Jessica continued. 'That night someone set fire to Mr Chadwick's house.'

Anthony grinned wider, continuing to remain silent.

'Do you know anything about either of those incidents?' Jessica asked.

At first she didn't think she was going to get a response but then Anthony's face broke and he started to laugh. His joy seemed unnatural, given the dishevelled nature of his appearance. Jessica and Reynolds sat impassively, waiting for him to compose himself.

'What is it you find so funny?' Jessica asked when he had eventually quietened.

Anthony finally fixed his eyes on her. They were wide and full of a humour that shouldn't have been there. 'Fire,' he said, grinning yet further.

It was an uncomfortable moment before Reynolds spoke. 'Are you admitting to starting the fire at Martin Chadwick's house?'

The man switched his gaze from Jessica to her supervisor. 'Fi-re,' he repeated with as much joy as before, making the word sound as if it had two extended syllables.

Both officers knew it wasn't a confession, certainly it wasn't strong enough to pass any kind of test if it ever got to court. Jessica asked where he was on the night of the first incident but Anthony simply shrugged and smiled before saying that he couldn't remember. Jessica was grateful to have something other than a one-word response but it still didn't get her anywhere.

'The graffiti sprayed at the Chadwick house was done in yellow paint,' Jessica said. 'We found an empty tin of yellow spray paint in the same shade in your shed. What would you say if I told you the pigment of the paint from the can matched what was sprayed on the house?'

It wasn't strictly true because that was still being looked into. In any case, Anthony smiled and said nothing.

'We also found a petrol can in your back garden the day after the fire was started using an accelerant.'

No response.

'Last night you were arrested close to where Martin and his son are now staying. That's three pretty big coincidences that end up with you being here, isn't it?'

Jessica hadn't known whether to reveal that the Chadwicks were staying somewhere central in the city. If Anthony's location was incidental then she didn't want to tip him off. On the other hand, she wanted to see his reaction to the news.

His face didn't change from the fixed half-smile he had been displaying. 'I don't know what you're talking about,' Anthony replied.

His unpredictability made it almost impossible for Jessica to read him. At times he seemed confused, as if still drunk. At others, he seemed perfectly aware of what was going on. At the present time, he had returned to staring at the spot on the wall behind her.

'Did you have anything to do with this?' Jessica tried one more time.

'He deserves all he gets,' Anthony answered with a snarl.

'That's not what I asked.'

Anthony burst out laughing again before dissolving into a coughing fit. Reynolds caught Jessica's eye, telling her without words that they were getting nowhere. Anthony had lifted his jumper to cover his mouth as he coughed. Then, much to Jessica's disgust, he blew his nose into the material. She couldn't prevent herself from pulling a face, which the man noticed and smiled more widely at.

If it wasn't an act, Jessica thought Anthony must be quite close to having some sort of personality disorder. He lurched from saying nothing and barely reacting to laughing himself hoarse. On the one hand he appeared to understand all of the questions being put to him and responded when he wanted. On other occasions, he would resort to one- or two-word replies, as if the language being used was too complicated. She had to remind herself that he had lost his son. She wondered what he was like before it happened. Was he similarly difficult then or had everything happened since?

'Do you think this is what Alfie would want?' Jessica said quietly.

Anthony's laughing stopped as suddenly as it had started. He focused his attention on Jessica, his eyes narrow and fierce. She realised from the pressure in her chest that she was holding her breath in the ensuing silence. Jessica looked up to meet his eyes, not knowing why she had said it but determined to get something from him. Above everything, she wanted him to deny it. She had now met him twice but on neither occasion had he outright told her the vandalism and now the fire was nothing to do with him.

'Don't you say his name,' Anthony said softly, his voice clearer than it had been at any point since he had been brought in.

Jessica knew she had crossed a line. 'I'm sorry but . . .'

'Don't. You. Say. His. Name.' Anthony's voice was louder and firmer, each word punctuated with absolute fury.

Reynolds stood and said he was ending the interview before announcing the time for the recording. The same officer returned to collect Anthony, who left silently without looking back at the officers.

Jessica hadn't moved from her seat but the inspector paced the room, his black shiny shoes clipping noisily across the surface. She didn't risk standing herself because she knew what was likely to be coming. After what seemed like minutes but was probably just seconds, Reynolds stopped and sat in the chair Anthony had been in across the table from Jessica. He was shaking his head, sucking on his bottom lip.

'What was that?' he eventually said.

Jessica untied her ponytail and started to twirl her hair, before tying it again. 'I just wanted him to say something.'

'That you achieved.'

The inspector didn't sound angry, more exasperated. Jessica didn't know what to say. She knew she had gone too far but sometimes it was that which got a response.

'What do you want to do?'

'With you?' he fired back.

'With Anthony.' Jessica figured it was better to play things straight, rather than dig herself a deeper hole by being flippant.

Reynolds ran a hand through the little hair he had. 'It's going to be hard to keep him in. As far as we can tell he hasn't done anything. The few things we have got are about as circumstantial as you can get.'

'He doesn't seem quite . . . right.'

The inspector fixed her with a gaze as if to say he wasn't surprised given the way Jessica spoke to him. 'That's not a reason to keep him in.'

'He still seems drunk to me. You can smell it on him.'

'He'd have to be taken to magistrates' court today or we would have to let him go.'

'Not if he was still under the influence . . .'

If someone arrested was still intoxicated, they weren't supposed to be released. Jessica knew that what she was suggesting was anything but by the book. Reynolds continued to glare at the floor. 'I don't think he would protest,' Jessica added. 'I reckon he's been sleeping rough.'

'Why do you want to keep him in?' he asked.

'I don't know. I think there's something we're all missing.'

'To do with him?'

Jessica stood, adjusting her jacket. 'I don't know.'

Reynolds raised himself from the chair with a grunt and walked towards the door, standing in front of it and blocking the way out. Jessica wondered if he had done it deliberately. 'Do you think he started the fire?'

It was the most direct question he could have asked.

'I think he's unpredictable,' Jessica replied.

The inspector smiled in the fatherly way she knew he could. It was how he used to greet her when they shared an office and he didn't have to control her. His head lolled onto one shoulder as he rolled his eyes and flashed his teeth. He stepped aside, clearing the exit and then put a hand on Jessica's shoulder. 'I'll have a word with the custody sergeant but you're going to be the death of me.'

Jessica thought about Reynolds's words throughout the evening. Whatever he had said in the other station had done the trick and, however the paperwork had been fiddled, Anthony Thompson was going to be sleeping in a cell until the following morning. Jessica knew it wasn't a particularly fair way to treat him but, as she suspected, he had offered no complaints.

At some point during the day, Adam had bookmarked a selection of potential wedding venues, which he showed her enthusiastically. She found it hard to look him in the eye as, every time she did, she remembered her confusion from the night before in thinking he was Sebastian. Largely because of that, she skimmed through the sites with him, saying all the right things about going to visit them.

Jessica couldn't stop thinking about the way Reynolds had looked at her in the interview room. He was someone she had always respected, even though she had never been as close to him as she was to Dave and Izzy. One time when she was a child, her mother had scolded her for crossing the road without looking. She had said that she wasn't angry, just disappointed. The inspector had given her that same look and she wondered why she was allowing herself to become so involved. In essence, it was a straightforward arson that might, at some point, be upgraded to an attempted murder. She had dealt with much more serious cases and not allowed herself to be drawn in the way she felt she was now.

Jessica struggled to hide her relief as the sound of her phone ringing interrupted their Internet browsing. She mouthed her customary 'sorry' as she took the call, strolling into the hallway as she had done the previous night. On this occasion, she barely had a foot on the bottom step before she turned and walked back into the living room to pick up her jacket from the chair where she had left it.

There was another fire.

14

In her old car, Jessica knew there was a good chance she would have been driving around in circles swearing at no one in particular before stopping to ask scared passers-by for directions. Another function of her new car that she actually found useful – when she could figure out how to use it – was the built-in satellite navigation device. That didn't stop her swearing at the eerie flat tone of the voice telling her which direction she should be heading in. Adam would have laughed as she shouted 'I just turned left, you mardy bitch', only to get the reply: 'Please turn around'. It also didn't stop her becoming furious every time it beeped to tell her she was approaching a speed camera. That was something which seemed to happen a lot around Manchester.

She discovered to her surprise that the journey was largely along one road. Boothstown was an affluent area she had rarely visited. Jessica had been to plenty of large properties south of the city but rarely in the west. Outside the M60 ring road, it was close enough to Manchester to enjoy the transport links but far enough away that it was almost inconceivable that grim, dark housing estates were barely a fifteen-minute bus ride away.

The distance between houses began to increase and, as she passed a golf club, smoke drifted across the road and

Jessica could smell the burned aroma she had tasted at Martin Chadwick's house. Ignoring the sat nav and following the smoke, Jessica arrived in front of a property with huge metal gates that were opened inwards. From the road she could see the flames. She parked close by, grabbed the jacket that she still hadn't returned from the back seat, and then hurried along the wide driveway towards where she could see the fire licking into the night sky.

In the light of the flames, Jessica could see three fire engines parked at the end of the drive, with large hoses pumping water as small groups of men gripped them. As she walked, she looked to her left where a large lush lawn stretched away from the driveway. Ahead of her, she could see the far sides of the house were untouched by flames. The sandstone ends were in stark contrast to the blackened centre, which was entirely engulfed by the fire. She heard a creak and then a crash, watching as the upper part in the centre of the house collapsed onto the ground floor.

Two of the firefighters darted backwards, shouting instructions over their shoulders. She could feel the heat on her face, although the wind was blowing the thick black smoke away from where she was walking. The property itself looked as if it would have at least five or six bedrooms. The window frames still untouched at either end were tall, showing off what she expected were large, high-ceilinged rooms.

As Jessica continued making her way slowly towards the site, she heard someone shouting and turned to her right where another fire officer was running towards her.

As he neared, he lowered his voice. 'No public, you've got to go back to the road.'

Jessica fumbled in her pockets for her identification. 'I've been called here,' she said. 'Detective Sergeant Daniel. I'm from Longsight.'

'What are you doing all the way out here?' he asked.

'Long story. Where's the owner?'

'On his way. He wasn't in.' The officer pointed over his shoulder towards the next property along which was shielded from view by a large hedge. 'We were called out by a neighbour. You might want to talk to them.'

Jessica heard sirens approaching and two marked police cars started accelerating along the drive towards them. The first one sped past, pulling up next to the fire engines, the second stopping alongside Jessica. She didn't recognise the police officer who got out of the car, although that wasn't a surprise. She wasn't sure exactly what division was responsible for the area she was in. It was right on the border where Manchester West CID would take over from her Metropolitan division, although the responsibility for uniformed officers was far more localised.

Either way, given whose house was on fire, there was no doubt she would end up dealing with the fallout.

The uniformed constable who stepped out of the car put his hat on, straightening it, and fixed Jessica with a suspicious look. He was somewhere in his mid-twenties and, from the way he looked at her, she knew the type straight away. He was the sort who would ask all the questions first in a time-sensitive situation and then realise that they had left it too late to actually do anything. Jessica was the opposite, although, with everything going on around her and Reynolds's clear indifference to her presently, she wondered whose way was best.

Before the constable could ask who she was, Jessica showed him her identification and gave him a 'piss off over there' look. She had honed it perfectly over the years. She combined it with her 'and don't come back until your bollocks have dropped' look, which was a new one she was working on.

'Who called you?' the fire officer asked as the other officer walked towards the house, suitably chastened.

'Someone at Longsight.'

Jessica didn't know exactly who had phoned it through but, given the location and the fact she wouldn't usually have been called, it seemed like someone in the central call centre was on the ball that night. That was certainly a surprise. She knew she hadn't answered the question the fire officer was really asking.

'So why are you out here?' he persisted.

'Because I'm currently investigating why the house owner's daughter killed herself.'

Reynolds and Rowlands each turned up within ten minutes. The inspector headed straight for the house, hoping to talk to whoever was in charge from the fire service as soon as the blaze was out. Meanwhile, Jessica and Rowlands went to visit the person who had reported the fire.

The neighbouring property was a similar size to Harley Todd's. Large green gardens stretched into the darkness and the gravel driveway had three large cars parked close to the house. As they crunched their way towards the front door, Rowlands said the one name that Jessica had in her mind – 'Ryan Chadwick'.

'Why would he do this?' Jessica asked.

'I have no idea but it's the second fire he's been connected to in under a week. Not to mention that suicide,' Rowlands replied.

Jessica agreed but couldn't bring herself to say it. She didn't know why he might have set fire to his own house, other than to frame Anthony Thompson, but all she could think of was the doodles on the pages Aidan had given her. She hadn't told Dave, or anyone, about those sketches but that decision now looked foolish.

'We can't connect him to the one at his own house and all we know is that he knew Sienna. That doesn't link him properly to either her death or this fire.'

She was saying it more to convince herself.

'Maybe,' Rowlands replied. 'But the timing's bloody uncanny. That said, we have another arsonist we're overlooking.'

'Who?'

Jessica felt stupid when the reply came.

'Ryan's dad, of course.'

With everything that had been going on, Jessica had almost forgotten the obvious fact that Martin Chadwick had only recently been released from prison after starting the fire that killed Alfie Thompson. Could he really be up to his old tricks? If so, why his own house and why this one?

Jessica didn't know if there was a connection from Harley to Martin in any way other than through their children. The only thing she did know was that Anthony Thompson was definitely innocent of this one, given that he was still in a cell somewhere at the Bootle Street station.

Before Rowlands could say anything else, Jessica rang the bell. There was a large wooden door, fixed to a mock Tudor frame that looked impressive, even in the dark. The door opened inwards barely a second after the bell had sounded. Standing inside was a tall man with ginger hair combed to one side. He was wearing a grey pinstripe suit with a blue shirt underneath. Jessica was confused by how quickly he had opened the door.

As if reading her mind, he said: 'I've been watching through the upstairs window to see what was going on next door. I saw you coming.'

His voice was husky and dry and he offered little to no emotion.

Jessica checked his name and confirmed it was he who had called the police. The neighbour invited them in, closing the door behind them as flecks of black ash drifted across the front of the house. He told them he had smelled the fire but had disregarded it at first, thinking someone was having a bonfire nearby. When he noticed the orange glow illuminating his lawn not long after, he had walked along his driveway until he saw the flames properly and then called the police. Jessica asked if he had seen anything suspicious but the man seemed more concerned by the possibility of it being 'kids' who might target him next.

Three times he repeated 'These bloody kids today' before Jessica asked him to confirm whether he had seen any youths.

Unsurprisingly, he hadn't.

'What do you know of your neighbour?' Jessica asked.

'Harley?'

'Yes.'

The man shrugged. 'We pretty much keep to ourselves. We invited him around for a dinner party when he first moved in but he didn't bother turning up. Then sometimes we would hear cars bringing his daughter back late . . . well, before . . .' He tailed off, apparently not wanting to mention her death, but he didn't seem overly concerned.

'Was there anything suspicious about the cars?'

'What cars?'

Jessica forced herself not to roll her eyes. 'The ones you said brought back his daughter.'

He shrugged his shoulders, eyes darting towards the door, evidently bored. He clearly had no interest in anyone other than himself and Jessica suspected his annoyance stemmed back to the dinner party snub. She could picture him moaning about it every day since, a typical busybody who took offence at any minute dispute. Jessica thought about leaving but figured it couldn't do any harm to push him a little further.

'What else can you tell me about Harley?'

'What do you want to know?'

Jessica raised her eyebrows, speaking firmly. 'That's what I just asked you.'

For a moment, the man didn't reply, chewing on his

bottom lip. 'He's not around much. I think he's got a job that takes him around the country. A lot of the time it was just his daughter in the house.'

Jessica wasn't hearing anything she wasn't already aware of but didn't want another rant about kids.

The man suggested they should leave an officer stationed at the end of his driveway just in case the perpetrator – or 'perpetrators', as he emphasised – should return. His gravelly voice made it sound as if he endlessly smoked either cigarettes or cigars and his attitude was pushing her buttons.

Jessica told him to call the police if he had any further concerns and then left the house when, for one of the few times in her life, she was pleased to see it raining. It was the drizzly nothing-type mist that was barely noticeable when out in it. If you got wet in the morning, however, you spent the rest of the day trying to dry out. There were still small scraps of burned black material being blown across to them and the raindrops almost seemed to taste of the blaze.

'Shite,' Rowlands said as they made their way down the driveway.

'Stop moaning,' Jessica replied, pulling the jacket's hood over her head.

Dave was wearing only his suit. He tried to yank the jacket over his head but it was a little too tight and he struggled to loosen it around his arms to enable him to lift it up.

Jessica laughed. 'Covering your hair isn't going to stop it going grey.'

Rowlands finally contorted his arm enough to free the jacket and he raised it over himself. 'I keep telling you I'm not going grey,' he said defensively.

'Maybe you're right . . . it might be white, I suppose.'

'Sod off, is it.'

As they reached the main road, Jessica could see at least three more police cars had arrived. Their blue lights were silently spinning as if to remind people that, if the fire engines and flames weren't enough of an indication, there had been a blaze.

They began walking along the adjacent driveway but it was clear the fire was either out or close to it. Only one of the hoses still appeared to be in use and most of the fire officers who had been tackling the blaze were now leaning against the side of one of the large vehicles sheltering from the rain and ash-like debris which was drifting on the breeze.

Jessica heard the car approaching before she saw it. She turned to see a large grey vehicle screech on to the drive-way and accelerate past them before squealing to a stop close to the fire engines and police cars. She saw the various officers jump to attention almost as one and, without knowing what he looked like, Jessica had no doubts the man who got out of the car was Harley Todd.

Jessica quickened her pace with Rowlands by her side, as Harley ignored the officers who were trying to talk to him. Jessica didn't realise how tall he was until she got closer to him. He was definitely over six feet tall and, even from the back, she could see he was in pretty good shape. His suit appeared to be custom-fitted, tightly hugging his waist. She would have guessed it cost a lot of money but

Harley didn't seem to care. He stood in the rain staring at the property, watching a thin plume of smoke rise into the air.

As they saw her approach, the other officers parted, almost as if Jessica was the welcoming committee. She suspected the truth was that none of them wanted to speak first.

'Mr Todd?' Jessica asked quietly but the man didn't flinch. She circled around his car, pushing the driver's door closed, and continued until she was standing in front of him slightly off to one side. She could see the raindrops dribbling down Harley's face, his eyes wide in disbelief. 'Mr Todd?' Jessica asked again.

The man mumbled a 'yes' without moving his eyes from the house.

'I'm Detective Sergeant Daniel. Would you like to come and sit with me somewhere dry?' Jessica spoke gently, placing an arm on his shoulder and finally drawing the man's eyes towards her.

'I . . . I don't know what to do,' he stammered.

Jessica gripped his upper arm and motioned for him to turn around. Slowly, he followed as she led him towards the back of a police van. Rowlands had stopped trying to protect his hair with his jacket and he walked quickly ahead of them, opening the rear doors and holding them for Jessica and Harley to step inside. Most of the vans in the police fleet were used to transport prisoners but this one had seats that ran lengthways and was used to take officers to wherever they were needed at speed.

A line of small white spot lamps were fitted to the

ceiling and Rowlands walked around to the front of the vehicle to turn them on as Harley sat on one side with Jessica opposite. She leant against the inside of the van, thinking of how long it seemed since she had been in the rear of a van with Martin Chadwick. Harley hunched forward, using one hand to support his head. Rowlands joined them shortly after, sitting next to Jessica. She could feel the dampness of his suit on the back of her hand as he brushed against her.

'I'm sure I didn't leave anything on . . .' Harley said, tailing off.

Jessica didn't know for sure whether it had been started deliberately but it seemed too much of a coincidence for it to be accidental. 'We have people who will look into what started it,' she replied.

'I just . . . my daughter . . . and now . . .' Harley stared at Jessica but she didn't think he was really looking at her. His hair, which appeared to have been heavily back-combed at some point, was now flat and damp.

'Get a blanket,' Jessica told Rowlands quietly. She knew there would be one somewhere on one of the fire engines.

As he climbed out of the vehicle, Jessica leant over to touch Harley's hand. 'I have to ask this,' she said delicately. 'Do you know someone who might have a grudge against you?'

His eyes drifted into focus and Jessica could tell he was now looking at her properly. 'Like who?' he asked.

Jessica said nothing in reply, not knowing what she could tell a man who had lost his daughter and property within a week of each other.

15

Jessica had not got anything of any real note from Harley Todd, mainly as he was in shock. She left uniformed officers to make sure he was all right, one of whom would take a formal statement at some point. She suspected it would not happen until the following morning at the earliest.

As she left the house, Jessica first checked with Reynolds and then called Bootle Street Police Station to tell them there was no reason to continue to hold Anthony Thompson. She told them he might argue he wanted to stay in so he could keep a roof over his head but he was too difficult to read. Most people would simply go home but Anthony was anything but normal.

She had only wanted him kept in to see if he might have anything else for them in the morning but, given what had happened, there was no way she would have time to return to see him for a few days.

In the morning briefing, Cole had received a provisional verdict from the investigating fire officer. As with the blaze at the Chadwicks' house, the officer believed some sort of accelerant – most likely petrol – had been used to start the fire at Harley Todd's house. The rain had helped put out the flames but wasn't helping with preserving the crime scene, so the chief inspector told Jessica there would be no formal verdict for a while. Either way, she didn't doubt that the two blazes were connected. Cole and Reynolds seemed less sure. Jessica thought about revealing the drawings Aidan had passed her of Ryan's but Reynolds's words about her growing obsession were stuck in her mind.

The other thing that wasn't helping was that the media had got hold of the story that the man whose daughter had committed suicide days earlier had now lost his home to fire. Their details were sketchy but the *Manchester Morning Herald*'s website in particular had pictures, with the rest of the news media – including television – also reporting from the scene. The *Herald*'s late edition led with the headline 'TWISTED FIRESTARTER', which wasn't exactly helpful.

Jessica excused herself from the meeting as her phone rang, with Andrew Hunter's name appearing on the screen. 'Sergeant Daniel?' he clarified, before she relented and told him to call her 'Jess'. She only made people who annoyed her use her title.

He asked if she knew about the fire, not knowing she had been there.

'Have you heard from Harley?' Jessica asked, walking down the stairs from the DCI's office towards her own.

'He woke me up at about five o'clock,' Andrew replied, although he wasn't complaining. 'He had checked into a hotel and sounded like a completely different guy. I didn't know what to tell him.'

'Why did he call you?'

Andrew sighed loudly. 'Honestly? I think he just

wanted someone to talk to. His daughter's gone, he left his wife and I don't get the feeling he's in the type of industry that appreciates you talking about those kinds of thing.'

Jessica opened the door to her office and was relieved to see it was empty. She moved to her own desk and leant back in her chair. 'What does he do?' she asked, realising she had no idea.

'He runs some sort of consultancy firm. I don't know the details exactly but I looked him up and it's all about finance. It's not the type of thing I would usually ask a client.'

Jessica thought that explained the wealth. 'Did he ever tell you about anyone who might have a grudge against him? A former business partner or something dull like that?'

Andrew ummed for a few moments before replying. 'So you think it's deliberate then?'

Jessica winced and was grateful no one had overheard her accidentally giving the information away. It would only be a matter of time before the media got hold of it properly but it wouldn't help if she was telling private investigators what they were thinking.

'We're looking at all the angles,' she replied, thinking it sounded fairly unconvincing.

Andrew paused for a moment in a silence Jessica thought sounded distinctly smug.

'The only person he's mentioned that has a grudge is his ex-wife.'

'It's not her,' Jessica said, relaxing into her chair. 'He mentioned her to one of the officers last night. She's in Mexico on holiday.'

'Could she have hired someone?'

She knew that possibility was being looked into, although there was no reason to think the woman had done. Jessica laughed, thinking it was partial payback for the cocky-sounding silence he had subjected her to moments earlier. 'You've watched too many TV shows and not done enough proper work,' she replied.

Andrew didn't sound as if he had taken it to heart. 'Do you have any other ideas?'

Jessica reminded him that she couldn't give him those details as he was a 'nobody'.

'No offence,' she added, knowing full well that anyone using those two words definitely did mean to be offensive. 'What are you going to do now?' she added, realising she was being hypocritical in asking his business while refusing to tell him hers.

He replied anyway. 'I'm off to see Harley at his hotel later. I'm not sure after that. It doesn't seem right taking his money any longer.'

Jessica told him he could ring her if need be and hung up. As she did, her phone flashed to say she had two missed calls – both from a number she didn't recognise. She slid the file that contained Ryan's drawings out from under the stack she had left it in and began to look through them, wishing she had passed them on in the first instance.

She understood why Reynolds said he wanted no part of them – but she was desperate to share her concerns about Ryan with people who might agree with her. Again, she tidied them away and pushed the cardboard folder back to the bottom of the heap.

Looking back to her phone, and knowing she would regret it, Jessica redialled the missed calls number. It only rang once before a voice she instantly recognised answered. 'Detective Sergeant Daniel,' the man said with a hint of sarcasm in his voice. 'How are you today?'

'How did you get my number, Sebastian?'

Even without seeing him, Jessica could tell he was smiling. She remembered the cheeky way he smirked at her in the electrical store's car park and the way his dark eyes matched the grin. 'I know people who know people,' he replied.

Jessica thought there was a certain news editor she would be having words with. 'What do you want?' she asked, trying to sound annoyed.

'I'm following up about last night's fire. I gather the person who the house belongs to is the same person whose daughter died last week. Is that correct?'

'That's what you printed so it must be true. Just like that story with the talking dog you had the other month.' Jessica didn't know why he was asking as the information was already out.

Sebastian didn't reply instantly but the fact she knew he was enjoying the conversation was winding her up. 'It doesn't do any harm to get a second source,' the journalist said. 'Okay, how about a link to the fire at Martin Chadwick's house?'

Jessica's first thought was that Sebastian must somehow know something she didn't about Ryan. 'How do you mean?' she asked, trying to keep her voice steady.

She could hear the man blowing through his teeth as a

soft whisper echoed down the line. 'Well, you have to admit it's a bit of a coincidence that a known arsonist comes out of prison and, within a week or so, his house and someone else's in the city has been burned down.'

Jessica didn't think it was a coincidence but she didn't want to tell him that. She picked up a pen and began tapping it on her desk. 'Why would someone burn their own house down?'

'I don't know. I didn't say he did. I just said it was a coincidence that two houses burned down shortly after his release.'

Jessica stopped drumming the pen and instead launched it across the room. It clanged off the edge of the bin, launched vertically into the air and then bounced off the wall, ending up a good metre away from the target.

'Shite,' Jessica mumbled.

'Sorry?'

'Not you. Look, what do you want me to say? I can neither confirm, nor deny, blah-di-blah, insert whatever quote you want here.' Jessica paused for dramatic effect. 'Just phone the press office. Why are you calling me?'

'I was hoping we could go out some time.'

'No we can't. I'm engaged and you're a knobhead. I don't go out with knobheads. Can we leave it at that? Don't call me again.'

Jessica removed the phone from her ear and struggled to hang up, at first waiting for the screen's light to turn back on and then forgetting which button ended the call.

She picked up the receiver from her desk phone then slammed it down just to prove a point. The problem with mobile phones was that you couldn't emphasise when you were hanging up on someone.

Jessica stood and walked across the room to pick up her pen, kicking the bin to protest at the way it had rejected her shot. She then stormed back to her desk and picked up her mobile phone before dialling Garry Ashford's number. He answered on the third ring with a friendly sounding 'Hello' but Jessica cut in.

'Why did you give my number to Sebastian?'

'Um, what?'

'You gave my phone number to that journalist Sebastian. Why?'

Jessica was annoyed – but more with herself for not being annoyed. Usually if someone had passed her details along without asking, especially to a journalist, she would have been fuming. As it was, she knew she wasn't that bothered – and that was frustrating her the most.

'I didn't, Jess, I've never given it to anyone.'

'How did he get it then?' Jessica snapped.

'I don't know. He's very resourceful.' Garry sounded sorry even though he wasn't apologising for anything.

Reluctantly, Jessica accepted he was telling the truth and sighed in defeat. 'Right, just tell him not to call me again.'

Jessica was ready for the end call button the second time and stabbed it in victory to hang up.

She thought of the smug, smiley, long-eyelashed journalist and the way he had popped into her mind a couple of evenings ago. 'Bastard,' she said out loud to the empty room and then bounded into the hallway to find someone to shout at.

'Have I done something wrong?' Rowlands asked. Jessica could see a mixture of amusement and bewilderment on his face.

'We have been working together way too long,' she replied. Dave wheeled the chair he was sitting in backwards as Jessica, who was perched on his desk, swung her legs around, narrowly avoiding kicking him in the knees.

'Who's annoyed you this time?' he asked with a sympathetic smile.

Jessica wasn't too pleased with the way he had apparently read her mood perfectly and deduced that her dumping a load of work on him was directly related to someone else annoying her.

She shuffled backwards until she was sitting fully on his desk. 'Never mind that, I still need this job doing. I don't care if you do it, or if you get someone else to do it.'

Rowlands reached forward and picked up a pad and pen from his desk. His smile had disappeared now he realised she was being serious.

'Go on, tell me again. I was too busy watching the steam come out of your ears last time.'

'Right, just for that, you're doing it. I want a list of all criminals in the Greater Manchester area who have links to arson attacks. They might have actual fire-related convictions or just be some stupid teenager who once set something on fire by accident. Pull all the names together and then see if we can cross-match them against any of Harley Todd, Sienna Todd, Martin Chadwick, Ryan Chadwick or Anthony Thompson. If we get any double matches, all the better.'

Rowlands screwed up his face in protest. 'That's going to take ages.'

'Well get on with it then. You're going grey as it is.'

He rolled his eyes and fake-yawned. 'That's a new one. Anyway, where are you going?'

Jessica stood up from the desk and reached around to gently knead her lower back where it was beginning to ache again. 'I've got someone to speak to. Call me if you find anyone who is connected to more than one person on that list.'

She turned to leave but the constable added: 'What's up with your back?'

She shook her head. 'Nothing.'

'It's your age,' Rowlands replied with a smirk.

Jessica grinned at him. 'Just for that I want full records for Lancashire and Cheshire as well. Now get on with it – chop, chop. One more word and it's Merseyside too.'

Jessica wriggled to get comfortable in her car seat, trying to ignore Rowlands's probably fair point about her back pain being down to her age and wondering how Andrew Hunter did what he did. She had been watching the garage Ryan Chadwick worked at for over twenty minutes and, aside from someone dropping off their vehicle, she hadn't seen anything of note.

After checking with Martin about his son's where-abouts, Jessica set off to have another word with Ryan, not entirely sure what she was going to say. She remembered Andrew telling her how he would watch and take photos of people, blending into the scenery and going unseen. Jessica thought all of that might be true but it was also pretty boring.

The garage was located just off Stockport Road roughly halfway between where Ryan's house had been and the city centre. The red brick of the building had turned grey-ish and a large set of double sliding doors painted blue were exactly in the centre, opening out onto the road. At one end was an office, with a smaller double-glazed door that had a sign in a matching blue over the top advertising cheap MOTs.

As she watched, one half of the blue metal doors slid open noisily. A mechanic wearing a grey sweatshirt and jeans that had long been abandoned to oil and dirt emerged. He walked over to a car that had been parked on the road and then climbed inside and drove it through the door, which moments later was hauled shut again.

Jessica was on the brink of phoning Andrew to tell him what she thought of his job when the door opened a small amount and Ryan emerged, closing it behind him. He was wearing a far cleaner pair of jeans than the previous person who had exited and he was in the process of pulling on an olive green army-type jacket which reached his knees. He pulled a mobile phone out of his trouser pocket and walked along the road talking into it. Jessica waited for a couple of vehicles to pass and then got out of her car, locking it behind her and hurrying after the young man.

The air was cool, a breeze blowing across her, chilling her face and making her shiver. Jessica pulled her jacket tighter and followed Ryan around a corner that led towards an alleyway she knew would open onto the main road. As she moved around the bend still trying to adjust her coat, Jessica collided with something and stepped back in surprise. Looking up, she saw Ryan glaring at her, his grey eyes narrow and formidable.

'Why are you following me?' he asked. His voice was calm but his top lip was twitching.

'Where were you last night?' she asked, ignoring his question.

He glared at Jessica, clearly struggling to control himself. 'Didn't you have someone taking pictures of me?'

'Should I have?' Jessica knew she had to be careful.

'Why aren't you out catching the man who burned our house down? You know who did it.'

Jessica knew she either shouldn't have come or should have thought through what she wanted to say. She struggled for words before eventually replying. 'We're still looking into it.'

Ryan swore and spat on the ground. 'You know who did it! He said in the paper he was going to.'

'We don't know.'

'So what's this all about? That slag Sienna? I told you I don't know anything.' Ryan shook his head and stomped on the ground. Jessica doubted he was aware he was doing it, but it was clear he couldn't control his anger.

'You shouldn't say things like that. She's dead.'

Jessica was trying to be sincere and Ryan clearly sensed it. He smiled broadly. 'Why are you upset over her? Is it all the dick she got? Do you fancy some too?'

He reached down to grab for his crotch but had barely touched himself when Jessica slapped him hard across the face. It was instinctive and something she instantly regretted. She stepped away as Ryan reached up to his lip where a small smear of blood had appeared. The teenager stared at the red liquid dribbling down his fingers and then back up to her.

'I'm sorry, I . . .' Jessica began but Ryan glared through her before turning and walking away. He hadn't said a word but he didn't need to as his eyes gave her a very simple message.

'You'll regret that'.

16

It was little comfort to Jessica as the verdict on Sienna's death was finally confirmed as suicide the following day. It wasn't that she had been hoping for something else, just that it made things harder to comprehend.

Jessica was sitting in a quiet corner of the station's canteen reading through the coroner's initial paperwork but there was nothing that jumped out at her, not that she would have expected it to. Knowing the information would make its way into the media sooner or later, Jessica called Andrew Hunter and told him the news.

He was silent for a few moments before responding. 'Have you told Harley yet?'

'Not me, no, but someone will do.'

She heard the investigator taking a deep breath. 'I saw him last night. He's in a hotel in the centre. He had a laptop on the bed and seemed determined to work non-stop. When I met him a few weeks ago he was this big, influential man but he doesn't have that aura about him now. I tried to tell him I didn't want his money but he wouldn't listen.'

'So what are you investigating?'

Andrew gave a small laugh but it didn't sound as if there was any humour to it. 'Honestly? I don't know. He seems to think there's this conspiracy involving his daughter and his house. It's not like I could stand there and tell the guy not to be silly. He practically forced me to carry on working for him.'

Jessica was beginning to warm to the man. She had no real opinion of the occupation, thinking that most private investigators were retired police officers. Aside from taking photographs of people, she didn't know what he actually did but he did seem to care about his work, which was more than she could say for a handful of people she worked with.

'What are you going to do?' she asked.

'I don't know. What do you think? Do you reckon the fire could be linked to Sienna?'

Jessica hadn't revealed her reasons for taking the print-outs of the photographs from Andrew, so he didn't know about the connection to Ryan.

'I'm not sure,' Jessica said. 'Why would they be?'

She was hoping Andrew might offer her something she hadn't thought of. The man sighed again. 'I was hoping you could tell me.'

If she hadn't have been feeling so hopeless, Jessica might have laughed. They were each relying on the other to provide some sort of reasoning for what had happened. Jessica said goodbye and told Andrew to stay in contact.

She walked back to her office, where Reynolds was heading along the corridor towards her. 'Bad news?' Jessica asked, reading the serious look on his face.

'Not really,' he replied, holding some papers out towards her.

Jessica took them, holding them to her side. 'What are they?'

The inspector smiled. 'You could try reading them.'

'I've got far more literate people like you to do that for me.'

'Let's go in here.'

Reynolds led Jessica into his office. She shared with DS Cornish but the inspector had one to himself along the corridor. Usually it was tidy but, as they entered, Jessica could see a row of files on the floor to her right pressed up against the wall.

'You're going to be as messy as me soon,' Jessica said, pointing to the items on the floor.

'No one in here is as messy as you,' the DI fired back, as he sat in the chair behind his desk. 'That's the report from the investigating officer from the fire at Martin Chadwick's house.'

Jessica sat in the chair across the desk from her supervisor. She glanced at the top of the document. 'Arson?'

'As we thought. At least it's confirmed now.'

'Is there anything about Martin's claims that his back door and window had been obstructed?'

Reynolds nodded. 'It might be hard to prove completely but there was a singed rope recovered on the ground at the back. There's so much damage to the property that we wouldn't be able to say where it came from but it might be true.'

'Someone actually tried to kill him then?'

It was the theory they had been working with but, now

it was as confirmed as they were going to get, it was still a shock for Jessica.

'Yes but I don't think we can start looking at an attempted murder investigation just yet. Maybe that will come when we pick someone up for the fire?'

'What about the blaze at Harley Todd's? It sounds like the report is going to be similar there – except that he was out when it happened.'

Reynolds shook his head. 'Aside from the fact they both appear to have been started deliberately, we don't know of another link. A known arsonist comes out of prison and we have had two houses burned down within a couple of weeks – including his. Door-to-door has given us nothing, we have no witnesses, no footprints, no anything.'

They looked at each other and Jessica knew neither of them had a clue where to go from there. They laughed gently at their situation. 'I've had Dave making a list of known arsonists in the local area. Everyone from kids upwards. I'll go see if he's managed to link any of them to the rest of the information we have.'

'What about Ryan?' Reynolds asked as Jessica stood.

For a moment she wondered if he somehow knew she had hit the teenager the previous day. 'What about him?'

'The other day you seemed convinced he had something to do with Sienna Todd's death and the fire.' The inspector was staring at her.

Jessica met his eyes. 'I can't find anything concrete.'

'Anthony Thompson?'

'I don't know.'

'I had an officer drive past his house last night and

there were lights on. I think he's back at home.' The DI paused before adding: 'Just so you know.'

Jessica started to walk towards the door but the inspector had another question. 'Why aren't you thinking about Martin Chadwick?'

It was a question she had been wondering herself. There was an insurance policy on his house which would likely pay out – although, according to him, it was now in Ryan's name.

'I don't think it's him,' Jessica said. 'I don't think he would burn his own house down and I don't think he torched Harley's either.'

Reynolds spoke precisely. 'I checked with the hotel Martin is staying in to see if he was in his room on the night Harley Todd's house was burned down.' Jessica felt a chill go through her, knowing what he was about to say. 'The person who was working on reception told me he left the hotel early evening and didn't return until after midnight.'

Jessica walked back across the room and leant on the back of the chair she had been sitting on. 'You can't think he burned his own house down? Why would he do that?'

'Not a bad cover, is it? If your place has been destroyed, everyone sees you as the victim.' Jessica knew he was speculating, trying to get her opinion on something he'd had in his own mind. She had been the only person to witness the emotional side of Martin as they sat in the rear of the van and couldn't see how he could go from that to burning down buildings.

'I'm getting someone to look into his background,'

Reynolds added. 'We know what he went to prison for but maybe there were arson attacks before that?'

'Will you let me know if you find anything?' Jessica asked.

Reynolds tilted his head to one side, fixing her with the protective stare she used to see a lot more often when they shared an office. 'Don't get involved, Jess,' he said firmly.

Jessica met his eyes and gave a small nod, before turning and leaving his office. She didn't know why she cared so much that whatever was happening was not down to Martin. It wasn't often that she allowed herself to become attached to the people she was supposed to be investigating but there was something about the moment she shared with him in the back of the van that she wanted to believe was real.

With all the people she dealt with and the horrific things she saw, it gave her some comfort that there was genuine remorse out there.

She chewed on her lip, hurrying along the corridors to the main floor where she could see Rowlands at his desk frantically clicking the mouse next to his keyboard. Jessica slid herself in front of him, blocking his view of the monitor.

'How are you getting on?' she asked.

Rowlands scowled at her. 'This computer system is absolute shite. I've crashed twice today already.'

'Yeah, yeah, a bad workman blames his tools and all that. What have you got?'

Rowlands shook his head but Jessica could see he was suppressing a smile. 'You're all heart, Jess.' He pointed to a lever-arch folder on his desk. 'These are the records of everyone in the area with priors for arson or anything similar. There aren't as many as I thought. I've been trying to do it through the computer but it's not having it, so it's back to paper. I've had two others going through the lists with me but we can't connect any of them to either of the Chadwicks, the Todds or Anthony Thompson. The best I've got is that one of them was in the same prison at the same time as Martin Chadwick. I checked their records and they were on different wings. It's tenuous at best.'

Jessica knew it was always going to be a long shot but it was something that had to be done. She stood, feeling another jolt of pain shoot through her back, but stopped herself from touching it to avoid any further age jokes.

'All right, good work,' she said.

Rowlands raised one of his eyebrows and grinned. 'Is that praise?'

'Let's call it an anti-bollocking.'

Jessica couldn't figure out if the man who was boring her was wearing a suit or a uniform. It was a little of each, with a red handkerchief sticking out from his pocket and matching sash around his waist that was the same colour as the hotel's logo. Jessica realised she hadn't listened to anything he had told her for at least the past five minutes, if not longer. She felt Adam's arm snake around her waist and heard him say, 'Can you give us a few minutes?', before leading her back towards the main doors of the hotel.

'What do you think?' he asked.

'As a wedding venue?'

'What else?'

Jessica struggled to hide her lack of enthusiasm, biting her bottom lip and shrugging. 'I don't know.'

Adam's face broke into a knowing smile and she was aware he had dealt with her apathy many times in the past. 'What don't you like?' he asked, smoothing the hair down on the side of her face, before sitting on the stone steps.

Jessica sat next to him, resting her head on his shoulder. 'I dunno. I think it's that bloke to be honest.'

Adam put his arm fully around her and laughed. 'What's wrong with him?'

'He's just so bloody happy and enthusiastic. Everything's "wonderful", "great" or "brilliant". Either that or "fab". Honestly, anyone that uses the word "fab" without being ironic deserves shooting.'

Jessica felt Adam pull her tighter towards him. 'There's nothing wrong with enjoying your job.'

'Not that much. I don't trust anyone who isn't thoroughly miserable when they're at work.'

She felt Adam's chest bobbing as he laughed. 'You're so weird.'

Jessica snorted. 'You're marrying me.'

She felt Adam's chest calm. 'Yes, I am.' He kissed the top of her hair. 'Not here though?'

'Nah, he'd drive me bloody crazy. What's that sash thing around his waist?'

'It's a cummerbund.'

'But why would you wear it to work? The guy's a lunatic. It wouldn't surprise me to find loads of people have gone missing from this hotel and their body parts are in his freezer. No one can be that cheery on a Sunday afternoon.'

Adam started laughing again, standing and holding his hand to help Jessica up. 'Now I know you're working too hard,' he said.

Jessica allowed him to pull her into a brief hug, before he released her. 'I should go and tell him it's not for us,' he said.

'I'll meet you at the car.'

Jessica began to walk across the car park, taking her phone out of her pocket to find no one had bothered to contact her in the time they had spent looking at – and rejecting – three potential wedding venues. After days with nothing other than confirmation the blaze at Harley Todd's house had been started deliberately, she thought it could be a distraction from an arson case that seemed to be going nowhere. Reynolds was still having Martin Chadwick's past looked into but nothing had come up so far.

Jessica sat in the driver's seat before Adam clambered into the passenger's side a few minutes later. 'Was he all right?' she asked.

'He didn't try to kidnap me and shove me into a freezer if that's what you're asking.'

Jessica laughed. 'That's exactly what I was asking.'

Adam reached across and tucked a loose strand of hair behind her ear. 'Are you all right? It's fine that you've not liked any of the places we've been to today but I wanted to make sure you still want to go through with it.'

In the instant he finished speaking, Jessica felt a lump in her throat and blinked furiously to stop herself from crying. She didn't know how to tell him what she was feeling. She wanted to marry him but, at the same time, something didn't feel right. Jessica wondered if it was butterflies that anyone might have, or something unique to her that was making her feel that way. She knew Adam loved her more than anyone had or probably would. The problem was that, increasingly, Sebastian was drifting into her mind. A man she had only met properly once. She knew it could be only a physical thing. Did it make you a bad person if you were seeing somebody but were attracted to someone else? It was the type of thing she might have spoken to Caroline about a few years ago, or maybe Izzy if she wasn't on maternity leave. It felt like the kind of knowledge she should have, given she was a grown adult, but she didn't remember the 'How do you stop yourself messing up a relationship' class when she was at school.

'I'm just waiting to see the right place,' Jessica croaked before turning the engine on. She pulled out of the car park and headed onto the main road. Adam hadn't seemed to pick up on her moment of insecurity and chatted about his week as Jessica made sure to say 'yes' and 'uh-huh' at the correct moments.

Within moments of joining the M60, Jessica felt her pocket begin to vibrate. 'Can you get that,' she said, lifting her hip up from the seat and angling it towards Adam. 'I forgot to turn the Bluetooth on.'

She felt Adam reach into her trousers and pull her mobile phone out before putting it to his ear. After explaining who he was to whoever was calling, Jessica heard him say, 'oh', 'right' and finally, 'all right, I'll tell her'.

'Who was that?' Jessica asked as she heard the beep to signal the call was over.

'It was Jason. He, um, had some bad news. He said it was all right for me to tell you.'

Jessica felt a rush of adrenaline in her chest, thinking it must be something to do with one of the Chadwicks. She certainly didn't expect the news he actually had.

Adam gulped, speaking gently and deliberately. 'Someone called Molly North is dead.'

17

It was only when Jessica saw scenes like the one in front of her that she struggled to conceive how Britain only stopped hanging people in the 1960s. It wasn't that she had any especially strong feelings for or against capital punishment – she understood the arguments from both sides – simply that being hanged in particular seemed so brutal. If state-sponsored killing was ever brought back, there surely had to be a more humane way to do it.

Molly North's bedroom reminded Jessica of her own from when she had been a similar age. While Caroline adorned her walls with posters of pop stars and one footballer whom she had a crush on, Jessica left hers plain. Instead, she had rows of books and a mixture of compact discs and cassette tapes shoved onto two shelves next to her bed. Unsurprisingly, she couldn't see any cassettes in Molly's room but there were rows of books lining the otherwise clear walls.

The lampshade was upside down on the carpet, with small flecks of blood next to it and a leather belt that had a neat cut mark through it. Although the body had been removed, it was the way the belt had been snipped which had Jessica thinking about her own childhood.

'What happened?' Jessica asked Reynolds, who was standing next to her.

'Her mum and dad went out for Sunday lunch, came home and shouted up to say hello. When there was no reply, her mum came up and found her hanging from a beam in her room. Her dad cut through the belt but it was too late.'

Jessica didn't know what to say, other than a pitiful-sounding, 'That's horrible.'

Neither of the officers moved, silently taking in the surroundings before the Scene of Crime team came in to catalogue everything and take photographs.

'What are you thinking?' Reynolds asked.

'I don't know. Two suicides, two fires, we don't even know if they're connected.' A thought occurred to her. 'Was there a note?'

'Not that anyone has found. The Scene of Crime boys will have a proper look around but you would have thought it would be left out in the open if there was.'

Jessica peered around the room from the doorway but, aside from the lampshade, blood and belt, the only thing that didn't seem quite right was how tidy it was. She wondered if it was always like that, or if Molly had cleaned her own room before hanging herself.

Reynolds walked across to the window and peered outside, before turning to face Jessica. 'Do you think she killed herself because of her feelings for Sienna?'

Jessica shook her head. 'I don't know. She seemed more savvy than that. Obviously she was upset but it's a large jump from that to . . . this.'

'Why else would she do it?'

Reynolds's question sounded more rhetorical than

something for her to answer. Jessica spotted two framed photographs next to the bed. She stepped carefully across the room and sat on the bed before picking one up.

It seemed as if it had been taken relatively recently, perhaps in the last year or so. Both young women were wearing shorts and small T-shirts and appeared to be in a garden or a park. Molly looked exactly as she had on the day Jessica interviewed her. The woman's short dark hair was tucked behind her ears and she had an arm draped around Sienna's shoulders. Jessica had only seen pictures of Sienna after her death but had to admit she was truly stunning. In the photo, her T-shirt was tied to expose her stomach with her shorts only just long enough to cover the area where Jessica knew she cut herself. Her long blonde hair fell seductively, framing her face. She had one arm around Molly's waist and was giving a thumbs-up to the camera with the other. Jessica struggled not to smile at the image. It reminded her of touring south-east Asia with Caroline when they left college. There were all sorts of photographs in an album or a box somewhere that were exactly like the one she was looking at: two young women hugging and grinning with their lives ahead of them.

She put the picture down and shuffled uncomfortably on the mattress, trying to get comfortable. There was a section close to the edge that felt softer than the rest and she had partially sunk into it. Jessica picked up the second photo in which Molly and Sienna were still children, perhaps eleven or twelve years old. They were on a beach but the framing was a lot tighter and Jessica couldn't see much more than their smiling youthful faces.

As she put down the second picture, for a reason she didn't want to think about, Sebastian popped into Jessica's mind again.

'You know what the news is going to say, don't you?' she said.

Reynolds caught her eye from across the room, telling her he knew. 'We don't have anything to say there's any sort of suicide ring going on around here.'

'I know that but it's not going to stop them writing it – or hinting and letting people put two and two together. Before we know it we'll have every parent with a teenager keeping them inside because they think they're part of some cult.'

'What can we do?' Reynolds replied. 'If we tell the press office to brief against this, it's going to risk giving the media a story they don't have. Even after that, there would be nothing to stop them writing it the way they want anyway.'

Jessica thought about his response for a few moments and then changed the subject. 'Are we going to be okay talking to the parents?'

Reynolds crossed back to where Jessica was standing, walking past her with an implication that she should follow. 'To a degree. They've got a support officer with them. The father wanted to talk earlier but we were waiting for his wife to settle. Ideally we would leave them for a while but if there is anything deeper going on here . . .' He tailed off without finishing his sentence.

As they made their way downstairs, Jessica thought she would never have known anything untoward had happened in the house if it wasn't for the items on the floor of Molly's bedroom. The hallways and stairs were covered with a thick, fluffy pink carpet and pictures of Molly and adults Jessica assumed were her parents lined the walls. It was very suburban, very normal.

Reynolds led Jessica into a living room where a support officer and two uniformed officers were sitting on chairs facing the people who Jessica had seen in the photographs. Reynolds introduced himself and Jessica to Molly's parents and apologised for their regular clothes. Jessica had dropped Adam at home before heading to the house still in the jeans and jumper she had been wearing all day. The inspector was wearing something similarly casual but the young woman's parents, who introduced themselves as Peter and Nicola, waved away their apologies.

The other officers left the room and closed the door as the Scene of Crime team arrived. Reynolds had already told Jessica they were running late because of a large traffic accident involving a lorry and a shop front in the city centre.

The paramedics had transported the body but the bedroom still needed to be examined.

Jessica was struck by how much Peter North looked like his daughter. He was somewhere in his forties but they shared the same facial structure and had a dimple in the same spot on their cheeks. Nicola looked older than her husband but Jessica put a lot of that down to the trauma of what had happened. Her eyes were red and swollen.

Peter did much of the talking, telling them more or less the same as what Reynolds had already spoken about upstairs. It was the little details that struck Jessica. He mentioned that they always went to the same pub for Sunday lunch because of the way they cooked the roast potatoes. He said they were ready to leave but met a couple they knew. Because of that, they stopped for an extra coffee they might not usually have had. Nicola hadn't looked up from the tissue she was holding until her husband said that, at which point she blew her nose loudly and burst into tears.

Reynolds caught Jessica's eye to say they would have to be quick in getting anything else they needed because the woman clearly wasn't up to it. As he comforted his wife, Peter explained that Nicola had gone upstairs when Molly hadn't responded to their arrival home. He rushed up after her when the screaming started.

'It was my belt,' was all he could conclude. Jessica knew that single detail would be something that would stay with him. What if he had worn different trousers and needed that belt? What if they hadn't stopped for the extra coffee? She knew there was nothing she could say that would make either of them feel any better.

'Did you have any reason to think she might be unhappy?' Jessica asked as tactfully as she could manage.

Peter shook his head. 'She was upset over her friend Sienna. They were so close. They had been friends for ages. Sienna used to sleep over here and then Molly would stay at theirs. Well, not recently. Not since her dad left her mum and bought the new house.'

'Do you know if the two girls had fallen out?' Jessica asked.

Peter went to answer but Nicola spoke across him. Her voice was throaty, dry, and sounded painful. 'They used to fall out when they were younger, much younger. But they grew out of it like most girls do.'

Jessica directly addressed Nicola. 'Do you know why either Sienna or Molly might want to do something like this?'

Nicola's bottom lip started to wobble again at the mention of her daughter's name. She shook her head. 'No.'

Peter stood and walked behind where they were sitting. The daylight had almost gone and he twisted a cord which closed the blinds before returning to sit next to his wife.

'Were there any other friends Molly was close to?' Jessica asked.

Nicola shook her head again. 'There were some girls she used to hang around with but that was because they were Sienna's friends. I know she didn't think much of them.'

As his wife tailed off, Peter spoke. 'I kept expecting her to bring home some boy I inevitably wouldn't like. At first it was a bit of a joke but then I just left her to it. You're not supposed to like your daughter's boyfriends, are you? I was always waiting for one not to like.'

Jessica watched the man gulp and wipe his face with the back of his hand. She glanced at Nicola, who caught her eye. It was only for a moment but Jessica could tell that Molly's mother knew exactly why her daughter hadn't been bringing home boyfriends. Jessica nodded a fraction to acknowledge what the woman was saying without words and, in that silent understanding, Jessica felt a lump in her own throat.

She blinked furiously, fighting back tears she didn't understand. She'd had the same feelings in the car with Adam earlier in the day but that was over a different issue and Jessica couldn't fathom why she was struggling to deal with her emotions. She had been able to put a brave face on most things through her career but, perhaps because they reminded her so much of herself and Caroline at that age, she was feeling attached to the two teenage girls.

Reynolds didn't peer towards her but it felt as if he was aware of her feelings as he took up the questioning, clarifying a few things they needed for their records and checking to see if the names of Molly's friends matched the ones they already had.

When he had finished, Reynolds stood and shook hands with Molly's parents. Jessica followed suit, again locking eyes with Nicola. She felt like hugging the woman instead.

Both officers left contact numbers in case either of the parents thought of anything else they might need to know. The support officer re-entered and Jessica could hear the investigating officers working upstairs.

She walked alongside Reynolds down the pathway towards their respective cars. 'Are you all right?' he asked.

'Sorry, I don't know what came over me. I just . . . I don't even know what to say. It seems like such a waste.'

As they rounded a corner to head towards where they were parked, Reynolds stretched out an arm and pulled Jessica towards him. When they shared an office, they had been much closer than recently. She rested her head on his shoulder briefly before pulling away. 'Thanks,' she said, meaning it.

He smiled. 'We should share an office again. I miss having someone leaving their mess on my side.'

Jessica laughed wearily. 'What on earth is going on?' she asked, knowing her question was as unanswerable as Reynolds's had been in Molly's bedroom.

The moment was interrupted as Reynolds's phone started ringing. He fumbled in his pockets before finally finding it in an inside section of his jacket. He reminded Jessica of her dad and the way he lost his glasses case.

Her moment of amusement didn't last long as she saw his eyes widen in surprise before he hung up. 'You didn't have plans tonight, did you?'

'No, why?'

'Someone just tried to set fire to Anthony Thompson's house.'

18

After the hours she had put in over the weekend, Jessica spent Monday morning sitting around the house having been ordered by Cole not to be at the station – or do anything relating to the job – until lunchtime. She knew he had done it because he wanted her to rest but being in the house she still thought of as Adam's when she would have much rather been at work wasn't good for her mood.

When they had spoken on the phone the previous evening as she left Anthony Thompson's house, the chief inspector's exact words had been, 'Get a lie-in'. Whether he was implying she looked as if she needed a good night's sleep was something that Jessica didn't want to ask. She knew the answer was 'yes' but that didn't mean she could flick a switch and suddenly start sleeping solidly again. Her late-night thoughts were haunted by Adam and Sebastian as well as Sienna and Molly. With the time she spent commuting and general problems with sleeping, Jessica was finding herself alone with her thoughts far too often.

When she lived on her own, Jessica had long watched late-night reruns of early-morning talkshows. She wouldn't have admitted it to her colleagues or friends but the family arguments, DNA tests and general confrontational nature of them was something she pretended to hate but secretly watched when it was just her. Since moving in with Adam, she had largely given up her vice but, with the television remote to herself and an empty living room, Jessica allowed the morning show to take her mind away from everything she had going on.

She pictured Anthony Thompson in one of the seats, with Ryan storming on. 'YOU BURNED MY SON, NOW I'LL BURN YOUR HOUSE' was the strapline across the bottom, with a DNA test at the end to figure out who the father of Sienna's baby was.

Just after midday, Jessica left the house and drove to the station, sitting in the car park to ensure Cole would not accuse her of cheating on his demand that she rest. He had scheduled a senior briefing for one o'clock where they could go over everything properly for the first time – including the events of the previous evening.

Jessica walked straight up to his office. Through the glass walls she could already see that Cole was sitting behind his desk, with DS Cornish, Reynolds and Rowlands packed into chairs across from him. Rowlands wouldn't usually be a part of such meetings, so his presence surprised Jessica as she entered. Because of how closely everyone was sitting, Jessica had to push the remaining empty chair out of the way so she could open the door fully and close it, before manoeuvring the seat back behind the door so she could sit. Realistically, there was only room for the DCI plus two other people to sit comfortably. She winked at Rowlands, who was wedged in between his two supervisors with his arms crossed looking awkward.

'We have got the good, the bad and the ugly squeezed in here,' Jessica said as she sat down.

'Who's who?' Cole asked with a smile.

'Louise is the good, obviously, because she's female. Dave's the ugly, because, well, look at him. And I guess that makes Jase the bad.'

DS Cornish laughed, with Rowlands scowling and unfolding his arms, throwing them up in the air in mock protest.

Reynolds replied with a smile. 'The black man's always the bad guy, is he?'

'Well, it's either that or ugly, so take your pick.'

The inspector looked from Jessica to Rowlands then back again. 'Fair enough. I'm the bad guy.'

Jessica saw Cole smiling broadly before he quietened them down. 'Did you enjoy your morning off?' he asked her.

'I slept all morning just like you said.'

It was clear from the chief inspector's raised eyebrows that he didn't believe her.

'All right then,' he said. 'We have had some information back this morning which will bring everyone up to date on the attack on Anthony Thompson's house last night.' He turned to Reynolds. 'Jason?'

The inspector looked at a set of papers in his hand and pushed his chair back slightly to make sure the others could see him better. 'Jess was with me last night, so she knows some of this but some of you are new, so I'll go through it all. Yesterday evening, while Jess and myself were attending to another matter, we got a call to say someone had tried to set fire to Anthony Thompson's house. The person who lives opposite spotted someone prowling around just after dark. They saw him hanging around Anthony's front door with something they said looked suspicious. They left their house and crossed the road, which led to the person running off. It was only then he smelled petrol and called us. No fire was started but large parts of the front of Anthony's house had been covered in it.'

'Was Anthony inside?' Louise asked.

Reynolds nodded. 'Yes but he didn't hear anything. He was a bit . . . wired.'

'How do you mean?'

Jessica answered: 'He's hard to read. You never know if he's drunk, high, or just putting it on. Sometimes it's like a combination of all three. He was there but he seemed oblivious to it all. His neighbour ended up cleaning the door for him.'

Louise seemed confused but Jessica thought she didn't know the half of it considering she hadn't met the man. 'Did we get any sort of description?' she asked.

Reynolds shook his head. 'Not really, just a man in dark clothing. Relatively thin, quick at running, that sort of thing.'

'What about a petrol can?' DS Cornish added.

'He ran off with whatever he stored the liquid in. It must have been fairly heavy before he emptied everything out of it, so he might have had a vehicle nearby. We have been going door-to-door this morning but can't find anyone else who saw it. No footprints or anything else on site either.'

Jessica knew Ryan didn't drive, but that didn't necessarily rule him out in her mind. Just because it was heavy, it wouldn't be impossible to carry.

'Do we have any obvious suspects?' Cornish asked.

Reynolds glanced quickly at Jessica before turning back to face the others. He knew she was thinking of Ryan Chadwick. 'We're not sure. Not really. Obviously there are connections to both Martin and Ryan Chadwick. I spoke to my source at the hotel they are staying at earlier who told me that neither of the two men were on site as far as they know. They're not completely sure about Ryan but Martin was definitely away. From what I'm told, he leaves the hotel late morning or at lunchtime every day and doesn't return until later in the evening.'

Jessica remembered her conversation with him in the back of the van, when he spoke about his drinking. She hoped he hadn't returned to that and, more than anything, she hoped he had an alibi and wasn't involved.

Louise had been working on a different case but Jessica assumed she had been brought in to listen to everything as a fresh set of ears. 'Do we have anything we might be able to bring him in on?' she asked.

Reynolds waved towards Cole. 'I don't know. We were talking about this earlier. The guy was released from prison and served his time so we have got to be careful. In essence, he has no connection to Anthony Thompson, other than what happened in the past. It's circumstantial that he wasn't at the hotel. We could see if he has an alibi but we don't want to be seen to be harassing him.'

He glanced at Jessica before continuing, clearing his throat. 'That said, I've had people looking into Martin's past and his old school was burned down a year before he was arrested for the fire that killed Alfie Thompson.'

It was the first Jessica had heard about it. 'Seriously?' she blurted out.

Reynolds nodded. 'Yes. He was never a suspect and, other than the fact he went there, there's nothing to link him to it. It's just something to bear in mind.'

'Let's not forget his house was burned down too,' Jessica reminded everyone.

All five officers looked at each other as if searching for inspiration. 'We're clutching at straws,' Reynolds said. 'Maybe someone's trying to set Martin up? Maybe someone's out for revenge on him or Anthony? If any of you have any theories, they would be most welcome.'

Again, no one said anything and Jessica could only think of Ryan.

Before the silence could last too long, Cole interrupted. 'Moving on for now, I've got an update on our two suicides.' He picked up a folder from his desk, before shuffling some papers around and picking up the one he wanted. 'I think you all know the details about Sienna Todd, the first victim. Jason and Jess visited the parents of her friend, Molly North, yesterday after a second apparent suicide. We have the early results in, which basically say all the signs point to suicide.'

'Did Molly have any self-harm marks?' Jessica asked.

'Nothing,' the DCI replied. 'No note found either, nothing untoward at the scene.' He turned to face Rowlands. 'David?'

Jessica hadn't expected the constable to speak but she

realised he must have been given her duties from the morning.

He looked apologetically towards Jessica for a moment and then spoke. 'I talked to Sienna and Molly's friends earlier this morning. To say they were no help would be an understatement.' He nodded towards Jessica. 'I know Jess and Jason spoke to the same girls at the school but I couldn't get anything from them either.'

As if reading Jessica's mind, Cole cut in, speaking to her. 'I asked Dave to do the interviews because I thought they might have felt drawn to someone male who is a bit younger than myself or Jason.'

'Did you get anything at all?' Jessica asked.

Rowlands shook his head. 'Nothing really. They all said they only knew Molly through Sienna. None of them seemed to think either of the girls were particularly depressed or anything like that.'

'Do you think it could be some vow of silence?' Cornish asked. 'Like a cult or a club or something like that?'

'I honestly don't know,' Rowlands replied.

Jessica thought of herself at that age and the way she and Caroline pretty much kept themselves to themselves. There were other friends they might do things with, but their secrets and worries were only shared with each other, if at all. Although she had found the other girls' attitudes hard to fathom, she could just about understand why they might not know the intimate details of each other's business.

'I don't know if it's relevant,' Jessica said softly. 'But Molly was most likely in love with Sienna. She might have killed herself because of that.'

'Did you question the parents?' Cole asked, slightly surprised as it was the first he had heard of it.

'I think her mother knew but her father didn't. It's not fair to any of them to bring it up now. If Nicola – the mother – chooses to tell her husband then it should be her decision.' Jessica spoke firmly enough to make it clear to the others that it shouldn't be negotiable.

For a moment, no one said anything, as if digesting her words, before Cole spoke. 'With the coroner's verdict confirmed on Molly North, I think we're all aware of what tomorrow's headlines might bring. Dual suicides of young girls and the like. I'll liaise with the press office about what to do if we end up with the worst type of coverage. We absolutely cannot allow people to think there's some sort of suicide cult.'

'What if there is?' Louise asked, quite reasonably Jessica thought.

Cole shook his head. 'Then we'll still tell them there isn't.'

Jessica had rarely seen him angry but he appeared close to losing his temper before composing himself. 'Because everything has been happening at once, we haven't yet put together a concrete plan of who should be doing what. I know that's my fault but let's sort this now.'

'Are we ruling out the possibility that everything is linked?' Jessica asked, knowing it wouldn't go down well.

She saw Reynolds and the DCI exchange the briefest of glances to confirm her suspicions that they had already talked about her while she wasn't there. 'I wouldn't say we're ruling it out,' Cole said, 'but we don't have any reason to think they might be connected. Obviously, there was a fire at the house of Sienna Todd's father but that could be bad timing.'

'Or it could be relevant,' Jessica replied, trying not to sound too aggressive. The inspector and DCI exchanged another glance, infuriating Jessica, who suddenly found herself raising her voice. 'Look, I'm not just picking on him but you've got to admit there's a link to Ryan in all of this. He knew Sienna. Molly and the other girls were nervous talking about him. He was angry over Anthony's interview.'

There were a few moments of silence before Cornish spoke. 'Why would he set fire to his own house? And what about the suicides? Are you saying he was somehow involved?'

Jessica's anger dissipated as quickly as it had erupted. She slumped into her seat. 'I don't know. I just think we're missing something.'

More silence.

'What are you suggesting, Jess?' Reynolds asked gently. She knew the inspector was trying to be delicate but she didn't like the idea of her colleagues trying to patronise her. 'We can't just follow Ryan around,' he added to emphasise his point.

'We can't,' Jessica replied. 'But I know someone who can.'

19

Andrew Hunter had been doing whatever he could to forget the case he didn't want to be working on. He took on a job running a pre-marriage background check for a man on his potential wife. Quite what that said about 'love' and 'trust' between the couple before their big day, he wasn't too sure. Either way, one of his contacts who worked for a credit rating agency had passed him some information which showed the woman in question had some debts her spouse-to-be didn't know about. Andrew passed it on and took his fee, realising more and more each day that he had probably made the wrong career choice.

He was sitting in his comfortable chair, spinning himself around in the absence of anything meaningful to do, when his mobile phone rang. The name which flashed up filled him simultaneously with excitement and a little fear.

'Sergeant Daniel,' he answered, before being reminded to call her 'Jess'.

'How are you?' Jessica asked, which was the first time Andrew could remember her asking him something similar. He was instantly suspicious.

'I'm all right. You?'

'Good, good,' he heard Jessica reply. 'Look, I've got something for you. A sort of "You scratch my back, I might be able to pass a few things discreetly your way"-type thing.'

'Is that how the saying goes?' Andrew asked, trying to make a joke.

'What?'

It was clear to Andrew that Jessica worked very much with one-sided conversations which she controlled. 'Nothing, don't worry about it,' he replied. 'What are you after?'

Jessica explained the only link she knew of between the suicide of Harley's daughter and the fire which destroyed the man's house. It was a young man named Ryan, whose father was a convicted killer and arsonist. He had been in the photos she had taken from him. As she spoke, Andrew reloaded the images on his computer so he could familiarise himself with what the teenager looked like. From the photographs he had, Ryan was the person who had fed Sienna chips.

'Obviously this call hasn't happened,' Jessica said. 'But I was just wondering if you could perhaps keep an eye on Ryan? You're being paid to find out information which could be relevant to him anyway and, of course, I'd be really grateful . . .'

Andrew almost laughed, wondering if the sergeant knew how fake her pleading voice sounded. She had the bollocking-angry one down to a T – but the one where she was trying to be nice needed work. He wondered if he should tell her but figured he didn't want to risk hearing the irate voice again.

'What am I going to get in return?' he asked.

'I've already given you information about Ryan which could help you,' she replied.

'Are you saying he could be the father?'

'Maybe . . .'

'You're not, are you?'

The line went silent for a moment before Jessica began to speak, her voice slightly harsher. 'No, probably not. Well, maybe. Look, do you want me to be honest?'

Andrew laughed. 'Go on then.'

'Basically, we don't have a bloody clue what's going on. We've got fires, attempted arsons, suicides, knobheads working at newspapers, all sorts. I suggested you might be able to help. The people I work with aren't so keen but I think they'll turn a blind eye as long as any shite ends up sticking to me, not them.'

Andrew couldn't stop himself from laughing again. 'That's a lovely picture you're painting.'

He heard Jessica join in and, for the first time since she phoned, Andrew felt as if she was being herself with him. 'People tell me I have a way with words,' she said.

Andrew suddenly realised he had missed something. 'Hang on, "suicides"? As in more than one?' It was the first he had heard of it.

'That's the other thing,' Jessica replied. 'Sienna's best friend, Molly, killed herself yesterday. We're expecting it to hit the news tomorrow. It might even be on TV tonight, I don't know. Our press office is trying to keep things quiet for now but it'll only stay like that for a while. That's where my knobhead at the newspaper comes into things.'

'Where are you from?' Andrew asked. 'You're not a Manc, are you?'

'No, why?'

'Because if you're going around calling people "knobheads", you've definitely been working here too long.'

He heard Jessica sigh. 'Yeah, you're right. Anyway, we don't know why these girls killed themselves. We don't know why Harley's house was burned down, or any of the other stuff I told you about. All we know is that Ryan is the only person we know who links it all together.'

'So you want me to follow him?'

'I can't ask you to do that.'

Andrew was confused. 'You don't want me to follow him?'

He heard the woman give an exasperated gasp. 'I don't think you heard me quite right,' she replied, annoyed. 'I can't ask you to do anything. If you do choose to do something along those lines and then call me regularly to tell me what's going on, that would be up to you. Obviously if that were to happen, there may be times in the future where I might be able to call you and pass on pieces of information you might not necessarily have. As a friend, of course. If anyone were to examine certain phone records, I would just be talking to an old mate on the phone.'

Andrew laughed, feeling stupid for not picking up on her initial hint. 'We're friends then?'

'Oh yeah, we go way back. You, me, my boyfriend, your girlfriend, wife, boyfriend or whatever. It's all dinner parties and that type of shite. Old, old friends.'

'All right but, if we're such old pals, you would know that I don't have a girlfriend or boyfriend.'

'Wife?'

'Yeah, she's just not married to me any longer.'

'Oh.'

Andrew heard Jessica pause. He wanted to make a joke of things to stop the conversation being uncomfortable. 'Trust me Jess, never get married,' he said as breezily as he could, not believing anything he was saying. 'Only fools get married. Or "knobheads" as you might say.' The silence from the other end started to become uncomfortable. 'Er, Sergeant . . . ?'

'It's Jess.'

'Yeah, sorry, erm . . . I was only joking. You're not married, are you? It's just you said boyfriend, so I . . .'

She replied far too quickly and Andrew knew he had said the wrong thing. 'No, no, it's fine. So, er, right. Are we all right, then? On the same page and all that?'

'Yeah, that's fine. I'll call you.'

'Thank you. Bye.'

The line went silent. Andrew stared at the screen for a few moments before it hit him. He remembered seeing the engagement ring on her finger the very first time he had met her in the service yard at the back of that electrical store.

He remembered Keira's engagement ring, bought when he had hardly any money. It was a thin strip of white gold fitted with the smallest of diamonds. Even given its size, he had to haggle over the price because he couldn't have afforded it otherwise. She insisted it was perfect but the look on her father's face when he saw it – half-amusement, half-disgust – was something Andrew had never forgotten.

'Sorry, Jess,' he said quietly to the empty room, hoping she had more luck than he had.

*

Andrew was beginning to regret the first decision of his day. Jessica had told him that Ryan didn't drive – even though he worked in a garage – and, given that, he thought it would be best if he got some exercise and used public transport. That was definitely his first mistake. Sitting in his own vehicle in traffic that hardly seemed to move each morning was a nuisance. Sitting in a vehicle with fifty or more strangers in traffic that hardly seemed to move went far beyond that.

There were the fourteen-year-old boys at the back of the bus in their ill-fitting school uniforms, swearing and scowling at anyone who dared to look in their direction. Then there were the young teenage girls in front of the boys, split into two both physically by the aisle and their attitude. A handful on one side were leaning over the backs of the seats, chatting to the lads, or applying make-up. The others were seemingly unhappy at both the other girls – and the boys.

After that, there were the people in suits on their way to work, constantly checking their watches and a few older folk looking slightly bemused. Probably thinking about how much things had changed since their day, Andrew thought before realising he had stereotyped everyone on the bus. The one thing which definitely wasn't just in his head was that everyone seemed to have a mobile phone in their hand – even the pensioners.

When the bus finally stopped in the city centre, Andrew hurried through the streets until he reached the hotel Jessica had told him Ryan was staying in. Although she hadn't been able to give him any specific details about the schedule the teenager kept, Jessica said he usually went to college in the mornings and worked at a garage in the afternoons. What he got up to in the evenings was anyone's guess.

Andrew sat in the window of a coffee shop across the road, sipping on a cappuccino and watching the world pass him by. Gentle rain started to fall as the pace of everything, from the cars buzzing past, to the speed at which people were walking, seemed to increase. The glass began to mist up, so he finished his drink and left the cafe before crossing to the hotel. Although he was confident of his ability to blend into most scenes, standing in the rain was always a guaranteed way to make yourself stand out.

And you got soaked.

The investigator walked through the revolving doors of the hotel, entering the lobby. A selection of empty wide lounge chairs was dotted around. He walked quickly across the area, checking where the lifts and stairs came out, before sitting on one of the chairs and taking his phone out.

He was consistently amazed at how you could get away with hovering almost anywhere unchallenged if you looked a little bit smart. It was all about seeming as if you had authority whether you did or not. Jeans and a T-shirt were a definite no. A well-fitting suit carefully matched with a plain tie would do wonders as long as you walked around in a manner that made it appear as if you knew what you were doing.

Andrew typed on his phone's keypad and stopped every few minutes to check his watch, looking frustrated enough that he might be waiting for someone but not agitated enough to make a scene. As expected, no one paid him any attention.

After fifteen minutes, Andrew spotted the person he had seen with Sienna in the restaurant. Ryan slouched his way out of the lift, looking at his own phone screen and not where he was going. He scowled at a member of staff he almost walked into and left through the rotating door, shoving his shoulder hard into the glass to make it move.

Andrew moved quickly from his seat, pulling his woollen coat around him before exiting into the drizzle. He couldn't believe his luck that Ryan was wearing bright white trainers and an almost luminous yellow coat. Losing him would be well-nigh impossible, especially because of the uninterested, slouching way the teenager walked. Andrew could see him across the road, heading towards the bus stop he had not long left himself. He walked swiftly through the foot traffic, keeping an eye on the bright yellow jacket as Ryan slowed to a stop by the bus rank. Andrew waited at the far end of the enclosed area, around twenty metres away, thinking it was going to be a long day.

By the time the daylight began to fade, Andrew was annoyed at himself firstly for allowing Jessica to talk him into the job and secondly for the crazy decision to spend the day on foot. As his thighs and legs began to ache, he kept telling himself how good it was for him to be getting so much exercise. The truth was he would have rather been in his car eating a meat and potato pie and brushing the crumbs into the foot well.

His journey had taken him to the college, where he spent the morning in the park next to the bus stop waiting for Ryan to finish. He knew there was a chance the young man could leave by a different route but, considering he knew where he worked, it wasn't the worst of his concerns. The only reason he hadn't gone straight to the workplace in the afternoon was because he wanted to get an idea of what Ryan's journey was like and to keep an eye on anyone he might be hanging around with. He had already scouted the location and knew the back of the college led nowhere. The front was essentially one enormous car park. From his position it had been pretty easy to see everything except inside the building. Realistically he was never going to get access there, so, by using his telephoto lens from the safety of the bushes just inside the park, he had done as well as could be expected without descending to significantly more subterfuge than he was willing to use.

From the college, via the bus, he arrived at Ryan's workplace. The previous evening, he had left his car parked on the side street opposite the garage, knowing he was going to end up there. Again, finding out what exactly Ryan did inside was a level up from what he felt was necessary but Andrew took photos of Ryan's workmates and each customer who came and went. At some point, he would share the images he had from both the garage and the college with Jessica to see if she spotted anything he hadn't.

The clouds had started to mass and with the light fading and his ability to take photos severely impeded,

Andrew was almost ready to pack up for the day when he saw Ryan hurrying out of the large sliding doors speaking into his phone. At first Andrew thought he was heading for the bus stop but the teenager turned left almost immediately into a side street. Throughout the day, he had only seen his target slouch but he was now moving quickly and something didn't seem right.

Andrew dropped the camera in his shoulder bag and stepped out of the car, pulling the lapels up on his coat to partially shield his face. He walked steadily but swiftly across the road, following Ryan's yellow coat from a distance as the teenager crossed another road and cut across a grassy area until he came to a bridge over the main road.

There were street lights at either end but none in the middle. Andrew hung back, away from the first lamp, squinting into the distance as Ryan stopped almost exactly in the centre of the walkway. From the far end, he saw another figure approaching. It was undoubtedly a young woman, roughly Ryan's age. She was wearing jogging bottoms and a large coat but her long blonde hair swished in the breeze.

Andrew edged as close to the bridge as he dared, not wanting to stand directly under the street light. The noise of the traffic passing underneath meant overhearing any of the conversation was impossible but the two people seemed to be having some sort of argument. The female waved her hands around and Ryan pointed an aggressive finger. The investigator peered towards them, trying to see if the girl seemed familiar from any of the photos he had taken.

As the duo's gesturing tailed off, Ryan unzipped his jacket and reached inside. From where he was standing, Andrew couldn't see exactly what he was holding in his hand but it looked like a folder or an envelope. He held it out towards the woman, who looked inside but didn't take it. Andrew closed his eyes for a moment and took a deep breath, before starting to walk confidently and quickly past the lamp over the bridge. He was careful not to arouse suspicion by looking at the pair as he moved towards them but glanced up briefly as he passed.

Ryan was shielding his body but his companion was clearly less aware of Andrew's approach. She was now holding a white padded envelope and, although he didn't catch the whole sentence, he heard her local accent say one line perfectly. 'Where the fuck did you get all this money?'

20

Garry Ashford wasn't answering his phone. Jessica first called from her mobile and then from the station's phone. With no luck, she tried using the prefix that meant the call showed up as 'unknown'. He obviously knew she was trying to get hold of him, which meant he was avoiding her calls. In fairness, she didn't blame him.

Jessica tried dialling his mobile one final time, staring at the *Herald*'s website on her work terminal. The words 'SUICIDE CLUB' leapt off the screen. They were the exact ones which had also been on the front of that morning's paper and had been picked up by national newspapers who had been calling the press office all morning. Even the television news, who had initially reported things fairly straight, were now using harder language so as not to be left behind by their print colleagues.

At first, she had thought about calling Sebastian to shout at him but held back, thinking he might enjoy it. She also knew from what Garry had previously claimed that the writer didn't create the headlines. It sounded sus-piciously made up and didn't stop her wanting someone to shout at.

Jessica clicked the 'contact us' button at the bottom of the news story and dialled the number on her desk phone.

A female voice answered sweetly on the second ring. '*Morning Herald*, how can I direct your call?'

'Garry Ashford, please.'

'One moment.' Generic instrumental music started playing, agitating Jessica even further. The line quickly clicked back to the woman's voice. 'Can I ask who is calling, please?'

'Yes, it's his mother.'

'Okay, one moment.'

The music returned as Jessica re-read the top few lines of the story, allowing herself to become more annoyed by it. After a couple of minutes, the tune finally ended and Garry spoke. 'Mum, I told you to call my mobile.'

'I did but you're not answering that, are you, Mr Ashford?'

There were a few moments of silence before the journalist realised he had been duped. 'Jess?'

'What the hell is going on with the headline?'

'Jess, I, er . . .'

'And since when do you ignore my calls? I've been dodging yours for years but that's not the point.'

Garry stumbled over his words before finally coughing to clear his throat. 'Sorry. I didn't write the headline but you can't say the story isn't true. Two teenagers have both killed themselves with apparently no good reason. Why shouldn't we report that?'

'It's not just reporting that though, is it? It's the implication there might be a string of other young girls ready to do the same.'

'Are you saying there's not?' Garry shot back.

'Are you saying there are?'

There was a pause before the journalist replied. 'I told you, I didn't write the headline, or the story for that matter. If you want to take it up with someone, call the editor.'

Jessica was surprised at the annoyance in his voice. Their relationship had always been very one-sided in her favour. 'I'm sorry, Garry,' she said. 'I know it's not you.'

When the journalist replied, his tone was a lot steadier. 'Jess, we know each other well enough that I understand you just wanted someone to shout at. But as I keep telling you, these decisions go above me.'

She felt a little silly, recognising he was right. 'Fair enough but we have now got people going into schools and colleges today to give talks and so on.'

'Maybe that's a good thing? If there is a wider problem, it will get people asking for help.'

When he put it like that, Jessica realised the morning's coverage wasn't entirely negative. 'You're a slippery little fellow, aren't you?' she said, lightening her tone to let him know she was joking.

Garry laughed. 'If I were you, I'd be more concerned by the morning's other revelation?'

'What?'

'The fact our secretary thinks your voice sounds like a sixty-four-year-old woman's. That can't be a good sign.'

Jessica couldn't stop herself from giggling, although his point did hit a little too close to home. 'All right, laugh it up,' she said. 'You've not been breaking any speed limits recently, have you? Tax disc in date? What about the tread on your tyres? Are they the correct depth?'

'Everything's perfectly in order. The police are dodgy around here so you've got to be careful.'

'Yeah, all right. We should go for a beer sometime. Just stop pissing me off, okay?'

'I think me breathing pisses you off, but I'll do my best.'

Jessica put down the receiver, feeling a little better, despite the lack of shouting. As she did, her mobile started ringing, with Andrew Hunter's name illuminated.

'You called at just the right time,' Jessica answered.

Her greeting obviously confused the caller, who could only reply with a, 'Huh?'

'If you had phoned ten minutes ago, I would have been less than my cheery, fragrant self.'

'Er, right . . . I've got something for you.'

Jessica realised the man hadn't had time to adjust to her sense of humour. 'Go on.'

'I was going to call last night but it got late and then your line was busy this morning. Yesterday I followed your Ryan lad. I wanted to see what his routine was. Anyway, I ended up following him to this bridge out by his work where he met this girl.'

Jessica couldn't stop herself from interrupting. She took a pen from her top drawer and turned over a scrap of paper. 'Did you recognise her?'

'I don't think so.'

'Did you get any pictures?'

'No, it was way too dark. Ryan gave her this large envelope. I didn't want to be too conspicuous but I heard her ask him where he got the money from.'

For a moment, Jessica didn't know what to say, before replying with a simple: 'Money?'

'Yes. I don't know how much. The envelope didn't seem particularly stuffed but I only saw it for a second.' Andrew went on to describe the girl.

'So she's about his age?' Jessica confirmed. 'Why would he be giving her cash?'

'I don't know. I was hoping you might.'

Jessica tried to think. If the woman was a similar age to Ryan, that meant she was also close to Sienna and Molly. Could that mean anything?

'Did you follow her?' she asked.

'I tried to but she walked off on her own and got in a car after separating from Ryan. I've got the number plate.' Jessica noted it down and said she would contact him if she managed to find anything out.

Because of the way rules had been tightened in recent years to prevent officers using various databases to check up on people they knew, Jessica wasn't sure if she should look into the number plate. Everything was traceable back to the person who made the request and, considering the information had come from Andrew – who was only working in an unofficial capacity – Jessica was even more wary. Her concern lasted less than twenty seconds as she figured she would deal with any disciplinary problems if they arose at a later date. She doubted they would.

She was in the process of noting down the car owner's name and address when Rowlands knocked and entered her office. 'Have you got a minute, Jess?'

'That depends who it's for.'

The constable laughed. 'Having a good day, are we?'

'I'm as much a bundle of joy as always,' Jessica replied, spreading her arms wide and offering him an over-the-top grin.

'Are we still on for later?'

'Yes but Iz told me to tell you to bring a balaclava.'

'Why?'

'Because if she's going to introduce you to Amber, she doesn't want the poor girl tortured by that face of yours.'

Jessica had always been a little scared of babies. The first fear was that she would somehow manage to break them. One time when she was in uniform, she had been sent to a property to interview a potential suspect. The furious mother had asked the two officers if they could keep an eye on her 'child' while she went out to drag her wayward son back into the house. What she hadn't said was that the 'child' was actually a seven-month-old baby. With her colleague flatly refusing to touch it, Jessica was left cradling the little girl.

The second fear was based on a far more irrational feeling that a child's head was simply too big. She had read somewhere that you had the same size eyes as a baby as you did as a fully grown adult. It sounded suspiciously made-up but, ever since, Jessica had been slightly creeped out by how large their heads were in comparison to the rest of their bodies.

As Izzy stood up from the reclining seat and offered

Amber to Jessica, both of the fears jumped to the front of her mind at the same time.

'It's just a baby,' Izzy said with a smile as she practically forced the child into Jessica's arms.

Jessica cupped the child's head with her elbow and awkwardly sat on the nearby sofa, thinking it would at least be less of a fall if she dropped the baby.

Rowlands was next to her, struggling to contain his laughter. 'It's just a kid, Jess, what do you think is going to happen?'

Izzy returned to her recliner, sighing loudly but grinning at the same time. 'If you want to keep her for a day or two, feel free. I'll just sleep.'

Jessica almost swore but had visions of Amber's first word having four letters in it. 'They're pretty small, aren't they?'

Both constables laughed. 'What, babies?' Izzy said. 'What did you expect?'

'I know they're small, but not this small. Look at the fingers. They're like real fingers just . . . littler.'

'They're still real fingers,' Izzy pointed out. 'They're not glued on.'

Jessica realised she couldn't think of a sensible way of putting it. She had seen babies before but rarely like this. 'So what do they do when they're this young?' she asked, thinking it was a reasonable question. She looked up to see Izzy staring at her, eyebrows arched, as if she were the child. 'What?' Jessica asked.

'She's a baby. She eats, she sleeps, she poos. She absorbs

everything that's going on around her. Then one day, she'll be in her thirties and be able to ask stupid questions about other babies.'

'All right, forget it,' Jessica said as Rowlands continued to laugh. She wanted to ask how long it would be before Amber would be walking but decided against it.

'You're thinking about the size of her eyes, aren't you?' Izzy said with a grin.

Jessica looked at the baby and then her friend. 'I've told you about that?'

'Lots of times. Apparently you reckoned one of your friends' babies looked like an alien. And said it out loud.'

'Er, yeah. That was a while ago.' Jessica didn't remember telling that story.

'So what do you think?' Izzy added.

'Very nice. Very baby-like. Pretty much what I'd expected,' Jessica said.

Izzy laughed. 'I'm glad you said that. Everyone keeps saying she's gorgeous and looks just like me and all that. She is gorgeous of course but I know people have to say that.'

'So how are you, Iz?' Rowlands asked.

'I'm all right. I thought I'd have Amber and want to be back at work straight away but I'm getting used to it now. It's a full-time job with more poo and less money. If you're not directly looking after her, then you're dealing with her clothes, or her food, or people are coming around to see her and so on.'

Amber gurgled slightly and Jessica peeked down at her, hoping she wasn't going to be sick. Instead, the child continued to sleep peacefully. 'How's Mal?' Jessica asked, referring to Izzy's husband.

Izzy smiled widely. Her long hair was usually dyed a bright red. It clearly hadn't been done in a while as the sharp crimson colour was now more of a faded auburn. 'Ha! I think you're the first person to ask about him in ages – and he's not even here to appreciate it. He was half-moaning, half-joking about it last night. Even when his own mum came around, all she wanted to do was fuss over Amber. I think he's feeling a bit left out because everyone asks about me and the baby. He's stuck making tea.'

Jessica looked at Rowlands and raised her eyebrows, being careful to support Amber's head. 'Are you taking notes? You're the tea-maker.'

'I don't know why you're telling me,' he replied. 'You're going to be up the duff long before Chloe.'

'Get out.'

'You're engaged and everything. What do you think is going to happen after that? One minute it's church bells, the next it's cribs and pushchairs. That's the way it goes.'

Jessica looked at Izzy, who shrugged. 'I didn't think I'd want kids. It was all Mal, my parents, his mum and so on who kept going on about it. But it's nice . . .'

Jessica thought about how things were going with Adam and her own unspoken concerns about marriage. Was her real worry not about getting married, but more about everything that would come after?

She looked up to see Izzy staring at her with a small

smile on her face, almost as if the constable had read her mind. 'It's all right, Jess,' she said. 'I'm sure you'll do your own thing. You always do.'

The new mother crouched next to Jessica and took Amber back before returning to her recliner. 'So how are things at the station without me? I've noticed that society hasn't collapsed yet, which is slightly disappointing.'

Jessica was somewhat relieved to not be holding the baby any longer. She loosened her shoulders. 'Dave spent two days moaning last week because I gave him a list of names to compile and cross-check, so he's definitely missing you.'

Rowlands was scowling. 'I knew you two would gang up on me if I came along. I wasn't moaning – it's just that you do it so much . . . better, Iz.'

Izzy gently rocked her child, nodding in acknowledgement. 'At least me being here means you actually have to do something, you lazy sod.'

'Is bullying really something you want to be teaching Amber?' he replied.

'If she grows up to pick on you, then yes,' Izzy said with a grin. After a moment, she turned to face Jessica. 'I've seen bits and pieces on the news and so on. Is there really a suicide ring out there?'

Jessica rolled her eyes. 'Of course there's not. We're looking into it all but there's nothing to suggest it.'

'What about the fires? Are you on that too?'

'Sort of. Jason has been dealing with it really. I just float around annoying him. I don't know how much you've been following it but everything has come so quick. I was escorting Martin Chadwick out of prison one minute and now we have had two fires and a close call.'

Izzy looked down at Amber. 'Where was the attempted one?'

'Anthony Thompson's – the guy whose son died. Everything seems to be connected to everything else but I can't figure out exactly how.'

'Do you think Martin's involved then?'

Jessica sighed. 'I wish I knew. Jason says there's something in Chadwick's past where his old school burned down but we don't have anything to suggest it might be him. It was years ago but it all builds a picture. I guess we're just watching and waiting for something else to happen.'

'You know how to pick 'em, don't you?' Izzy said.

Jessica laughed. 'I'm thinking of retiring early to a sleepy little village in the back end of nowhere. My mum and dad took me for tea to this little place called Martindale in the Lake District the other week. Not much seemed to be going on there.'

Rowlands snorted. 'You'd be bored within a week.'

'I know . . .'

'What I don't get is what someone gains,' Izzy said. 'I only know what you've told me and what I've seen on TV and so on. With most things we get involved with, there's always a clear motive, even if we haven't quite figured it all out. Usually it's revenge or something like that. But who gains from this? Houses burning down, all the suspicion being pointed from Martin to Anthony and back again. No one's winning here.'

Jessica didn't know how to reply because her friend was right. If it was Martin or Ryan who was involved – or even Anthony – they were each ultimately going to lose. Sienna and Molly's parents had already lost.

'We should probably go,' Jessica said, standing up. Izzy started to get up but Jessica motioned for her to remain sitting. 'You stay there. We'll let ourselves out and come back soon.'

Jessica kissed the constable on the forehead and Rowlands gave her a peck on the cheek. 'See ya, Iz,' he said.

As they walked out of the house, Jessica felt her phone begin to vibrate in her pocket. She didn't need to answer it to know it was going to be bad news.

21

When she first met him, Jessica thought Martin's wrinkles and thinning hair made him look older than his fifty years. For some reason, the large dark bruises around his eye and bandaged wound on his forehead seemed to de-age him. As he sat up in his hospital bed and tried to smile, Jessica could see the muscles twitching in his face as he forced himself not to wince.

'We can leave you and come back if you'd prefer?' Jessica offered.

Martin shook his head slightly. 'I'd rather do it now so I can get some sleep.'

Jessica sat next to the bed, Rowlands perching next to her with a pad and pen. 'Can you start by telling us what you remember?' she asked.

He closed his eyes and sighed. 'I'd been out for the day and was on my way back to the hotel.'

'Where had you been?' At first Martin said nothing but then he looked away from Jessica, unable to meet her eyes. 'Have you started drinking again?' she persisted.

His voice was quieter than before. 'I've tried not to . . .'

Jessica thought about their conversation in the van and how Martin had said stopping drinking had helped him sort his life out.

'Why did you start again?' she asked, knowing it wasn't really any of her business.

'It's not as easy as you think. When you're inside, everything's decided for you. Out here, you have to start making decisions. Then, with the fire at the house and everything . . .'

Jessica realised there was little point in dwelling on something that was going to upset him – at least not until she had the information she needed. 'Okay, so you were out for a drink. Were you on your own?'

'Yes.'

'And you were making your way back to the hotel . . . what happened then?'

'The hotel they've got us in is in the centre but I was out at this place Longsight way. I was going to get the bus but thought I'd walk it off. I was most of the way back. There's this alley opposite the hotel next to a coffee place. I was cutting through and felt something hit me from behind.'

Jessica already knew he had been found barely metres from the hotel in a pool of his own blood. Even though he was resting on it, she could see a bandage at the rear of his skull. 'What else do you remember?'

Martin shook his head. 'Not too much. I fell forward and hit my eye on the kerb.' He reached up to touch the blackened area. 'I think someone kicked me but . . . that's it.'

'Did you see anyone or hear anything? Maybe you passed someone on your way into the alleyway?'

'No.'

'How about your route home? Have you been cutting through the same spot more than once recently?'

'I guess. Why?' Martin was beginning to speak more slowly, his words slurring into each other.

'If someone had been watching you over a period of days, they might have known that was the way you were going to return to the hotel.'

'You think someone could have been following me?'

'I don't know. Have you seen anything suspicious in recent days?'

Martin seemed embarrassed by his response. 'I'm not always aware of it all . . .'

Jessica thought the sobering nature of his words jarred strongly with the way they overlapped each other, almost as if he were thinking more quickly than his body would allow him to talk.

'Do you know of anyone who might want to harm you?'

Martin met Jessica's eyes, as if putting the name 'Anthony Thompson' telepathically in her mind. He never said the words but the implication was there.

'I didn't see anyone,' he said, as if following up his unspoken suggestion with the acknowledgement that he felt as if he deserved what had happened to him.

'You can say if you know who did it,' Jessica assured him.

He shook his head. 'I didn't see anyone.'

Jessica could see the same guilt in his eyes as when they had shared the back of the van together. She didn't know what else they could get from him. An additional, more formal statement might be taken at some point but, if he continued to insist he hadn't seen anyone, there was very little they could do other than check the CCTV cameras in the vicinity. She didn't expect them to reveal the attacker.

'Has someone contacted Ryan?' Jessica asked.

Martin nodded, wincing painfully and no longer trying to hide it. 'I think he's on his way.'

'Right . . .'

'I'll deal with him,' Martin added.

Jessica felt as if he had been a step ahead of her at every stage of their conversation. She was going to say she would hang around to speak to Ryan, in order to make it clear there should be no form of retaliation.

'He's going to have to let us deal with things,' she said.

'I know. I'll talk to him. He'll listen to me.'

Jessica stared into the man's eyes and saw that he meant it. With a small nod, she stood, Rowlands following her lead. 'Can you give us a minute, Dave?' Jessica asked, not looking at the constable.

Rowlands ummed for a few moments and then touched her gently in the small of her back to let her know he would be outside and available if she needed anything.

As he left, Jessica continued to hold Martin's eyes. 'Can I ask you a question?'

'Go on.'

'As I'm sure you can understand, with everything that has been going on, we have been looking into a few things from your past.'

Martin said nothing, his face not changing.

'That pub you burned down with Alfie inside wasn't the first building you set fire to, was it?'

He continued to stay silent, holding Jessica's eye and licking his lips.

'How many places?' Jessica asked.

Martin winced, his eye flickering shut, before opening again. 'You wouldn't understand.'

Jessica broke eye contact, sitting back in her chair and staring at the ceiling. 'I wanted to believe you when we were in the back of that van. I wanted to think people could change and do good things after bad ones.'

'What really excites you?' Martin asked. The question took Jessica by surprise and the room suddenly felt heavy with menace. Before she could think of a reply, Martin continued, 'Maybe it's chocolate, maybe it's rollercoasters? Perhaps you like driving really fast? I have no idea. We're all different but for me . . . I find enjoyment from other things.'

His voice had cleared again and Jessica wondered if the slurred speech from before was either put on, or a figment of her imagination.

She didn't reply straight away, wondering if he had anything else to add. 'Are you saying you like setting fire to things?' she asked after the pause.

Martin said nothing, shuffling in his bed and attempting to roll over. 'I think I'd like to get some sleep now.'

Rowlands knew her well enough not to ask why Jessica had wanted to talk to Martin by herself. Instead, as they exited the hospital, he turned his phone back on and made a call. Jessica got the gist of the conversation from his half.

'Jason not having much luck?' she asked as they arrived at the car.

'No. He says Anthony was too drunk to talk when they first went round. They've been letting him sober up and they're going to have another go soon. Are we going back to the station?' Rowlands asked, starting the engine.

'Not yet. I need you to take me somewhere but we have only been to the hospital if anyone asks.' At first Jessica thought he was going to query why but he simply asked for the address.

Despite the way she ribbed him, Jessica knew it was moments like this that showed her how good a colleague and friend Rowlands was. He had left her alone without knowing why and then agreed to drive her somewhere simply because she had asked.

She didn't know the area they were heading to but told the constable to keep driving past the house after she had spotted it and then pull up at the end of the road.

'Are you okay to wait here?' she asked.

'Are you sure you're going to be all right?'

'I'll be five minutes.'

Jessica got out of the vehicle and walked towards the house. She double-checked the number on a piece of paper and folded it back into her pocket.

The car with the number plate Andrew had noted down was parked on the road directly outside the house. Jessica walked along the pathway and knocked on the door.

A scowling young woman soon answered, her long blonde hair tied into a loose ponytail. Her baggy jogging bottoms and matching top would have made it look as if she had just got up, except for the thick layer of make-up. She eyed Jessica up and down, casually holding a cigarette in her free hand. 'Who are you?' she asked harshly.

'Morning, Lara, how are you?'

The woman's eyebrows arched further in annoyance. 'How do you know my name?'

Jessica hadn't known it for sure but, from Andrew's description and the fact the address matched, it seemed a fair bet.

'A lucky guess. I'm clever like that. I'm Detective Sergeant Daniel. Can I have a few minutes?'

Lara screwed her face up further, causing a heavy line to appear on her forehead. 'You're police? What do you want?'

'Just a quick word . . . as I, er, said . . .' Jessica couldn't resist the sarcasm, thinking that was probably why it was 'always you' as Rowlands pointed out.

'I ain't done nothing.'

'I never said you had. I just wanted to ask you about Ryan Chadwick.'

Lara looked surprised at the mention of the name. 'Ryan? What about him?'

'I was thinking maybe we could have a girly chat. Compare notes. You know, what do you think about Ryan? What's he up to? Why is he having illicit meetings in the dark on bridges in the middle of nowhere? That kind of thing.'

Jessica got the reaction she wanted. Lara's eyes widened in amazement. She took a long drag from her cigarette before throwing what was left at her feet and putting one hand on the door. 'What are you on about?'

'I was wondering how you know Ryan.'

'We're mates.'

'How about Sienna Todd and Molly North? Do you know them?'

Lara's eyes rolled upwards in thought before she replied. Jessica wasn't sure if it was because she was trying to decide what the best response might be, or because she was genuinely trying to recall if she did know the other girls.

'I don't know. I sort of know the names. Maybe they're friends of Ryan?'

It sounded plausible. 'Are they friends of yours?'

'No. Why are you asking?' Lara's demeanour had changed completely from being aggressive to hugging her arms across her chest. The absence of the cigarette had left her biting her bottom lip. Jessica started to speak but the sound of a baby crying began somewhere behind Lara, interrupting them. The young woman half-turned, looking back to Jessica. 'I've got to go. What do you actually want?'

Jessica locked eyes with the woman but tried to sound sympathetic. 'I want to know that you're not involved in anything you can't get yourself out of.'

For a moment, Jessica thought the woman was going to break but another wail from the unseen child seemed to change the woman's mind. 'No, I'm fine,' she said, starting to push the door closed. 'I've got to go.'

Jessica turned and walked back towards the car, wondering if she should have asked Rowlands or someone else to handle talking to Lara. She hadn't wanted to ask specifically about the money but she did want to let the woman know that she knew something was going on. The one thing that both Lara and Molly had in common was the awkwardness when Ryan's name was mentioned. She couldn't place what it was but it matched the uncomfortable feeling she had when she was around him.

As she sat in the car next to Rowlands, it was clear something had happened. 'I didn't know if I should come find you,' he said.

'What's up?'

'Jason says Anthony Thompson has confessed to attacking Martin.'

22

Jessica and Rowlands arrived at the police station just as Anthony Thompson was being led through the side entrance towards the cells. Jessica caught Reynolds as he was walking across the car park.

'What did he say?' she asked.

The inspector seemed a little frustrated and she didn't know if it was due to her – or because he had spent the morning with Anthony. 'We asked where he was last night, the usual thing. At first he said he couldn't remember. I took a gamble and told him Martin had been attacked and he just laughed and said he enjoyed doing it.'

'Shite. Do you believe him?'

Reynolds held open the station's door, letting her and Rowlands enter. 'I don't know, that's why we brought him in. If he repeats it on tape, we'll have it formally. There's something wrong with him. At first we thought he was drunk but then he seemed fine. Sometimes he slurs his words, sometimes he's completely clear. You never know what you're getting.'

It all sounded very familiar. Jessica told Rowlands she would see him soon, before following Reynolds along the corridor towards the interview room.

'What are we going to do?' she asked.

He stopped, shuffling into a doorway away from the

main area. 'I'm not sure you should be involved in this.'

Jessica felt stung. He had never said anything like it to her in the past. 'Why?'

'You're too close, Jess. I'm not sure you even see it. Jack and I were thinking . . .'

'You're talking about me behind my back?' The aggression in Jessica's voice surprised even her.

'No, we're not. We know how good you are with people and at your job. But there's something about Martin, Anthony, Ryan and these girls that seems to have affected you. You're connecting dots that aren't there to be joined.' He lowered his voice, leaning in closer. 'You suggested using a private investigator to do our dirty work. Dirty work we're not even sure needed doing. Don't you see how that all looks?'

'What if I'm right about Ryan?'

'What if you're not, Jess? What do you think he's been up to? Burning down houses? Attacking his own dad? Killing girls and make it seem like they've done it themselves? How far are you going to go?'

Jessica couldn't meet the inspector's eyes. She knew he was saying things for her own good but he didn't know the half of it. He hadn't seen the doodles she had been given by Aidan. He didn't know she had gone behind his back and got Andrew to follow Ryan anyway. He hadn't been there when she had followed and slapped the teenager. She tried to steady her voice. 'Let me sit in with Anthony. You talk, I'll listen.'

'No.'

'Why not?'

'Because I know you, Jess. I know you won't be able to stay quiet and it's not as if I can turn around and tell you to stop once we're in there.'

'Trust me.'

Reynolds sighed, staring at the ceiling before shaking his head slightly and affectionately resting an arm on Jessica's shoulder. 'Fine – let's go.'

As they readied the interview room, the two officers barely spoke. Jessica knew the inspector had been as delicate and discreet as he could. In previous years, she might have flown into a rage, storming up to the chief inspector's office to find out what the problem was. She had largely moved past that but his words hurt more than they angered her.

An officer knocked on the door to say that Anthony was refusing his right to speak to a solicitor and seemed content to sit quietly in the cells. Reynolds told the officer he may as well bring the man upstairs in that case.

Jessica couldn't remember feeling nervous ahead of an interview but, as she sat slightly behind Reynolds in a position that felt unfamiliar, she could feel a twinge in her stomach. 'Are you all right?' the inspector asked, sensing her unease.

'I'm fine.'

'You don't have to stay silent. If you've got something to mention, just say it.'

Before Jessica could think of anything appreciative, there was a knock on the door and Anthony Thompson was led into the room. He looked almost the same as the other times Jessica had met him, his matted hair hanging untidily around his shoulders, but his face was even redder than on the earlier occasions. She saw him smirk slightly before realising he was being filmed.

Reynolds ran through the initial details from the previous night, asking Anthony where he was. Jessica immediately began to feel edgy when he wouldn't be more specific than 'town'.

After a frustrating series of exchanges, Reynolds eventually moved onto the questions Jessica would have started with. 'What happened as you were returning home?' he asked.

Anthony grinned, showing his discoloured yellow teeth. 'You know what happened. You told me. I beat him into hospital.'

'Who?'

'You know. Him.'

Jessica could feel the inspector tensing. In her own mind, she was counting to ten.

'Martin Chadwick?' Reynolds persisted.

'Yes.'

'So you beat him up?'

'Yes.'

'What exactly did you do to him? Did you punch him? Kick him? Hit him with a weapon?'

'All of them.'

'What kind of weapon?'

Anthony scratched his head, as if thinking. He stuck out his bottom lip before smiling again. 'I don't remember. You tell me.'

Jessica knew they were wasting their time. Anthony

hadn't attacked anyone, he was simply enjoying hearing the details of how Martin had been attacked.

'Did you hit him from the front or the back?' she asked.

If Reynolds was annoyed, he didn't flinch.

'I don't remember.'

Jessica was going to speak again but the inspector beat her to it. His voice was raised and frustrated. 'Answer the question. You've got a fifty per cent chance of getting it right. Front or back?'

Anthony pushed his chair back, leaning into it. 'Front. I caved that fucker's head right in.'

Reynolds looked to Jessica and raised his eyebrows before turning back to Anthony. 'You do know we could charge you with wasting police time?'

The man shrugged. 'Do it.'

Jessica knew it wouldn't happen, largely because they were already in a battle of sorts with the media. Considering the coverage Martin's original release from prison had generated, the last thing they wanted was everything being blown up further by charging Anthony.

Reynolds shunted his chair backwards with a noisy scrape. He announced formally that the interview was over, adding dismissively: 'Go home, Mr Thompson.'

Jessica watched the man turn from Reynolds to stare at her. It didn't seem as if he was going to move. She reached across and stopped the tape recording.

'Why don't you talk to me, Anthony,' she said gently. 'Just tell me whatever you want to.'

She thought about everything the inspector had said to her and realised they had done nothing but accuse

Anthony of doing various things – even right from the beginning. He might still be responsible but no one had asked him what was going through his mind.

Anthony eyed Jessica, his head at an angle. He had stopped grinning, his eyes studying her intently. 'Let's just talk,' she added, holding her hands out to show she was hiding nothing.

The man nodded towards Reynolds. 'What about him?'

'He has to stay – but you can just talk to me if that's what you want.'

Anthony nodded slowly and Reynolds slid the chair away from the desk so it was in front of the door. He sat and Jessica could feel him staring at her.

'You didn't attack anyone last night, did you?' Jessica said softly. The man leant forward, resting his elbows on the table, shaking his head. Jessica was going to ask why he'd claimed he had but the answer was obvious – he wished he'd done so.

'What about the other things we have spoken to you about? The brick? The fire?' Anthony shook his head again but didn't speak. 'What would you like to tell me?' Jessica asked.

Anthony ran his hands through his hair, getting one of his fingers caught on a knot, before aggressively yanking it free. 'Do you have children?'

'No.'

He looked up from the table and waited until Jessica met his gaze. 'Do you know why Alf was sleeping in the pub the night he died?'

'No.'

'We'd had an argument. A stupid thing about him getting a job because he was twenty-one and still living at home. I was only joking – I knew he was trying but there was nothing around. He was a clever kid. He wanted to work with computers, not work in a shop. Me and his mum would have let him live with us for as long as he wanted. It was just one of those things where you joke about something so often, it begins to sound serious. I'd been going at him and he walked out one afternoon.'

Jessica could guess the rest of the story but didn't want to interrupt the man's flow. From his grinning, almost mocking performance earlier, she knew he was being as sincere as he was capable of.

Anthony scratched just above his eye so hard that Jessica thought he might draw blood. 'When he didn't come home at night, we thought he was with one of his friends,' he continued. 'It was only when you came knocking the next day when we realised something had happened. From there . . . well, what do you want me to say? My wife blamed me and left. Meanwhile he walks out of prison as if everything's all right just because he's spent a few years inside.'

'I'm sorry, Anthony, but this has to stop. All of it. I'm not saying you've been involved in what has happened to Martin but we both know what you told the journalist. I know it isn't down to you what they wrote but it could have been that which inspired someone else to target him.'

'I know.'

'Can I ask you a few questions now?' Anthony rocked himself gently forwards and backwards, nodding his head.

'We found a tin of spray paint and a petrol can at your house. Was the damage to Martin's house anything to do with you?'

'No.'

'Why were those items at yours?'

'I don't know.'

'They're not yours?'

'No.'

Jessica believed him – but that only left them with more questions they would have to think through.

'Why didn't you tell us that?' she asked. Anthony shrugged but Jessica knew the answer was because he hadn't forgiven himself for the way his son had died. She suspected he wanted to get himself in trouble. It was why he hadn't protested about being left in the cells at Bootle Street station.

'Why did you go missing when we came to find you?' she asked.

Anthony smiled for the first time since they had begun to talk properly. 'Booze.'

'But why were you near to Martin's hotel?'

The man shook his head. 'I didn't know I was until you told me.'

'Anthony.' Jessica waited until they were staring at each other.

'Yes.'

'I know you might look at me in this suit and you hear me introduce myself as "Detective Sergeant" and you might think I'm someone I'm not. The thing is, away from here, my name is Jessica. You asked if I have children. I don't – but I've got a mum and a dad. I've got friends and I've got a fiancé who's bloody fantastic.'

Jessica felt a lump forming in her throat but continued, even as she felt a dampness around her eyes. 'I don't know what I'd do if someone wanted to hurt them, let alone if they actually managed it. I don't want to patronise you and say, "I know how you feel" and all that shite, because I don't. Anyone who tells you that is a complete dick. But you have to see that this is your chance to let go. When we open the door, you can go home and you can do what you want with your life. If that means drinking yourself to death, that's up to you. I believe what you've told me – but, even if you're not involved with what's happened to Martin, you still would have wished it upon him. You have to let it go.'

Jessica was thinking about Adam and how she would go on if anything happened to him. Just the idea of him being hurt was making her feel a type of grief she hadn't experienced since her colleague and friend Detective Constable Carrie Jones had been killed. She dabbed her eyes with her sleeve but didn't stop looking at Anthony.

'You can't just flick a switch,' he said.

'I know.'

Jessica saw the man's Adam's Apple begin to bob up and down. Her mind flashed back to the same thing happening to Martin in the rear of the van they had shared. Anthony burst into tears. At first, Jessica thought about comforting him, but the man raised his arms and covered his face with his sleeves. She looked sideways at Reynolds, still trying to dry her own eyes. He gave her a small nod.

'Anthony?'

The man swiped the sleeves of his top across his face, trying to calm himself. He met Jessica's eyes again. 'Yes.'

'Are you going to be okay?'

He didn't speak, nodding instead. Jessica motioned to move her chair backwards but Anthony interrupted her. 'I've never told anyone this before.'

Jessica had her hands resting on the desk but stopped. 'What?'

'That afternoon, I'd got home from work and Alfie was watching some rubbish on the TV. I'd wanted to put on the racing and we had this stupid argument. That's when I told him he should get a job if he wanted to stay at our house. I said he could watch what he wanted when he started paying rent. He was so angry. He threw the remote at me and stormed out of the room. Just before he slammed the door, do you know what he shouted at me?'

Jessica thought it was a question he was asking himself but it was clear Anthony wanted her to respond. 'No.'

Tears had begun to form around Anthony's eyes again. He gulped before replying. '"Fuck off, Dad". That was the last thing he ever said to me. I never got the chance to say I was sorry. Just "fuck off" and then he was gone.'

Jessica tried to think of something she could say but instead the sobs she had been trying to suppress were drowned out by Anthony's eruption of tears.

23

Jessica sat alone in the interview room, directly underneath the security camera so that it couldn't see her. The tears felt embarrassing but relieving at the same time. The ends of her sleeves were feeling pretty damp by the time Reynolds returned.

'I thought you were going to listen, not talk,' he said with a smile.

Jessica snorted and coughed. 'You know me. I've got a big mouth.'

The inspector came close to Jessica and held his arms out. She allowed him to cradle her onto his shoulder. 'Are you all right?' he asked.

'I'll be fine. I don't know what's happening to me.'

'It's called being human, Jess. Welcome to the race – it's taken you long enough.'

His arms were strong and Jessica felt as if a large weight had been lifted from her – even if she didn't know what the burden had been in the first place.

'I sorted out one of the cars giving Anthony a lift home,' Reynolds said, releasing her.

'Do you think he'll be okay?'

He shrugged. 'Who knows? I think he's been waiting to tell someone about it for a long time.'

'If he didn't burn down Martin's house, who did? And I

believe him when he said the paint and petrol can weren't his. So who left them at his house? And who attacked Martin? Plus someone poured petrol over his front door too.'

The inspector smiled weakly. 'I'll talk to Jack and we'll meet upstairs.'

'I'll see you in five minutes,' Jessica said. 'I've got something to pick up first.'

Cole's office was a little less crowded than it had been a few days before as Cornish was working on an armed robbery case. When Jessica arrived, the chief inspector was behind his desk as usual, Reynolds and Rowlands across from him.

As well as collecting the item she wanted, Jessica had visited the toilets to make sure it wasn't too obvious she had been crying.

'I've told Jack about the interview with Anthony Thompson,' Reynolds said. 'I don't think either of us really suspect him but we have another problem too.'

Cole spun around his computer monitor so Jessica could see it. In large capital letters was the headline 'ARSON MAN BEATEN', with the same picture of Martin Chadwick that the media had used to report his release from prison.

'Bloody Internet,' Jessica said. 'A few years ago, you'd at least manage to wait until the next day for these things to get out. How did they find the story?'

Cole shook his head. 'I don't know. Our press office

were just working on a release when it broke. Someone at the hospital probably? Maybe even the hotel? There were plenty of bystanders too. Martin has been all over the news, so it's not as if the doctors, nurses and receptionists would struggle to recognise him. I don't know if they copied it off each other but it's been on the news channels too. Everyone has the story.'

Jessica read the first few lines of the piece before sitting back in the seat. 'I've got something to show you,' she said, reaching into the cardboard folder she had been keeping in her office and handing Cole the papers with the doodles in the margins.

'I know it isn't proof of anything,' she added. 'But Ryan Chadwick's form tutor gave me these. I don't know all the data protection or privacy stuff but I'm guessing I probably shouldn't have them. Either way, it's too late now.'

Cole looked through the pages before passing them to Reynolds to scan. No one said anything as Rowlands flicked through the pages, before handing them back to Jessica.

'What do you think they show?' the DCI asked, but Jessica interrupted him.

'There's more. When I mentioned about that private investigator the other day, I know you told me not to but . . .'

She could feel the other two officers' eyes on her but it was Cole she stared at. 'Sorry,' she offered, knowing it sounded pathetic.

Cole sat up straighter in his seat and glanced towards Reynolds before returning his gaze to Jessica. She couldn't read his face. 'Did you . . . ?'

'Yes . . . well, sort of.'

Her supervisor rolled his eyes and shook his head but she still couldn't tell if he was angry. 'What have you got?' he asked.

'You've seen the drawings. It can't just be me that's concerned about the flames Ryan drew?'

From the moment Cole said 'Jess', she knew what was coming. 'This is nothing,' he stated. 'You must know we could never use it as evidence.'

'Of course I know. It's just something to bear in mind along with everything else that's going on.'

'What about the investigator?' the chief inspector asked.

'I asked him to follow Ryan for me. I didn't bring any of you into it. He saw Ryan giving money to this girl. She's the same age as Sienna and Molly. It was all secretive and away from people.'

'Do you know who the girl is?'

'Yes. I spoke to her. I think she wanted to talk but got distracted.' Jessica realised she was sounding desperate.

Cole didn't look annoyed, just confused. 'What are you saying he's up to?'

'I . . . I don't know, just something. You have to admit it all looks bad. The link to the fires, the girls, the drawings, the money. There's something going on there.'

There was a short pause and Jessica realised she had badly misjudged the mood of her colleagues. It was Rowlands who spoke which, in many ways, made her own desperation worse. If either of the other two had said something, they were her superiors. She not only outranked the constable but considered him one of her closest friends.

'Jess,' he said quietly.

'What? I'm not saying all of this is down to him. I'm just saying we're missing something.'

'But this can be so easily explained. Most people draw, write and doodle when they're bored. Just because his are flames, it doesn't show anything. And as for the money? I don't know, it could be for anything. Maybe he'd bought something from her?'

'But what if it's more?'

Cole interrupted. 'We can't keep having this conversation, Jess. We all love you here but . . .'

As Jessica was about to reply, Reynolds spoke. 'Remember what you told Anthony about letting go? Whatever's going on, you've got to get on and do the job. If we find any proper evidence to say Ryan is involved with either case – the fires or the suicides – then we'll move on it. But we don't have anything. No witnesses, no forensics . . .'

Jessica knew she was in an argument she wasn't going to win. 'I just wanted to tell you everything that was going on,' she said. 'We don't have any other suspects or clues for either of the cases. Before they get dumped to one side as unsolved, I wanted to tell you what I had.'

Cole nodded, although she wasn't sure if it was to accept her explanation or simply to shut her up. 'You've got to tell this investigator friend of yours to stop doing whatever he's doing if it's on your behalf. We can't get tied to something like this. Other than that, we'll just have to dig deeper. You might be right that we're missing something, so let's go back to the beginning and look into Martin himself. Jason says his old school burned down – let's see if we can find any way he could be connected to that, or anything else suspicious he might be connected to. When we're done with him, we'll move onto Ryan. If he was in a children's home, there must be people out there who know him and paperwork to chase. If we can't come up with anything, we'll look further afield.'

Jessica knew that much of what he had suggested had already been done. It wasn't as if they had sat around doing nothing for the past few weeks. She suspected he had said it for her benefit.

'Sounds good,' Jessica said, thinking that it didn't.

It wasn't often that Jessica arrived home before her fiancé but, as she opened the front door to a silent welcome, the irony of Adam not being home on one of the occasions she needed him wasn't lost on her. The biggest problem was that she knew her growing obsession with Ryan was getting out of hand too. She had felt it festering inside her from the moment he had looked at her in his house and the way those grey eyes had stared through her. It sent a shiver down her spine at the time and it felt as if it was still happening.

Jessica went into the living room, curling up with her feet underneath her on the sofa. She took a laptop out of a drawer and turned it on. It was one of the few new things she and Adam had bought together. They'd both had bulky desktop computers, which they each donated to charity, before investing in something smaller.

Before the computer had finished booting up, Jessica's phone started to ring. She scrambled across the room to pick it up, expecting it to be Adam, but instead Sebastian's name flashed. Her thumb hovered over the answer button before she let it ring off, waiting for a couple of minutes before listening to the voicemail. Sebastian sounded breezy, asking if she fancied a chat, emphasising that it would be for professional reasons, although it didn't sound like it. Jessica deleted it, trying not to picture his face in her mind.

Back at the computer, she read through the news stories about the attack on Martin, including Sebastian's on the *Morning Herald*'s website. She never ceased to be amazed at how the stories got out; whether via hospital staff, the hotel workers, an eyewitness or any number of other people, somehow the things they tried to keep quiet always found their way into the news.

As she continued to skim through the articles, the front door slammed, with Adam shouting 'hello'.

'In here,' Jessica called. As he entered, she couldn't stop herself from laughing. 'How red are your cheeks?' she giggled, standing up and walking across the room towards him.

'It's cold out there and the wind's howling.'

'You look like a bloody robin trapped in his nest. Look at the state of your hair.' Jessica grabbed some strands that had been blown around and pushed them back into position, before giving him a hug and nestling her head into his shoulder. 'I've been waiting for you,' she said.

She gulped as Adam pulled her tight and squeezed. 'Bad day?'

'How'd you guess?'

'That grumpy, moaning look on your face.'

Jessica pulled away and playfully slapped Adam in the chest. 'Oi, you're supposed to be nice to me.'

'I am nice to you. Now where's my tea?' Adam grinned widely. Although she had been getting better – and despite a Christmas dinner she had cooked for her friends – she still didn't do much in the kitchen.

'Ha! Cheeky sod. Get your own tea. I'm busy.'

'Fine. I will.'

Adam went to turn but Jessica reached out and grabbed his arm, pulling him back towards her. 'Adddddaaaa-aaaammmm,' she purred as seductively as she could manage.

'What?'

'Can you make me something?'

Adam laughed. 'I knew you were going to say that. What do you want?'

'I dunno. Something.'

'Well, that narrows it down. You're a bloody nuisance.'

Jessica grinned. 'Yeah but that's why you love me.'

'All right but if I make you tea, do I finally get to see you in that dress?'

Jessica stared doe-eyed at her fiancé and smiled. 'Maybe.'

When she and Adam had moved in together, they had had something of a clear-out which largely involved her sorting his clothes into three piles. The 'stay' pile was fairly sparse. The 'okay but I'd rather you got rid of it' mound contained the bulk of his wardrobe and the final 'throw it out now, what on earth were you thinking?' stack was quite large too. After protracted but rather one-sided negotiations, where Jessica flat-out refused to give any ground at all, Adam relented and disposed of everything she suggested. She suspected it was because she promised to buy a 'hot dress' to sit in the newly cleared half of the wardrobe. She wasn't a big fan of clothes shopping but Adam had chosen an outfit he deemed 'hot' enough during a trip to Manchester city centre one weekend. As she promised, the dress did indeed sit in the wardrobe. But, as she consistently pointed out to him, although she said she would buy something, she had at no point promised to wear it.

'I know that "maybe",' Adam replied. 'It sounds like "maybe" but it's actually saying "no".'

'How about if I say "perhaps"?'

'Nah, I'll just cook my own tea.'

Jessica stuck her bottom lip out in protest. 'Oh Addddd-aaaaaaaammmm . . .'

'All right, stop moaning. Yeah, I'll make you something.'

As the evening wore on, Jessica managed to put most of her thoughts and emotions from the day to the back of her mind. If anything, telling Anthony – who was essentially a stranger – that she cared so deeply for Adam made it feel more real. The baby-talk with Izzy was making her think that her previous nerves were down to what other people's expectations of her might be, as opposed to her own or Adam's.

After they ate Adam's stir-fry, they played a game of Scrabble on their phones, which Jessica lost badly, before settling down to watch television. Jessica had her head resting on Adam's lap as he snacked on chocolate buttons.

'Are we going to visit some more possible venues this weekend?' Jessica asked.

'I've got a few more we can look at,' Adam replied, dropping a button towards Jessica which hit her in the eye.

'Oi, my mouth's here,' Jessica said, as she picked the chocolate from her face and swallowed it.

'I did have an idea,' Adam said.

'I told you we're not getting married at a bloody sci-fi geek convention,' Jessica said. 'And before you ask, no, I'm not dressing up as Princess Leia.'

Adam laughed. 'Not that – although I'll bear it in mind. I was thinking maybe we could do something abroad? We're only going to be inviting your mum and dad anyway. Maybe Caroline and Dave?'

Because she had been avoiding thinking about the potential date, the idea of going overseas hadn't occurred to Jessica. She reached up and snatched a button from Adam's fingers and threw it at his face, laughing as it bounced off his nose. 'Ha. That's for getting me in the eye. Anyway, yes, maybe? Let's look at some places this weekend and then make a decision. I reckon my mum and dad would be up for something in the sun.'

'Have you thought about when? It's loads of planning. Most people take eighteen months or so.'

It wasn't the first time he'd asked but this time Jessica was in the mood. She snatched another piece of chocolate and replied as she chewed. 'Sod that, I'll put my mum on it. She'll get people sorted out.'

'Are you sure you don't want to do more of the planning? Most brides go a bit crazy as the day approaches.'

'Yeah, I'm not most brides though, am I?'

Adam laughed. 'I don't think you've ever said anything more true.'

As the show they were half-watching finished – and Adam had finished picking up chocolate buttons from the surrounding furniture – he heaved Jessica to her feet. 'Come on, let's go to bed,' he said.

'Are you going to carry me?'

'Not after all the chocolate you've just put away.'

Jessica jumped up from the sofa and stuck her fingers just below Adam's ribcage in the spot she knew he was most ticklish. He squirmed away from her. 'Oi, that's cheating,' he protested.

'I told you, I'm a cheat.'

'You lost at Scrabble.'

'Maybe you're a bigger cheat?'

Jessica reached out to try to tickle Adam but he grabbed her arm and picked her up. 'Ah, so you are going to carry me upstairs,' she declared.

'Yeah, if it'll shut you up.'

Jessica wrapped her arms around Adam's neck as he opened the living-room door with his foot and steered her around the corner. 'Watch my head,' she reminded him.

'Stop wriggling.'

Jessica grinned and locked her hands behind his neck. As Adam hoisted her higher and said that he loved her,

Jessica couldn't help but hate herself for the thoughts of Sebastian which filled her head.

As her mind slowly drifted awake, Jessica coughed slightly. She had the beginnings of a headache which was pounding in her head. At first she wasn't sure if the throbbing was something she was dreaming, or it was real. She opened her eyes as little as she could get away with in an attempt to look at the numbers on her alarm clock. Instead of the red glow, the area it should have been in was dark. Jessica reached onto her bedside table and picked up her phone, pressing a button on the side that made it light up and show her that it was 3.31.

The bright white stung her eyes and she quickly closed them again, putting the phone back on the table and coughing gently a second time. She wondered whether there was a problem with the clock or if they had simply had a power cut.

Shuffling sideways, Jessica reached out towards Adam and wondered why he never seemed to wake up at the silly times she did. She rested a hand on the base of his back before realising the pulse in her head wasn't just a headache, there was actually something making a noise below them. Jessica rolled onto her back and sat up, staring towards where the clock should be glowing.

She had never been the best morning person but her head felt woozier than usual and her throat was dry. She reached out and took a drink of water from the glass next to her. 'Adam,' she mumbled, reaching out to touch him again. When he didn't stir, she shook him gently. 'Adam, there's something making a noise downstairs. The power's off.'

Again he didn't move, so Jessica swung her legs out of the bed and stood up. Her bare feet brushed across the carpet but, despite the fact she was only wearing a pair of shorts and a large T-shirt, she didn't feel cold. She breathed in, coughing heavily again. Although she sometimes got the sniffles and minor colds like most people, there was something that felt different as she breathed in and tried to clear the dryness in her throat.

Jessica stumbled towards the door and flicked the light switch up and down but nothing happened. There was still a noise coming from below but she wasn't awake enough to understand what was happening.

'Adam, where's your fuse box? The power's off,' she called but he didn't move.

She turned back to the door and, in the fraction of a second it took to open it, she found herself falling to her knees as thick smoke poured through the gap into her lungs.

24

Jessica collapsed onto her back and kicked the door closed. She wanted to scream at Adam to wake him but her throat was so dry she couldn't swallow. In the dimness of the street lamps shining through the curtains, she could see a thin cloud of smoke billowing above her.

It seemed so obvious now that the beeping was the smoke alarm placed on the living-room ceiling directly below them. To begin with, her drowsy brain hadn't made the connection. Jessica stared at the ceiling, desperate to move but struggling to clear her head and breathe. She rolled away, pushing her face into the carpet and inhaling slowly and as deeply as she could. She spluttered slightly but the mildly stale taste of the floor was preferable to the smoke drifting around the room.

With her head marginally clearer, the warmth of the floor suddenly became obvious. She knew there was a fire burning directly below her.

Feeling weak, Jessica crawled along the floor before reaching out and taking a large gulp from the glass of water. She knew she had to get out of the house but staying calm and trying to breathe slowly was the only way she was going to be able to manage it.

She picked up her phone and switched on the torch, sending a bright white light onto the ceiling. Jessica looked up again, where she could see the remnants of the swirling smoke she had let into the room. She shone the light around until it was pointing at the door. Thin wisps of dark mist were cascading under the frame and drifting airily upwards.

Jessica swung the phone around and reached up onto the bed, breathing slowly but deeply and closing her eyes before pulling as hard as she could until the duvet fell on the floor. Her eyes felt heavy, her arms ached, but she used her feet to push the duvet across the carpet until it was blocking the gap under the door. She shone the light around the rest of the frame and, although fragments of smoke were seeping through at the top, the bed linen was blocking most of it.

Clambering onto the bed, Jessica rolled Adam over on his back. She shone the light across his closed eyes while shaking him as hard as her weary arms would allow. 'Adam,' she hissed into his ear but he didn't respond.

She felt tears in her eyes again as she slapped him across the face. Her arm felt limp but, despite the lack of force, she knew it should have been enough to wake him. She held the light close to his face and lifted one of his eyelids, not knowing what she was looking for but hoping he would respond in some way. His pupils had rolled back into his head and Jessica allowed his eyelid to droop. She rested her head on his chest, feeling it rise and fall ever so faintly, wanting to cry but knowing she had to get out of the house first.

Still resting on Adam, she flipped her phone around and dialled 999. She spoke quietly, thinking it might conserve more oxygen if she didn't raise her voice. The female operator took her address as Jessica said she was a police officer, hoping the woman would contact someone at Longsight.

Jessica's voice was croaky and, although the operator said she would wait on the line, she hung up, wanting to use the torch again. She kissed Adam on the forehead and climbed across his body until she was at the window. Her legs felt weighed down from the effort of moving and she knew the way she was trying to conserve the oxygen could only last her so long. Her brain seemed alert but her limbs were languid and sore. She lay on the floor, reaching up and pulling open the curtains slowly from the bottom.

As the faint light from the street lamps outside dribbled into the room, Jessica could still hear the beeping of the smoke alarm through the floor. Her eyes were desperate to close but she fought it by focusing on the noise.

She reached up and grabbed the curtain, heaving herself gradually to her feet. When she was nearly standing, she heard a crack and suddenly found herself falling. Things seemed to happen in slow motion as she collapsed onto her back, the curtain and rail landing on top of her. For a moment, Jessica struggled to comprehend what had happened. Thoughts seemed to flood her head but figuring out what they were telling her was hurting.

She rolled back towards the bed, shaking herself free of the curtain and only then realising she had pulled it down. Jessica lay on her back, staring at the ceiling. She could feel the weight of her phone in her hand and shone it upwards, trying to count to ten and calm her thoughts. When she reached five, she twisted her body around until she was on her knees, using the corner of the bed to raise herself up.

Even with small breaths, the air instantly felt harder to digest. She knew she had to stay low, so she crouched and stepped across to the window. As she turned, she peered towards Adam. He was spread-eagled on his back, his eyes closed, one arm hanging limply off the bed. She knew she would have been in tears at any other time but her throat was so raw that it felt as if there was no moisture in her system at all.

Jessica pressed herself against the window, the glass cool against her skin. She let the phone drop onto the window sill. Her eyes again felt heavy, as if willing her to sleep, but she put a finger and thumb above and below each eye, physically pulling them apart. Jessica coughed heavily, huge heaves of thick phlegm rolling up her windpipe into her mouth before she spat it onto the floor. Her throat was still sore as she pressed her thumb onto the button of the window's locking mechanism.

Usually, she would have been able to push it in and twist the handle. As she tried, Jessica felt a slow sense of panic flowing through her as she realised the button wasn't giving way. With the tip of her thumb, Jessica could feel the outline of a small keyhole and recalled that Adam made a point of locking all the windows when they weren't at home. She remembered him telling her the previous weekend just before they left the house that he was going to check everything was locked. She'd sat in the car complaining about the length of time he was taking but now wished she had gone with him.

Jessica fell to her knees, partly through exhaustion but also because she knew she had to stay low. She reached onto the sill, fumbling for her phone and pulling it towards her. She shone the light along the length of the frame, hoping to see the key somewhere nearby. She could picture what it looked like. It had been a silver colour at some point but was now faded to a scuffed grey and was barely larger than the fingernail on her big toe.

Just in case she had somehow swept past it, Jessica ran her hand the full length of the sill but there was nothing there. She sank down until she was sitting directly under the window facing the rest of the room. A thought ran through her head that she could smash the window if she could find something heavy enough but the part of her brain still thinking rationally remembered a locksmith once telling her how hard it was to get through double-glazing.

She closed her mouth and tried inhaling steadily through her nose. As she shone the light upwards, she could see there was a greater amount of smoke drifting around the top of the room. Jessica couldn't resist shining the light back to Adam's body. He hadn't moved since she had tried to rouse him but she crawled back across to the bed and pulled herself near to him, placing her ear close to his mouth. She was hoping to hear him breathing but there was nothing. Her mind drifted back to primary school where her class had been taught how to take a pulse. She had been at the back punching Peter Jenkinson hard on the shoulder to see if she could bruise him. He would grimace and then punch her back. Jessica wished she had paid attention. Even through the police training, taking a pulse was something she had never mastered.

Jessica shone the light back down to his chest and felt her heart skip as she watched his chest rise a tiny amount before falling again. She rolled onto her back, resting her head next to Adam's and trying to think where he might have left the key. It had to be in the room because it didn't fit any other window. She knew what Adam was like and leaving the key near to the lock so he didn't lose it was something he would do.

Although he would have left it close, he definitely wouldn't have left it within sight. She remembered telling him about a case where someone had used a hook to steal car keys through a letterbox and he had made a point of keeping things out of sight ever since then.

Jessica could still hear beeping from below her, knowing fire engines would arrive without sirens at this time of the morning. She closed her eyes, fighting the tiredness but trying to picture the layout of the room. Adam slept closest to the window, which meant the key would almost certainly be somewhere in that half of the room.

She slid onto the floor, opening her eyes and lying as flat as she could comfortably manage. She doubted he would have left the key in the wardrobe at the foot of the bed and, if it wasn't on the window sill, the only other place it was likely to be was the bedside table next to him. As Jessica pressed her palms into the carpet, she could feel the heat from underneath. It was almost too hot to touch but Jessica's aching limbs wouldn't allow her to move any quicker.

Slowly, she edged along the side of the bed until she could reach out and touch the cabinet. Somewhere along the line she had dropped her phone but she wasn't sure she had the energy to find it. Her eyes felt painful and she could not force them to stay open.

Jessica ran her hands across the front of the wooden bedside table and fumbled the top drawer open without opening her eyes. She reached inside, pulling out socks and underwear, letting them drop to the floor and listening for the clang of a key.

As she removed the final item, Jessica smoothed her hand along the inside of the drawer but could not feel anything metallic. She shuffled back to the floor, pushing the items of clothing around and groping underneath in case she had accidentally pulled out the key already.

Feeling like giving up, Jessica returned to the cabinet, opening the next drawer and reaching inside to feel metallic bottles that must have been deodorant cans. She forced her eyelids apart but her head was heavy and the rush of air seemed as if it was stabbing her in the eyes. With her phone lost, there was barely enough light from the window to see the contents of the drawer but Jessica fumbled for each item one at a time, taking out the toiletries and dropping them onto the floor.

As the final one fell, the rush she had felt moments ago disappeared, almost as if it had a physical presence which had been taken away. Jessica's mouth was parched and she wanted to cry so much that her stomach ached. She rested her forehead on the top of the cabinet, reaching in the drawer and tracing along the edges. There was nothing at the front but as she reached towards the back left corner, her fingers felt something cool.

She tried to tell herself to stay calm but, in her rush to pull the key forward, Jessica could only shunt it further into the drawer. She could feel her entire arm shaking with anticipation and frustration and settled herself to try again, this time taking the small object between her thumb and forefinger and moving it into her palm.

For a moment, Jessica wanted to relax and enjoy the success of the moment but the warmth of the floor was telling her she had to keep going. She used the bed to help pull herself up and felt her foot touch her phone. Bending down, she picked it up and staggered back to the window, dropping the phone and key on the sill.

Under her breath, she mumbled 'concentrate' but instantly wished she hadn't as it launched her into another coughing fit. Jessica could feel the pressure through her chest. Part of something was coming up her windpipe each time she coughed. Again, she rested her forehead against the glass, allowing its coldness to keep her alert. For the first time since she had woken up, a chill went through her.

Jessica picked up the key and reached up to the window lock. She tried pushing it in, but couldn't make her fingers obey as the metal scratched either side of the hole, instead of sliding into the centre. She stopped, closing her eyes and counting to ten.

As she reached the final number, she opened her eyes as wide as they could go, and the blue rotating lights of the fire engines appeared at the bottom of their small front garden.

Jessica thought she could see people moving but her vision was hazy around the edges. Focusing all her effort on the lock, she pushed the key in and turned it, before wrenching the handle up and shoving the window outwards.

The tears she had been desperate to cry finally erupted as Jessica gulped in the clear night air. It was cold and hurt her throat but she had never felt anything as refreshing in her life. She leant out of the window, drinking in the oxygen, tears streaming down her face.

The ground below her was a mix of bright blue and a dim orange and she could hear voices. Their words all blended into one but someone appeared to be shouting towards her. She tried to respond but the combination of the pain and dryness of her mouth along with the clean air meant she could do little more than cough.

As Jessica struggled to keep herself conscious, she felt a noise somewhere close by and realised a ladder had appeared next to where she was resting. Everything within her was telling her to allow herself to sleep but she could hear metallic vibrations of footsteps climbing the rungs. She felt an arm on her and someone telling her she was fine but, when she attempted to open her eyes, she could see only vague grey shapes.

Jessica felt a sensation of being lifted but wasn't aware of whether she was awake. She felt a sense of weightlessness, as if she was floating, but she couldn't decide what was real and what was in her mind. All of a sudden, there was a damp sensation on her back, quickly replaced by someone covering her with what she thought was a blanket. Jessica forced her eyes open but felt dazed by the blue light. Her feet felt warm and, as she tried to sit up, she realised she was half-lying on the lawn at the front of their house. Someone was supporting her and she could hear voices and a vehicle screeching to a halt.

She looked up at the house, taking large gulps of air as she realised someone must have carried her down the ladder. Jessica didn't know if she had been asleep but whoever was sitting next to her was stroking her back and holding a bottle of water close to her lips.

Jessica felt someone kneel nearby but the person with the water simply said, 'There's one more'.

At first it didn't register what they had said but Jessica's mind slowly started to put together what was going on. The person who had knelt close to her was wearing a green colour and was likely a paramedic. 'Adam,' Jessica croaked.

'It's all right,' a female said as they continued to stroke her back. 'Drink.' Jessica did as she was told, the liquid rushing down her throat and making her cough painfully. 'Slowly,' the person said. Jessica had no idea who they were but she could sense the concern in their voice. She tried sipping the fluid and it felt much better the second time, easing the ache that was throbbing through her body.

'Adam,' Jessica tried again. She could tell she had said it more clearly the second time. She wanted the woman to tell her everything was fine but her eyes closed involuntarily and Jessica rested her head against the paramedic.

She wanted to be able to respond to the words she heard shouted but her body refused to let her move.

Instead, the anguished cries from someone nearby of 'he's not breathing' sent her off into a deep, dreamless sleep.

25

Once a week when Jessica was a child, her mum would shoo everyone out of the kitchen and thoroughly bleach everything. Because you couldn't get to the living room without going through the kitchen – and she wasn't allowed past – she would have to choose where to spend an hour while everything dried out. She would usually opt for her bedroom but the smell would drift through the house wherever she was. Whenever she heard anyone talking about cleaning, she could almost sense the aroma from when she was a child, its pungency as strong as ever.

Jessica knew she was awake as she breathed in the smell of disinfectant. For a moment, she thought she was a child again, sitting in her room as her mum mopped and dusted below. She knew she was lying somewhere comfortable but her eyelids seemed to have weights attached. Wherever she was, everything felt peaceful. Wondering if she would be able to fall asleep again, Jessica allowed her airways to relax, breathing in the scent that made her think of home.

And then she started coughing.

At first it was a slight tickle at the back of her throat but then it shook her entire body. She could feel the heave starting somewhere in her stomach, pains shooting through her chest as she sat up, a thick liquid being pushed upwards into her mouth. She opened her eyes, dazzled by the bright lights, but with an overwhelming sensation that she was going to be sick. She was trying to stop her body from trembling and instinctively found herself rolling over until she was on her hands and knees. The softness of the surface told her she was on a bed but it felt unfamiliar. Someone nearby was saying her name and, although she tried to swallow it, the pain was too much as Jessica spat the mucus towards the floor.

Her mouth felt disgusting; the smell of disinfectant, which once was comforting, now made her feel nauseous. Her vision began to drift into focus, the white of the lights overhead fading into the colour of the room as shapes began to form. Jessica blinked furiously and the outline of Rowlands filtered into view.

'Dave . . .'

'Jess, you're awake . . .' She felt him move before she saw him, almost as if her brain was telling her something was happening before her eyes could register what it was. Her head was spinning as the constable's hand touched her shoulder. 'You should lie back down,' he said. 'I'll get someone.'

'No, stay.'

Jessica's memory was hazy but she felt a need to have someone close by.

'Okay, okay, but you have to at least sit.'

After he pointed it out, Jessica realised she was still on her hands and knees on a bed, but it was only then she realised her arms were aching. She felt her colleague's hands on the upper part of her back as she turned herself over and relaxed against the headrest.

'Am I at yours?' she asked, her words grating on her throat.

The constable didn't answer immediately but she knew her voice hadn't sounded right. She felt him pressing a glass into her hands. 'Drink,' he said gently.

Jessica first sipped the liquid but as it eased the pain in her throat, she drank more quickly, taking large gulps until she was coughing again.

'Slowly,' she heard his voice saying.

As her spluttering slowly evaporated, Jessica felt his warm hand on her forehead, pushing hair away from her face. 'You should sleep,' he said, his words soft and calming.

Jessica felt something familiar in his words but her mind wasn't alert enough to process them. She slid down under the bed sheets and felt someone rearranging the covers around her. As they moved to draw away, she gripped their hand, holding tight before closing her eyes and allowing the tiredness to envelop her.

Jessica jolted awake as another cough ripped from her stomach. Her body contorted involuntarily into a sitting position as she struggled to catch her breath before, finally, her chest calmed. She opened her eyes gradually but the room felt darker than she remembered.

Her thoughts were sluggish as she tried to recall where she was. The silhouette of Rowlands swarmed into view, although he didn't look quite right. Usually he had spiky hair but the shape of him was wrong. Jessica tried to work out how much wine she had drunk because she couldn't remember being this tipsy for a while. She giggled unwillingly. 'You look like a twat,' she croaked.

She expected something barbed in return but instead she realised she was holding the man's hand. 'Jess . . .' he said soothingly, gripping her more tightly.

'Dave?'

'How are you feeling?'

'I . . . I don't know. How much did I drink? Am I at yours?' Her final words sent a wave of déjà vu rushing through her and then she remembered how the rest of the conversation went. He would tell her to 'drink', she would cough and then he would say 'slowly'.

Then she remembered a woman's voice saying the exact same words.

Jessica flipped herself upwards until she was sitting rigidly; her eyes were wide. 'Adam.'

She could feel one of Rowlands's hands gripping hers even tighter, the other on her back. 'Jess, you should rest,' he said.

Jessica wanted to move quickly but her body was betraying her. She thought she was swinging her legs over the edge of the bed but only her top half moved. 'Adam . . .' she moaned, unable to stop herself crying. She squeezed her friend's hand as hard as she could, until she heard him squeal. 'Where's Adam?' she implored.

She felt his other hand move from her back onto her face, sweeping away a strand of matted hair. Her eyes tried to focus on the man who was with her. Rowlands's voice was restful. 'Relax, Jess. You've got to focus on yourself.'

Jessica could feel tears on her cheeks, itching as they rolled down her face. Memories of what had happened fell on her in one go as, instead of recalling things bit by bit, the whole terrifying night flashed into her mind.

'Oh God. There was a fire. There . . . Adam . . .' The room swam into view, everything becoming visible. She could see the pale walls, the white bed linen, a closed door at the foot of her bed and Rowlands's concerned face staring into hers. Jessica tried to speak but her throat felt hoarse. 'Is he . . . ?'

The constable's hand brushed tears away from her face before finally saying the words she had been crying for. 'He's alive, Jess.'

It was the greatest sentence Jessica had ever heard. It surged through her, the pain in her throat and stomach dissolving into a grin she didn't want to fight, no matter how much her head was hurting.

'He's alive?'

Rowlands's hand left her face and, although the second one twitched, she continued to hold it as tightly as she could manage. 'Yes, he's alive but you have to think about getting yourself better first. He's got doctors and nurses and all sorts of people around him.'

Jessica thought about what she was being told and then realised what the constable hadn't said. 'Is he awake?'

Dave's voice faltered. 'He's . . . no. Not at the moment. But he's breathing on his own and they say he's going to be all right.'

Jessica didn't know how to reply. She still felt cloudy. 'What time is it?'

Rowlands tried to withdraw his hand from hers but she wouldn't let him, even though it felt clammy. 'Jess . . .' he cooed. She released him and, even though her eyes had closed again, she could sense him looking at a watch. When he took her hand again, there was less sweat and she knew he must have wiped it. 'It's five o'clock,' he said.

'In the morning?'

'No, in the evening. You've slept all day.'

'Oh . . . I'm tired . . .' Jessica found herself giggling but didn't know why. The laughter dissolved into a mix of tears and coughs. She didn't know if she was happy or distraught.

'I want to get up,' she said, managing to move her legs in the direction she wanted second time around. She heard the constable stuttering and saying something about getting someone but she continued to hold his hand, putting her other one on his shoulder and using his body to pull herself up. He let go of her hand but used both of his to steady her hips. It was only as he held her that she realised she was wearing a gown, which she presumed must mean she was in hospital. It seemed silly that she could have missed it but it hadn't registered that was where she was.

The material felt thin against her body and the way Rowlands held her felt slightly unnatural at first, until he pulled her towards him into a hug. His hands were on her back as she clung to his neck, at first loosely and then with all the strength she could manage. She heard him whisper her name.

Her sense of time felt warped and she didn't know how long it was before she finally released his neck. He let go of her body, allowing her to use his upper arm to support her weight. 'I love him so much,' Jessica said, trying not to cry.

'I know you do. He's going to be fine.'

'I want to see him.'

'Jess, you shouldn't . . . just wait and I'll get someone.'

'No . . .' Jessica held his hand again, desperate not to be on her own.

'Okay, okay. But let's tidy you up a bit.'

She felt him tugging her gown, straightening it around her shoulders and then tightening it at the back after she had reluctantly let him go.

'Have you been here all day?' she asked.

'I got a sandwich earlier but . . . yes.'

'That's nice.'

She saw him shrug. 'It's you,' he replied delicately.

Jessica didn't know exactly what he meant but figured it was because her mind still wasn't functioning fully. He started to laugh.

'What?'

'You gobbed on my shoe earlier. When you first woke up. I was panicking and thinking I should get a nurse. You started coughing and I wanted to help, then you just spat this black mucus stuff onto my foot.'

Jessica began laughing herself but it soon gave way to another cough. She waved her colleague away, not wanting to sputter anything else on to him. As he stepped backwards, she knew her mind was still playing tricks as someone she knew couldn't be Rowlands whispered that he loved her.

26

'If you didn't want to marry me, all you had to do was say.' Jessica squeezed Adam's hand, willing him to smile at her. It certainly looked as if he was trying but he motioned for the oxygen mask and took a deep breath.

'I love you,' he whispered hoarsely.

'So you should. And next time, leave the key for the window next to the bloody window.'

Adam's eyes crinkled but he again didn't smile as she was willing him to. 'What happened?' he asked.

Jessica wanted to continue making jokes, knowing that, if she stopped, the tears that had felt close since she woke would return. 'There was a fire, that's all we know. People are looking into it.'

'Your people?'

'Yes.'

'So someone did this to us?'

Jessica closed her eyes to stop herself crying. 'To me.'

She felt Adam's hand twitch in hers, as if he were trying to console her, but there was no strength to his grip. 'Who?'

Jessica didn't want to say but she could hear the pleading in his voice. 'I don't know. Probably the same person who has been in the news for the other fires.'

Adam took another breath from the oxygen, before

Jessica took the mask and did the same herself. It felt dry on her throat but nothing except water seemed to offer any relief – and that only lasted for as long as she was drinking.

'What happened with the window?' he asked.

Jessica didn't want to think about it too much but, in trying to make her joke before, she had already told him half of it. The nurse had told her she couldn't spend too long with Adam because he needed to rest.

'We were trapped in the bedroom. The smoke alarm woke me up. The hall was full of it. I managed to open the window and a fire guy helped us both out. But you'd put the key in one of your drawers so I had to go looking for it.'

'Sorry.'

Jessica smiled. 'The only reason I know where to find it is because I know how your mind works. It's probably a good job I didn't go hunting under the mattress on your side of the bed, isn't it?'

He still didn't smile.

'What about Grandma's house?'

Jessica had forced Rowlands to give her the story. He said he had been called by Reynolds after someone had alerted the station that she was in trouble. Apparently, Cole, Reynolds, himself and everyone who was on duty and not otherwise occupied converged on her house.

'I'm sorry, it's almost all gone. Everything on the bottom floor was burned. The back bedroom collapsed. We might be able to salvage some things from our front bedroom but we won't know about smoke damage until we get to see it.'

Adam said nothing for a few moments. Jessica passed him the oxygen but he waved her away. 'What about the attic?'

'I . . . I don't know. Why?'

'It's where all the pictures of Nan are.'

Jessica smiled and stroked his face. 'I love you too,' she said, finally returning his declaration.

Adam reached out towards the glass of water. She helped him to hold it as he sipped slowly. She wondered how he knew that was the right way to drink, flashing back to the moment she had gulped and ended up coughing.

'Am I allowed to leave?' he asked.

'Maybe in a day or two? Didn't the doctor tell you?'

'Yes but I want you to tell me.'

'Why?'

'Your voice is all husky and sexy.'

Jessica slapped him gently on the wrist. 'Are you really coming on to me now?'

Adam took a deep breath from the mask before replying. 'Always.'

Jessica couldn't do anything but laugh. 'The oxygen mask doesn't do it for me, sorry.'

'So can I leave?'

Jessica rolled her eyes but kept holding his hand. 'Not yet. You weren't breathing when they took you out of the room but they managed to get you going again fairly quickly. I don't know what happened.'

'Where were you?'

'I don't know. An ambulance I think. They say there's

no lasting damage but that's probably because you had such a stupid pea brain before, there wasn't anything left to harm.'

Adam finally broke into a smile.

'See, I knew I could crack you.'

She felt his hand twitching again. 'What happens now?'

'Now? Now you get better.'

'Where are we going to live?'

Jessica realised that, in all that had happened, it hadn't crossed her mind.

'Just get some sleep and leave the worrying to me.'

'Jess, I . . .'

She leant in, kissing him on the forehead and whispering softly in his ear. 'Sleep.'

Jessica made her way back to the small side room she had been offered. Rowlands was waiting with a carrier bag, which he held towards her. 'Chloe says you can have these. She reckons you're about the same size.'

Jessica didn't want to seem ungrateful but she did have a peek inside before accepting it. She had met the constable's girlfriend a few times and some of her clothes were more revealing than she herself might ever choose to wear. She was relieved to find a sensible-looking pair of jeans, a vest top and a jumper.

'Thanks. I'm going to go back to the house tomorrow to see what's left. I'll need some work stuff too.' She noticed Rowlands narrowing his eyes. 'What?'

'Jess, you can't go back to work straight after this. Even

if you did, there's no way you can work on the case. Not now. You're a victim, a witness. You can't investigate it too.'

It was another thought that hadn't registered. 'Jack's not going to stop me,' she said aggressively.

Rowlands put a hand on her wrist and gently eased her into the seat next to him. 'It's not as if it's his decision. That's just it. I don't think he'll let you come back for a while but, even when he does, you'll be on other things. It's not about him stopping you. It's just what's allowed.'

Jessica knew he was right but it didn't change the fact that, of anything she had ever worked on, this was the most important case she needed to solve herself.

'They tried to kill me,' she said.

'I know.'

'Burn me. Burn Adam.'

'Jess, I know.' She felt his hand grip her more tightly and realised she was shaking with a mixture of fear and fury. Rowlands raised himself up and reached into his pocket. 'I found it on your lawn,' he said, handing over her phone. 'I don't know if you dropped it but I knew it was yours because of the way it's scuffed.'

Jessica took it from him and put it in the bag of clothes. She wanted to change out of the gown but didn't want to finish the conversation. 'I don't remember . . . I . . . was anyone else hurt?'

'No. Your neighbour's house has a bit of damage but everyone got out.'

'What have we got to go on?'

'We?'

Jessica continued to glower at him, refusing to give ground.

'Fine,' he eventually said. 'Currently, not much. Jack's there with the investigating team but it looks the same as the others. The front door is almost entirely destroyed, as are the window frames – so probably petrol or diesel.'

'But how did they know where I lived? Was I followed? Is it someone I know?'

Dave shook his head. 'Jess . . .'

'What?'

'You've got to slow down and let us sort this out. You have to focus on getting better.'

'I am better.'

Jessica could see he was torn about what to say but she couldn't stop her mind from whirring. She knew Martin Chadwick was in hospital himself, so it definitely couldn't be him. She didn't think it would have anything to do with Anthony Thompson – which only left Ryan. She remembered slapping him and the way he looked at her as if to say he would get her. Had he really done this as revenge?

'I'm going to get changed,' Jessica said.

Rowlands nodded. 'Okay.'

'Er, do you want to leave?'

The constable stood up, having clearly missed the point before. 'Oh right, sorry. I'll wait outside.'

'Can you help me with the back before you go?' Jessica turned around, letting him loosen the ties at the rear of the gown. His hands felt reassuringly warm on her skin as he slid them down to the base of her back.

'Is that okay?'

'Yeah, ta.'

As he closed the door behind him, Jessica dropped the robe to the floor and pulled out the clothes Chloe had left. They were a tiny bit too tight but would do until she could get back to the house to see if anything was salvageable. Luckily, the battered pair of black trainers at the bottom of the bag fitted perfectly.

Before she was ready to leave, Jessica turned on her phone, ignoring the 'Switch It Off' signs. As it connected slowly to the network, Jessica began to think of the every-day things she had lost. She wondered how she would be able to charge her phone, where they would get mail delivered to, what would happen to all the burned items. Were they hers and Adam's responsibility, or did the council help clean things up? She realised that, now she was the victim, she knew so little when it came to what happened after crimes had taken place.

The phone screen blurred into life and, one by one, the device buzzed to announce the arrival of messages and missed calls. Most of them came from people at the station although there were none from either Caroline or her parents, which was something of a relief as it meant she could contact them herself and say she was fine. There were text messages from both Sebastian and Garry.

Ignoring Sebastian's, Jessica called Garry, who answered before she had even heard it ring.

'Blimey, you're keen,' she said.

'Jess?'

'Who else?'

'I heard about . . . well, we all did. Are you all right?'

Jessica tried to sound as upbeat as she could, knowing tears would not be far away if she attempted to be serious. 'I'm fine. Adam's fine. I was trying to reply to your message but the predictive text kept changing the word "knob" to "know", so I thought I'd call instead.'

It was clear from the pause and Garry's gentle tone that he wasn't believing the bravado. 'I'm glad you called. I wanted to phone you but Dave said you were in hospital. I thought I should tell you about our front page tomorrow . . .' He tailed off guiltily.

'What are you writing?' Jessica asked.

'Nothing bad, we're just saying what's happened with you and your house and everything.'

'Are you using my name?'

'Yes, we have to. That's the story. I'm sorry, Jess.'

Jessica didn't know how to feel. It was another in her long list of things she hadn't considered. She knew the fire would get coverage and the fact she was one of the officers investigating the series of arsons made it even more of a story.

'What's the headline?'

'I didn't write it.'

Jessica paused for a moment, wondering why she wasn't feeling angry. 'Just tell me, it's fine.'

She heard Garry take a deep breath before replying. '"Arson nut burns down hero cop's house".'

Jessica thought about the words for a few moments. 'I guess it could have been worse. How do you know they're a "nut"?'

She heard Garry snort slightly. 'Christ knows. I didn't write it.'

'And what about "cop"? We're not in bloody New York.'

'I know but it's nice and short for a headline.'

'"Hero"?'

Garry sounded pensive. 'I suggested that bit.'

'Why?'

'Because you are a hero, Jess. Everyone knows the cases you've been on in the past. Randall, Doherty, the Marks brothers . . .'

Jessica felt a lump in her throat, embarrassed that she could solve other cases but, when it came to someone who had tried to burn her in her sleep, she either didn't have a clue – or couldn't pin it on the person she suspected.

'Cheers,' she said quietly before lurching into a cough. Again, it started deep inside her and she couldn't control how long it lasted. She dropped the phone on one of the chairs, using both hands to cover her mouth. When she finally stopped and pulled away, there were flecks of blood and black in her palms. She winced at the sight and, in the absence of any tissues, wiped them on the underside of the seat before picking the phone back up.

'Garry?'

'I'm still here. Are you okay? That sounded bad.'

'Nah, just a little tickle.'

The man paused briefly. 'Jess, are you sure you're all right?'

Garry was using the same concerned tone as Rowlands and it was beginning to annoy her. She ignored his question. 'What picture of me have you used?'

The journalist clearly hadn't anticipated her question and stumbled over his words. 'I don't know, a normal one.'

'I don't look like a moron?'

For a moment, she thought he was going to say 'no more than usual'. She almost implored him to, wanting him to treat her normally. Instead, his reply was measured. 'You just look like you, Jess.'

Jessica swallowed but her throat was drying out again. 'All right. Thanks for calling anyway. I appreciate it. Don't make a habit of it though.'

'Okay, I was just concerned . . .'

'I don't mean that – I mean tipping me off about stories. If you're nice to me too often I'm going to have to stop thinking all journalists are ambulance-chasing shits.' Garry laughed but Jessica knew her bluster hadn't duped him in the same way it hadn't fooled Rowlands.

After hanging up, she dialled Andrew Hunter's number. He sounded sleepy as he answered. 'Er, hello?'

'Andrew, it's Jess. Are you going to be in your office tomorrow afternoon?'

'Um, I guess . . .'

Before he could say anything else, Jessica cut across him. 'Good, because I'm coming over.'

'Okay . . .'

'You should probably read the papers in the morning too.'

With that she hung up and called Rowlands back into the room.

'You took a while,' he said.

'It takes time to look this good.' She saw a smile crack across Dave's face and realised she must be a mess. Her hair felt dirty and the clothes didn't quite fit. She knew she needed a shower.

'You should go home,' she said. 'It's late and I'm feeling all right. One of the nurses said they'll sort out a room for me so I can get some sleep and I'll call you all tomorrow.'

'You only just got dressed.'

Jessica didn't want to tell him that she had put clean clothes on to feel normal – or that the reason she wanted him to leave wasn't because she was going to sleep but because she wanted to be by herself.

'I just wanted to make sure it all fitted,' she said.

Dave nodded. 'Okay, but make sure you call tomorrow.'

He turned to leave but Jessica touched his arm and pulled him towards her, resting her head on his breastbone and wrapping her arms around him. 'Thank you for staying with me.'

At first, he seemed reluctant to reciprocate but then he put his arms completely around her, holding her and resting his chin on the top of her head.

Jessica eventually pulled away. 'I'll see you or talk to you tomorrow,' she said.

She could tell he was forcing a smile as he motioned to leave for a second time. 'Don't come anywhere near work or Jack will go mental.'

'Okay.'

Jessica watched him leave and then found one of the nurses. They allowed her to look around the door of Adam's room but he was asleep. For a moment she stood transfixed by his chest rising and falling before the nurse brushed her arm and brought her back to reality.

She led Jessica to a small ward just along the corridor from Adam's, where they said she would be able to stay the night. The smell of disinfectant was strong and, after she had been left alone, Jessica found it hard not to gag. Her mind was a mixture of things she definitely knew had happened and flashes of those she wasn't so sure about.

Jessica removed Chloe's clothes and entered the shower cubicle adjacent to the room. She turned on the water, adjusting the temperature until it was so hot that even holding her hand underneath it made her wince. Jessica closed her eyes and held her breath, stepping under the cascading water. She jumped as the heat burned the back of her neck but stayed underneath the jet, opening her eyes and staring at the plughole. As the black water swirled and descended through the holes in the floor, Jessica couldn't hold back the tears any longer. They had been close ever since her senses had returned but now, finally, she let go.

She crouched and then sat under the spray, watching the water slowly turn from black to grey and eventually run clear as the enormity of what had happened dawned on her.

Someone had tried to kill her.

27

As Jessica entered Andrew Hunter's office, she couldn't help but scowl at his open-mouthed welcome. 'Are you all right?' she asked. 'You look like you've seen a ghost.'

He hastily looked away as she sat down, brushing a copy of the morning's paper off his desk onto the floor.

'Subtle,' she said sarcastically.

'Sorry, I . . .'

'It's fine.'

'Is there anything I can do?'

Jessica wriggled in the seat. 'Getting a new chair would be a start.'

'Sorry, I've got one on order.'

'You told me that last time.'

'Er, yeah . . .'

'Forget it. Look, I need you to do something for me. I'll pay whatever your rate is but it's all unofficial, nothing to do with the police, it's not CID, it's a personal thing.'

Jessica could see the man looking uneasy in his chair. He glanced nervously away from her. 'I don't want your money,' he said.

'Why?'

'Aren't you going to need it? With the . . .'

'You can say "fire".'

Jessica was becoming annoyed by the way everyone

skirted around the issue. After emerging from the shower the previous evening, finally clean of the soot and smoke, she had resolved to get on with sorting things out and, regardless of what Cole said, finding out who had tried to kill her.

'Sorry . . .'

'And stop apologising!' Andrew seemed suitably chastened and Jessica felt bad about raising her voice. 'Shall we start the conversation again?' she suggested.

Andrew offered his hand across the desk and they shook. 'I still don't want your money,' he said.

'Why?'

'Honestly? I don't need it. You might not believe it given the state of this place, your broken chair and the fact I come to work each day – but I've got money. I could stay at home and live off it if I wanted. I'm not massively rich but I could get by if I invested it sensibly and lived off the interest.'

Jessica was stunned by his revelation. For the first time, she properly eyed Andrew's appearance. When she had first seen him at the scene of Sienna's death, she had thought he was so plain, she would struggle to remember what he looked like. That was still true but he did have something appealing about him too, although it was hard to pinpoint what. He had sand-coloured hair that was cut short and had been left to fall in no discernible style. His clothes seemed too tight and his suit certainly wasn't an expensive one given the way it was cut.

Andrew must have noticed her interest because he smiled – and Jessica knew what it was that made him stand out. It was when he grinned or joked. Unlike most people, he only seemed to show the beam on one half of his face. The right side of his mouth would crinkle upwards, the left unmoving. It was an odd yet strangely attractive feature.

'It's not that hard to believe, is it?' he added.

'Did you win the lottery or something?'

Andrew laughed again. 'I wish it was that simple. It's complicated but, because you've got bigger things to worry about, let's just say I was married, now I'm not. I just have money instead – that's why I don't need yours. Whatever you want doing, it's fine.'

'Can I ask a question?'

'Go on but I didn't kill her, if that's what you're wondering.'

Jessica laughed. 'No, but at least you think like one of us. I was wondering why you haven't got a better bloody chair over here if you have money.'

It was Andrew's turn to snigger. 'Money I've got. I'm just lazy. Sometimes I think I'd rather this all fell through so I could just stay at home. Maybe I don't really want clients? I have no idea.'

Jessica thought about his reply for a few moments. 'That's pretty honest.'

Andrew shrugged dismissively.

'Would you like to hear about my morning?' Jessica asked.

Andrew leant forward slightly, offering the half-smile she now associated with him. When he replied 'go on', she felt a tingle of relief she only partly understood. He was largely a stranger but she could see something behind his eyes that she felt herself. It was probably because she now knew him in the context of something happening with his ex-wife. As he'd mentioned that he had previously been married, she had seen in his face that he was still in love with whoever the woman was. She could understand wanting to hide emotions through work.

'It's been pretty shitty to be honest,' Jessica said, feeling her voice croak before correcting herself. 'This morning I had to phone my parents to tell them I was fine. They live in Cumbria so luckily don't get the papers or the same news as us. Before I'd even finished talking, my mum had jumped on the Internet and seen the pictures. They wouldn't believe that I was fine. I think my dad already had the car keys in his hand to come down before I managed to talk them around.'

'That's good though, right?'

'Oh yeah, I didn't mean it like that. I see all sorts of shite mums and dads and people who couldn't care less about their kids. Mine are amazing. It was just that moment in their voice where you tell them something bad has happened. It's like you're breaking their hearts. I hated it.'

'My parents loved my wife . . . ex-wife . . . Keira. I don't think they've ever come to terms with us not being together any more.'

Jessica wondered if she should ask what happened but Andrew stared at her, clearly expecting her to finish explaining her day. 'That was just the first thing I did,' she continued. 'Then I had to go to the house. Have you any idea what it's like to go to a burned-out house?'

'No, I never went to Harley's.'

'It's just . . . horrible. There are these fire investigators who first check the scene. They had already decided it was started deliberately and then you're allowed back onto the site. One of the fire guys escorted me around. I don't know if they do it for everyone or if it's just because it was me. It's everything you can imagine but worse. Everything's black, even the bits that aren't burned, because of the smoke. You see fragments of your things, part-burned, part-not. It's not even those items that you think about – it's the memories that come with them.'

'Was there much left?'

'Unbelievably, most of the things in our bedroom. It sounds stupid but I keep my phone charger next to the bed and you wouldn't have known anything had happened. Most of Adam's clothes are fine. Some of mine. A lot of the things we might need day-to-day are all right. Some of them are smoke-damaged but the ceiling didn't collapse and the guy said it was lucky we lived in a house built just after the war.'

'Why?'

'He says the new homes have thin walls and thinner doors. That the fire just goes straight through it. Either way, I've got a carful of clothes. It was lucky I left my car keys in a pocket, else they would have been downstairs too.'

'Where are you going to stay? I might . . . ?'

Jessica didn't know what he was going to offer but she waved her hand. 'I've sorted it. One of my friends, Caroline, she's got this place on the Quays. She broke up with her husband and it's up for sale but it's empty for now. I'm going there after here to dump everything.'

'That's nice of her.'

'Well that's what I've realised this morning. It was horrible being at the house but, beyond that, people are bloody good. I've had my mum offering to drive a few hundred miles just to give me a cuddle. My mate's letting us stay in her flat for free. I spoke to one of my colleagues who is on maternity leave. She was telling me I could have all her clothes because they don't fit anyway. She practically ordered me to come over for tea. She's got a baby to be looking after but she was going to do that anyway. My phone's not stopped going all morning – it's a bloody good job I found that charger. Sometimes I think I forget that people are generally pretty decent. I just end up dealing with most of the shits.'

'So what do you do now?' Jessica started to reply but couldn't stop another coughing fit charging through her. Andrew handed her a tissue as she doubled over. Unable to stop herself, she checked it afterwards, seeing more flecks of black and spots of blood.

'Are you okay?' he asked.

Jessica nodded but only answered the first question. 'Now? Now I have to sit around. I spoke to my DCI too. He told me he doesn't want to see me for at least a week and, even then, assuming they haven't solved it by then, I won't be working on the case about who burned down the house and whether it's connected to the other ones – including Harley's.'

'Why?'

'Policy? I don't know. I told him I'd speak to the super-intendent and he said he already had – and that they were in agreement. I said I'd go to the chief constable but he'd done that too. Aside from the Home Secretary, there's not much else I can do. Basically, that's it. Unless he changes his mind, I'm off for six more days and then I go back as if nothing's happened.'

'But . . . don't you think you should take the time off? Is your fiancé doing all right?'

Jessica knew the newspaper article, and presumably the news broadcasts, had only made a passing reference to someone other than her being involved in the fire.

'We both slept in the hospital last night,' she said. 'I saw him before leaving this morning and dropped in again before coming here. The doctor says he's doing okay but he probably won't be released until tomorrow.'

Andrew spoke nervously. 'Maybe he'd like to spend the week with you . . . ?'

Jessica knew what he was saying was true. She had been telling herself the same thing but above that was an over-riding feeling that she wouldn't be able to feel safe until whoever had set fire to her house was caught. She ignored him, finally moving onto the reason she was there.

'What have you got on Ryan and the people he hangs around with?'

The investigator seemed surprised by her abruptness, certainly by the fact she had changed the subject so quickly. His eyebrows shot upwards as he looked off to one side as if thinking. 'I'm not sure. Only what I've told you.

I gave you the number plate of the girl but never heard back from you.'

Jessica knew she shouldn't be passing on the information but, given what had happened, didn't even hesitate. 'It belonged to a nineteen-year-old woman called Lara Sullivan. I visited her house and although I didn't specifically ask about the money, I did ask her about Ryan.'

'What did she say?'

'Not much. Every girl I mention his name to has a similar response. I'm not sure if it's fear or unease but there's something there.'

'I don't have anything else. I've not been following him everywhere but I've kept an eye on him in the evenings. He's not been doing much.'

Jessica gave him Lara's address and the details she could remember. 'Will you see if you can find anything on her?' she asked.

'Wouldn't it be better if someone you knew from the station did that?' he asked.

'They won't work with me, let alone help.'

'I'll do what I can but it won't be much.'

'I want you to keep following Ryan too. I would but he knows me. If he meets this Lara again, call me.'

'Do you think he was the one who . . . ?' Andrew tailed off, clearly not wanting to say, 'burned down your house'.

'I don't know. But there's no one else I can think of. His dad was in hospital. I know my colleagues are going over his past to see if there's anything else but they either haven't got anything – or won't tell me.'

'What's he got to gain though?'

Jessica didn't want to mention that she had slapped him. She wondered if that was reason enough.

'Say fire was his thing,' Andrew continued, 'I guess that could be a reason but what about the other things you were talking about with the girls and everything? What could he be involved in?'

'Money and girls have always made the world go around,' Jessica said.

'True but what would he have been paying Lara for? Sex? How would that connect to the other girls? Do you think he paid them too?'

'I don't know but everything has happened since his father was released from prison. That can't be a coincidence.' Andrew shrugged as if to say he couldn't think of a reason to disagree. 'Is Harley still paying you?' Jessica added.

'Sort of. He is but I'm putting all the money in a separate account and I'll either give it back if he'll take it or give it to charity. I've told him there's nothing I can do. He's been so different. When he first hired me, he was short and to the point, now he wants to have conversations. I don't know what to say. He's lost his house and daughter, it's not like I can take him down the pub to drink it off. He keeps asking what can possibly happen next.'

'When was the last time you saw him?'

Andrew shrugged sadly. 'Not for a while. He'll call but I think he's embarrassed about being seen. I asked if he wanted to meet and he couldn't get off the phone quickly enough. I think the biggest thing is that he has no closure because he doesn't know why it all happened.'

It was something Jessica could understand as well as anyone. 'Perhaps if you can get to the bottom of everything that's happening with Ryan, Lara and whoever else, you'll find him an answer after all?'

There was very little that annoyed Jessica more than having to act girly. In order not to be recognised from the morning's coverage in the papers and on television, she wore her hair down and found a low-cut top in the pile of clothes salvaged from the house. Rather than wear something over it, as she would usually, Jessica wore just that and a skirt to ensure the garage owner would be looking at her chest and legs as opposed to her face.

She kept her phone in her hand just in case Andrew called, explaining to the person who worked there that her vehicle was making 'a funny sound'. She giggled and flirted in a way that disgusted her but it at least had the desired effect as she noticed the man's gaze constantly drifting down towards her chest before he realised what he was doing. If he knew the amount of padding that was being used to create the illusion, Jessica suspected he wouldn't be quite so impressed.

'Do you want us to give you a bell when it's ready, love?' he asked.

'I'll just wait around, it shouldn't be long, should it?'

The mechanic took one final glance across at her chest before replying. 'No, I'll start on it right away.'

Jessica's plan to poke around the garage Ryan worked at wasn't exactly high-tech. Andrew was keeping an eye on the college waiting for him to leave, while, after dropping her clothes off at Caroline's flat and checking in on Adam, she had driven to the garage and made up something that sounded plausible. Andrew had pointed out the flaw in the idea that her face was all over the news and someone could recognise her, which had led Jessica to the current position she found herself in.

She remembered her old vehicle and thought that, if she had brought that by, it could have been a good two or three days before she saw the beloved thing again. With her new car, she knew there was nothing wrong with it.

As the mechanic and someone else went to work under the bonnet, Jessica looked carefully at the surroundings. There were large plastic cans marked 'petrol' and 'diesel' pushed into the far corner and another area held cans of spray paint. Jessica didn't check them any more closely but it didn't really matter if there was a yellow one now because there could have been at some point. She wondered if Ryan could have tried to frame Anthony by leaving the items in his back garden and the shed. Could he have burned down his own house for the same reason? It seemed far-fetched but then there was a likely insurance payout to come – and it could have landed Thompson in trouble. It didn't explain why the back of the house had been blocked to try to keep Martin inside but she was sure there would be a reason somewhere.

Jessica made her way through to the garage's reception area and then outside into a small car park. She took out her phone and called Rowlands. As it rang, she huddled close to a wall, trying to keep warm. Although the late afternoon wasn't exactly cold, her outfit wasn't really suitable for the time of year.

'What took you so long?' Jessica said, showing her agitation when the constable answered.

'Sorry, I was busy. What's up?'

'That's what I was phoning you to ask. What's going on?'

Rowlands paused for a second. 'Jess . . . you're supposed to be off.'

'Sod off, Dave, just tell me.'

He sighed. 'You know I shouldn't but we're all working hard for you. People are going over your statement, we're checking the times, we have spoken to your neighbours. We have got the initial report from the fire investigator. Honestly, we're doing everything we can.'

'But you've not got anywhere yet?'

'Jess . . .'

'There haven't been any other suicides, have there?'

'No, but . . .'

Jessica was too annoyed at his stalling to let him finish his sentences. 'Will you call me if you find anything?'

Rowlands sighed again. 'Jess, don't put me in this position. Just get yourself better and we'll see you soon.'

Jessica knew she wasn't going to get anywhere. 'All right, fine. Bye.'

She hung up and put the phone in the bag she was being forced to carry because there were no pockets in what she was wearing. She went back into the reception area and sat looking around at the various posters on the wall.

'Are you all right, love?' asked the female receptionist. She was only a teenager herself and Jessica could see her holding a puzzle book as she stared over the counter.

Jessica nodded. 'Fine, thanks.'

'You seem familiar.'

Jessica looked at the coffee table she was resting her feet on and noticed a copy of that morning's *Herald* with her photo on the front. She stood, stepping between the table and reception desk. 'Do you watch morning chat shows?' she asked.

The woman put her puzzle book down and beamed. 'Oh God, yeah. I love 'em.'

'I was on one a few weeks back. You probably know me from there.'

'Oh wow, you're famous! Which one were you on?'

Jessica turned around and picked up the newspaper, casually folding it over as if she were reading but shielding the picture from view before turning back to face the woman. 'It was called "My brother's really my dad".'

The woman's eyes were wide with surprise. 'Really? Your brother's your dad?'

'Yeah and my aunt's my uncle. It was this big thing they did over two days. My brother, who is really my dad, ended up having a fight with his brother, who's really his cousin.'

'I think I remember that one.'

Jessica had made it up but, if it had been a real subject, she wasn't surprised. 'Anyway, that must be where you saw me. I was sat at the back.'

The woman's mouth was open, staring at Jessica. 'Can I have your autograph?'

'Really? I was only at the back.'

'Yeah but you were on TV.'

The woman held out her puzzle book and pen. Jessica dropped the newspaper in the bin next to the desk but the woman was so in awe, she didn't notice. Jessica took the pen and signed 'Davina Rowlands' on the back of the book before handing it back.

'I'll get it framed,' the woman said, staring wide-eyed at the signature.

'You're welcome,' Jessica replied, before taking her seat, while thinking England really was a strange place.

28

Jessica's attempts to involve herself in the investigation were not going well. Shortly after her conversation with Rowlands, Cole had called to tell her to take an extra day off on top of the week he had already ordered. For most people, the time off work would be a blessing, but he knew Jessica wanted to get back as soon as she could. He said that each time he heard a report of her speaking to anyone at the station he would make her take another day off. He also reiterated that the next phone call would come from the superintendent, the one after that from the chief constable.

She knew there would be the offer of counselling sessions when she did return – but even so she wanted to get back as soon as possible. Even if they did force her to work on other cases, she would still easily be able to catch up on the gossip.

The next morning, she put her focus on Adam, although what was going on at Longsight was constantly in the back of her mind. It hadn't helped that the day's news coverage, although not entirely devoted to her, extensively recapped recent events. It linked all of the blazes and mentioned that Martin's release from prison had preceded everything.

Outside the hospital, Adam was determined to get into the passenger seat of her car by himself but she saw him wince as he crouched. Aside from the coughing, she pretty much felt back to her old self but Adam's voice was still deeper and rougher than it should be.

'You're going to like Caroline's flat,' Jessica said. 'There's a great view.'

'I'll sort something out so we don't have to burden her.'

'Take it easy, you know what the doctor said.'

'You're one to talk.'

When she had first seen the flat, Jessica was relieved that her friend had good taste. Much of Caroline's furniture was still there, which she suspected was because no one was too keen on trying to get it back downstairs in the lift. Caroline said they could treat the place as their own and that, as yet, there were no offers so they would have a couple of months at least to sort themselves out.

After they arrived, Jessica showed Adam around but, as much as she tried to talk up the benefits, she knew they would never be able to call it home. For Adam, the destruction of the house had meant he'd lost many of the memories from his childhood and beyond.

As they settled into Caroline's wide leather sofa, Jessica pulled a pair of boxes out from under the coffee table. 'Look what I found.'

Inside were the photographs and certificates that had been in the attic. She heard Adam cough gently but he was grinning as he began to look through the items. She knew there were photographs of his grandma from when she had been younger, as well as ones of Adam as a child too. 'Aww, look at the little thing,' Jessica said, pointing at a photo of a naked Adam as a baby.

Before Adam could reply, her phone began to ring, Rowlands's name flashing up. Jessica stood and walked into the open-plan kitchen.

'Look who it is, Judas Rowlands.'

'Hey, I didn't tell Jack you were calling me yesterday. I was in a meeting with him when you rang.'

Jessica thought his story sounded plausible but she wasn't entirely convinced. 'Adam was released today,' she said. 'You remember my friend Caroline? We're staying in her flat that's up for sale over on the Quays.'

'Did you get a call from Hugo?'

Jessica laughed. 'Hugo' was the stage name for a magician friend of Rowlands who she had come to know well. 'He said me and Adam can go stay in his flat any time we like.'

Dave snorted. 'You know he's still living above that bookies'?'

'I know. I said we would let him know if we needed somewhere. For one, it's just a one-bedroom place so who knows where he thought we'd all sleep. Secondly, he's still got all those stuffed animals and everything. There's no way I'd be able to sleep there. I'd be terrified of one of the mice coming back to life or something. Nice of him to offer though.'

'He's got a one-night-a-week residency at this comedy club in town. He does tricks and stuff. We should go some time.'

'I'll see what Adam says. I'm not sure either of us are in the mood for much comedy at the moment. Anyway, what's going on?'

'Jess . . .'

'Just tell me, you've called anyway.'

Dave sighed. 'All right, fine, but don't tell Jack. We're trying our best. We have been going as far into Martin's background as we can but there's nothing there that couldn't be explained away through coincidence.'

If they delved deeply enough, Jessica knew they would find most people could be linked to a crime simply by being in the wrong place at the wrong time. Just because a person was in a town when there was a robbery or a fire, that didn't mean they had anything to do with it – but when the police looked into histories as thoroughly as they were examining Martin's, something would come up.

'Did you link him to the fire at his old school?'

'Nothing that would stick. He was released from hospital today. I wasn't there but apparently it's mainly cuts and bruises. They did all the brain scans and everything and he's fine.'

'What about Ryan?'

'We found a little about him – a couple of fights while he was in care but nothing serious.'

'What about anything found at the house?'

'Nothing. Because you have a lawn at the front, anything, such as footprints or something, would have been destroyed as they needed the ladder to get you out. People would have walked on it. Your neighbours were all sleeping, as you'd expect.'

'What about Sienna and Molly?'

'It's sort of been sidetracked. Apparently calls to those

helplines are up, so the media coverage has had one good effect. There haven't been any other deaths.'

'So the world's still turning without me in the centre of it?'

She heard Rowlands sniggering. 'We're all missing you, Jess. Get better and then come back.'

Jessica hung up and rejoined Adam in the living room. She wasn't used to being off work during the day and, although it was barely lunchtime, she felt at a loss. 'There was something else which survived the fire,' she told Adam, kissing him on the forehead before taking his hand.

'What?'

Jessica led him towards the bedroom. Caroline had come by the previous day with clean sheets and helped her change everything because Jessica knew neither she nor Adam would feel comfortable in someone else's bed.

'You know most of our clothes were okay?' she said.

'Yes.'

'There's a certain dress I've been promising to try on for quite some time . . .'

The bedroom curtains were wide open as Jessica and Adam lay watching the sky slowly darken.

'It's better when it's sunny,' Jessica said. 'Caroline reckons that you can see mist forming underneath you on the water on the cloudy mornings. Her exact words were, "It's beautiful, just bloody cold".'

'What are we going to do?' Adam said, wrapping an

arm around Jessica and pulling her closer to him on the bed.

'We'll get a place of our own and start again.'

'What about getting married? We can't do that and then come back here. Everything's going to take so long to sort out with the insurance and so on.'

'You don't know that,' Jessica said.

'Neither do you. I just . . . I want you to be happy.'

Jessica moved her head further onto his chest, being careful not to press too hard. 'I'm going to be. We will be. At least we both got out.'

'Do you remember it?'

'Bits.'

'I'm sorry I couldn't protect you.'

Jessica wriggled up and straddled herself across Adam's stomach. 'It doesn't matter. If you hadn't tested those bloody smoke alarms once a week when I was trying to watch TV, neither of us would have got out. It's as much down to you as me.'

'It doesn't feel like that.'

Jessica rested her hands on his chest and began to smooth down the hairs. 'Ad, what matters is that we're both out. You don't have to be a knight in shining armour. You'd piss me right off if you were. You're just you.'

Adam put his hands on her hips and pulled her into an embrace. 'You're so cool,' he whispered before dissolving into laughter which inevitably became a very unsexy chesty cough.

As Jessica tried to stop herself from joining in, her phone rang, Andrew's name flashing on the screen.

Adam was doubled over and unable to protest, so Jessica answered.

'What's up?'

'You told me to call if I saw Ryan and Lara together again?'

'Where?'

'The pub next to the hotel he's staying in.'

'I'll be right there.'

29

Jessica didn't spot Ryan on her first sweep of the pub but on the second she saw him sitting with Lara in a booth towards the back. Andrew had met her outside and said he would wait around the front in case she needed him.

The booths were circular with an entrance only just wide enough for one person to walk through. A soft seat took up the rest of the circumference with a similarly round table in the centre. Jessica walked directly up to the booth she had seen the pair in, squeezed herself through the gap, and sat next to Lara across the table from Ryan.

'This is cosy,' she said as both teenagers eyed her with a mixture of shock and, in Ryan's case, outright anger.

'You?' Lara said, recognising Jessica from the time she was door-stepped.

'You know each other?' Ryan exclaimed furiously, seemingly trying to address both women at the same time.

'Old pals, me and Lara,' Jessica said with a grin. 'We have lovely little chinwags all about you, Ryan.'

'Fuck off, do we,' the girl replied angrily. 'What do you want?'

'Just a little chat.'

Jessica could see Ryan was livid, his arms tense, his fists no doubt balled under the table. 'How did you know where I was?' He barely moved his mouth as he spoke.

'Lucky guess. Your hotel is next door, so I thought I'd drop in and see if you were around.'

'Weren't you in the papers yesterday?'

Ryan didn't exactly sound as if he was gloating but he certainly knew he had something over her.

Jessica didn't want to let him get under her skin. 'Don't go telling me you can read? Or did you just look at the pictures?'

Ryan glanced towards Lara. 'Can you give us a few minutes?'

The girl leant forward. 'Seriously? Just tell her to piss off.'

'Wait over there. I need a few minutes.'

Jessica realised she had never heard Ryan sound assertive until he addressed the woman a second time. He'd been angry and aggressive but now his voice was lower and more serious with a tone she hadn't recognised before. Jessica slid out to let Lara pass as the teenager gave her the dirtiest of looks and muttered a very audible 'bitch' as she walked towards the tables Ryan had indicated.

'She's a lovely girl,' Jessica said, sliding back into the booth.

'How did you know where I was?' Ryan asked again. 'Do you have someone following and taking pictures like before?'

'Should I? Have you got something to hide?'

Ryan sighed. His arms were no longer tense and he seemed more frustrated than angry. 'Just tell me what you want.'

'I want to know who Lara is to you and why you're giving her money.'

The man's mouth fell open. 'How do you know about that?'

'I just do. Now let's stop all the bollocks and tell me.'

'I didn't nick it.'

Jessica swore. 'I never said you did. I'm here because I'm sick of everything that's going on. The fires, the girls dying. All of it. Yes I was in the paper yesterday because someone set fire to my house and tried to kill me and my fiancé. I'm here because I want it to stop before someone else gets hurt.'

Jessica was shaking as she finished speaking. She hadn't thought any of her words through but something about how Ryan had spoken to Lara made him sound less hostile. She was seeing him in a way she hadn't before.

'You think it was me?' he said, eyebrows raised.

'Just tell me what the money was about.'

Ryan shook his head and sighed. 'It was for my little boy. Lara and me, we . . . we have a kid. It wasn't planned or anything, it just happened. We're not even going out. She was going on about going to the child-support people and all that, so I gave her some money to shut her up. I don't know how you know.'

Jessica stared at him, thinking he at least appeared to be telling the truth. She figured there was little point in him lying considering she could just ask Lara anyway.

'Where did you get it?'

'I work in a garage.'

'I know but they can't pay that much.'

'No but it's not as if I spend it, is it? My college is free, I buy a bus pass once a month, the house was mine and the hotel's paid for by the insurance.'

When she thought about it, Jessica realised he was right. Apart from food and transport, he would have nothing to spend his money on. The stupidest thing was that she and Adam had been in the exact same situation, because he had inherited the house with no mortgage from his grand-mother. Somehow she had failed to see the parallel.

'So why were you meeting again tonight?' Jessica asked.

Ryan was scowling. 'Nothing. None of your business.'

'No, you're right, sorry. It's just . . . those other girls.'

'Who?'

'Molly and Sienna.'

Ryan was clearly struggling to comprehend what she was saying. 'What about them? Do you think they were something to do with me?'

Jessica felt as if she were drowning. She knew that, to an outsider, between the two of them, Ryan would seem like the rational one.

She shook her head. 'I don't know. It's just from the moment we first met, you were so angry and then every-thing spiralled from then. The fires, the suicides – and you're central to everything.'

Ryan looked away and bit his bottom lip. 'If I've been angry, then don't you think this could all be why? When we first met, I was pissed off because you lot weren't going to do anything about those threats against my dad. And I was right, wasn't I? Look at what happened. Why didn't you have someone protecting us?'

'That wasn't my decision.'

'Fine, but why pick on me after everything? Of course I was fuming. Someone had tried to kill my dad and you were standing around chatting.'

Jessica knew that wasn't exactly true but, now he said it, she could understand why he had viewed it that way. Rowlands's 'why is it always you' comment was bouncing around her head because she could see so much of herself in Ryan. The first impression he gave of being abrupt and combative was likely the way lots of other people viewed her. The parallels were almost too embarrassing for her to think through.

'I'm sorry for slapping you.'

Ryan reached up to his lip. 'You can't half hit for a girl.'

Jessica didn't know if she should take it as a compliment. She knew she was in the wrong. 'Thanks.'

'When I got in that night, I was all for reporting you but then . . .'

'. . . you didn't want to admit you'd been hit by a girl,' Jessica said, finishing his sentence.

Ryan smiled. 'Exactly, so I let it go. Why were you following me?'

'I don't know, instinct. It was the night after one of the fires and I was keeping an eye out.'

He picked up what was left of the pint of beer he had on the table. 'Do you at least believe that it's not me now?'

Jessica looked into his eyes but she already knew the answer. 'You don't help yourself. You never had an alibi . . .'

Ryan sipped the drink. 'I was with Lara those nights.

She can probably tell you. Well, maybe not you but some-one.'

'I thought you weren't going out?' Ryan raised his eye-brows as a response that Jessica read clearly. 'Oh, it's like that.'

'So can I ask you some questions?' Ryan said.

Jessica shrugged. None of the conversation had gone the way she had expected.

'Why would I burn my own house down?'

'To implicate Anthony and get the insurance money?'

'I suppose but that's a lot of hassle.' Jessica laughed but Ryan continued. 'It's true,' he said. 'I've got better things to do than all of that.'

'People have gone through much more "hassle" than that to get revenge.'

'What do I want revenge for? Some dick telling a news-paper he's got it in for my dad? All I wanted was for you lot to warn him off.' Jessica nodded, willing to accept his explanation. 'Why do you keep mentioning Sienna and Molly to me?' he asked.

'You called Sienna a slag, you said she was filthy. There was so much anger there. Why do you think I was asso-ciating you with her? She had just died and you were effectively saying you hated her. Meanwhile I had a photo of her sucking your fingers as if you were involved. Those are some pretty mixed messages.'

Ryan shrugged and nodded. 'Sienna was all about mixed messages.'

'How do you mean?'

'Well she hung around with a lesbian for a start.'

'Molly?'

'Yeah, everyone knew about it.'

'What's wrong with that?'

Ryan smiled but there was nothing cruel about his expression. 'How old are you?'

Jessica felt compelled to answer. 'Thirty . . . something.'

The teenager laughed. 'I don't know about you being at school or college or whatever but what do you remember the kids being like? Did you ever have a lesbian at your school? Or someone gay? Or someone really tall? Or short? What happened to them?'

Jessica couldn't believe she was being lectured by an eighteen-year-old but she knew exactly what he meant. To her, it wasn't significant if people were of different races or sexualities. To a teenager, especially an immature one, it was something to pick on.

'You think they were bullied to death?' she said.

Ryan stared at her as if she had overlooked the most obvious point. 'Of course not. Sienna was the one everyone looked up to. All the lads wanted to f—, go out with her and all the girls wished they were her – especially because her old man had money.'

Jessica still didn't understand. 'Right . . . what am I missing?'

'Sienna loved the attention. She would snog you and let you touch her tits and so on. It was just the way she was.'

'But why were you so aggressive about her if that was the case?'

Ryan sighed. 'Will you get me another beer?'

'I thought you had money?'

319

'I do but surely I deserve something for all of this?'

Jessica motioned to stand, nodding towards Lara. 'All right but send her home. I can't take any more of her staring me out from across the room.'

A few minutes later Jessica returned with two pints and slid in across from Ryan. 'How'd she take it?' Jessica asked.

'How do you think? She's only bothered about the money now she knows I have some. I just want to see my kid. My name's not even on the bloody birth certificate.'

'Why not?'

Ryan glanced sideways. 'Let's just say there were a few candidates and she didn't know whose it was at first.'

Jessica wasn't surprised. 'Does your dad know?'

'Not yet. I didn't tell him straight away because I wanted it to be a surprise when he got out of prison. After the bricks and the fire, the hotel, the attack and everything . . . I got used to keeping it a secret.'

Jessica nodded in acceptance and sipped the froth from the top of her glass. 'So why were you so aggressive about Sienna?'

Ryan looked at the table before picking up his drink and downing half of it in one. 'Because I liked her. I thought when she was teasing me and leading me on that it was because she actually liked me. Then she would do it to my mates in front of me too. You got used to the way she was.'

'But it didn't stop you liking her?'

'Of course not.'

'Did you ever sleep with her?'

Ryan shook his head and drank some more. 'Some of

my mates said they had shagged her but . . . I don't know. I think she was too much of a tease to actually go through with things.'

Jessica thought about the self-harm marks on the insides of the girl's thighs and knew that if she had been sleeping with a host of boys, they would have been mentioned by someone at some point. She doubted they were the type of scars Sienna would have been happy with other people knowing about.

'Do you know she was pregnant?' she asked.

'Only because you asked some of the girls about it. They came into class and told us all.'

'Why?'

'I dunno. You tell me. Women are weird.'

Jessica suspected the answer was that, as Molly had suggested, the other girls weren't really Sienna's friends and were simply clinging on because of the wealth of her father. With that gone, it didn't matter if they gossiped a little.

'Do you know why she might have killed herself?' Jessica asked.

Ryan shook his head, wiping his eye, although Jessica couldn't see any tears. 'No.'

'What about Molly?'

The teenager shrugged. 'I dunno. Everyone said she was trying to cop off with Sienna.'

Jessica already knew that but it seemed a big leap to make from Molly's secret crush killing herself to Molly doing the same.

Ryan finished his drink with one final gulp. Jessica had

barely had two sips from hers and slid it across the table towards him. 'You sure?' he asked, nodding towards the glass.

'Yeah, you only have to stagger next door, I have to get all the way back to Salford.'

'Anything else?' he asked.

'When I spoke to Molly about you, she . . . well, she wasn't too willing to talk. The same with Sienna's other friends. And Lara.'

Ryan shrugged. He seemed to be getting friendlier the more he drank, another parallel Jessica saw with herself. 'I guess I have that effect on girls,' he said. 'Molly hated me because I was a bit of a twat. I'd call her a dyke and all sorts and then Sienna would still hang around with me.'

'What's changed?' Jessica asked, curious about his attitude.

Ryan scratched his head. 'I guess you just grow up at some point. Especially when you have a kid and your house burns down.'

'What about the reactions from the other women?'

He shook his head. 'I dunno the girls you spoke to but, basically, they all hated us lads who would hang around with Si.'

'What about Lara?'

Ryan snorted. 'You've seen what she's like. She's bloody nuts.'

'So why did you hang around with her?'

He raised his eyebrows again. 'She does this thing with . . .'

Jessica cut him off. 'All right, I can imagine.' She almost

added 'kids today', before realising how old that would make her sound. She recognised he had good answers for all of her questions. If they did ever need to check his alibis, she thought Lara would be able to provide one. The edginess in the young women's responses to him seemed understandable in the circumstances.

'There's one làst thing,' Jessica said.

By the time they had finished talking, she knew she had all but solved one major part of the puzzle.

30

Jessica knocked on the front door and stepped backwards. She could hear the television being muted from inside before the locks were noisily unbolted. The man who stood at the door in his dressing gown eyed her suspiciously through a small crack before opening it fully.

'I'm sorry, I know it's late,' Jessica said.

'Why are you here?' he asked.

A woman appeared in the background and Jessica acknowledged her with a smile before turning to the man. 'I was just hoping I could come in for a short while. I promise I won't be long.'

'Do you have any news about . . . ?'

Jessica shook her head. 'I wish I did.'

The woman walked over to stand next to her husband. 'You can come in,' she said, pulling the door wider and stepping aside.

Jessica wiped her feet, desperate not to make a bad impression before asking the one question she had.

'Are you all right?' Nicola North asked. 'We saw you on the news because of the fire and everything. It looked bad.'

'I'm okay,' Jessica said. 'I was wondering if you might allow me to look around Molly's room?'

She saw Peter exchange a slightly panicked glance with his wife. 'I . . . don't . . . why?' he said.

Jessica made sure she looked them both in the eye as she spoke. 'It sounds stupid but, when I was in her room before, it reminded me a little of my own from when I was that age. I just wonder if something was missed.'

Nicola replied. 'There was a group of your people in there for almost a day . . .'

'I know, it's not that. I'm looking for something different. Have you changed much around since . . . ?'

Nicola shook her head. 'We tidied up after the police left. It's as it was.' She looked at her husband, who turned to Jessica.

'What are you looking for?'

'I'd rather not say – just in case I don't find anything.'

Nicola spoke before her husband had a chance. 'It's fine. Let us know when you're finished. Take as long as you want.'

Jessica couldn't read Peter's face but he didn't object. She turned and walked up the stairs, remembering how she had felt when she had made the opposite journey what seemed like such a long time ago.

Molly's room appeared almost exactly as she remembered it, except that the light fixture had been repaired and the blood stain on the carpet was now only visible if you knew where to look.

The bed seemed pristine, as if it had been made that morning, and the light-coloured linen creaseless. Jessica slid her hand under the mattress, before picking the whole thing up, resting it against the wall so she could see beneath. There were wooden slats running the width of the bed frame but there was nothing on them. Jessica lowered the mattress and re-made the bed, trying to make the corners as sharp as they had been.

She moved to the bookcase and started removing the books one by one, checking inside and then replacing them. Molly's literary choices were wide-ranging, everything from biographies to romance novels to science fiction. She seemed to read a bit of everything but, after flicking through each one, Jessica couldn't find what she was looking for.

She looked down the back of the radiator and then, although she suspected the other officers would have already done it, Jessica searched through the chest of drawers and wardrobe.

She tried to stifle a cough but ended up making it worse, sputtering small spots of black and red onto her hand. She took a tissue from the box on the dressing table and wiped her palm and then pocketed it. She didn't want to admit to anyone that her throat was constantly sore but she had been coughing up blood and bits of black ever since the fire. She knew everyone would tell her to go to the doctor, but she couldn't face talking about it any more. The truth was, through her dreams and daytime flashes, Jessica had remembered more than enough and wasn't sure if she could cope with reliving everything that happened.

She scanned around the room, looking for any other hiding place and partly wishing she hadn't come. When the idea had struck her after the conversation with Ryan, she knew it was a long shot. She had seen the hope in

Nicola's eyes that she might have visited to bring them news, or offer the longed-for closure.

At a slight loss for what to do, Jessica crouched and crawled around the room, feeling into the corners of the carpet to see if there were any areas raised higher than they should be.

She ended up sitting in the centre of the room peering at the ceiling, although she couldn't see a loft or anything similar. As she stood, she felt her back twinge and instinctively reached around to hold it. She cursed under her breath and sat on the edge of the bed, sinking into the same spot she had on the previous occasion.

Jessica put her palms on either side and pressed down into areas of the mattress which felt firmer. She moved back onto the floor, ignoring the pain in her back, and untucked the sheet, running her hand along the edge of the mattress before finding a small hole. Jessica could just about squeeze her hand in, rummaging between springs and soft sponge-like material before her fingers touched the edge of something solid.

Jessica withdrew her hand, re-adjusted the way she was sitting and then tried reaching in again. This time her arm slid in more comfortably and her fingers closed around the object. As Jessica withdrew the book, small dots of fluff followed it out of the hole, dropping onto the floor.

In her teens, Jessica had kept her diary underneath the carpet which sat under her bed. As far as she knew, no one had ever found it and she burned the contents shortly before turning eighteen. Back then she had found her writings embarrassing and childlike but now she suspected they would be funny.

Jessica wasn't expecting a humorous read from Molly's diary but, as she scanned from the most recent entry backwards, she did find the solution to at least one of the cases she wasn't supposed to be working on.

31

Jessica knew there was no good way to contact Cole that night, so she reluctantly left it until the following morning. As he refused to answer her call on his mobile, there was only one thing for it. She had never heard the chief inspector swear in the entire time she had known him and he had raised his voice fewer than half-a-dozen times. After telling the operator she was his wife and being put through, the DCI broke the habit of a lifetime by both swearing and shouting at Jessica in the same sentence.

If she hadn't had something so serious to tell him, she would have felt strangely proud.

It was only because of the content of what she had that he didn't threaten any further disciplinary measure. Jessica told her supervisor everything she had found – and said she would bring him the proof, assuming she was allowed on the premises.

Reluctantly, he not only agreed to that but, with her standing firm, he said she could take part in the questioning if Reynolds agreed.

Jessica knew he would.

After driving to the station and talking Cole, Reynolds, Cornish and Rowlands through what she had discovered, Jessica allowed them to take Molly's diary. She wanted to make the arrest but the chief inspector gave her the choice of either sitting in on the interview – with special emphasis on 'sitting in', not 'taking part' – or simply going back to her flat to rest.

Jessica took the interview option, although everyone was aware the chances of her sitting quietly were slim.

Within a couple of hours, the suspect had been arrested, brought to the station and had spoken to a solicitor. Jessica was waiting in the interview room, as Reynolds made sure the recording equipment was working.

'Are you going to be all right?' he asked.

'Definitely.'

'Jess, I'm serious.'

'Me too. I'm fine.'

'You know you shouldn't be here.'

'None of us would be here doing this if it wasn't for me.' Jessica wasn't trying to brag but she wanted to make a point.

'If you're sure.' They sat in silence for a few moments before the inspector added, 'Dave's been missing you, by the way.'

'Rowlands?'

'Yeah, who else?'

'What's up with him?'

'Something about him breaking up with his girlfriend.'

'Chloe?'

'I don't know. What you kids get up to is your own business. I try to stay out of it all. He's spent the last few days moping around though.'

Jessica didn't have time to reply before there was a knock at the door and it swung open. A solicitor in a smart suit entered first, followed by his client. They sat in the chairs opposite the officers, as Reynolds announced everyone's name. The inspector had given up any hope of keeping Jessica quiet and allowed her to take her usual seat. As she pointed out, she knew the case better than anyone anyway.

After the announcements had been made, Jessica stared at the person in front of her. 'How are you doing, Aidan?' she asked. 'Long time, no see.'

'I don't know why I'm here,' the tutor said, looking to his solicitor for guidance.

Jessica knew she couldn't specifically talk about Ryan's drawings because she shouldn't have had them in the first place.

She realised her mistake at the college. She suspected that, after they had asked the tutor about Ryan, Aidan had sketched them himself as a way of deflecting their investigation. He knew they could never be used as evidence.

Instead, Jessica mentioned the other reason they had brought in the teacher. 'Sienna Todd.'

Aidan seemed instantly defensive. He shuffled backwards in his seat, crossing his arms. 'What about her? I thought it was a suicide?'

Jessica opened a cardboard wallet and took out the photocopies they had made of Molly's diary. 'I'm just going to read you a few things and you can say if they sound familiar. I'll go from the earliest entry, if only to give your solicitor the full picture. Is there anything you'd like to say first?'

Aidan said nothing, staring at Jessica with his mouth open. She could tell he was terrified.

'Okay, well, if you're sitting comfortably then I'll begin,' Jessica said, then started to read.

'I know there's something that Si isn't telling me. She's been weird ever since that time she told her dad she was staying over at mine but really didn't. I keep wanting to ask her what's going on but don't want to fall out. At first I thought it was because Rebecca was telling people that Si fucked two lads in the college toilets. I don't know why Si puts up with it. It's not as if being a virgin is anything to be ashamed of. Everyone thinks she sleeps around. If only they knew.'

Jessica looked up at Aidan. 'Anything to say?' She glanced across at the man's solicitor and, from the nervous look on his face, she knew that he must have a good idea where things were going.

'Nothing?' she continued. 'All right then, how about this from five days later.

'Oh my God. I can't believe it. I feel like crying. Si told me tonight that she's not a virgin any longer. She didn't want to say who but it's definitely a boy. I can't even think about it. Some of the lads are going around school saying horrible things but it can't be any of them. Si told me she was only stringing them along. I wish she would tell me the truth but maybe it's my fault for not telling her how I felt sooner?'

Aidan still wasn't reacting and Jessica knew she was going to have to read everything she had. 'This next one's around eight weeks later,' she said.

'Today I've spent most of the day in my bedroom with Si. Usually that would be brilliant but I finally found out why she's been feeling ill all week.'

Jessica raised her eyes. 'Just for your benefit, this next sentence is in capital letters,' she said.

'*SHE'S FUCKING PREGNANT. As in there's a baby inside of her. It's a good job Mum and Dad were out because there's no way they wouldn't have heard. Si went through almost a whole box of tissues. She didn't want to say who the father is but she didn't want her dad finding out either. She spent the whole day stressing. I was trying to say it was going to be all right but we both knew that was bollocks. I don't know what she's going to do.*'

Jessica took a breath and brought out another sheet from the wallet. 'I'm skipping through a bit here but you'll get the gist. Anyway . . .

'*I didn't think she was going to do it but Si eventually told her dad about being pregnant today. She asked me to be there with her, partly because she thought he might shout a bit less. Fat chance! He was horrible to her. He called her a slut and a slag and said she was a whore just like her mum. He screamed at her to tell him the name of the boy but she wouldn't. I think he might have killed whoever it was if she had. Eventually, he just said he'd pay to make it go away. I felt really bad because Si was going to go to the clinic without telling him but I thought she would feel better if she told her dad. I didn't know he would react like that. Si said she was all right but I don't know how she could have been. I thought it was just a jab or something but there are these sit-down interview things. I've told her I'll go with her wherever she wants.*'

Aidan was white as Jessica finished reading. He was star-ing at the back of the sheets of paper she was reading from, as if he could somehow see the words. 'Just a couple more,' Jessica said.

'*I don't know what I thought an abortion was but I didn't think it would be like that. It's really messy and poor Si just cried and cried. I don't think it was the procedure itself, more the fact she had to go through everything with just me. Her dad was somewhere else on business and she said the father refused to come. I asked her who it was, expecting her to say nothing like always. I actually felt guilty when she told me because it felt like I'd taken advantage of her when we were sat in the waiting room. She just said, "It's Aidan." At first I was like, "Aidan who" but then it dawned on me that she meant our tutor.*'

Jessica heard a small sob come from the man but she didn't want to interrupt the flow.

'*I've always found him a little creepy. It's the way he looks at some of the girls. Sometimes you'll see him watching them leave or whatever. I know he's always had something for Si. I think she probably knew too. It turns out that, on the night she told her dad she was at mine, she was actually at his. Si didn't want to say because he's married. She feels really bad about it. She reckoned there were pictures of his wife in the living room and everything. I really don't know why she went through with it. Apparently Aidan's wife was on a work trip or something but I don't know why she chose to lose her virginity to him. I said that she should tell someone but she didn't want to. I think she's in love with him. Either that or she thinks she is.*'

Aidan's solicitor interrupted. 'What are you hoping to achieve through all of this?'

Jessica looked at Aidan, ignoring the other man. 'Do

you want to tell him or shall I?' Aidan said nothing but reached for a tissue from the table.

'Fine,' Jessica said.

'I didn't know if I would be able to write this down but I figured maybe someone will read it one day. I know I should go and tell people but I have no proof. I've been hoping Si told someone else what was going on but, if she did, no one else is saying it. I don't know how to even write this because it somehow doesn't seem real. Maybe I'm hoping that, by writing it, it helps me to figure out what happened. I know I'm going to re-read these next few words over and over but . . . Si is dead. It sounds like she killed herself but I don't know. She said she was going to the cinema with Rebecca but then I don't know what happened. They're saying she slit her wrists. I can't believe it. I've just read the last sentence over and over and I still can't believe it. My phone rang earlier and I thought it might be her, even though she's gone. She told me Aidan was going to leave his wife for her but then she seemed really upset yesterday and didn't want to talk about it. She was avoiding me this morning but I think it was because she knew I would ask about things. I don't know what to do. I've already told the officers I don't know anything. I think they'll be back but, if I tell them something then, it will seem suspicious. I just want to cry. I wish Si was here.'

Jessica's throat was feeling dry. She took two long sips from a cup of water on the table, carefully watching Aidan. His solicitor had been furiously making notes throughout the previous entry but the tutor seemed largely unmoved. The earlier tears had stopped but still stained his face as he continued to stare at the photocopies Jessica was reading from.

'A couple more,' she said.

'*I went to see Aidan today. I told him that I knew about him and Si. I don't think I've ever seen anyone so scared. He asked me what I was going to do. I said I wanted him to tell the headteacher and if he didn't, then I would. He asked if I could leave him over the weekend because he'd have to tell his wife. I thought it sounded fair enough.*'

Jessica shuffled onto the final page. She flipped it around to show both men. 'I could read this out for the tape but I won't. As you can both see, the "c" word has been written over and over in capital letters. I'll continue from the next page.

'*I went to see Aidan again today. He lied about talking to his wife. He said that I had no proof and that, if I thought about going to the head or the police or anyone else then he would "fucking do me". He said that he would make sure no university would take me and that he would spread rumours through the school. At first I thought he wasn't serious and tried to say I'd tell the police anyway but he grabbed my arm and spat in my face. He told me not to mess with him and kept going on about how I have no proof. The thing is that he's right. All I've got is Si's word and she's not here. I miss her so much. I started writing a poem about her last night but couldn't finish. Mum and Dad have invited me out with them for lunch tomorrow but I can't stand it. It's not them, I just don't know what to do. I wish there was someone I could talk to.*'

Jessica put the pages down and looked up, waiting until Aidan caught her eye. 'Molly North killed herself the next day,' she said quietly. A fury was raging inside of her but she kept her tone calm. 'Are you proud of yourself?'

Before Aidan could speak, his solicitor cut in. 'This is ridiculous. How are you ever going to convince a court those words you've just been reading aren't something you've made up? What are you even going to charge him with? As far as I can tell, from everything you've described, no criminal offence has taken place.'

Jessica didn't want to speak, partly because her throat was hurting but also because she didn't know if she could stop herself from saying something she would regret. Taking the hint, Reynolds cut in and spoke to say he was ending the interview. Aidan and his solicitor looked on, each as confused as the other.

Both officers stood up. 'You can leave,' Reynolds said, nodding towards the door.

Aidan slowly got to his feet, his solicitor packing the pad he had been writing on into his briefcase. 'Did you really just bring us here to read all of that?'

Jessica watched Reynolds stare at Aidan. Because of the way he usually acted like a mixture of her father and older brother, she had forgotten how fearsome he could be.

'No, we brought you in here to let you know that we know what you did,' Jessica said. 'Whether we can prove it – and whether it's technically a criminal offence – is another matter.'

The solicitor took his client by the wrist and led him out of the room. Jessica started to speak but Reynolds barely let her get a word out. 'Not here.' In silence, he led her along the corridors until they were in his office.

'What do you think he's going to do?' Jessica asked.

'I couldn't care less. We could go into abuse of trust or

something like that but Sienna was over eighteen and the only proof we have of anything is the diary of a dead girl. We already knew that. Neither of us really thought he'd confess, not with a solicitor there.'

'It was worth a try though. He'll be looking over his shoulder every time he sees a blue flashing light now.'

'Oh, he'll be doing more than that.'

Reynolds had spoken with a fearsome tone in his voice and Jessica felt intimidated by such a change in the man she thought she knew.

'What are you going to do?' she asked.

'I'm going to send photocopies of this diary to every newspaper and TV channel in a ten-mile radius. I don't even care if it comes back to me – there's no way he's getting away with this.'

'I'll do it,' Jessica said.

'No you won't. If I end up getting it in the neck for this, I want you to get my job.'

'Why would you do that?'

The inspector put an arm around Jessica. 'Because you've already done enough.'

32

Jessica relaxed into the large reclining chair and put her feet up on the desk. 'About time you got a new one,' she said approvingly.

She watched Andrew relax into his own matching chair. 'I didn't think I could put up with you moaning about it any longer.'

'How did Harley take the news about his daughter and her teacher?' Jessica asked.

'I don't know. I called him the night before you told me it was going to drop in the papers. I thought he'd be angry, which he sort of was, but I think he's been through too much to really take it all in. He said he'd pay me. I kept telling him it was nothing to do with me but he wouldn't listen.'

'What are you going to do with the cash?'

'I don't know. Give it to charity probably. He still doesn't know what happened with the fire and, even though I'm sure he'll have the insurance, it doesn't feel right taking the bloke's money.' Andrew caught Jessica's eye. 'Sorry about mentioning the, er, fire.'

'It's fine.'

'Do you know anything yet?'

'No, we're looking into things.'

Andrew stood and walked to the window. 'You should quit and do this.'

Jessica spun around in her chair and snorted. 'What, follow people around for a living? I'm all right.'

'The money's better and I'd bet it's far less hassle.'

'It's not about the money.'

'What's it about? Putting yourself in danger?'

Jessica realised Andrew was being serious. She thought of the people she had come across over the years and the number of times she had been in trouble. 'It's about mates,' she said. 'I get to go to work with my friends every day and, even when they're being dicks, they're still my mates.'

'You could come to work with me? I'll pay you well. We'll set up our own joint agency.'

Jessica grinned at him. 'It's a really nice offer but I'm all right, thanks.'

'You've got my number if you change your mind.'

'I won't.'

Andrew went back to his desk and hunted through the top drawer, before picking out a newspaper and placing it on the table between them. 'What do you think is going to happen?'

Jessica picked it up and scanned the front page before turning to the inside and laying it flat. 'I have no idea but I did hear that Aidan Barlow resigned last night.'

'Do you think he'll sue?'

Jessica shrugged. 'Who cares? I spoke to the guy I know at the paper. He says that if the guy does try legal action, they would be able to produce all the diaries in court.

Because it's a civil case, it's on the balance of probabilities, not beyond reasonable doubt. He might still win but more and more details would be revealed each day. The papers only printed that he had an affair with a student who later killed herself. If it got to court, everything else would be released about his threats to the second student.'

'Sneaky.'

'Yeah, it wasn't entirely my idea. I would have leaked the whole lot.'

'Are they going to know the information came from your station?'

Jessica shrugged again. 'Probably. But again, if they complain, they risk the rest of the information coming out. I reckon Aidan will keep his head down and hope his wife forgives him. He's got off lightly.'

'He'll have to watch out for Harley too.' Jessica didn't want to comment, thinking that Aidan deserved everything he got but not wanting to condone anything else that might happen. 'I bet sales of the *Herald* are up today,' Andrew said, flipping over to the next page of the paper. 'They got five pages out of it and it's been on the news all morning.'

'Yeah, my mate Garry will be happy.'

'I didn't think you were supposed to be friends with journalists?'

'We're not really but they can be helpful sometimes. I said I'd take him out for a beer but he'll be buying after this.'

Andrew laughed but stopped himself when he realised Jessica wasn't joining in. 'Are you okay?' he asked.

Jessica jumped up from the chair and took her phone out of her pocket. 'Sorry, I've got to make a call. Are you going to be free later?'

'I guess.'

'Good, because I might have one final job for you.'

Jessica sat staring across the rippling water. The gentle waves were illuminated by rows of lamps along the water's edge, the bright white moon reflecting from the surface. The evening was cool but Jessica left the flat's balcony door open, her feet resting on the handrail.

She knew something had changed. She didn't know if it was down to her, perhaps a natural progression as she got older, or if her relationship with Adam had matured her. She wanted to feel angry but instead she felt calm. The fact that she recognised her attitude had altered made her all the more certain that things weren't quite right.

It didn't matter how much she thought about the fires – and the fact someone had tried to kill her and Adam; she couldn't raise the fury in her that she knew would have come so easily barely months before.

Instead, she couldn't forget Rowlands's words. 'Why is it always you?' Over the course of her conversation with Ryan and the way she had uncomfortably begun to realise that they were very similar people, she thought she had stumbled across the answer. It was always her because she couldn't stop herself. Everything about her personality was act first and think later. If she had thought first, she wouldn't have lost Adam originally. If she had thought first, she would never have ended up alone in her flat with a mass murderer. If she had listened to Izzy, her flat would never have burned down.

Her thoughts were interrupted by the sound of Caroline's doorbell. Adam had been saying that perhaps they could think about buying the flat – but Jessica knew she could never stay there long-term. The house they had been living in felt like Adam's and this place felt like Caroline's. She wanted somewhere of her own to call home.

Jessica closed the balcony door just as her phone begun to ring. She checked the caller and smiled, walking to the front door. The man standing there was cradling his phone to his ear with his shoulder, holding onto a stack of newspapers under each arm.

'You're late,' Jessica said.

He tried to enter but bounced off the doorframe, spilling one of the piles onto the floor. As he wobbled and tried to stop the first few falling, he accidentally released everything from under his other arm, leaving a mound of papers covering the area in between the hallway and the flat. He crouched down, swearing under his breath and trying to pick everything up.

Although he had come to see her for a serious reason, Jessica couldn't stop herself from laughing. 'I thought the sign downstairs said no free papers?'

Garry Ashford looked up from the floor as he tried to re-stack what he'd dropped. 'Ha ha, you're very funny. Are you going to help?'

'If by "help", you mean take pictures and laugh, then yeah.' Jessica stooped and began to pick up some of the papers herself before they eventually moved everything onto the floor inside the flat.

'Nice place,' Garry said, wandering to the window and peering over the water.

'It's nicer when the sun's out.'

'How's Adam? I heard he was out of hospital.'

'He's all right. I asked him to go out for the evening so we could work.'

Jessica sat on the floor next to the stacked papers and opened the lid of the laptop she had borrowed from Andrew.

Garry sat on the sofa. 'Do you know what I had to go through to get those out of the office?'

'I dunno. You left with them under your arm and managed not to drop them? How hard can it be?'

'I had to sign them out because they're part of our archive. It was only because I said I was working on a story that they let them go.'

Jessica shunted the laptop to one side and picked up the first paper. 'Do you remember the last time we did this in my old flat?'

Garry clearly did. It had taken the combination of the two of them both to figure out who had been killing seemingly unconnected people in their own locked homes.

'Is that why I'm here this time?'

'Yes.'

'Do you know who started those fires?'

'Probably.'

'Then why aren't you out . . . I don't know . . . getting them?'

344

Jessica shrugged and looked away, unable to admit that it was because she wasn't sure if she trusted her own judgement any longer. 'I want to know what you think first.'

'Why me?'

Jessica beckoned the journalist over, so he was sitting next to her on the floor. She put the paper down and pointed to the page she had loaded from the *Herald*'s website. 'What do you think?'

Garry leant forward and squinted at the screen, reading the headline and first few lines. 'What am I looking at?'

Jessica flicked onto a second page and let him read again, then onto half-a-dozen more. Garry turned to her, obviously confused. 'Stories about the fires, your fire, Martin Chadwick being released . . . I don't get it.'

'How far back do these papers go?' Jessica asked, pointing at the pile.

'It's what you asked for – about seven months or so. I've not got them all because there would have been way too many.'

'Do all the stories you print go on the Internet?'

'No, not the smaller ones.'

'Okay, let's start at the beginning.' Jessica reached across Garry and started sorting through the papers.

'What are you doing?'

'Looking for the earliest one.'

Garry half-heartedly picked up the papers closest to him and began sorting them. 'Are you going to tell me why?'

'I want you to see it.'

Jessica needed Garry to work things out. If he could, it

would offer some sort of justification for her actions and thought process. She flipped over the pile of papers and took the one from the bottom, checking the date, and then skimming through the first two dozen pages. 'Not this one,' she said.

'What am I looking for?'

'Just wait.'

Jessica flicked through eight more newspapers before finally handing one to the journalist. 'That one.'

She waited as Garry looked through the same sections. He looked up at her curiously. 'Jess, I . . .'

Jessica continued working her way through the first pile, picking out three more and passing them to Garry and then choosing another five from the second. When she was finished, she tidily stacked the ones she had used in date order and sat on the sofa, looking to where the journalist was going through the items she had given him.

After the final one, he stared up at her, holding his palms upwards. 'I don't get it.'

Jessica closed her eyes and leant back in the seat. 'Just look. Read what I've given you and read what's on the Internet.'

As Garry looked back at the stack of papers, she could tell he was thinking that everything had got to her. She could almost hear his mind working, wanting to ask her if she was all right.

'Just read,' she whispered quietly.

33

The man reached into his jacket pocket and fingered the ignition of the lighter. He felt a thrill of excitement surge through his chest as he rubbed the grooves of the circular part with his thumb, gently rotating it slowly enough so that it didn't produce a flame. He kept one hand on the object, holding his phone with his other as he walked briskly through the maze of alleyways he had so carefully remembered.

He felt proud of the way he had evolved. In the early days, there had been no planning at all. He would drive to the site, do what he had to do and then get in his car and head home. It hadn't taken him long to figure out that he would find it hard to explain things if any witnesses reported his number plate close to more than one of his targets.

What he also started doing was buying fuel at a different petrol station each time, allowing him to refill his petrol can without arousing suspicion.

Not using his car at the scene solved one problem, but it left him with the issue of how to get the canister to the target without being seen. Public transport was obviously out and walking was not only impractical because of the distances but also due to how heavy the petrol was. He had thought about using something else to get the fires started but he hadn't come across anything that was so quick to burn while, at the same time, being so easily available.

There was something about the smell too.

The aroma was perhaps the best part: the thick scent of power hanging in the air before he used the lighter. It offered more satisfaction than a match. The enjoyment as he quickly scuffed his finger along the round ignition was so much more thrilling than simply flicking a match along the side of a box.

Hiding the can close to the victim's house had come to him in a moment as close to genius as he thought he had ever managed. He would find a nearby spot during daylight and then return to hide the can not long after it went dark. He would leave it under a hedge or somewhere similar that the public paid no attention to. With that done, he would park around a mile away in the early hours, hurry through the collection of side streets and back alleys he had memorised, and then retrieve his prize. After lighting the flames he would race back the way he had come and be in his vehicle before someone had even called 999.

At that time of the morning, it was almost always clear and by the time anyone arrived to start investigating what had happened, he was well on his way home.

Well, that was how it worked now.

Martin Chadwick's house had almost been a big mistake. The early evening timing had been utterly naive, but at least it had guaranteed the target was in – and allowed lessons to be learned.

The man was glad it was spring, the early morning

temperatures were relatively comfortable and the ground wasn't frosty and slippery. He also didn't have to wear a thick coat, making it harder to run.

He crossed a road, ducking under an overhanging branch before hurrying through a ginnel and emerging onto the cul-de-sac he had chosen. The hiding place for the fuel had been pretty easy this time around. Purely by accident when he had been driving to check the location earlier, he saw that it was bin day. Residents had already started to leave their large grey wheelie bins at the end of their driveways ready for collection the following morning. The man had left his can in the one belonging to the house opposite and then driven off.

He put his phone into his jacket pocket and raised the bin lid, reaching inside and lifting the petrol container out. He had deliberately not filled it all the way, knowing how heavy it would be otherwise. Making his way across the road, he could feel his hands trembling with anticipation.

At the end of the target's drive, he stopped and placed the can on the floor, unscrewing the lid and inhaling just enough to enjoy the sensation without clouding his senses. His heart was pounding as he walked towards the front of the property and began dribbling the liquid in a thin trail towards the main door.

The faint glow of the nearby street lights glistened from the liquid as he watched it seep into the ruts of the paved drive before he reached the front of the house. He continued to trickle it gently as he never felt comfortable glugging the liquid over doors and window frames. The noise sounded wasteful, as if the fuel were simply being hurled away, rather than being used for a legitimate purpose.

He was lost in his thoughts, the smell gradually reaching the point of empowerment when he heard the front door open. The man was so surprised that as he spun around the can slipped in his hand and noisily clattered to the ground. He glanced up to see Detective Sergeant Jessica Daniel standing in the doorway. The liquid gushed out of the container over his shoes. He could feel a squelching sensation as he took an involuntary step backwards.

Jessica hadn't left the doorstep but the man could hear movement behind him. He turned to see someone he didn't know standing at the edge of the driveway. Looking from one person to the other, he heard Jessica saying his name, telling him not to be stupid. Desperately, he tried to think of an innocent explanation for why he happened to be there but there was clearly none.

He knew it was game over.

His hand shot into his pocket and pulled out the lighter in an attempt to keep the man from advancing down the driveway towards him. He held it in the air in a silent threat, trying to think what to do next. He wondered how they knew. Was it Jessica or was it the man he didn't know who had figured it out? He thought he had been careful enough but there must have been something he had overlooked.

He turned to see the stranger advancing one step at a time. He shouted 'Stay back', and held the lighter higher, his thumb resting on the trigger. Jessica still hadn't moved but she was saying his name again, telling him to think about what he was doing.

He could feel the fumes drifting into his nostrils. As the stranger took two steps closer, he flicked the switch, feeling the heat of the flame close to his thumb. 'Stay back,' he shouted again, looking from side to side and wondering if there was somewhere he could run. He eyed the hedge that bordered the adjoining property. He might have been able to jump it but where could he go then? If he somehow escaped, he wouldn't know where to hide long-term. Even so, it was surely a better idea than simply standing still?

His feet squelched again, this time uncomfortably, as he edged away from the two people towards the hedge. Jessica called his name again, seemingly sensing what he was thinking, but the stranger was now moving quickly towards him. He stepped backwards without looking and clipped his heel on an uneven part of the driveway.

Everything seemed to happen in slow motion. The man felt himself tumbling while instinctively putting his hands down to stop himself. The stranger leapt sideways. The man turned just in time to see Jessica dashing into the house. As the lighter slipped from his grasp, he thought the flame was out. He stretched forward to catch it but couldn't control his falling body as he landed on his backside, the lighter dropping onto his foot.

For a moment he thought nothing was going to happen but then he felt the heat. Somehow the flame had ignited and, as he felt pain surge through his body, he stared down in disbelief at the fire that had engulfed his feet.

In the weeks that had gone by, the power of the flames had entranced him in their initial moments before he had to run off. He could barely comprehend the sight of the blaze that was covering his lower half. He couldn't even scream as the heat and the pain overwhelmed him.

He tried to roll before he heard a woman's voice shouting and then something hammered into his legs. He heard the liquid hitting him before he felt it but, as he scrambled onto his back and stared down, he saw Jessica holding a fire extinguisher and spraying white foam over his lower half. He couldn't feel anything except for an intense pain and didn't even know if he was screaming.

The man breathed in, desperate for clean air, but all he felt was a gagging sensation in his throat as the stench of his own burned flesh tore through him.

A FEW DAYS EARLIER

Garry Ashford looked up from the newspapers. 'Are you saying what I think you're saying?'

'That depends on you,' Jessica replied.

'You know it can't be him.' The journalist was wide-eyed with shock and Jessica could see his hand shaking.

'Why not?'

'Because . . . well, why would he?'

Jessica shuffled onto the floor so she was sitting next to Garry and took the paper from him. She opened it at the relevant page and spread out the rest of the stack she had isolated, finding the articles she was looking for.

'I went to see my friend Izzy the other day,' she said. 'She's just had a baby. She's not had much sleep and she's hardly stopped since the birth but she looks amazing. She's younger than me but it feels like she's the grown-up. While I was busy trying to figure all this out, I've been fussing over other things and allowing my own personality to get in the way. But she asked the simplest of questions. It was the one we all should have asked at the beginning – but we were so caught up in the pace of everything and the things we thought were obvious, that we ended up missing that one issue.'

She paused, not for effect, simply because she thought

she might cough. Garry asked the obligatory 'what?' as Jessica allowed her throat to settle.

'Who gains?' Jessica replied. 'And Iz was right. Who gains from all of this? Martin didn't, he lost a house. Anthony had already lost his son and could have lost his liberty. Ryan got his dad back but could have lost him again. What about Harley? He lost his daughter and then his house. I couldn't see past that – because I couldn't understand how the two things couldn't be connected. No one is that unlucky. It was too much of a coincidence.'

She picked up one of the papers. 'When you look at these, though, you realise it didn't happen by chance – because there was always one person at the centre of it all. One person who gained.'

'But what kind of person would go that far?'

Jessica pointed to the picture byline underneath the story about the fire at her house. 'This guy,' she said, pointing to the photograph of Sebastian Lowe.

34

Izzy grinned at Jessica. 'You don't have to hold her if you don't want to.'

Jessica held out her arms and cradled Amber to her body, relaxing back into the sofa. 'They're not too bad after all. She still has big scary eyes but at least they're closed.'

Izzy sat in the recliner and curled her feet underneath her. 'Can you stop saying my only child has enormous body parts, please?' she said with a smile.

'Okay, let's just say she has her mother's eyes.' Jessica looked up at her friend and grinned.

'Come on then, let's hear it.'

'Is Amber going to mind if I say it all in front of her?'

'Well, firstly she's asleep and secondly she's a tiny, tiny baby, so I think she'll be all right.'

Jessica hugged the baby closer to her. 'I know Dave's spoken to you about the case a bit but, in the end, I figured it out by working my way back to what you said. It was so confusing because we were looking for the link from Harley and his daughter to Martin and his son. There was no way it could be a coincidence but we missed the obvious connection – Sebastian.'

'He's the reporter, yeah?'

'Exactly. To be honest, I think things just got out of

hand. We went through all of his stories. There are around a dozen crimes we think he may be responsible for, which he then reported. There was this old lady bashed over the back of the head three days after he started at the paper. He got the story before anyone else because he somehow knew where the woman lived. At the time no one there questioned him. After the assault had been reported, we didn't pay much attention to the coverage. It was only going back now that we could see there was no obvious reason for him to know her name and address – we only gave out the woman's age. We assumed she had approached him about the story but she says he came to her.'

'What else have you got?'

'A few things we're not completely sure of but which seem likely. There's a shop robbery where the person was wearing a balaclava. The physical description matches Sebastian but we would never be able to prove it. But then the fire stories started. He wrote something about this disused off-licence being set on fire a couple of months back. It wasn't even something on our radar and we never put out a press release, yet he wrote about it. When he stumbled across the legitimate story about Martin, it gave him ideas. When Anthony made those threats, that meant there was a motive. The attack on Chadwick in that alley kept it in the news – and kept them on edge over each other. When the first attack on Martin's house happened, we went straight to Anthony's. We found a paint tin and petrol can which I guess Sebastian left there. I unscrewed the shed door to get in, so he may well have done the same.'

'So he set the fire at Martin's?'

'I think so. Sebastian is in hospital with burns. He set fire to his own feet. The doctors don't know if he will ever walk again. He hasn't been talking. I think he literally just wanted to light the fuse and see what would happen between the two men. To us, it looked like Anthony waging war and Ryan or Martin fighting back. Really it was just one guy attacking both sides.'

'But why would he want to burn down the house of that girl who killed herself?'

Jessica pulled up the blanket to cover Amber's ears, just in case the baby could somehow understand what was being said. 'I reckon he got the bug after that. When I spoke to Martin in hospital he talked about the addiction he had to the flames. For some people it's booze or fags, for him it's fire. I wonder if that's how Sebastian felt after he tried it the first time? My theory was that he was just targeting people in the news, which would then generate bigger stories.'

'And that's how you found him?'

'Pretty much. I'm mates with this private investigator guy. He followed Sebastian over a couple of days and saw him leave this petrol can in a wheelie bin opposite Peter and Nicola North's house. We had to be careful so we made sure there were fire extinguishers around. We wanted to catch him doing it, of course. I waited in the house, Andrew was just around the corner, and our other lot were at the end of the road out of sight.'

'Wow, he was really going to target those poor people?'

Jessica nodded. 'Horrible, isn't it.'

'And why you?'

It was something Jessica didn't want to think too deeply about. 'Same reason, I guess. Think about the coverage it got. Everyone was reporting it.'

Izzy reached onto the coffee table and picked up her mug of tea, interlocking her fingers around it and taking a sip. 'When you arrested him, were you scared . . . after what happened to you?'

Jessica ignored the question. 'The stupid thing is that, in the end, I don't know how much more he was going to gain. He got a promotion, he looked good among his colleagues, but what else was he going to do? With me, everyone reported it so there was no personal gain to him. I think he started by doing this to make himself look impressive but, by the end, he was addicted to what he was doing.'

'Dave told me you put the flames out when Sebastian was on fire.'

Jessica shrugged. 'Yeah.'

'Did you think about . . . ? I dunno. After what he tried to do to you . . . ?'

For a few moments, Jessica said nothing and then she changed the subject. 'Did you see the story about the teacher who had the affair with the student who killed herself?'

Izzy stared at Jessica, pausing before replying. 'I saw.' she replied. Amber wriggled gently in Jessica's arms and gave a slight gurgle. 'Just rock her,' Izzy said. Jessica began to bob the girl delicately up and down. 'You'll want one of your own soon,' Izzy concluded.

'Did you hear that Dave split up with Chloe?' Jessica asked, again deliberately changing the subject.

'Yes.' Izzy shook her head. 'He said it had just reached a natural end and tried to laugh it off but I think there's something more. They were living together and talking about marriage and stuff. You don't just do that.'

'Did he say anything else?'

'Not really. I got the impression there was someone else.'

Jessica had been trying to catch some time alone with him but it was proving elusive. 'Who?' she asked.

Jessica thought she saw her friend's eyebrows raise but, if they did, it was only for a moment. 'No idea,' Izzy said. Her tone sounded unconvincing but, as Jessica softly rocked Amber back to sleep, she didn't think it really mattered.

35

Jessica tapped her hand on the top of the steering wheel in frustration. 'Lorry drivers really are knobheads,' she said.

'What's wrong with them?' Adam asked, although Jessica suspected he didn't particularly want to know the answer.

'It's just one dick overtaking another dick for five miles, and meanwhile we're all backed up trying to go around.'

Although she was watching the road, she could sense Adam rolling his eyes. 'So where are we going?' he asked.

Jessica eased onto the brake to let a car pull out in front of her. 'Wait and see.'

In the week since Sebastian Lowe had been arrested, Jessica had been trying to convince herself that the reason she had been picturing him in her dreams so often was because it was her subconscious trying to tell her something that, deep down, she already knew. When she thought about it like that, she could almost feel justified for the way he consistently intruded into her thoughts.

She figured that it might eventually feel true if she repeated it enough times.

As she finally accelerated past the lorry and pulled back into the second lane, she eased off the accelerator. 'Are you all right?' Adam asked.

'Yeah, you?'

She heard Adam breathe in deeply before he finally spoke. 'Why did he do it, Jess?'

Jessica could feel the anguish in his voice. 'I'm not sure you'll ever get the answer you need if that's the question you ask.'

It was something she didn't know the answer to, despite telling Izzy and her other colleagues what her suspicions were. Adam said nothing for a few moments as Jessica indicated and moved to the inside lane, ready to exit at the next junction. 'What should I ask instead?'

'You should ask when I want to get married.'

'Um . . . okay. When do you want to get married?'

Jessica indicated again, this time crossing the dotted line and slowing as she entered the bend of the slip road. 'What sign did we just pass?'

'The airport.'

'Yep. Guess where we're going.'

Adam made an 'um' sound as if ready to play along and then said in a panicked voice: 'I don't have my passport.'

'Don't worry, I've got both of ours. It's a good job we kept them at the bottom of the wardrobe. Anyway, hurry up and guess.'

'Er, I dunno. Paris?'

'Nah, further. The other way.'

'America?'

'Well, yeah. But it's a pretty big place. I don't think they're going to drop us out somewhere in the middle and see where we land.'

'New York?'

'Further.'

'Er, Orlando?'

Jessica laughed. 'Hang on a minute, do you want to go to Disney World?'

Adam snorted. 'I've always wanted to get in a fight with one of those mascots.'

'You want to get in a fight?'

'Not really. I just fancy rugby-tackling one of them. You know the guys in the big furry suit things.'

Jessica was trying to focus on the road but, considering she had never known Adam display anything approaching a violent side, she sneaked a sideways look at him. 'Why?'

'I dunno. Just one of those things.'

'Right . . . And you say I'm the weird one. Anyway, we're not going to Disney World.'

'Texas?'

'Too hot.'

'LA?'

'Nah, we would both be mega-fat there.'

Adam paused for a moment and as Jessica waited at the traffic lights to turn into the airport car park, she knew he had the answer. 'Oh,' he said.

'So are you going to ask me again when I want to get married?'

She turned to face him as the light hovered on red. 'When would you like to get married, Jess?' he asked with a smile.

Jessica turned back to the road but couldn't stop herself smiling. 'As soon as we get to Vegas. And you better get ready to carry me over the threshold because my back has been bloody killing me.'

Afterword

I'll start by saying that if you've skipped to the back without reading the story, you should really stop reading now to avoid spoilers.

Honestly, stop reading this sentence and go back to the part you were at before jumping to this bit.

Have you done that?

Really?

Honestly?

You're going to spoil the story if you don't stop here . . .

All right, good. There are sections of this book that are far more personal to me than the other stories I have written, largely because I have been in a house fire. It was nowhere near as serious as the one described here but a lot of the after-effects were similar. For instance, I inhaled a large gulp of black smoke and felt that moment of confusion and dizziness where your head just won't clear. For anyone who has experienced it, you'll know what I mean. I spent weeks coughing up little bits of black 'stuff' and simply became used to that heavy feeling in my chest. That was from one gulp.

At the time, I was living in a large house which had been converted into flats. I lived on the top floor in the attic, while beneath me were three apartments on the ground floor and another three on the first. The fire started in the kitchen shared by everyone on the bottom floor. The electricity in my flat went out and, for some reason I'll never know, I went to the window to see if there might be an explanation. What I saw was around half-a-dozen people pointing and staring at the house.

Obviously that wasn't a regular occurrence.

I went down the stairs, where there were small amounts of grey smoke and a young Polish girl screaming and crying. She pointed to the kitchen door and said she had put some chips on to fry and then gone back to her bedroom and fallen asleep.

No, I'm not making that up.

Stupidly, I shunted open the kitchen door, which is when the thick cloud of black smoke poured out into the hallway. It took me a few seconds to clear my head and it's only since then that I've been able to understand why people say it's the smoke that kills you. You can feel it inside you, like a parasite. Your breathing feels heavy, your voice doesn't sound right and you simply can't stop coughing.

Luckily, the door was the type that swings back into place, so it closed itself. I managed to call 999 and told the girl to get out and then left the house myself. With the fire brigade on their way, it only then dawned on me that others might still be inside, so I went back into the building and knocked on every door.

At first I thought it was fine but in the flat directly below where I lived another Polish woman, who was around twenty or so, answered the door. You might think that 'fire' is a universal word. Either it isn't, or she simply didn't understand my dulcet West Country tones.

Some people have told me that they think Jessica sometimes doesn't appear to take things too seriously. That may be a fair criticism – but then I am a person who has stood in a burning building playing what can only be described as a piss-poor game of charades with a half-asleep woman in her pyjamas who didn't speak English.

Either way, through a combination of me waving my hands around and saying the words 'fire', 'flames', 'hot' and 'out', I somehow managed to convince her it was a good time to leave the house.

What has that to do with the story? I'm not sure. Perhaps this is just my public safety message telling you all to check your smoke alarms?

In any case, I hope you enjoyed book five in the Jessica Daniel series.

Kerry Wilkinson

COMING SOON

THICKER THAN WATER

Jessica Daniel Book 6

When Cameron and Eleanor Sexton arrive home to find their babysitter missing but their child and property otherwise untouched, Detective Sergeant Jessica Daniel is sent on what she thinks is a fool's errand to find out what happened.

But Jessica is left confused as the teenager's body turns up in the bath of a different house, seemingly at random – a puzzle which only deepens when a journalist points out that someone placed an obituary for him days before he went missing.

With one colleague leaving while another returns, plus a local businessman taking an unhealthy interest in her, Jessica turns to home to find the one person she can rely on. But is that trust misplaced?

This is Book 6 in the Jessica Daniel series, following on from *Locked In*, *Vigilante*, *The Woman in Black*, *Think of the Children* and *Playing with Fire*.

An extract follows here . . .

ISBN 978-1-4472-2342-9

1

Cameron Sexton's finger hovered over the standby button on the television remote control. He thought about calling upstairs to see if his wife was almost ready but figured he might at least be able to watch the kick-off before having to leave the house if he kept quiet.

He glanced at the teenager fidgeting nervously in the armchair across the room.

'Are you all right, Ollie?' Cameron asked.

The young man looked up from the television, nodding a little too enthusiastically. 'Yes, Mr Sexton,' he said. 'Thanks for calling me.'

'It's Cameron and thank you. It's always nice to have a reliable babysitter. How are your mum and dad doing?'

Oliver nodded, offering a vague 'all right', which Cameron thought could mean either 'they're absolutely wonderful, never been better', or 'they've split up and are living at opposite ends of the country', depending on which way the teenager's hormones were raging.

The sound of a whistle and an overly excited commentator took Cameron's eyes back towards the television screen. If he had remembered that the football was on, he would have suggested a different night to go out for a meal with his wife.

Cameron leant back into his seat as the commentator's voice plus the oohs and aahs of the crowd broke the uneasy silence between him and Oliver. He tried to focus on the screen, resisting the urge to tug his suit trousers into a more comfortable position. They were feeling a little tight around his waist, although he tried to tell himself it was because they must have shrunk slightly at the cleaners, as opposed to his forty-something stomach being less forgiving nowadays.

The match was dull and Cameron felt his mind wandering. It was strange to be leaving your child at home in the hands of someone else, especially a person you didn't know that well and who wasn't technically an adult. Using Oliver had been his wife's idea. Eleanor knew his mother and, because he was about as polite and sensible as a teenager could be, they had asked him to look after Lara for an evening a few months ago while they went to the pub around the corner for a meal.

That had now become a monthly event that was both enjoyable and tentative. If anything, Cameron would have thought his wife would be the one nervous about leaving Lara – but she kept saying they were going to have to get used to it, which was true but also a bit of a shame.

Cameron squinted so he could read the match time in the top left corner of the screen and was surprised to see the game had already been going for five minutes. He stifled a sigh before standing and reaching across to hand the remote to Oliver.

'Here, you take this. We should be off out any minute. Well, whenever Eleanor is ready. You've got all this to come with girls and the like . . .'

Oliver took the control, shuffling in his seat, clearly uncomfortable with the topic. Cameron didn't know if the teenager had a girlfriend, or possibly even a boyfriend. The young man didn't seem overly confident but Cameron knew from his own experiences of being that age that very few seventeen-year-old lads had the bravado to talk to girls first. The ones that did were usually the biggest prats going, covered in gel and too much deodorant, not realising they were a couple of years away from ending up in some dead-end job for the rest of their lives.

Wondering when exactly he'd stopped knowing how to talk to the younger generation, Cameron offered a weak-sounding 'you can watch what you want', before adding: 'I'll go see where she is.'

He headed out of the room, moving quietly up the stairs until he saw his wife standing in the doorway of their daughter's room, her outline silhouetted by the night light from inside. Cameron stepped towards her, placing his hands on her hips and pulling her tightly as she gave a yelp of surprise.

'You scared me,' Eleanor said with a smile, playfully slapping his chest.

Cameron waggled his fingers in her face. 'Oooh, yes, I'm really scary.'

Eleanor giggled and turned around, pressing her back into him and resting her head on his breastbone. They stood silently in the doorway, watching their daughter's chest rise and fall, her eyelids twitching. Cameron found himself breathing in time with the young girl before his wife spoke softly.

'She's okay, isn't she?' Eleanor said.

'Well, she has got my genes. Let's just hope she ends up with my looks, intelligence, charm and charisma.'

Eleanor suppressed a laugh, spinning around, snaking an arm around her husband's waist and butting his shoulder gently with her head. 'As long as she doesn't have your head size.'

Cameron hugged his wife with one arm, using the other to pull the bedroom door until it was almost closed. 'And are you okay?' he asked.

'I can't believe she starts school in September. It only seems like yesterday we were in the hospital. Tomorrow she'll be dyeing her hair black and refusing to speak to us.'

As he smoothed down his wife's hair, Cameron tried not to laugh. 'Is that what you were like as a teenager?'

'I never dyed my hair but basically, yes.'

'At least we'll know where she gets it from then.' Cameron loosened his grip, kissing his wife on the top of the head. 'Come on, let's get going, or we'll never leave.'

Eleanor peered up at him wearily. She looked as tired as Cameron felt. When they had talked about having a regular 'date night', they'd agreed that regardless of his job, or how exhausted either of them felt, they would ensure they had one night a month for each other.

'Is Ollie all right?' Eleanor asked.

'I left him in charge of the TV and he knows where everything is. I made sure the baby monitor was working earlier, so he's all set. I even put a pizza in the oven for him.'

'Wow, my hero,' she mocked with a grin. 'Let's hope Lara grows up to have your culinary skills as well as your giant head.'

*

Cameron glanced at his watch as discreetly as he could, not wanting to let on that he was in any way concerned about the time.

'How long ago did we order?' Eleanor asked.

Realising he had been caught, Cameron tried to reply in a way that didn't betray how annoyed he was. 'Around forty-five minutes,' he replied, knowing it was over an hour.

'I'm tempted just to say "sod it" and get a burger on the way home.'

Cameron failed to suppress a grin. 'Classy.'

Eleanor was trying to stop herself smiling too. 'You're the one checking the time.'

'I was checking out the back of my hand actually.'

She rolled her eyes. 'They're still hairy and clumsy, if that's what you're worried about.'

Before Cameron could respond, a waiter appeared over his wife's shoulder. 'Risotto?' he asked, before placing that plate in front of Eleanor and offering the steak to Cameron. 'Any sauces?'

Cameron couldn't avoid his wife's disapproving stare. 'No, fine, thanks,' he said, before waiting for the man to walk away. 'What?' he added innocently, looking at her, even though he knew exactly what she was thinking.

'You don't ask for ketchup in a restaurant,' Eleanor said.

'I didn't.'

'No but you were thinking about it.'

Cameron shook his head but could not stop himself smiling. 'What are you, the thought police?'

'When it comes to you, yes.'

Cameron cut into the meat, feeling his stomach rumble as

a small amount of juice oozed onto the plate. Despite the time it had taken, he did have to admit the steak looked perfectly cooked and had no doubt the thick, chunky, skin-on chips would be excellent too.

'Is it nice?' he asked his wife, nodding towards her bowl.

Eleanor chewed with her mouth tightly shut but nodded.

'Worth the wait?' Cameron added as he put a forkful of meat into his mouth.

She swallowed, taking a sip from her glass. 'Maybe.'

'What is a risotto anyway?'

He looked up to see Eleanor narrowing her eyes in the way that made the top of her nose crinkle. A strand of blonde hair fell across her face. Cameron thought she looked as gorgeous as ever as she moved it away. 'How old are you?' she asked.

'Forty . . . ish. What's that got to do with anything?'

Eleanor swallowed another mouthful. 'It's a rice dish. How can you not know that?'

'I don't know, I've never had it.' Cameron picked up a slice of steak with his fork and held it in the air. 'I eat man food.'

His wife smirked. 'Is that why your trousers are too tight?'

Cameron pulled a face of mock indignation, trying to think of something funny to respond with.

'Forty . . . ish,' Eleanor reminded him.

As they ate and chatted, Cameron risked another glance at his watch. They weren't running late as such but neither he nor his wife wanted to stay out any longer than they had to. He remembered the first time they had left Lara with Oliver, they had wolfed down a main course and then rushed home barely an hour later to find their daughter sleeping peacefully and the babysitter watching a film.

They had stayed out progressively longer on each subsequent date night. Somewhere at the back of his mind, each time Cameron expected to arrive home with the house a mess and Lara nowhere to be seen. It wasn't that he distrusted Oliver in any way, just that the irrational voice in his head always seemed to have more prominence than it should. They never went to the cinema because neither of them wanted to have their mobile phones on silent just in case they missed something. Even when they went to have something to eat, Cameron would make sure there was good phone reception and ensure Oliver had the restaurant's landline number just in case. He knew it was overdoing it but nothing would stop that little niggle that told him he should not leave his daughter.

He drifted back to the present as Eleanor put her fork down, picking up her napkin before starting to dab at her mouth. 'Are you okay?' she asked, apparently noticing his distraction.

'Fine, just thinking about dessert.'

Eleanor clearly wasn't taken in. 'She'll be fine.'

'I know.'

She tilted her head to one side, smiling widely. It was the exact expression that had made Cameron fall in love with her. She had a way of both grinning and chiding at the same time, one eye twinkling, the other attentive. 'I'll go phone the house while you look at the puddings,' she said, standing up. 'I'm not letting your trousers out for next time though.'

Cameron watched her walk away, her hips swaying, wondering if she would still be awake by the time he had managed to give Oliver a lift home. With those thoughts in mind, he was considering if dessert was a good idea after all. It wasn't often he saw his wife dressed up nowadays; the years of maternity wear, sensible shoes and breast pumps had become a necessary – albeit not too appealing – part of their lives.

As he took a cursory glance at the back of the menu, Cameron kept an eye fixed on the direction Eleanor had gone in. He had expected her to be barely a minute or two but began to feel something building in his stomach completely unrelated to what he had eaten. Putting down the menu, Cameron watched the doorway. After a few minutes more, Eleanor finally emerged but he could see immediately that something was wrong. The smile from a few minutes before had disappeared as she walked quickly, the sway absent from her stride as she stared at her mobile phone. She didn't sit as she arrived back at the table.

'What's wrong?' Cameron asked, standing himself.

'No one's answering.'

'Did you try the house phone?'

'Of course.'

'What about Oliver's mobile?'

'That too – no answer.'

Cameron started patting his pockets, wondering which one he had put his car keys in. 'Shall we call the neighbours?'

Eleanor spoke with a forced calmness. 'No, let's just go. I'm sure everything is fine.'

The wait to pay was excruciating and Cameron could barely tolerate the silence during the car journey home. Each red traffic light and delay to give way at a roundabout seemed to occur in slow motion. He cursed any driver in front of him who was not going at least 10 m.p.h. over the speed limit. He could sense Eleanor in the passenger seat holding her breath as she tried to call the house. Each time, he could hear the phone ringing without being answered until his wife would hang up before trying again.

Neither of them spoke.

When they first moved in, Cameron had spent months struggling to reverse his car onto their driveway each time he arrived home. The thick brick pillars on either side seemed to have been placed deliberately to make life difficult and Eleanor would make jokes about his parking ability. Without even thinking, he drove in front first and switched off the engine, opening the door in one fluid movement. Eleanor was out of the car before it had stopped, heels clip-clopping across the tarmac as Cameron watched her climb the steps two at a time to their front door. He reached the bottom as she got to the top, a small cry escaping her lips.

'What?' Cameron asked, louder than he intended.

Eleanor was standing still as he joined her on the top step. She didn't have to say anything because he could see it himself – the front door was unlocked and open. Cameron looked at the fear in his wife's eyes. He was too scared to speak, in case saying it out loud would make it more real.

Gently, he eased the front door open, not knowing what he would see on the other side. Cameron realised he had been holding his breath and exhaled loudly as he stared into the hallway to see everything exactly as it should be. Eleanor's bright pink coat, which he so hated, was still hanging from the row of hooks on the right-hand wall. Lara's wellington boots and trainers were neatly placed on the floor under-neath.

Cameron felt Eleanor pushing past him, heading for the stairs. Lara's bedroom was the natural place to visit first but, for some reason, he felt drawn to the living room. As he heard his wife's shoes ascending the wooden steps, Cameron slowly opened the front-room door, peering around it.

The room was bathed in a bluish haze with the glow from the television creeping into the darkened corners. Cameron stood for a few moments, staring at the screen, before remembering where he was. He blinked rapidly, glancing around the empty room which was, apart from the absence of Oliver, exactly as he had left it. Cameron noticed the house phone undisturbed on the side table, before he picked up the remote control and switched the set off, allowing darkness to engulf him.

He turned to walk back into the hallway but his foot brushed across the top of something hard. He bent down and picked up a mobile phone, examined it and put it back in his pocket, stepping into the hallway. Cameron felt his stomach gurgling uncomfortably as he rested one hand on the banister at the bottom of the stairs. His house had a different aura about it in a way that was difficult to describe. He remembered when the new-born Lara was first brought home, and Eleanor spent the best part of two days sleeping. Owning a property wasn't about the bricks and tiles, it was about those memories, and now they suddenly seemed tarnished.

Cameron held on to the banister, eyes tightly closed as he slowly started climbing the stairs. He winced at every creak, listening out for the scream of anguish he knew would soon be coming from above.

As he neared the top, Cameron opened his eyes one at a time. He fully expected to see his daughter's bedroom door flung open with a pile of clothes or toys on the floor. Instead, Eleanor was standing in the doorframe staring inwards, illuminated by the night light in an almost identical fashion to a few hours previously.

'Ellie?' he said softly.

His words echoed around the hallway, unanswered. Cameron stepped closer to his wife until he was standing directly behind her. He peered over her shoulder until he could see the room clearly. He blinked rapidly, wanting his eyes to confirm it was true.

Even from the doorway, he could see Lara's chest rising and falling as she slept soundlessly.

'She's okay,' Eleanor said gently as Cameron pressed into her back. He felt his wife push into him before relaxing her muscles so he was supporting her weight. 'I thought . . .'

'I know.'

They stood in silence watching their daughter breathe. Cameron would have been happy standing there for the rest of the night but his wife turned and nestled her head into his shoulder. 'Where's Oliver?' she asked.

'I don't know. He's not downstairs.'

'He wouldn't have just gone home . . . would he?'

Cameron rubbed the bottom of the woman's back soothingly. 'His mobile phone was on the floor.'

Eleanor pulled away and met her husband's eyes for the first time since they had left the restaurant. She asked the question they were both thinking. 'So where is he?'

2

Detective Sergeant Jessica Daniel finished chewing the chip she was eating and scowled at her friend across the canteen table in disapproval.

'I'm not rising to it,' she said.

Detective Constable Isobel Diamond laughed. 'You always rise to it. There's no way you're going to let it go.'

Jessica picked up another chip and put it in her mouth, shaking her head. 'I'm a changed woman.'

Izzy laughed again. 'Not that changed if you're still talking with your mouth full.'

Jessica swallowed. 'That was just a treat for you. Anyway, I'm not rising to it.'

'I'm just asking if you're ever going to take Adam's last name.'

'Yes but you're not really asking, are you? You're stirring.'

Izzy giggled further. 'I am a bit, yeah.'

Jessica looked across the canteen table at Detective Constable David Rowlands. 'What's up with you anyway? Nothing funny to say?'

The constable had been swishing his cup of tea with a teaspoon absent-mindedly for around five minutes. 'Jessica Compton would make you sound like a farmer's daughter,' he concluded, not looking up from his mug.

Jessica raised her eyebrows and met Izzy's surprised stare. 'That's a bit rude,' Izzy replied.

Dave shrugged, picking up his tea and downing what was left. He offered a half-smirk as he raised his gaze to their eyes. 'It does sound a bit *farmy* though, doesn't it? It's like you should be working somewhere in Alabama throwing hay bales around.'

'Have you ever been to Alabama?' Jessica asked.

'No, you?'

'Surprisingly no, but I doubt they throw hay bales around.'

'Anyway,' Izzy said. 'Are you changing your name or not?'

Instead of replying, Jessica picked up another chip and chewed it deliberately slowly. 'It's your first day back, Iz,' she eventually said. 'You've returned earlier than anyone expected. Haven't you got more important things to be getting on with?'

'Not really, no. Everyone's being particularly nice and offering to carry stuff or take work off my hands. I might have a few more children if this is what everyone's reaction is like.'

She raised her eyebrows in a silent suggestion.

'Don't even say it,' Jessica replied. 'You either,' she added, turning to Rowlands.

Izzy snorted with laughter. 'It's going to happen, Jess. You're married. It's kids, grandkids, great-grandkids, the lot from now on.'

'My mum's been dropping hints,' Jessica confessed. 'After she got over us flying to Vegas, she started talking about us figuring out somewhere more permanent to live so we can "sort out the spare room".'

Izzy giggled knowingly as Dave kept a straight face. 'Are you still living at your mate's flat?' he asked.

The house Jessica had lived in with her boyfriend Adam

had burned down and they had been staying in an apartment owned by Jessica's oldest friend. 'For now,' she replied. 'We're looking for places but it's bloody boring . . .'

'. . . And you wouldn't know which name to write on the mortgage,' Izzy interrupted.

Jessica tried to stop herself smiling but Izzy's mood was infectious. 'There's nothing wrong with keeping your own name,' she insisted.

'Adam could take yours,' Dave suggested unhelpfully. 'Adam Daniel.'

'I did mention that but it didn't go down well.'

Izzy swished her long red hair behind her and tied it tightly. 'I've missed all of this.'

'What, winding me up?' Jessica said.

'Pretty much, yes.'

Jessica grinned. 'At least you're honest. How is Amber?'

Whether it was deliberate or not, Izzy shuffled in her seat until she was sitting up straighter. Her smile widened. 'I'm missing her. I know her grandparents are looking after her fine but you get used to spending every day together.'

'When I saw you last, it didn't look as if you'd slept in a week,' Jessica pointed out.

Izzy shrugged. 'Amber's sleeping a bit better now and doesn't wake up so often in the night. You get used to it.' She paused for a moment, before adding with a wink: '*You'll* get used to it.'

Jessica ignored her. 'My mum reckons she used to give me a tiny amount of whisky on my dummy whenever I couldn't sleep. You should try that.'

'I'm not giving my baby alcohol to make her sleep.'

'It didn't do me any harm.'

'Aside from the chronic wine intake nowadays, you mean.'

Jessica ignored the dig. 'Are you sure it's not just a massive scam to get extra presents? Not only do you get gifts for Christmas and birthdays, you now get Mother's Day stuff as well. It's one big cycle of getting free stuff.'

'Yeah, you're right,' Izzy replied sarcastically. 'That was my first thought when I found out I was pregnant.'

Jessica grinned. 'You're quiet,' she said to the other constable.

Rowlands, who was fiddling with his empty mug, shrugged dismissively. As Jessica took another chip, he locked eyes with Izzy. There was an awkward silence as Jessica glanced up and caught them.

'What?' she demanded, wondering what she was missing. Dave quickly looked back at the table. 'Are you two up to something?' Jessica persisted, although neither of the constables replied.

'So are you going for Jason's job or not?' Izzy asked.

Jessica paused for a moment, wondering whether to let the obvious subject change go. After a very deliberate pause to let her friends know she was on to them, even though she wasn't, Jessica replied. 'I've been asked to apply but I don't think it's for me.'

Both constables groaned together. 'Jess, you'd be perfect,' Izzy said. 'You practically do the job already.'

Jessica shrugged dismissively, although she knew it was true. Ever since Detective Inspector Jason Reynolds had been suspended for leaking sensitive information to the media a few months earlier, his workload had been spread out among his colleagues – with Jessica and Detective Sergeant Louise Cornish taking the brunt.

Their bosses had already been looking for an additional inspector but whoever got that position would end up doing it in place of DI Reynolds instead of alongside him. That was until the results of his disciplinary were through, which would be months, if not longer.

'They're interviewing over the next few weeks,' Jessica said. 'But I don't want to end up sitting around here all day. I'd rather be out there annoying people.'

'You are very good at being annoying,' Rowlands replied.

Jessica wiped up the remaining brown sauce with her final chip and bit it in half. 'Thanks, I'll take that as a compliment.'

'So you're definitely not going for it?' Izzy continued.

As she finished the final part of her lunch, Jessica pushed the plate away. 'Nope. I'd be jealous if anyone else got to order Dave around. That's my job.'

'It's not because you're thinking about the pitter-patter of tiny feet, is it?' Izzy asked with a smile.

Jessica rolled her eyes. 'You're not going to let it go, are you?'

Before Izzy could reply, Jessica saw Detective Chief Inspector Jack Cole striding into the canteen. He didn't need to speak before she was on her feet. 'What's up?' she asked.

He was biting his bottom lip, unsure how to phrase his words. 'I'm not sure,' he finally admitted. All three officers were now standing. 'It's good to have you back,' he added, turning towards DC Diamond.

'Thanks, Sir.'

'What do you need?' Jessica asked.

The chief inspector cleared his throat. 'You know the usual policy on missing persons is to wait a day but we've had something this morning that is a little different . . .'